"I WANT YOUR SPUNK," SAID RORY

"You're not beaten, are you? You haven't realized yet that failure exists. Tracy—" Rory stopped himself, burying his nose in her wildly curling hair. A shudder rippled through him, but he managed to control himself. With a choked sigh, he added inadequately, "You've got something I need, Tracy."

Perhaps he didn't realize what he was saying. At least he had been honest. He wanted Shamrock Air, and Tracy was apparently part of the bargain.

Aching with reluctance, Tracy spread her hands on his chest and pushed. The pressure was weak, but insistent. When Rory loosened his grip on her, Tracy kept her head down, her eyes hidden from him. Her laugh was tremulous. "I'll bet you say that to all the airlines."

WELCOME TO...

HARLEQUIN SUPERROMANCES

A sensational series of modern love stories.

Written by masters of the genre, these long, sensual and dramatic novels are truly in keeping with today's changing life-styles. Full of intriguing conflicts and the heartaches and delights of true love, HARLEQUIN SUPERROMANCES are absorbing stories—satisfying and sophisticated reading that lovers of romance fiction have long been waiting for.

HARLEQUIN SUPERROMANCES
Contemporary love stories for the woman of today!

Nancy Martin
FLIGHT INTO SUNSHINE

Harlequin Books

TORONTO • NEW YORK • LONDON
AMSTERDAM • PARIS • SYDNEY • HAMBURG
STOCKHOLM • ATHENS • TOKYO • MILAN

Published September 1984

First printing July 1984

ISBN 0-373-70133-0

Copyright © 1984 by Nancy Martin. All rights reserved.
Philippine copyright 1984. Australian copyright 1984.
Except for use in any review, the reproduction or utilization of
this work in whole or in part in any form by any electronic,
mechanical or other means, now known or hereafter invented,
including xerography, photocopying and recording, or in any
information storage or retrieval system, is forbidden without
the permission of the publisher, Harlequin Enterprises Limited,
225 Duncan Mill Road, Don Mills, Ontario, Canada M3B 3K9.

All the characters in this book have no existence outside the
imagination of the author and have no relation whatsoever to
anyone bearing the same name or names. They are not even
distantly inspired by any individual known or unknown to the
author, and all the incidents are pure invention.

The Superromance design trademark consisting of the words
HARLEQUIN SUPERROMANCE and the portrayal of a Harlequin,
and the Superromance trademark consisting of the words
HARLEQUIN SUPERROMANCE are trademarks of Harlequin
Enterprises Limited. The Superromance design trademark
and the portrayal of a Harlequin are registered in the
United States Patent Office.

Printed in Canada

CHAPTER ONE

TRACY REGAINED CONSCIOUSNESS on the bathroom floor. Distant piano music and the strong aroma of coffee awakened her. She opened one eye and focused blearily on her left hand, fingers clenched instinctively around the key to somebody's twin-engine Cessna. The checkered tile of the floor began to move. Wow. The squares were swimming, first weaving together, then fanning away kaleidoscopically. Oh-oh.

She grabbed for the rim of the tub and hauled herself upward, bringing herself to a sitting position. What a night. If this was being drunk, it was no fun. Somebody had left a half-cup of coffee on the edge of the tub, and Tracy stared at it for a long moment. No way. This situation definitely called for a bath. Unsteadily she reached for the taps and let a rush of hot water come splashing into the tub. If half a dozen cups of coffee and a hot bath didn't fix her, nothing was going to do it.

Ten minutes later, a little improved and unpleasantly sober, Tracy staggered from the bathroom, tugging her fluffy pink bathrobe around her slim body.

At that moment, she finally realized that the piano music was live, not on the radio at all. Tracy froze. She braced her back against the doorframe and exhaled one long cautious breath, and a whispered, "Holy Cow."

He was sitting on the piano bench. At her low, moaned exclamation he turned though, and eyed Tracy with an unsmiling, steely gaze. He removed the smouldering stub of a cigar from between his teeth. His voice was almost a growl. "Sober yet?"

Tracy clutched the bathrobe instinctively to her chest. She was stark naked underneath. "Who are you?"

Still no smile. The slate-blue eyes darkened, then slipped appraisingly down her figure. His gaze lingered on the long supple length of leg that peeped provocatively from the bottom of her robe. Appreciation dawned before he returned to hold Tracy's eyes with a new light in his own gaze. "Nice of you to ask, Miss O'Hara. I wondered how well acquainted we were going to get before we introduced ourselves."

Tracy knew the tone. She'd been around enough men to recognize a contempt for her youth and a respect for her female endowments. She summoned her poise and swiftly tied the belt on her robe. Her voice was steady. "What are you doing in my house?"

He glanced around the room. Darkness filled the tall windows that overlooked the airstrip, but the floor lamp by the old wing chair was on. The place was cluttered with books and tagged aircraft parts, an extra coffee cup or two, a pair of boots and a Jeppesen manual torn apart with the notebook pages scattered all over the dining table. But he was looking at the walls: the photos, dad's Purple Heart, the Korea medals, and the wooden propeller from their first Piper Cub. He said, "This is your house? I thought it was a museum. Or a memorial. Why do you keep all this stuff?"

Angry then, Tracy deftly yanked the belt tighter and advanced into the room. "It's my house," she snapped, turning arrogant as usual. "I keep it the way I like it. Right now I'd like to throw you out, mister."

"Now, now," he cautioned with a sardonic mildness, squinting slightly through the blue smoke. He put the cigar back in his teeth and smiled coldly around it. "Let's not talk about throwing out until we're sure you're not throwing up. Coffee's in the kitchen." He turned back to the piano, apparently uninterested in her response.

Tracy stared. He was big—probably more than six feet—and powerful through the shoulders as well. His size, combined with the unquestioned ring of authority in his voice, almost caused Tracy to obey his command to get the coffee. She resisted the impulse, however, and glared at his back. Her habitual quick tongue wasn't going to work with this character, she guessed. Tracy hadn't the faintest idea who he was. He was wearing a white shirt, though, and a loosened striped tie. His trousers were charcoal gray, and his suit jacket had been slung over the ladder-back chair. Not the usual type to hang around the airport.

His profile was lean and clean-shaven, marked by dark, mobile brows and a straight aristocratic nose. Conservatively cut, his short dark hair was ruffled from the evening breeze. The sleeves of his starched shirt had been rolled up over hard, tanned forearms, but the casual treatment of his clothing did not disguise their very good quality. Tracy guessed him to be in his early thirties. Definitely the visiting executive sort, except for the cigar.

But here on Lake Ontario? In a little town like Port Barnett? And worse yet, here in her house? With Tracy herself half-dressed and barely in command of her wits? Too many questions boiled in her already dizzy head, and nausea rose suddenly in her throat. She put a steadying hand out to the doorjamb and concentrated on not throwing up. Yes, some coffee now might just do the trick.

The kitchen light was off, and Tracy's shaking fingers flicked on the switch. Then she winced at the fluorescent glare and clapped her hand over her aching eyes. She had never been a drinker, that was sure. Not like dad, anyway. Liquor tasted bad and invariably made her sick. Tonight had been an unprecedented binge, an angry reaction to what had happened today with.... No, no. Tracy had hoped to erase the day's events with a good drunk. Obviously, it had been a disaster, but she didn't want to think about the airline just yet.

Tracy poured coffee—he must have made it, she realized—and immediately drank from the scalding mug. She gasped, eyes watering, but the effect was good. The long, wisping bangs of her russet hair were wet, and she smoothed the curling tendrils behind her ears. She must look like a half-drowned setter, she decided. Appearances had never meant much to Tracy, but modesty did. She pulled the collar of her bathrobe more snugly around her throat. With the coffee mug in one hand, she went back out to the music.

He was playing something bluesy. He wasn't bad. Maybe an amateur, but clearly more than just a dabbler. The piano, unfortunately, hadn't been tuned in six years.

Tracy perched on the end of the dining table a safe ten feet away. She drank her coffee and listened to the mellow music, waiting. Her head began to clear again.

The tune slowed, lost its syncopation, and the final note, beautifully plaintive, hung in the air. Before the haunting sound died away, he tipped his head and glanced around.

Tracy met the look without blinking.

"So," he said into the silence as he turned on the bench to face her. "Feeling human?"

"Not yet," Tracy responded with a chill in her tone. "But I think I can handle things from here."

One eyebrow arched. "Ordering me out?"

"Yep." Tracy nodded. She took another sip of coffee and tried to look bored.

"Without a thank-you?"

She hesitated watchfully. This guy could be trouble. "For what?"

The smallest smile began to tease the corner of his mouth. He lifted the cigar away. "Don't you remember?"

Tracy cleared her throat to dispel her momentary nervousness. "If you—if I made any overtures to you, Mr.—"

"Buchanan," he supplied blandly.

"If I gave the impression of—of picking you up in the bar, Mr. Buchanan, I assure you it was a temporary lapse of my sanity."

The smile appeared for real then. "I did the picking up, Miss O'Hara. You were passed out in a bowl of peanuts, and the men still hanging around the bar were flipping a coin over who got to carry you over here. I lost. Or won, depending on how you look at it. A fellow named Spinelli allowed me to bring you home."

"Remind me to fire Spinelli in the morning."

"Am I staying that long?"

A quick look. His face was expressionless again,

and she couldn't tell if he was kidding or not. Briskly, Tracy said, "Well, thank you for escorting me home, but now—"

"Escorting?" he repeated, amusement growing lighter in his eyes. "Miss O'Hara, I've carried sacks of corn over my shoulder that had more life than you did. With sacks, though, I don't risk the possibility of having my back upchucked on."

Tracy's eyes popped at that, and she automatically looked around at his jacket. A blush stung her cheekbones, and she closed her gaping mouth with a snap.

"No, no. Rest easy. You weren't sick. Not yet, anyway. You were charmingly irate," he went on smoothly, "when I dunked your face in the sink. You're truly one of those females who looks beautiful in a fury."

"Cripes!" Tracy muttered viciously. She set her mug quickly on the table and stood. "Listen, Buchanan, I'm just not the sort of woman you're looking for, so—"

"In fact, you're hardly more than a girl, are you?"

"I'm old enough!" she snapped, head high.

He laughed then, a rich chuckle as he admired the fire in her eyes and the straight, stalking walk that brought Tracy to stand before him. "You're old enough," he agreed with a slow grin. "Yes, indeed."

"And I'm tough enough to toss you out," she

went on fiercely, catching the plush fabric of her bathrobe more tightly across her breasts. "If you're looking for action, I suggest you drive to Niagara Falls. Or up to Rochester, or something. This town has nothing to interest somebody like you."

"Oh, yes it does," he corrected mildly, meeting her eyes with deliberate intensity. A moment passed, and his meaning was unmistakable.

"Wait." She held up her hand as if he had started to get up. "I've already explained that I'm not interested in anything to do with you. I employ half a dozen guys just as big as Spinelli who are still over in the bar. They'll come running if I yell, so let's avoid an ugly scene and you—"

"Miss O'Hara," he said quietly, cutting across her rejection with a menacing sort of calm, "I think you're soon going to be very interested in me."

"I am?" Tracy demanded sarcastically, haughtily. "Just who the hell are you, anyway?"

He put out his hand. "Rory Buchanan."

Tracy eyed him with wariness. "Rory? What kind of a name is that?"

"A corruption of Roderick. It's my grandfather's name."

Taunting him, Tracy repeated all three syllables slowly. "Rod-er-ick." She took the final pace and accepted his hand.

His grip was firm and very warm. Directly, he

delivered the rest of his introduction, "I'm Northstream Airlines."

Her stomach dropped. Tracy swallowed hard and nearly lost her voice. "I see."

Buchanan's sharp gaze never left her face. "You weren't expecting me."

She shook her head, unable for one long foolish moment to tear her eyes from his vivid, mesmerizing gaze. He was decidedly handsome, she realized, and the reputation that followed the Buchanan name finally popped into her head. This was one suddenly very touchy situation. She said, "Not you specifically, no. They told me I'd get popular with the big boys. I didn't think it would start so soon."

"Am I the first?"

Aware that she had held his hand overlong, Tracy disengaged herself and took an automatic step backward. She knotted her fingers in her bathrobe, holding it tightly to her body. "No," she said, her voice abruptly turning to an odd whisper. "You aren't the first."

"I'm here now, however," Buchanan continued blandly, transferring his cigar back to his right hand. "And I think we could do some business, Miss O'Hara. That is, if you're sober now. I'd hate to find myself in court—"

"I'm not doing business with anybody," Tracy objected swiftly, striding with long-legged steps to the center of the room. She was thinking fast, frantically scrambling her brains back into order.

"I'm not selling my planes or my airport slots to anybody, so you can all just take your corporate jets back to your big fancy offices."

"I hear that you haven't much choice anymore, Miss O'Hara. You're in bad shape. It's common knowledge."

"I am not!" Tracy countered, arguing with herself as much as with the voice behind her. "Maybe the big airlines need to make huge profits and buy pretty new planes all the time, but I'm just a little commuter line, and we're doing just fine. I'm not selling anything yet!"

"Yet," he repeated.

Tracy swung on him. "I know what all you guys are after. I'm not a stupid little country girl, you know."

"Aren't you?" he asked, still watching her with that unswerving, measuring gaze.

She pointed at him. "You don't want my planes or my territory. You just want to buy my landing slots at Montreal and Pittsburgh. All the airlines are expanding, and you need to run more flights to those airports. Since they're not taking any more customers, you've come looking to buy my landing rights."

He nodded once. "Exactly."

"What is this?" she exploded, throwing her hand out to indicate the airport around them. "You expect me to roll over? Give you my business and come home to knit?"

"Do you have a choice, Miss O'Hara?"

"Damn right I do!" Tracy shouted.

He cocked his head skeptically. "I don't believe you."

"I don't have to quit the business," Tracy snapped, spinning away from him again. "My father was flying people around the country before anybody ever heard of United or USAir or Northstream. This airline has been around for decades."

"And you haven't made a profit the whole time."

"The hell I haven't!"

"How much?" he challenged, looking around them at the modest A-frame cottage. "Enough to pay your bills, and that's about it."

"I don't need to squeeze nickels out of the public so I can sit around in my hot tub, buster."

"That's a shame," he mocked her, again glancing pointedly at her long slender figure. "You'd look very nice in a hot tub, little lady. And you might find it a lot more enjoyable than keeping a couple of old airplanes together with rubber bands and glue."

Enraged, Tracy glared at him. "My planes are every bit as safe as yours, Buchanan. Maybe better too! The Fairchild Metro can fly forever, if it's expertly maintained. Don't you try making me look incompetent with airplanes! I can fly circles around any pilot on your payroll, and I know my way around every plane that's built. I will not be intimidated out of the airline business!"

But he was leaning back on the bench, his back comfortably against the piano, as if enjoying the show. He flicked his ash on the floor and observed, "Somebody must have done some intimidating today, Miss O'Hara. I know a happy drunk from an angry drunk, and tonight you tied one on for a reason. Care to tell me about it?"

"Why should I?" Tracy snapped, lifting her nose higher still. "The grapevine will be sure to spread the news around very quickly."

Buchanan grinned at her. "Let me guess. My competition is either Crown or Piedmont, or maybe even Midcontinental coming east—"

"Wrong," Tracy sneered, abruptly childish. "Try the great Hallis Air!"

Buchanan whistled, not surprised, but countering Tracy's mood with some mild sarcasm. "The really big boys—or girls. Isn't it nice to be wanted?"

Tracy was pacing by then, trying valiantly to sort her thoughts as she walked. "Wanted? Cripes, even the almighty boss lady showed up to see me today. Marjorie Hallis herself came swishing in here in a suit that probably cost as much as her Lear jet. Just like you, she figures she's dealing with a girl who just came in from milking the cows. Throwing around stuff like 'balloon payments' and 'amortized returns' and all that financial crap that's supposed to impress me. Does she think I don't understand the financial page in the New York Times?"

"Do you?"

"Not yet, but I'm damned sure going to figure it out!"

Buchanan laughed at that, the ringing sound halting Tracy in her tracks. She glared at him, forcing from her mind the thought that here was a man who was too attractive for his own good. His smile was crooked, slipping off to one side of his face into a groove that ran the length of his cheek and spoiled the symmetry of handsomeness. Tracy had seen this before. Wait—yes, it was a real Clark Gable dimple!

Buchanan had braced his hands on his knees, hands that were strong and long fingered, tanned even, though probably from a jaunt to the Caribbean or Acapulco with some giggly stewardess. He wore no rings. His upper body was built for strength and looked slightly incongruous in such a dressy shirt and tie.

He got to his feet with the lithe grace of confidence. He was indeed very tall, suddenly filling the cottage with his height. Instinctively, Tracy retreated around the wing chair.

If he saw her momentary uncertainty, Buchanan gave no sign. He took a short, appreciative pull from his cigar and studied her through narrowed eyes while the smoke cleared. "Let me tell you a story, Miss O'Hara, and you tell me if I've got the facts straight."

"What kind of story?" she asked suspiciously.

"Your old man came back from the war and hung around the airplanes because he thought he knew all about them. He must have known more than the average Air Force retiree, judging by this quaint display of his accomplishments." Buchanan gestured at the picture of Frank O'Hara with Harry Truman. "Your dad had some change saved up, so he bought some airplanes and started running a shuttle back and forth to Montreal. You came out of the cabbage patch and got caught up in the mystique of flying—the romantic part of climbing into a cockpit and soaring off into the sunset. The two of you must have made quite a pair. Right so far?"

Tracy didn't answer. Her blazing green eyes and stiff, straight mouth were enough. Inside her pocket, she clenched her fingers around the sharp contours of the Cessna key.

Buchanan sauntered along the wall and looked casually at the memorabilia hanging there. "So for a few years he flew and made just enough cash to keep the planes in the air and supply himself with a fifth of booze every night. Then—"

"Hold it right there!" Tracy objected hotly.

"Then your dad started going up in his plane when he was soused, and one day he just missed the runway on his way down—"

"He was trying an outside loop, damn you! An almost impossible maneuver in a Cherokee Six!"

Buchanan shrugged, coming to a halt at the end of the wall. He put one hand into his trouser pocket and faced Tracy across the table. "So he got himself killed and left you to run Shamrock. You've been messing around with it for a couple of years now, right? And the finances have gotten steadily worse. You've got loans due, and your planes are getting old. It's time for a change. What's it going to be? Declaring bankruptcy and getting out with the shirt on your back, or selling your assets to somebody like me and making a few hundred thousand?"

"I am not selling." Tracy enunciated each word with precision. "We can fly for years before things get bad."

"And what are you paying mechanics like Spinelli with? The joy of flight? Free booze in the company bar over there? This is an airport right out of a 1942 movie. You just need Tyrone Power to come swaggering in here in a flight jacket and silk scarf."

"Is that the part you hope to play?" Tracy asked, her tone full of acid. "Have you come to sweep the boss's daughter off her feet?"

Buchanan met her eyes, smiling slightly at the fire he must have seen there. Benignly he asked, "Are you looking to be swept?"

She blushed then, much to her fury, and flounced

away to the window to hide it. "I don't intend to get my hormones mixed up in this, so don't rev your engines yet, mister."

"Good," he said tranquilly. "You're not so bad when you're not about to throw up. Very tempting, if I was sure you weren't jailbait. I'd still like to keep this visit strictly professional, though. Every time I get mixed up with a woman in a business deal, I get burned."

"So I hear," Tracy said over her shoulder.

The silence that greeted that remark was deadly.

Tracy risked a peek around and found him studying her again. "So?" she asked saucily. "You've come looking for another female to seduce, haven't you? Seems to me your track record is pretty obvious. You bought a commuter line out in Chicago from some lady you romanced, and then a few planes from Libby Stone at Rocktown Manufacturing. You get around, don't you?"

"My reputation is overrated."

Tracy laughed rudely. "Yeah? So every stewardess that comes through here is lying?"

"Stewardesses? They haven't interested me since I was your age."

"You're a legend in your own time, Buchanan. Enjoy it. Fame is fleeting."

He had strolled to the other side of the wing chair, and he casually rested one hand on the upholstery. "How come you're so interested in my sex life?" he asked, amused. "The boys in this neighborhood aren't appreciating your charms?"

"I'm not the tiniest bit interested in your sex life," Tracy retorted. "Just so long as it doesn't get mixed up with mine."

He grinned. "Are you old enough to have one?"

"I'm twenty-four, for crying out loud! There! Feel like a senior citizen?" Tracy's green eyes blazed at him. "State your business and hit the runway, pal. You're starting to bug me."

He nodded agreeably, still smiling at her firebrand manner. "Fair enough. Shall we sit down?"

"Is that the first step? We could just skip that and go right to bed, if that's where you're headed."

He burst into laughter at that. "You're a pistol, aren't you?"

"Just suspicious, that's all. The episode with Marjorie Hallis clued me in to what's going on. I'm real important all of a sudden, aren't I?"

"Yes, ma'am." Buchanan nodded, his eyes holding hers. "Exactly what did Marjorie have to say?"

Tracy sauntered back out into the room, heading for her coffee mug again. "Don't get cute, Buchanan. I'm not about to tell you what your competition had to offer. Let's just say that she thinks she's being very generous, but she's got icicles in her eyes, you know?"

"Yes," he said, "I know."

The coffee was still warm, and Tracy took a sip. "She wants the whole thing: the planes, the hangars, the landing rights. She's calling it a merger, but I know better. She's buying me out."

"For how much?"

Tracy glanced at him, thinking. "I guess it won't do any harm to tell you. Two million."

He didn't react. "And how much debt do you have?"

Tracy nodded. "Two million."

Buchanan let his smile appear again. "Well, that keeps your arithmetic simple, doesn't it?"

But she had begun to lose her humor. She did not return the smile. The afternoon meeting with the owner of Hallis Air, one of the major eastern United States commuter airlines, had been rough on Tracy. She'd never admit it, but she didn't understand a lot of what was happening. Until now, running the small commuter line had been relatively easy. Just keep the planes in the air and the ticket window open. Passengers weren't beating down the doors to fly to Montreal and Pittsburgh, but the traffic had been enough to pay her bills. For three years since dad died, she hadn't taken any new loans, but hadn't paid off any old ones either. The snowball had kept building. Things were tight now, and Tracy wasn't sure how to handle it. Her knowledge was in airplanes. A balance sheet didn't make much sense.

Marjorie Hallis had talked fast and smiled a lot.

Tracy had almost liked the woman. The industry-renowned Ms Hallis was not much past thirty herself and already a big success—most of which Tracy had decided she owed to her charm as much as her brains. She had spoken fondly of Tracy's dad, as if she had known him. There had been lots of flattery, too, talk of Tracy's flying skills and close involvement with the airline. Marjorie had played at being her friend, though she must have been eight or ten years Tracy's senior and aeons older in terms of sophistication. That had made Tracy suspicious. And the fact that too much was happening too fast was starting to make Tracy nervous.

"Let me guess," Buchanan said after a long moment. He had been watching Tracy's expression change. He put the remains of his cigar into the ashtray on the windowsill before continuing casually, "Marjorie offered to do all the paperwork, handle the details, and give you a check when it was all over with. Since your debt is so high, she must have promised you something nice, something more personal."

Tracy stared at him.

"What might that have been?" he went on, studying her with speculation as he stood with relaxed strength, arms folded across his chest, a few yards away. "A trip around the world? No, I suppose that would have been too obvious, even to someone your age. How about a nifty new plane, just for you? Where do you get your kicks, Tracy O'Hara? If I know Marjorie well enough, she researched you until she found your weak spot. What did she promise you?"

"You're a slick son of a bitch, aren't you?" Tracy snapped, glaring at him anew.

"No," he disagreed. "Just well informed. Am I right?"

Tracy shrugged, heading for the kitchen and more coffee. "Maybe so."

"Ah, now you've piqued my curiosity," he said, following in Tracy's wake as she left the room. "Just looking around, I'd say your heart's desire is probably something Marjorie can't supply."

"What's that?" Tracy asked, reaching for the coffeepot.

He paused in the doorway, hands in pockets and bracing his shoulder against the refrigerator. "Looks to me like all you want in life is to have your daddy back."

Tracy swung on him, cracking the mug down on the counter and splashing coffee in all directions. She was furious. "Who the hell are you to come poking your nose into my life? The bunch of you can go straight to—"

"Take it easy," he commanded sharply, his voice rising to match hers. "If you want to get out of this fix, little girl, you had better pull your pretty red head out of the clouds first. You've got a lot to lose here!"

"Tell me about it."

"I will tell you about it, if you'd just step out of your adolescence long enough to listen." He came a pace closer, effectively backing Tracy against the counter. "You're in the big league now, whether you like it or not. You're ripe for the picking, and somebody's going to do it, because you haven't any alternative! You're not going to solve your troubles by getting drunk with a bunch of mechanics. Time to grow up, Tracy."

"And I suppose you're the only one who's going to treat me fairly? You're my savior? The one who's going to rescue me from all the other dastardly airlines coming here to pick my bones?"

Amazingly, Buchanan put his hand to his forehead and rubbed, turning away from her to mutter to himself. "Why am I doing this? Rory, you're a fool and always have been."

"I'm not arguing with that!" Tracy snapped sarcastically.

"Maybe I'm slitting my own throat, but I can't steal candy from this baby. I've done some sneaky things in my time, but this would be too low." He faced her again, dropping his hand away. "Look, Tracy, you're a sitting duck. You're uninformed, you're inexperienced, and above all, you're letting your emotions get tangled up in what should be a clear-cut business decision. Have you got a lawyer?"

"My cousin Sean graduated twelfth in his class at Harvard last year," Tracy said proudly.

"Great," he responded with total lack of enthusiasm. "So you don't have a lawyer. Have you got an accountant?"

Tracy was frowning. "I write the checks and Spinelli does the books. We work together on it."

"Terrific," Buchanan commented ironically. He began opening cupboard doors, looking until he found a clean coffee cup. "I suppose he flies the planes while you serve the drinks to passengers?"

"I fly the planes myself," Tracy objected swiftly, getting out of his way as he pulled the coffeepot toward himself. "I've got three pilots plus myself to fly the commercial runs. Spinelli just flies the charter plane. He's busy with the ground work most of the time."

"Humph," Buchanan noted, pouring. "Does he sleep with you?"

"Oh, take a hike, for crying out loud!"

He looked down at her, unimpressed. "It's an honest question. You've got a cozy little family business here. It makes things a lot more complicated if anyone's ego or virility is at stake—"

"No, I'm not sleeping with Spinelli!" Tracy snapped, angrily jerking at the belt on her bathrobe. She stalked within the few square feet of kitchen space, fuming. "Not that Spinelli hasn't been trying for five years or more! He probably sent you over here with me, hoping that you'd get me started—" She bit off her own words and stopped.

Buchanan took a short sip of coffee, watching. "Yes?"

"Forget it," she said sharply. "So what have you got to offer, Buchanan? Aside from your sex appeal, that is? I assume you have come to see me with more to trade than what you keep in your pants?"

"Judas!" Buchanan set his cup down with a bang. "If you were any relation of mine, I would whip your backside until you screamed! What a mouth you've got!"

Tracy tipped a wicked look up at him. "Into that kinky stuff, are you?"

He swore again, shaking his head in disbelief.

Laughing, Tracy teased him. "I thought you were the hotshot lover from Chicago! What's the matter Rod-er-ick? You've come to seduce me, and now you're losing your nerve?"

"I think I'd rather seduce a mountain lion than—no, you're more like those little cats—what is it? A bobcat!" He snapped his fingers. "You're like a bobcat, all spit and fire, and about the size of a minute!"

"I'm not so little! If you weren't as big as a gorilla—"

Buchanan was grinning at her, openly appreciative. "You probably torment the hell out of poor Spinelli, don't you? No wonder the guy has to stay on the ground all the time."

"Don't you worry about Spinelli. He deserves

what he gets." Tracy folded her arms across her chest, smothering her smile. "What have you got to offer, Rod-er-ick? Since I'm not classy enough to fool around with the likes of you, what's it going to be? Can you top Marjorie Hallis's two million?"

He toyed with the handle on the cup, spinning it on the counter for a moment. "What makes you think you're not classy?"

Tracy glanced up and laughed. She was playing with fire and didn't care just then. "Oh, so I'm sexy enough after all?"

"You're very sexy, little girl. More than you know. Cleaned up a little, you'd be a knockout. There's something about you that's even more appealing than your pretty face and kitten mouth, though."

Buchanan reached and touched her chin, lifting Tracy's face to the light. The spark in her eyes flashed from jade to emerald, hard and fiery. "That's it," he said softly, noting the spirit in her unflinching gaze. A tremor, perhaps barely checked dismay, shivered down through her, and he felt it. Quietly, he went on, "I'd hate to see you lose that fire inside, Tracy O'Hara. You can lose your airplanes and your property, but this—this is something very special."

Tracy held very still, allowing him to appraise. He caressed the delicate softness of her cheek, his thumb making slow and gentle whorls there. His touch was hesitant, almost unwilling, and into Rory Buchanan's blue-gray eyes came a haze, a faraway look at once both sharp, yet distant, as though his thoughts were suddenly troubled.

"Having second thoughts, Rod-er-ick?" she mocked lightly, watching his face.

He tipped her chin a fraction higher, hypnotized, it seemed, by the curve of her mouth. "About you?"

"About seducing me," she corrected mildly, permitting his slow perusal a moment longer. Tracy's conscience was telling her—no, screaming at her—to pull away, but she foolishly wasn't listening. His touch had become deliberate, tracing from the rise of her cheekbone back down to the sleek point of her chin, a mesmerizing sort of caress.

"No," he responded slowly. "I don't want to seduce you."

She waited, and soon enough, he touched her mouth, the full, bowing lower lip and then the arching, too-short upper curve. Tracy felt her mouth tremble once, partly from the expression she read in his eyes, and partly from the butterfly-soft contact. She parted her lips slightly, and breathed, her fear pushed aside. Maybe the lingering effects of the booze were enough to make her bold. She murmured, "Would you care to have the tables turned this time?"

He laughed at that, clearly shaken by his own

sudden reaction. Her teasing tone jolted him back to the present. "No," he said, taking his hand away. "You're flattering me now, Miss O'Hara, and—"

Tracy laid her hand on his chest. The touch stopped him. Her smile was slow, slanting upward into his face. He didn't need to know that her heart was thumping out of nervousness, not arousal. Tracy took a step closer, letting both hands slide tantalizingly up his chest. The neckline of her bathrobe tipped open slightly, enough to show a glimpse of curving breast. Tracy's thighs were soft against his. "You're not bad for an older man, Rod-er-ick. Are you game for a little preliminary negotiating?"

He took her wrists firmly in hand. "Do you know what you're doing, Miss Tracy?"

She smiled, the wicked light shining in her eyes. "Maybe not. Would you like to teach me?"

"How drunk are you?" he asked, holding her off momentarily.

"Not very. Kiss me once, will you?" Tracy blinked lazy lashes and lifted her mouth. "Please?"

The sight was more than almost any man could resist. A young, unspoiled kind of beauty with a fair, fair skin and the greenest eyes Rory Buchanan had ever seen. She was prettily tousled, her red-gold hair curling in a great halo of color around her slim face. Against his, her body was lithe and lean except for the luscious fullness of soft breasts that seemed to nestle on his chest. She could be gorgeous with some subtle makeup to accent her cheekbones and thick lashes. Her mouth especially, with its arching cat's lip and lush lower surface, was surely delicious, sweet with the fire that burned inside her. This was a girl on the verge of a startling plunge into womanhood.

But Rory did resist, setting her firmly away from him despite the surprised anger that flashed in her gaze. "No," he said in a voice that had turned ridiculously hoarse.

"No?" Tracy demanded, mocking him with yet another glinting smile. "No?"

"This is a test, isn't it?"

She flushed and caught her balance on the counter again. "You're a—a—"

"A gentleman," he supplied for her, dusting his hands, as if he had just finished a dirty job. He turned away. "It surprises me now and then, but deep down, I guess I'm just a nice guy. Go try teasing your friend Spinelli, little Tracy. You're not going to play those games with me."

"Why not?" she said pouting, following him to the doorway. After she'd been so brave this character was going to walk out like nothing had happened! Tracy was relieved, yet outraged at the same time. "Are you afraid a younger woman might be too much to handle?"

"Don't challenge me over this," he warned,

pausing in the doorway to give her another short appraisal. "I always accept challenges, and I usually win."

Saucily, Tracy leaned against the refrigerator and blinked slyly up at him. Feeling safe, she taunted him one last time. "Couldn't prove it by me."

The sight of her wickedly sparkling eyes fired some volatile emotion in Rory. He caught Tracy's wrist, his grasp closing over her with a strength borne of aggravation. He muttered, "I haven't the faintest idea why I'm doing this."

With that, Rory Buchanan pulled Tracy to him and wrapped one arm around her body. For one senseless moment, she tried to arch away from him, to escape the punishment, but it was too late. His tall frame was solid and unyielding. He tangled his other hand in her hair and pulled gently to tip her face to his, eyes blazing suddenly with the excitement of holding her so roughly. Watching the fleeting spark of fear pass through her emerald gaze, Rory swooped and took her mouth with his.

He was hard and draining, seeking to force her capitulation in one long passionless kiss. She struggled against him, but the contact of two lithe and vital bodies was suddenly wonderfully sensual. Tracy's lips parted, half at his demand, and half in response to the surge of a nameless instinct that rose within her. Unconsciously she molded to his frame.

Rory felt the tremor go shuddering down through her body, and the quickness of her reaction surprised and strangely pleased him. She was warm and womanly in his arms. Her breath caught oddly in her throat, almost a moan, and the soft sound had a quick and liberating effect on him. He tasted deeply of her mouth, savoring the mixture of sweet innocence and fiery liquor. He rolled her tongue with his, and wove his fingers luxuriously through her hair. It curled in his hands with the texture of silk. A subtle scent of soap and autumn air clung tantalizingly to her fair skin, and a headier, muskier perfume rose from the plush folds of her bathrobe.

She was lovely and soft and pliant, and desire flashed within him like the first stabbing rays of sunrise. Expertly he lifted her chin higher still and tore his lips from hers. A moment later, Rory explored her throat, his mouth hot as he felt for her pulse in the fragrant flesh.

Tracy closed her eyes and wound her arms around his shoulders, hardly able to stand unaided. Her breath was shallow and fast, her head light. This was a need as she'd never felt it before, so suddenly had it come upon her. To be mindless in a man's arms and yet to cause such mindlessness in him was more intoxicating than any liquor. Beneath the crisp fabric of his shirt, his shoulders were wide and taut. By contrast, his hair was soft between her fingertips. The sandy surface of his cheek rasped along her throat, and Tracy winced away, both from the tiny pain and the wonderfully twisting sensation the contact wrought.

He was all man. Too much man, of course, for the likes of her. Tracy realized his intent almost too late, when Rory backed her into the refrigerator and eased one knee between her thighs. He passed a long, practised caress down the curve of her side, coming to ride gently on her hip. The message was clear and insistent. Menacing.

Abruptly frightened by the speed of such a storm, Tracy wedged both hands between them and pushed against his chest. She gasped, wriggling, and in a moment, he released her. Tracy slumped, spent, against the refrigerator, her eyes wide and full of turmoil. She had certainly bitten off more than she could chew!

Laughing suddenly at her bewildered expression, Rory let her go as quickly as he had snatched her up. "Proof enough, little Tracy?"

Tracy hastily spun around and laid her trembling hands flat on the counter. She had to catch her breath. What a lesson! That ought to teach her for trying to act more experienced than she really was! This shaken reaction was ridiculous. And embarrassing. Tracy manufactured as much worldliness as was possible and said the first thing that came to mind. "You passed the first test, Rod-er-ick."

"That's good," he said behind her. "At least my reputation is intact."

Tracy glanced around at him, her eyes furious again. "Not for long."

"Now what's got you spitting fire?" he demanded on a rude laugh. "You pushed until you got what you deserved just now. If you didn't want me, then what in blazes were you trying to prove?"

"I've got a business to run, Buchanan. That was my little way of testing your methods. If you really mean to compete with Marjorie Hallis to get my company, you'll have to do it without any funny business." The theory sounded good. Venomously Tracy added, "You're going to have to play it straight with me from now on!"

He met her eyes, mystified by her sudden change of manner. Then, his own expression hardening, he promised curtly, "Count on it." He turned on his heel.

"Wait a minute. Aren't you going to make an offer?" she asked, amazed that he was leaving. Gathering up the folds of her bathrobe, Tracy hustled after him into the living room. "How much money are we talking? Two and a half million? Three?"

"Are you kidding?" he asked, letting the mocking grin appear again. "What's the sense in that? I'll match Marjorie's two million, and that's it."

"That's it?"

"Sure. With my sex appeal thrown in, of course." He lifted his brows, laughing at her. "I'll be here until tomorrow evening. If you decide to sell between now and then, get in touch with me at that establishment across the highway that somebody with a sense of humor calls a motel. I'll stop in for a visit in the afternoon, just to answer questions."

Tracy stuffed his jacket into his hands and glared up at him. "You're a sneaky son of a gun, aren't you?"

Rory Buchanan lifted his shoulders, unconcerned. "Maybe so. Lately, I don't even recognize myself. Good night, Miss O'Hara. Be sure to take some aspirin before you go to bed. It will make a tremendous difference in the morning."

CHAPTER TWO

NEVER HAVING BEEN A PERSON who took advice gracefully, Tracy did not take any aspirin and consequently felt lousy the next morning. So lousy that she did not get out of bed until nine o'clock, an unheard of hour at the airport. She endured a lot of razzing when she finally showed her face in the hangar. The boys all whistled and called rude comments to her, but Tracy just waved them off and kept walking, her high-heeled boots clipping on the shiny concrete.

Spin was not with the rest of the boys underneath the Metro, but he had been waiting for her in the cool dimness at the back of the hangar. Thin and tough, Vincent Spinelli looked like the quintessential aviator, complete with Air Force-issue flight jacket and Oklahoma cowboy boots. He had one shoulder leaning against the wall and the phone propped against his ear when she arrived.

"Yeah, okay," he said into the phone. His accent, the speech that nearly all pilots affected, was laid-back Oklahoma. "We'll skip the eleven-thirty run and book those passengers on the three o'clock.

If they don't like it, send them to the bus station."

The hangar was cold, and Tracy bundled her calfskin jacket closer around her throat. Then she shoved the sleeve up over her wrist to check the time as she reached for the clipboard hanging by the phone. She reviewed the daily chart. The 6:00 A.M. plane to Pittsburgh had been nearly full, but the late-morning flight only had four reservations. If they sent the plane anyway, they'd lose a significant bundle of money. Not smart. Combining passengers and canceling flights wasn't good policy either, but it was a question of economics.

Spin hung up the receiver and waited for Tracy to speak first. He stuck a toothpick in his mouth and waggled it around to the corner of his lip, eyeing her straight, slim figure. He was sure to notice that she had washed and brushed her hair, for this morning it was unusually fluffy and pretty, not the usual braid down her back. Spin made no comment about her appearance, however.

"Hello," Tracy said coolly, dropping the clipboard back into place. "Everything smooth this morning?"

"Sure," Spin said, leaning negligently against the corrugated wall. "Isn't it always?"

Tracy didn't glance at him. "Not since yesterday. Any phone calls from Miss Neat-as-a-pin Hallis?"

Spin shook his head. "Nope. But Rory Buchanan called once already, just to see how you were, of course. He sounded really concerned. You two must have got real chummy."

"Well, I have you to thank for that, don't I?" she asked flippantly. She stepped to the file cabinet, pretending no interest in Spin's presence. "I hear that you sent him home with me last night. Nice, Spin. Really nice of you."

Spin laughed. "He minded his manners, didn't he?"

Tracy was silent, digging into the battered file drawer for the copies of her landing rights. She had a lot to do today.

"He did, didn't he?" Spin repeated.

"What do you care?" Tracy asked, her voice sounding bored and airy.

Spin glanced warily at the mechanics who worked just twenty yards away. He didn't want to be overheard, so he came closer with wiry quickness and poked Tracy's shoulder. "Don't pull that cute act on me, Tracy. I was good and angry with you last night. I let that Buchanan character take you home so you'd get a scare. I hope it worked."

Tracy faced him, her eyes flashing. "What are you trying to scare me into doing, Spin? As if I don't have enough to worry about these days."

"Trace, Trace!" he pleaded, catching her hand in his and pulling. "I want to protect you! Look after you, just like always!"

But Tracy shoved him away with a straight-arm block. "Don't give me your usual line today,

Spin. I ought to fire you for what happened last night!"

"Okay, okay, I'm sorry," he said, immediately apologetic. He kept his voice hushed. Perhaps he still thought they were hiding something from the rest of the Shamrock employees. A major shouting match took place at least once in a fortnight, and the relationship between Spinelli and Tracy never seemed to progress from that point. Everybody realized it but Spin himself. He pleaded, "Trace, it's just that you're driving me nuts! I spent the whole evening with that chick Buchanan brought along with him—"

"Chick!" Tracy objected. "Oh, for crying out loud, Spin!"

"I can't help it!" he cried, throwing up his hands. "She's not a girl and she isn't exactly a lady if she's with him, is she? I bought her a few drinks while Buchanan was over at your place and—"

Tracy swung around. "You mean he's got a woman here with him? He brought along a date or something?"

A smirking grin developed on Spin's face. "I dunno. Do you bring a date to a merger?"

Tracy blew an exasperated sigh, and walked to the storm door, thinking. "It's going to take some doing to figure that guy out!"

"Why?" Spin asked, going to his pocket for cigarettes. "Is he looking to buy this place, too?"

"Of course he is, you dope!" Tracy blew up. Her head was throbbing, and she controlled herself before continuing with venom, "Do you think he came here to watch our operation in action for its efficiency?"

Spin shrugged, unconcerned. He took the toothpick out of his mouth and replaced it with a filter tip. "You never know," he remarked carelessly.

"You may never know, but I do!" Tracy retorted. "We could be in a real jam pretty soon, Spin. We're going to end up doing business with Hallis or Buchanan or somebody just as slippery. I'm getting worried."

"Aw, Trace." He came behind her and wrapped a sinewy arm around her waist. "Don't worry, huh? Everything's going to turn out okay."

Tracy shook her head, gazing almost sightlessly out the door's window at the long stretch of runway that ran for a mile to the southwest. The wind sock was barely stirring in the September air. Nothing else moved on the landscape, and Tracy knew every stone and tree and crack in the pavement. She had been raised at this airport, and it meant more to her than she'd ever be able to explain to the upstart likes of Vincent Spinelli. She sighed and said quietly, "I don't think so, Spin. Nothing's going to go right unless we make it happen."

"Take it easy." Spin ruffled her hair playfully.

"If you've gotta sell, you've gotta, right? Looks like we've got an auction going. Hallis bids, then Buchanan makes a better offer, then somebody else comes along and—"

Tracy pushed away from him again. "That's just it. Buchanan knows the Hallis offer was two million, and that's just what he bid also. Something's fishy, and I don't know what. I'm going up to see my cousin Sean this afternoon. I'll take the five-thirty to Montreal."

Spin shook his head, digging a dime-store lighter out of his pocket and fingering it. "I don't know, kid. That's the flight that the travel agency booked for some tour, so it's full. Unless there's a cancellation, you'll have to go by yourself."

"I don't want to waste the gas. I'll co-pilot on the commuter, if I have to. Who's on the flight?"

"Harvey and Lester. But Lester's gotta go, because he's taking his wife for the weekend. And Harvey's playing the football pools again and needs the money, so he's taking every flight he can. You promised him yesterday he could have that one."

Tracy rubbed her forehead tiredly, trying to force the pain away. "Right, right. I'll figure something out. Don't light that thing in here, please. All we need right now is an explosion."

"Okay. Listen, there's been a couple of things going on this morning that I thought you'd want to know about," Spin went on, pocketing the lighter again. He took the unlit cigarette out of his mouth. "Let's see. We need you to co-pilot to Pittsburgh at one. Pete's got to take his kid to the dentist or something. If you don't want to go, I could take it, I guess."

"Hmm," Tracy responded, noncommittal. She wasn't listening very carefully.

"And the ticket agent in Montreal wants to talk to you. Some glitch in their computer. No big deal, I think. And what about Buchanan, Trace? He had a look around the hangar last night, but he's gonna want to see the whole setup today, I'm betting. You want to take him around?"

"No," Tracy said quickly. "I don't want to see him yet. I need some time to think. Yes, I'll take the plane to Pittsburgh. With any luck he'll be back in Chicago before I get home."

"Don't bet on it," Spin said dolefully. "The guy acts real determined, Trace."

She sighed again, kicking absently at the door with the toe of her boot. "I've got to think, Spin. And we've got to try to remember every bit of gossip we ever heard about him. If he really has womanized his way to the top of commuter airlines, I want to know before I'm the next target."

Spin glanced closely at her. "You don't sound opposed to the idea."

Tracy looked at him, aware that she had started to blush. "Put it in your ear, Spinelli."

"What is this?" Spin pressed, crushing the cigarette in his fist. He took a pace closer again. "The guy has been here less than twelve hours and you're in love with him? I thought you had him figured out! He thinks the fastest way to a lady's wallet is through her pants—"

"Just shut up!" Tracy shouted, her voice ringing in the cavernous hangar. At that outburst, the mechanics looked around, but not for long. Tracy's volatile temper was a fact of life around the airport. They went back to work in no time. Ignoring the potential audience, she snapped at Spin, "Just mind your own business for once, all right? I know exactly what I'm doing!"

Spin swore softly.

Tracy dropped her voice. "I know he's probably here to repeat what he's tried with every other woman in the industry, Spinelli. I've got the jump on him. The minute he tries anything remotely resembling romance, I'll know he's just a sharpie. Until that happens, though, I have to treat him just like the rest of the airline big shots that come to see me. I've got to listen to everybody before I make a decision about Shamrock!"

Spin's mouth began to twist into a grin. "So what's your plan, Trace? You gonna tease this guy until he makes a move?"

Tracy shrugged. The idea hadn't occurred to her until just then, but Spin didn't need to know that. She said casually, "The faster I figure him out, the faster we get rid of him, right?"

Spin laughed. "You little witch! He makes one false move with you, and he's out on his ear?"

Tracy permitted a smile at her friend, getting bold once again. "It would save a lot of time if he'd just try his sleazy stuff now, wouldn't it? Then we'd be done with him and be able to devote our attention to the serious bidders."

Smiling and shaking his head, Spin said, "I only wish you could do that with Hallis Air and anybody else who waltzes in here!"

"Marjorie Hallis will have to be your department, lover boy," Tracy shot back, patting the sleeve of Spin's jacket. "Maybe we've found the best way to weed out the con artists!"

Spin let out a long breath, and it whistled in his teeth. His quick gaze had gone beyond Tracy to the yawning door of the hangar. "Maybe so, kiddo. I think I'll give it a shot on that babe Buchanan brought along."

Tracy turned to look. Just outside the hangar on the tarmac stood Rory Buchanan looking composedly around the premises. He had changed from his suit of the night before into a pair of casual whipcord trousers and a fleece-collared bomber jacket that suited the surroundings. His head was bare, and his dark hair stirred handsomely in the morning air. He had his hands shoved deeply into his trouser pockets, and his habitual cigar was in his teeth.

At his side was a very pretty young woman. She

was blond and dressed in a blue cashmere sweater that, even from a distance, complemented the azure color of her eyes. Her skirt was full, yet clinging to her legs in a stylish swirl. A pouchy handbag, the sort imported from Italy, hung from her shoulder. She had a camera with a long zoom lens around her neck and a pair of sunglasses resting on the crown of her head. She tipped her head and said something quickly to Rory, who laughed pleasantly and agreed. He put his hand at the small of her back.

Aware of the tightness that suddenly gripped her throat at the sight of that gesture, Tracy piped up, "Don't bring that cigar in here, Buchanan!"

He hadn't made a move to come into the hangar, and he did not budge at Tracy's shouted command. He lifted his head to see her, though, and the smile broadened. "Good morning, Miss O'Hara. Feeling better?"

Manly laughter rose from the mechanics under the Metro.

Tracy ignored them. "I'd feel a lot better if you'd say your piece and clear out of here!"

He lifted his shoulders. "Just having a look around the place, that's all. If you have objections, we'll certainly leave—"

"Look all you like," Tracy retorted. "Just don't get in anybody's way, all right?"

He shrugged again, acquiescing.

Tracy turned to Spin again. "I'm going to have

to think about everything for a while, okay? I'm going to take the Pitts up for an hour or two. Can you hold the fort?"

Spin nodded, tossing his toothpick into the corner. "Sure. Weather's nice. I'll radio you if something turns up. What do I do with Buchanan while you're gone?"

"Let him do what he pleases. Show him the blasted passenger lists if he wants!" Tracy started away. "If I've got to sell out, it better be to somebody who appreciates the quality of our work!"

Tracy strode across the hangar floor, heading for the opposite corner.

The plane that rested there was a Pitts Special. It was Tracy's own, her pride and joy, a gift from her father on her eighteenth birthday. The Pitts, a quick little terrier of an aircraft, and one of the few biplanes still manufactured, was a homely little plane that Tracy had come to love like an ugly pet. Used primarily for aerobatics, the single-propeller Pitts had taught Tracy many of the subtleties of flying. Surprisingly, it continued to teach her. The plane had also become her friend, a silent companion with whom she could spend hours of solitude.

Tracy made the exterior preflight check. Seeing her intention, a couple of the men who had been tinkering with the larger Metro came over to her, rubbing their greasy hands in the rags kept in the pockets of their coveralls. The three of them put their shoulders to the wings and tail, turning the Pitts so that it was facing out onto the runway.

Tracy thanked them and ducked under the prop. She came up to find Rory Buchanan at the left wing. He had come automatically to assist in shifting the plane and had sensibly left his cigar outside. Tracy's step faltered when she came face to face with him, but he did not seem to notice her hesitation.

He was looking over the stunt plane. "Little beauty you've got here," he noted, running one hand up the skin of the wing.

"It's not for sale," Tracy said waspishly.

He heard her tone but didn't acknowledge it, except to smile slightly. Casually he patted the wing and said, "I'm not in the market. I'm not the kind of pilot in this league, frankly. This yours, I guess?"

"Yes," Tracy said stiffly, waiting for him to get out of her way. "It's mine, and nobody else flies it."

He leaned against the wing then, and folded his arms across his chest to take the time to look her over properly. His half smile, the mocking, annoying kind, teased at his mouth. His eyes were heavy-lidded, but amused at her brashness. "You must be quite the expert pilot, Miss Tracy."

"I think so," she countered lightly, flinging her bright hair away from her face. "But then, you might be surprised at a lot of the things I know how to do."

He laughed at that. "Surprised? I doubt it. Pleased, perhaps!"

Tracy made a noise of disgust and moved to cut around him.

Buchanan put out a hand and stopped her. His touch on her chest, just below her collarbone, was electric. Too slowly, he dropped his hand away. "Where are you off to? I thought you and I could have a talk this morning."

"I think we've said all of the important stuff," Tracy said. She settled her hands on her hips, holding her ground though he towered over her. "Unless you'd like to change your offer now that you've seen a few things?"

"Except for you, I haven't seen anything that's worth two million," he countered lightly, clearly enjoying teasing her. His eyes were vivid with morning sunshine, and in that dazzling light, he didn't look quite as old as he had the night before. Perhaps thirty-one or thirty-two. Beaming an amused smile down at her, he asked, "Why don't you stick around this morning and show me your assets?"

Tracy must have made an instinctive move to slap him, for in the next instant, Buchanan had her wrist captured firmly in one hand. His grin was broad and crooked. "Easy there! I was talking about your planes, little girl!"

"If my father was still alive, you wouldn't be so city smart!"

"Probably true," he agreed, still holding her tightly. In fact, he began to pull Tracy slightly closer to his body. The biplane concealed them from the others in the hangar, and he was taking advantage of the moment alone. "But then, I don't suppose I'd enjoy doing business with your father. You're looking much better this morning, Miss Tracy. I'm beginning to regret leaving you alone last night!"

"It looks like you weren't too lonesome, though." Tracy jerked her head to indicate the woman he had brought along. Her sneer was faked, a reaction to the quickening sensation that resulted from Buchanan's proximity. She braced her thighs against his and tried to arch backward. His tall frame was at once both warm and menacing, eliciting an odd sort of excitement deep inside her. Tracy kept her chin up and her gaze steady in spite of the surge of nervousness. "Did you bring her in case I didn't pan out in bed?"

His brows arched in amusement. Perhaps he could see how this sudden body contact confused her. "Tracy!" he exclaimed softly. "Are you jealous?"

She didn't answer. The muddle of heated sensations inside was too strange, too disconcerting. Abruptly afraid of losing the upper hand, Tracy wrestled herself from his grasp. "Just don't expect me to take advantage of your sexual expertise when you've got her waiting in the wings, buster!"

He laughed at that and let her go. "I'll remember that in the future."

"Do that!" Tracy pushed past him, her hair flouncing in the breeze.

But Rory spun her around again, his grip hard but brief on her upper arm. "I really don't want to play any games with you, Tracy. I meant what I said last night. I'll put my offer on paper if you like. I need this airline. I'm not in town to maneuver you into bed. Nothing was further from my mind when I got here."

"And now?" Tracy sassily blurted the question.

"Now...." He looked into her eyes, and the turbulence of blue eyes meeting green was intense. He slipped his hand up the curve of her arm, a caressing sort of touch that ended when his fingers met the soft tips of her hair. Startled by the sudden power of the charge that passed between them, Rory said without thinking, "Now I'm not so sure."

"Which is more important?" Tracy shot back, in spite of her own quailing courage. She saw the smoky cloud of indecision in his eyes, and the too-gentle contact of his hand in her hair was indeed confusing. Spin had never touched her so cautiously, so unwillingly. It was as if Rory was afraid of the consequences of caressing her, but was unable to stop himself. Tracy stood very still and let her own gaze bore straight into his with all the power she could muster. "Do you want to get this airline or another female scalp on your belt?"

"Tough question," he said quietly, lifting his thumb to test the softness of her cheek. He drew a slow brushing line up the delicate rise of her cheekbone. His touch sent a shivering sensation down her body, an invisible reaction that he could not have seen, but must have felt. The memory of what had happened the night before created an electric current between them. The attraction had been instantaneous then, and the situation had not improved. Tracy felt her nipples tingle and come erect beneath her thankfully thick flight jacket.

Rory's eyes were sharp on hers again, for he had noted her involuntary intake of breath. Half to himself, he said, "I should take this airline and run, but you—you're not what I expected to find here, Tracy O'Hara."

"As long as we're being honest," she said, surprised that her voice wasn't quavering as she taunted, "Rod-er-ick, you're not what I expected either. I figured you'd at least have the brains to be subtle about this seduction."

He laughed, shortly this time. He let her go and stood back. "I haven't been using my brains for a long time, I've decided. Go on. Fly your plane. I'll send you some papers. We can probably conduct this business over the phone from now on."

He walked away then, leaving Tracy to stand at the wing of the Pitts Special. What had just happened? Tracy's head was whirling, and she put her hand on the wing to steady herself. The merest touch from him had sent her senses into an uproar. Was this a hangover, or was this man different from the others she had come to know? Her legs were trembling and weak. Inside, an awful ache began to twist in her stomach as Tracy realized the truth. Something strange and very powerful existed between the two of them. He had a magnetism Tracy had never encountered before, never came close to experiencing before. Rory Buchanan lighted some kind of fire inside her, a fire that she wasn't able to control. He was very dangerous.

Angry suddenly, Tracy threw herself away from the wing and climbed up into the cockpit. She needed time to think, time to be alone. The seat of the Pitts was familiar and comforting, and as Tracy snapped the first switches, she felt the return of common sense. Beyond the windshield of the plane, she could see Rory Buchanan walking out onto the tarmac toward the woman who stood there. He had handed her his cigar apparently, and she gave it back to him with distaste, making some joke. He laughed with her and stuck the cigar back in his teeth. He turned then, to watch the Pitts.

Looking quickly away from him, Tracy fired up the engine and readied the plane for taxiing. The great, burbling roar of the Pitts sounded like the voice of a friend to her. She advanced the throttle and taxied slowly out onto the tarmac. The long empty runway stretched before her. The sight was wonderfully welcome.

IN THE AIR, time passed very quickly, and Tracy had barely executed her usual warm-up routine before she noted the lateness of the hour. Like an athlete in training, she had a system, a daily exercise of maneuvers she liked to practice. But she was low on gas, so she skipped her usual series of rolls and went directly into a long inside loop. The plane rounded out beautifully and roared up the valley with several thousand feet to spare. Nicely done, she congratulated herself. The airport came up quickly, and resisting the impulse to buzz the place—Rory Buchanan would have the conceit to think she was showing off for his benefit—Tracy flew directly into the landing pattern and set the Pitts down as lightly as a feather.

There was work to be done then, and later Tracy co-piloted the commuter run to Pittsburgh. She did not see the owner of Northstream Airlines before she left, and Spin happened to mention that Rory had taken his girlfriend out to lunch at a relatively good restaurant not far from the airport. Assuring herself that she was glad to have seen the last of him, Tracy left for Pittsburgh.

The flight was a little less than two hours in the Fairchild Metro. Once on the ground after the passengers disembarked, Tracy and Harvey supervised the fueling of their plane. Another group of passengers boarded within the hour, and the return trip was under way. Flying north from Pittsburgh took slightly longer than the flight down, but the Metro crossed over the New York State border only four minutes off the advertised time. The autumn afternoon had remained as clear as the morning, and on the horizon they easily saw the mist from Niagara Falls. Below the aircraft ranged a network of power lines that carried the electricity generated by the Falls in every direction.

Soon enough, however, the landscape changed in character to wooded hillsides and smaller, rural communities. The planned flight took the Shamrock plane over Buffalo, and at the higher altitude, they made up some flight time. Right on schedule, the small airstrip appeared below them, and Spin's voice crackled on the radio. Without mishap, they touched down and taxied to the block building that served as a terminal for Shamrock Air.

Tracy and Harvey turned the plane over to the mechanics for night maintenance. Harvey decided to hang around to chat with the other men, but Tracy left and went looking for Spin.

He was on the phone, as usual. He had propped a bottle of soda pop on the top of the wall phone, and he was munching a sandwich from the dispenser in the terminal. "Yeah," he was saying into the telephone. "We must have forgot what date it was. We'll get you a check first thing tomorrow, okay?"

The bank, Tracy guessed. She knew exactly what date it was: the loan payment was due, and they didn't quite have enough cash to cover it yet. Maybe by tomorrow there would be enough. She took half of Spin's sandwich and perched on the stool by the door, waiting for him to get off the phone.

"Yes, Miss Harcastle," he said, sounding patient. He rolled his eyes at Tracy, who smothered a laugh. "I'll bring the check to you personally, if that's what you'd like. Right. Okay, bye."

Tracy laughed at his expression. "You're getting quite a relationship going with our Miss Harcastle, aren't you?"

Spin snorted and snatched his sandwich back. "The things I do for you! Let me eat my own supper, all right? I'm flying the charter tonight, and I need my energy!"

Tracy stretched and took his soda instead. "Oh, yes? Where are you going? Taking Miss Harcastle some place romantic?"

Chewing, Spin glowered at her. "Not on your life. As a matter of fact, I'm taking your Buchanan buddy to Montreal. Want to come?"

"Him?" Tracy exclaimed, sitting up straight. "He's still around here?"

"He's ready to go any minute," Spin explained, intent on consuming his supper. "He wants to get up there before dark, and—"

"To Montreal? Why? To see our operation up there?"

Spin shrugged. "Don't ask me why. There isn't much to see but a ticket counter, so he must have another meeting or something. I'm betting he's got another merger cooking up there with Air Norland. He has to go, so I'll take his money and be his charter pilot if he's in such a hurry to get there."

Tracy looked around to the window. "That's nice for us. That fare will give us enough to pay Miss Harcastle's stingy bank, anyway. Why doesn't he take his own plane? That's his Cessna, isn't it?"

Spin nodded, retrieving his soda from her hands and taking a swift drink. "Yep. He was pretty disgusted earlier this afternoon. He flew it in here himself last night, but now he can't find the key! What a hoot! He says he had it last night, but today he can't even unlock the cockpit! He sent to Chicago for another, but it won't get here until the first flight gets back from Pittsburgh tomorrow morning."

The Cessna key. Tracy had found it in her own hand last night in the bathroom. She had put it in the pocket of her bathrobe. It was still there. How she'd gotten it away from Buchanan in the first place was the uncomfortable question.

Spin was looking at her. "Pretty funny, right?"

"Oh, yes," Tracy agreed quickly, managing a

grin. "Hilarious. The airline owner can't keep his own keys in his pocket."

Spin nodded, enjoying the thought also. "But good for us, like I said. I'm taking off in about fifteen minutes."

Well, it didn't hurt to take a rich man's money, Tracy decided. If they flew to Montreal, they'd make a few dollars, and then Tracy could "find" his key for him when they got back.

"You want to come?" Spin asked. "You said this morning you wanted to go see your cousin up in Montreal. How about it? I could use the company."

"Sure," Tracy agreed, sliding off her stool. "I'll call Sean and ask if we can stay at his place tonight. I have to talk to him about this airline stuff. If I'm forced to sell everything, I think I'd better have a lawyer advising me. Let me go get some things packed."

At her house, Tracy stuffed her toothbrush, another sweater and some clean underthings into her nylon knapsack. She took a minute to make a stack of ham sandwiches, grabbed a bag of chocolate cookies and a couple of bottles of root beer, and headed back to the hangar. Might as well have a snack on the plane.

The charter plane was an old Grumman G1, a used corporate plane that Tracy's father had purchased secondhand a few years before his death. It was a propeller-driven aircraft, old now, but still in excellent condition, thanks to the TLC provided by the crack mechanics Shamrock had always employed. When either of the two Fairchild Metros was having trouble, the Grumman was a backup plane for the commuter flights. It was an expensive plane to use, primarily because it didn't accommodate very many passengers in its club-style seating arrangement. It was a nice plane to ride in, though. Rory Buchanan would have a comfortable flight.

Tracy found Spin already doing his preflight check. She climbed into the co-pilot's seat. "Hi. I brought us a picnic. I'm starved!"

"Great," Spin said distractedly, noting the positions of several dials and checking them against his clipboard. "We can take turns later, if you don't report me to the FAA."

"Trust me," Tracy said, buckling in. "Where's Buchanan?"

"On his way."

"Listen, Spin, can we keep it a secret that I'm on board?" Tracy asked. "I'd rather that Buchanan thinks I'm still on the ground."

"Sure." Spin glanced at her. "What's this? I thought you were all set to play Lolita with him?"

She smiled nervously and shook her head. "Not yet. I want to talk with Sean first before I get myself into trouble."

"That's surprisingly cautious of you," Spin

said lightly, going back to his clipboard. "Cold feet?"

"Maybe so," Tracy said softly, turning her attention to the matter at hand. "Did you check the fuel yet?"

The plane was ready to go in minutes, and by that time Rory showed up with his girl. They got on board, and Spin went back to speak with them briefly.

Just hearing his voice as he spoke with Spin gave Tracy a case of the jitters. Either she was getting it bad for this character, or she hadn't recovered from the night before yet! Tracy wondered at herself. Had she been so sheltered growing up at this airport that the first virile male to show his face was the one she should fall for? Granted, the two years at community college hadn't exactly given her a good look at the big, wide world, but Tracy thought she had enough sophistication to meet a man and not go all goo-goo eyed over him! It made her angry to think she was so weak. She was fuming when Spin climbed back into his seat beside her.

"Ready?" Spin asked, snapping the headphones around his ears.

Tracy gave him a thumbs-up signal, and he started the engines.

"Let's go," Spin said, sounding happy. "I think we've got a good flight ahead of us."

CHAPTER THREE

THE GRUMMAN CLEARED ROCHESTER in minutes, and swinging east, Syracuse wasn't much farther than that. They hadn't been climbing more than twenty minutes when the gold-and-green velvet hillsides of the Adirondacks began to stretch almost endlessly before them.

"Sure looks pretty," Spin commented, settling back in his seat once they were through the high-traffic area and flying on a steady north-northeast course.

"Just keep your eyes open for mountains," Tracy joked. "Unless you want to show off for the lady in the back and buzz a few treetops around Lake Placid."

"What's that supposed to mean?" Spin demanded, sounding startled. His eyes were concealed behind mirrorlike aviator glasses.

"Nothing," Tracy shot back, laughing at his quick response. "You spent a long time giving the preflight instructions to that pretty lady back there. Or were you exchanging pleasantries with Buchanan?"

"You're dreamin'," Spin snorted, eyes on the sky before them.

The sun was over his shoulder, and it threw the colorful autumn expanse below into exaggerated relief. It was a beautiful sight—forests of tall trees punctuated with slim ribbons of water that wound in shining curls through the woods. Spin wasn't looking down, however. A moment later, he glanced across at Tracy. "Hey, do you smell something?"

"What d'you mean?" Tracy asked, instantly alert.

But she didn't have to ask. In that moment, she too caught a whiff of something acrid. Without hesitation, Tracy said, "Take her down, Spin."

Spin was already dropping altitude. The plane descended through the clear sky with a stomach-heaving drop.

Tracy was busy, scanning the dials and looking frantically around the small cockpit. A second later, she breathed, "Oh, God."

There was smoke. Not much, but a thin wisp of gray seeping around her feet.

Spin swore. "Outside? Is it outside, too?"

Tracy craned out the windshield. "I can't see. It wouldn't show from here, though. Spin, we must be burning!"

Nothing could scare a pilot as much as fire on board. Unlike a car, it wasn't possible to stop and get out. They were eighteen thousand feet in the air and dropping, but still minutes from the ground. The speed of flame in volatile aircraft fuel, Tracy knew, was instantaneous. Automatically she began the emergency procedure and dropped the oxygen masks.

Spin cut the engines back to idle and grabbed for the microphone. Amazingly, his voice was laconic, infinitely calm. "Ladies and gentlemen," he said, as if he was half-joking, "we've discovered a little something up here, so we're going to take this pretty little plane down a ways. Just in case y'all get a little light-headed, we're gonna drop the oxygen masks. Go ahead and use 'em, if it suits you. The ride's gonna be kinda wild, so fasten your seat belts and hang onto your hats."

He clicked off the mike and said, "I'll dump the pressurization. See if that ventilates us a little. Roll her over for me, Trace."

Tracy snapped her oxygen mask over her nose and mouth before she reached for the wheel. Her hands were steady but cold on the control column. She was calm, too, though it surprised her. Under her command, the Grumman rolled in classic wingover into a steep dive. Suddenly they were nose down, dropping to the ground on a nearly perpendicular course.

"Got it," Spin said, taking the column again. He held on for dear life, face taut. "I'll watch the numbers."

He meant the altitude and speed. They had to

get down fast, but could not exceed 295 knots. The Grumman wasn't designed to go faster than that. If the plane didn't blow up from the fire, they were sure to break up from stress on the aircraft's structure. Coughing once to clear her lungs of the thickening smoke, Tracy peered at the spinning hand of the altimeter. "Fifteen thousand feet. Air speed two hundred seventy-five knots. Cripes, Spin, watch the speed! We're getting close to Never Exceed."

The Grumman fell out of the sky, air tearing around the windshield. Spin held the controls, fighting to keep the plane at the maximum rate of descent. "We're approaching two-ninety air speed. The faster we go, the quicker we get down."

"Eight thousand now. Seven. Air speed is almost two-ninety-five. Pull up some, Spin. Just a little."

She counted off the numbers, indicating that the altitude was dropping, the speed holding steady. Completely unconscious of the radical angle of the diving plane, Tracy mentally ticked off the seconds. Never had a minute seemed so long.

"I've gotta pull her up," Spin said, sounding suddenly faraway through the thick fog of smoke. "A little help on the pullout, Trace. Here we go."

Tracy grabbed the wheel with him and together they pulled up the nose. The cockpit was full of smoke. Gradually, the plane leveled, speed holding at two ninety-five for another few seconds, then starting to fall.

"Damn!" Spin exclaimed, thinking frantically. "See any flames yet? We going to fry, Trace? Where's that smoke coming from?"

"It's got to be coming from up in the nose. But what—?"

"Not much up there by avionics. Trace, cut the radios. See if that helps."

Still watching the altimeter through the clouding smoke, Tracy obeyed, snapping switches. "Got it. Radios aren't much use to us at the moment anyway."

"Controlled glide now," Spin reported. "Maintaining two eighty air speed."

Her eyes stinging, Tracy called, "Can we land it?"

"Look for a road, a field—anything but a power line."

But there was nothing on the ground but trees. Eyes burning now, Tracy concentrated on the ground, quickly searching for a flat place on which to set the plane. She pointed. "There! See it?"

Spin tore off his glasses and shouted, "Can't see a damned thing!"

"Easy now. We're close. Get the speed down some more. Now shove her to the right. No, some more."

"We gotta slow her down some—"

"Landing gear!" Tracy remembered. She groped through the clouding smoke for the controls. "It ought to act as a speed brake."

"If it extends at all. Will it drop at this speed?"

"Yes!" Tracy cried. "Got it! Now, see down there? It's a road, I think."

Spin craned in his seat and spotted the path through the trees. "Too narrow, right? We'll shear the wings—"

"Just get it down," Tracy commanded, her voice cracking. "The hell with the wings. If they hit some trees, it ought to slow us down a little. Here goes!"

Spin cut the engines. Neither spoke.

The road came up with a rush, trees whizzing by the wing tips at a hundred knots. Something whipped the bottom of the plane and was gone. Spin took the plane lower, lifted the nose, and set her down, the trees still barely beyond the wingtips. The wheels bounced once, twice. Tracy cut the main power switch. Spin and Tracy both stood on the brakes, fighting the controls. The careening plane roared too fast along the rutted road. Both tires exploded. The nose wheel hit the ground with a tremendous jar. The landing gear snapped and the wheel collapsed. The nose of the plane struck the road with a hideous screech of tearing metal.

The plane bucked, lurching thunderously sideways. The left wing crashed against a tree. The plane skidded, throwing Tracy violently into the harness of her safety belt. The windshield burst. A tree smashed against the fuselage and tore along the right wing. From back in the plane a voice screamed and was cut off.

The plane crashed straight into a pine and stopped.

"Cripes!" Tracy said, catching her breath for the first time in three minutes. She ripped off her oxygen mask. Her fingers were clumsy on her belt, and in a moment Spin was there, tearing her free and hauling her out of the seat.

They were both coughing, grabbing one another and pushing out through the back and for the cabin door. It was open already, and with Spin's arm around Tracy's body, they were out and sucking great gasps of fresh air.

Outside they collided with the woman and Rory, who took Tracy's arm with a grip like steel and bullied her straight across the rocky ground. Spin was dragging her too, and in seconds they were yards from the plane. Spin slowed first, looking over his shoulder and finally turning, still running, to look for flame. Behind them was quiet.

Tracy dug in her heels and stopped. The rest of them staggered to a halt around her, and the whole group turned to see the plane. Still nothing.

The woman with Rory was sobbing, and she collapsed against him. He reacted automatically, with arms around her, but he also watched the plane. Around them, the forest was deadly silent, beautifully golden in the fading autumn light.

"Doesn't look like she's gonna burn," Spin said finally, and he coughed horribly.

Rory caught his breath and demanded, "What happened?"

"Smoke," Tracy gasped, bracing her hands on her knees and bending over like a spent marathoner to steady her pounding heart. "The whole place filled up with smoke. It didn't smell like fuel, though."

"Didn't smell like anything I know," Spin added.

Smoke was still wafting up around the nose of the plane and pouring out the shattered windshield pane. The Grumman leaned precariously against a tree, one wing ripped and hanging, the other propped up on a boulder.

"I thought we were dying!" the young woman cried out, blue eyes wild and streaming with tears.

"Me, too," Spin said on a breathless laugh. "Man, what a ride!" He swiped a smear of blood from his cheek and looked at it in surprise.

"Nice flying," Rory said, also smiling now that the danger was past. He held the blonde tightly to him and grinned over her head at Spin. "You want to come work for me?"

"No way!" Spin said, reaching to pat Tracy on the back as she coughed. "This lady is my good-luck charm! I almost didn't ask her to come."

"Then she's everybody's good luck," Rory said, his tone changing.

Tracy looked up at them then. "Who's talking about good luck? I just lost a half-million-dollar plane, fellas!"

"Maybe not," Spin corrected. "She hasn't blown up yet."

"She'd better," Rory said, taking another look at the plane. "After a ride like that, I'll feel cheated if she doesn't burn."

"We need a big finish," Tracy agreed. "Anybody got a match?"

The blonde had managed to control herself by that time, and she blinked tearfully around the small circle. "How can you be joking at a time like this?"

Rory hugged her hard, with real affection. "Sorry, old girl. You okay? Not hurt?"

She shook her head, but the movement turned abruptly to a shuddering sob. "J—just scared out of my head! I never want to get on a plane again in my life!"

Spin was bleeding for real. Tracy caught his arm and turned him toward her to have a look at his face. Glass from the windshield must have gotten him, for his cheek was torn, and blood was streaming from his scalp as well. On his forehead, a sizable red bruise was erupting.

"Hey, you may get a Purple Heart out of this," Tracy said lightly to him. With authority, she dug into his hip pocket where she knew he kept a handkerchief. Finding it, she shook out the white square and stretched to dab his cheek. She took a look at the bruise. It was a whopper, swelling fast.

Spin's breath hissed at her touch. "Hey, watch it!"

"Everybody else okay?" Tracy asked the group, going on tiptoe to press the handkerchief to Spin's head wound. She tipped a glance around. "Buchanan? You didn't bump your brain or anything?"

He shook his head, eyes direct and brilliant on her. "No, ma'am. You? You were in the driver's seat." Then he seemed to remember and loosened his embrace on the other woman. "What the hell were you doing with us in the first place?"

"I came along for the ride," Tracy said flippantly. "Looks like I picked the wrong plane to stow away on."

"More jokes!" the blonde objected with irritation.

"Have you two met?" Rory asked, amused by the situation. "M.A., this is Tracy O'Hara. Tracy, meet Mary Alice Cooper."

"Hello," Tracy said blandly. "Sorry for the inconvenience."

Mary Alice stared, and Rory laughed at that.

"Now what?" Spin wanted to know. He took the handkerchief from Tracy with hands that were beginning to shake. He looked at the stained handkerchief for an instant, as if trying to focus his eyes. "We're in kind of a jam, if you ask me."

"I guess so," Rory agreed, looking around them for the first time. "Where are we? Anybody know?"

"I can guess," Tracy offered, dusting the residue of the stinking smoke from her flight jacket. "We're somewhere in the Adirondacks. Could be a mile or two from the nearest town."

"Or thirty miles," Spin added, giving Rory a significant look, the kind men exchange in the process of establishing command of situations. Gingerly he pressed the handkerchief into his own scalp.

Rory glanced in the direction of the still-smoking plane. "What about the ELT?"

"It should be working now," Tracy said. "But nobody's going to look for us in the dark."

"What's ELT?" Mary Alice asked.

"Emergency locator transmitter," Rory explained. "It's a device that functions automatically in a situation like this, immediately transmitting a signal that searching aircraft can hear and follow. We should be found very shortly."

"Not before morning," Tracy objected flatly, shaking her hair out.

Mary Alice looked frightened at that, and Rory threw Tracy an exasperated now-you've-done-it look.

"Maybe not even then," Spin added, not noticing Mary Alice's reaction. Spin was very pale suddenly. He swayed then, and put his other hand to his head, wincing. "Wow...."

Tracy grabbed his arm. "You don't look so hot. Sit down."

Spin obeyed without a word, abruptly sitting on the nearest rock that projected from the forest floor. Dazedly, he looked at Tracy. "Sorry, kid. I guess I don't have the stomach I thought I had. I'm kinda shook up."

"Me, too." Tracy's smile was tremulous as she patted his shoulder. Spin was truly in pain, and the sight upset her. Putting up a brave front, Tracy grinned and said, "I don't do this sort of stuff every day, you know."

"Let's hope you never do again," Spin added firmly, taking her hand in his. "That was too close for comfort!"

"I want to know what happened," Tracy said. Thoughtfully, she stared across at the plane. "If there was a fire, how come we never had any flames? Where did the smoke come from?"

Mary Alice pushed away from Rory finally, having gotten control of herself in an admirably short time. She came to Spin's side and purposefully took the handkerchief from him. She peeked at the cut on his scalp and then the frightening bruise on his forehead. "I think we've got more important things to be concerned with right now," she said. "You've really bumped your head, I think. Does this—?"

"Oww!" Spin yelped, ducking away from her instinctively.

"You hit your head on the steering column," Tracy said, relinquishing the nursing duties to Mary Alice. "I heard the clunk when the wheel collapsed. He hit pretty hard."

"I remember now," Spin muttered, wincing once again under Mary Alice's ministrations. "Listen, it'll be okay. Give me a minute. Then we'd better start thinking about what to do. It ought to be dark in less than an hour."

"We'll have to start a fire," Mary Alice said briskly. "It'll be terribly cold tonight. And there must be some first-aid equipment in the plane, right? And blankets? Water?"

Tracy looked her over speculatively. In spite of her elegant clothing and smart, stylish haircut, it seemed that Mary Alice Cooper had a brain after all. It hadn't taken her long to get a grip on the situation and on her own composure. And she certainly looked efficient as she tended to Spin's head. "Yes," Tracy answered finally. "There are a lot of supplies in the Grumman. I'll have a look."

"Not yet," Rory objected firmly.

Tracy turned on him.

"Don't get that look on your face," he admonished darkly, seeing the flash of emerald in her eyes. "The plane may blow up yet, so keep your distance, young lady."

"For crying out—"

"Do as I say," he commanded, no-nonsense. He blocked her path to the aircraft. "Don't go near the plane for half an hour."

"And in the meantime?" Tracy demanded with unconcealed hostility. "Shall we twiddle our thumbs while Spin bleeds all over the place?"

"Bleeding's almost stopped," Mary Alice reported. "Rory's right. A few more minutes won't make much difference in treating his injuries, and we don't need to risk getting killed in an explosion."

Annoyed, Tracy thrust her hands into the pockets of her jacket. It hadn't taken anyone long to forget her role in landing the plane and to start treating her like the youngster in the group.

"I'll have a quick look around," Rory said to Mary Alice, once he was sure Tracy was going to obey. "We'll look damned silly if we spend the night here, only to discover a major city over the next hill."

"Good thinking," Mary Alice agreed, all business as she checked Spin's wound once again and returned the handkerchief to it firmly. "See if you can find some firewood or something."

"Right."

Tracy sighed, feeling useless suddenly. Not only that, but she was decidedly sore, too. The crash landing must have slammed her around more than she first thought. But Tracy shoved aside her own injuries. She wasn't about to show anybody her weaknesses at this moment. When Rory went striding off along the road they had just come down on, she determinedly set off in the opposite direction, heading uphill through the thicker part of the forest. No sense standing around.

The trees were tall and ancient, bare of branches for thirty feet before leafing out into great, outstretched boughs. Underfoot, the ground was soft with moss and a deep, undisturbed layer of leaves and pine needles. As Tracy strode through the crackling carpet, a flock of crows set up a raucous uproar that reverberated in the silence of the deserted forest. From the unspoiled appearance of so beautiful a place, Tracy guessed that they were very far indeed from any civilization. She walked for several hundred yards and finally climbed up on a huge outcrop of lichen-coated rocks.

Nothing. Nothing but trees. Tracy scanned in every direction, but there was no sign of man. Before the light grew any more dim, she started back for the plane. Golden rays from the setting sun showed her way, streaming through the trees like some kind of heavenly illumination. If the circumstances were not so unfortunate, she might have appreciated such serenity.

Mary Alice had insisted that Spin sit more comfortably on the rocks, his head resting back and eyes closed. He was deathly pale, though speaking to her, so Tracy did not run to his side. Better not make him think his injuries were worse than he suspected. Instead, Tracy advanced on the plane.

The smoke had dissipated, and Tracy decided to first see about the medical kit. She climbed up into the cabin and unlatched the first cabinet in the small entranceway. The kit was there with a package of flares and a somewhat battered foil packet of dehydrated eggs. Tracy went to the hatch of the plane and called to Mary Alice. Carefully, Tracy tossed the kit to her. Mary Alice caught it deftly, and then mouthed, "Thanks!"

Back inside the plane, Tracy started to explore the usual gear that was kept aboard the aircraft, but with a fresh perspective on the uses of the stuff. Three blankets had been stowed in one compartment. A tank of water, probably nearly full, was underneath. Tracy hunched down and looked it over. Ouch. Her neck was stiffening up already. The last thing she needed was to be hurt at a time like this.

"You're a determined little idiot, aren't you?"

Startled, Tracy jumped and swore.

"And gracious, as usual," Rory noted ruefully, climbing the rest of the way into the cramped space. "What have you found?"

Tracy tried to appear cool again and jerked her head to indicate Mary Alice outside. "Some first-aid stuff. It ought to be complete. What about you? See any nice restaurants in the neighborhood?"

Rory laughed shortly, glancing around the small hatchway. "Not exactly. Two rabbits and a lot of very noisy birds. I think we're out of luck, if you want French cuisine tonight."

"Humph," she sniffed, going back to the water tank. "I'll have to speak to my travel agent about this."

Rory hunkered down beside her and ducked to look at the tank. "Will that come out?"

"I think so." She glanced up at him and was disconcerted to find him so close. Fortunately her voice did not quaver when she said, "We could probably leave it here, though. I think the plane is safe."

He nodded in agreement. "All right. I think your buddy Spinelli needs a drink in the meantime. Any cups around?"

"Sure." Tracy extended her hand without thinking, and Rory grasped it and hauled her to her feet.

For an instant they were face to face and squeezed into the space between compartments. Rory hesitated, not moving from before her.

Surprised, Tracy looked up into his face, her eyes clear and wide and puzzled. He was very attractive, and standing so close to him, Tracy felt something stir inside her. Fear again perhaps? Tracy held very still, and then he dropped his hands on her shoulders.

"Steady now," he said, voice low and cautious.

"This isn't a seduction, believe me. Tracy, I think we're in a deeper mess than it seems."

Tracy held his gaze and did not speak. All her senses sharpened to the point of straining.

"As far as I can figure, we're smack in the middle of Adirondack Park. Do you know anything about this area?"

Tracy shook her head.

Rory sighed, his grasp on her shoulders turning gentler. "I don't either. Except that it's very big and very empty. We could be here for days before anybody finds us."

"Spin is in bad shape, isn't he?"

Rory met her eyes, but did not hesitate with the truth. He sighed once, shortly. "It doesn't look good. He could have just a headache, or maybe it's a concussion. He's not feeling too well just now."

"Your girlfriend isn't a nurse or anything, is she?"

" 'Fraid not," he admitted. "And time could be a big factor, you know."

Watching his eyes, Tracy cocked her head and said with a flick of sass in her tone, "I'm not the type to sit around and wait to get rescued, Rod-er-ick."

He pulled a grimace, looking pained. His hands slipped down unconsciously to hold her by the arms. "Somehow, I knew you were going to say that."

"Spin should be kept still, I'm sure. But if he needs to get to a hospital...."

"I know what you're thinking," Rory intervened, voice urgent, but still hushed to keep the conversation secret. "It's plain stupid to start running around these woods in the middle of the night—"

"But somebody's got to go!"

Rory sighed reluctantly again and nodded. "Yes."

"And somebody ought to stay here with Spin."

"Mary Alice is quite capable."

Staring at him, Tracy demanded, "You think you're a candidate for hiking around the woods in the dark?"

"You don't think any of us is going to let you go traipsing off all by yourself? Including Spinelli?"

"I can do anything I please, and he knows it!" Tracy shot back, wriggling finally to escape his light grasp. It was no use. He held her fast. She went on vehemently, "I'm sure as hell not going to sit around the campfire and wonder what happens next. I'm just not that kind of person!"

"So I'm discovering," he muttered, giving her a little shake, annoyance showing. "I don't like this."

"Fine." Tracy shrugged blithely. "Stay here, then, and—"

"Forget it. Somebody's got to keep you from

killing yourself. M.A. can look after Spinelli. You and I are going to start walking."

"Just walking," she said emphatically. "And not a thing more."

"Are you still spooked about one little kiss in your kitchen, for crying out loud! Hell, if we'd done half as much as I've been thinking about since then, you'd—"

"All right," Tracy said sharply, cutting him off. It was stupid to be so foolish about one kiss, after all. She had had too much to drink and probably had blown everything out of proportion. Surely other people didn't react so immaturely. Unwillingly, Tracy looked up at him through her lashes. It was just plain dopey to get all bent out of shape over this. Risking a swift pat on his chest, Tracy nodded once. Her own heart felt light suddenly, and she smiled, having no idea how winsome the expression looked on her sprightly features. "Shall we go looking for that French restaurant?"

The tension snapped, and Rory laughed. He reached and chucked her admiringly under the chin. "You're a hellion, Tracy O'Hara. But in this situation, I'm glad you're not the shrinking-violet type."

Tracy pushed him back and reached for the blankets. Why were her hands shaking all of a sudden? Was this guy going to unnerve her so easily? A kind word and she was as tongue-tied as a teenager on a blind date! To herself, Tracy muttered, *"Sometimes I wonder just what type I am!"*

Rory heard it, and the question made him grin. "I think you're in a category all your own, little Tracy—no, I can't call you that anymore. You're anything but little in every sense of the word. Is there anything you can't do?"

"Just don't plan on finding out," she snapped abruptly, shoving the blankets into his chest. "Shut up and go make yourself useful!"

She knew he was staring after her, maybe even laughing, but Tracy didn't stop. She ducked into the cockpit and left him standing in the hatchway. Sliding into Spin's seat, she began to study the controls. It was a full minute before her brain could function, and that fact made her angry. What was it with this Buchanan character? Did he have to get her so flustered just by paying her an almost-compliment? Shaking her head at her own silliness, Tracy got to work, having a long detailed inspection of the plane. Something peculiar had caused the smoke, and she wanted to know what. The others could see to Spin's needs and set up a camp.

Preparations were quickly made. By the time Tracy got out of the plane, Rory had a fire started, though there was plenty of smoke, and Mary Alice had rigged a comfortable spot for Spin with two of the blankets and some seat cushions from the plane. She had purposefully pushed her sweater sleeves up and was giving Spin sips of water from a Styrofoam cup. Darkness was falling fast around them.

Tracy handed her knapsack to the other woman. "Here. I packed some sandwiches before we took off. And there's root beer, too. Maybe I should pack something stronger in the future."

Spin looked up at that, a trace of his old grin appearing. "Don't let her fool you, Mary Alice. Tracy is strictly an amateur when it comes to booze. Root beer is enough to get her dancing on the tabletops."

"Shut up," Tracy told him with a smile.

"You must have had a premonition about this," Mary Alice said, giving Tracy a friendly look as she accepted the knapsack. "Sandwiches may come in handy, indeed."

"I was starving an hour ago," Tracy admitted, turning a little shy in front of so sophisticated a lady. "But now the thought of food couldn't be more remote."

Mary Alice laughed and rubbed her own back as if to demonstrate her own sore body. "You're so right!"

Spin tugged at Tracy's jeans. "What's this about you leaving us?"

Tracy pretended to jerk away from him. "Don't play big brother with me, Spinelli! I'm not going to sit around here toasting marshmallows and listening to ghost stories! I want to check out the neighborhood, so just keep your advice to yourself!"

He squinted at her, not quite sure what to make of her attitude. "This isn't for my benefit, is it? I'm gonna be fine in a few minutes, so—"

"What an ego!" Tracy exclaimed, blustering. She stuffed between her knees the sweater she had been carrying and began to peel off her jacket. "Who cares what happens to you? I just don't want to waste any time getting that plane into the repair shop! I'm losing money every minute any aircraft sits idle, you know."

"What's wrong with it?" Spin asked, trying valiantly to act normal in spite of his deteriorating condition. He was sweating now and looking white. "A fire after all? Something in the wiring?"

Tracy shrugged. She tossed her jacket on the ground and took up the sweater again. Pulling it over her head, she said, muffled, "I don't see a damn thing wrong with anything, and that's fishy! Who looked the plane over before we left?"

"I did, and Mark, of course," Spin said, passing a trembling hand across his brow. He winced, surprised by the pain, then tried to concentrate on the conversation. "Harvey was hanging around, poking his nose into things, too. One of us would have spotted something really serious."

Tracy had been watching Spin's face, not paying attention to his words. He looked very sick, and that frightened her. Spin was Spin: always there when she needed him and talking tough in every situation. Tracy looked up and met Mary Alice's gaze.

The other woman must have seen the panic in Tracy's green eyes, for she reached over to touch Tracy's arm. Her voice was cheerful, contrasting with the meaningfully direct expression on her face. "Well, don't fuss about that silly plane now. It certainly deserves to be in the junk heap, in my opinion! You and Rory go for a walk and see what you can find. Vincent and I will have a quiet evening here by the fire. Goodness, Rory! All this smoke!"

"Sorry." Rory joined them, dusting his hands on his trousers. "All I could find was rotten sticks or green stuff. I'm burning a couple of magazines first, just to get it started."

"Outdated issues anyway," Spin interjected feebly. "We're strictly low budget."

"Speak for yourself," Tracy said, zipping her jacket over two sweaters. She glanced at Rory. "You ready?"

He nodded, looking around. "Let me get another sweater. It's going to get chilly tonight, and I don't suppose you're going to want to share any body heat."

"What a comedian," Tracy said sideways to Mary Alice as Rory headed back to the plane.

Mary Alice laughed and began digging through

the knapsack. "Here. Take half the sandwiches, all right? And we'll split the flares, so we can signal any planes in the area. I'll put one of the blankets in here for you. I'm sure you'll have to rest before morning. Want a root beer?"

The two of them quickly reorganized the knapsack, and Tracy slung it around her shoulders.

Rory came back. "There was a road atlas in one of the seat pouches. I tore out this page, in case we can figure out which road this is."

Mary Alice took it from him and placed it in Tracy's knapsack. Her voice full of concern, she said to Rory, "This is the second time you've left me in Vincent's care, you know. Are you trying to tell me something?"

"No," Rory said with a sincere smile. "Except that I'm sorry I got you into this, M.A. Are you going to forgive me sometime?"

"Probably," M.A. said. "Unless you get yourself hurt or something. Be careful, will you? Stick to the roads and don't wander off into the woods. We may never find you if you do."

Joking, Rory wrapped one arm around Tracy's waist and pulled her against him. "We may never want to be found! Well, Tracy? Trust me in the dark?"

"Of course not," Tracy shot back, meeting his crooked grin with a careless smile of her own.

Spin roused himself, sitting up on one elbow. "Watch yourself, Buchanan. If there's one hair on her head that's mussed up when this is over with, I'm going to put the blame on you."

"Take it easy," Tracy commanded, punching playfully at Rory's midsection. "He'll have his hands full with me."

Dragging her off into the darkness, Rory said. "This is sounding better and better. M.A., don't send a search party for a week at least!"

CHAPTER FOUR

THEY HAD THEIR FIRST ARGUMENT not two hundred yards from the plane.

"No, I already walked in that direction for at least a mile," Rory said, "and there wasn't so much as a tire track. We go this way."

"That's stupid," Tracy said with contempt. "It's uphill, for starters, and—"

"You're tired already?" he demanded, halting in his tracks.

"No!" Tracy faced him crossly in the darkness. "The pioneers always followed water when they made towns, and water travels downward."

"The pioneers?" he repeated, not sure he had heard correctly.

"Any towns that we come across are going to be near water, so we should walk down hills whenever possible. This way." Tracy set off determinedly, walking with long brisk strides.

In a moment, Rory caught up. "I don't believe I'm doing this."

"What's the matter? Never took advice from a woman before?"

"You'd be surprised what I've taken from women before."

"Oh, honestly! If you're going to—"

"Simmer down." He took her elbow as they matched steps, their boots crunching in the loose stone of the road. The moon was already on the rise, shining some pale light on the narrow cleft in the trees. Rory said, "I suspect I'm better at taking advice from someone who knows more than I do. You, on the other hand, are so accustomed to running your own show that you act like a spoiled child in the pettiest situations."

"I am not spoiled!" Tracy objected hotly, yanking her arm free. "Or petty! Just—just strong willed, that's all."

Rory laughed. "Who told you that? Your father?"

"No, my father told me I was spoiled. Spin tells me that I'm strong willed."

"I see."

Tracy glanced up at him then, discerning in the meager light a cynical smile on his face. Full of suspicion, Tracy asked, "What do you mean? What've you got against Spin?"

"Not a thing." Rory looked down at her, surprised. "Brother, you're touchy."

"You think he's not as good as you, don't you?"

"My dear girl, he might be the next president, for all I know. Just what have the two of you got going?"

"Why should you care?" Tracy challenged, stuffing her hands into her jacket pockets again.

"All right. Forget I brought it up."

"He's been very good to me," Tracy snapped, as if the argument had continued. "He's the closest thing I have to family, so watch your mouth!"

"If he's so damned wonderful, then why haven't you married Prince Charming? Or is he too old for you?"

Tracy shot daggers up at him.

"He's obviously crazy about you," Rory went on mildly, obviously curious. "And he watches every move you make. What gives? Not enough of a man to suit you?"

"You are disgusting."

"Disgusting? You haven't seen anything yet."

Tracy swung at him.

He dodged her blow easily, laughing. "Sorry, sorry. That just slipped out. What about Spinelli? Aren't you a little nervous about leaving him back there with M.A.? She's quite a lady, you know."

"No details, please."

"Let's just say that she is an available woman, and aside from his concern about you, Spinelli hasn't taken his eyes off M.A. practically since they met last night. An obvious case of lightning striking—"

"You're dreaming!"

"Ah!" Rory noted with a knowledgeable chuckle. "You are jealous of her, then?"

"Of course not. There is nothing between Spin and me."

"You're not in love with him?"

"For cripes sake," Tracy exploded. "No!"

Her strangled shout had surprised the both of them. Except for the echoing rhythm of footsteps in the darkness, there was nothing but silence. They walked and walked, perhaps covering yet another hundred yards.

Finally, embarrassed by her outburst, Tracy added in a restrained voice that came close to sounding apologetic, "I guess I am touchy about Spin." She cleared her throat nervously. "You see, I have a feeling that he's my brother."

Rory didn't answer. They walked a little farther.

"I see," he said finally.

"I'm not absolutely sure," Tracy said then, glancing furtively up at him again. Imperceptibly, her steps slowed as she explained. "I just—it's just a feeling I get when I look at him sometimes. There's something about him that's so much like dad."

"Your father never said anything?"

"No, no. Spin showed up about two years before dad was killed. I was just a kid then and—don't laugh at me!"

"Sorry. Go on. You were just a kid...?"

Distrusting that crooked smile of his, Tracy frowned. After several more strides, her expression gave way, though, and she answered, "I was very young. Spin never looked twice at me then, and I was caught up in plenty of other things, so—"

Archly, Rory interrupted, "So your father probably figured there was lots of time to tell the both of you before something—shall I say unnatural?—took place."

Tracy was silent again, thinking. The night around them was close, eerily dark with streaks of blue-white light. Tracy felt very alone with Rory. Before, at her house and in the hangar, she had been totally unnerved by him. Now, despite the barbed humor, it was as if they were friends. They had become confidants in spite of the sarcasm that peppered the conversation. This realization was equally unnerving.

Swallowing hard, Tracy shook her head and asked, "Why am I telling you this?"

"Damned if I know," Rory said, taking her arm again automatically, as if they were out for a stroll on Easter Sunday. "But there's something very peculiar about you and me, Miss Tracy. It's—I don't know."

"Unnatural?"

Rory laughed, the pleasant, ringing sound bouncing with spooky resonance in the trees. His body was warm and hard against her, though, and Tracy didn't mind being held firmly at his side. It was comforting, actually. Tossing her head up to tease him as they walked, she said, "Okay, I've told you my deep dark secret. Now it's your turn."

"One quality I'm beginning to like about you, Miss Tracy, is your complete lack of sophistication."

"No stalling."

"A deep dark secret?" Rory mused, thinking. He kicked at a stone in the road. "All right. Tonight I had every intention of asking Mary Alice Cooper to marry me."

"Good grief!" Tracy exclaimed, startled.

"Not juicy enough for you?"

"Plenty juicy. I just—" She wagged her head. "I don't know. I figured you'd go for something more showy. Not quite so maternal."

"Showy?" he repeated on a laugh. "M.A. is an old friend and a good friend. She's bright and witty and very attractive, but no, she isn't showy."

"Well, in a day or two you can go ahead and ask her," Tracy said, conscious that her voice was too cheerful. "Sorry for the delay."

"No," Rory said thoughtfully. "I've reconsidered."

Tracy laughed. "Because of Spin? Come on!"

"No, no," Rory admitted quickly. "Hasn't a thing to do with the way that relationship seemed to take off. I've reconsidered my reasoning, that's all."

"That sounds very cold-blooded," Tracy observed, sending him a derisive glance.

"I suppose so," he said, and he was quiet for a while, thinking.

Into that long and pregnant silence, Tracy asked slyly, "Are you the love-'em-and-leave-'em type, Roderick?"

"That's not the way it is," Rory said harshly, clearly angry with someone other than Tracy—himself perhaps. After a moment's consideration, he added, "I'm not exactly sure what's in the wind at the moment."

"Are you usually this confused about your love life?" Tracy inquired.

He smiled wryly. "Not usually. You see, I've decided that marrying M.A. would suit my purposes very well, but it just wouldn't be fair to her. She's one of the nicest women I know, and I've decided I'm the worst possible husband for her."

"Not enough sex appeal to suit her, huh?"

Rory wrenched playfully at her arm, hauling Tracy for a few steps.

"I give up!" Tracy cried, laughing. "I take it back!"

"So you think I haven't got any sex appeal, Miss Tracy?"

"I never said that!" Tracy shot back, prancing away from him in the darkness. "You're plenty appealing, Rod-er-ick. Too appealing, if you ask me! What a smoothie!"

"Well, if your limited experience extends only

to the aw-shucks type like Spinelli, I can see why I've shocked you."

"You haven't shocked me!" she claimed indignantly, halting in the road while he caught up. "You just act too cocky, pal, like you expect me to fall at your feet and start tearing off my clothes in a frenzy."

"That hasn't happened to me in at least six weeks," he said, laughing. "So go ahead. This night could use some livening up."

She punched him, laughing also. "See what I mean? Too cocky."

He wrapped his arm around her and pulled Tracy against him once again, smiling as they walked together down the center of the road. "I haven't got half the chip on my shoulder that you've got on yours. What an attitude! You're a regular spark plug, you know. Very refreshing."

"You're just jaded. I'm a nice girl who doesn't take any guff from anybody."

"Good for you. You're a scrappy little thing, and if I wasn't afraid you'd bite me for it, I'd probably try something very natural out here in these woods tonight."

"Forget it. I don't want pine needles in my pants or ants crawling—"

"Okay, okay," he soothed, still amused. "Forget I even suggested such a thing. Tell me some more deep dark secrets."

"I told you the only one I've got. What you see is what you get with me."

"Hmm," Rory said, studying her with a pretended frown. "I see a very pretty young lady who ought to have a dozen boyfriends loitering in the hangar. What gives with you?"

"I'm not abnormal," Tracy retorted emphatically.

He laughed. "I can see that for myself. Could it be that you're actually shy behind this blustering bravado?"

"I wasn't so shy last night in my house," Tracy said proudly, with a look up at him.

"Your big seduction scene?" Rory shook his head. "That was an act, pure and simple."

"How do you know?" Tracy demanded.

"There's nothing wrong with being a little shy."

"I am not shy! My love life hasn't been totally...I mean...."

"So tell me about your love life if it's not abnormal."

Tracy shot him a measuring glare. "You want a few vicarious thrills since you're getting nowhere with me?"

"Forget I brought it up!" Rory exclaimed in laughing exasperation. "Is there any topic of conversation that's safe enough for you?"

"Let's talk about you some more," Tracy suggested with a wicked grin. "Likes and dislikes? Perversions?"

"All right," he said promptly. "What do you want to know?"

"I don't know." Tracy shrugged and kept walking. "How did you get into the airline business? You don't look the type."

"Because I haven't got grease under my nails?" Rory asked archly. "I'm a businessman, Tracy. And times have changed very quickly. Successful airlines aren't run by old barnstorming pilots anymore. It's a very competitive industry now, a fact you had better wake up to."

"Is this going to turn into a lecture, after all?" Tracy yawned gustily. "Tell me something I don't already know, please, Rod-er-ick."

Rory blew an exasperated sigh. "You're impossible, aren't you?"

"Yep. Talk, Rod-er-ick. Something interesting this time."

"Okay." Rory stuffed his hands into his pockets and threw his head back, breathing in the crisp night air. Out of the blue, he plucked a subject. "I hate French cooking, and I'm glad we haven't found a restaurant yet."

"Why do you hate French cooking?"

"Too rich. Too heavy. I've got a delicate digestive system."

Tracy punched at his stomach, laughing.

"I inherited it from my mother," Rory added, joking. "I like Chinese, though."

"You've been eating old-fashioned French cooking."

He laughed at her imperious tone. "How would

you know? The young lady who brings root beer and ham sandwiches along?"

"I was fresh out of Châteauneuf-du-Pape and melon balls. Come on, Rod-er-ick, keep me awake. What else do you like?"

So they talked and taunted and walked for a long time. Hours, in fact, must have passed while they plunged into a startlingly intimate exchange of information. Tracy told him about her mother who had divorced Frank O'Hara when Tracy was fifteen and had gone off to Montreal to rejoin her family there.

"My mom and dad met in France when dad was stationed there after the war," Tracy informed him. "They got married, and brought her parents to live in this country, but granddad wanted to go to Canada. There are more people from France there, I guess. So most of our family's in Montreal, and I'm down here."

When the divorce had taken place, Tracy had chosen to remain with her father. The decision had hurt her mother, but the bitterness subsided after a few years. Granted, they were long years for a young girl. Tracy visited her mother from time to time. The ex-Mrs. O'Hara had remarried, but Tracy was her only child.

Rory, with a little prodding, admitted that he had an older brother and two sisters. His parents still lived not far from Chicago, and all the Buchanan children kept homes within the same ten-mile radius. "We weren't very close as kids," he told Tracy after a while, "but now we're best friends, it seems. Kind of funny the way things turned out."

And he spoke about his father, a retired salesman for a multimillion-dollar aircraft manufacturer. "He got out of the business shortly after I got into it," Rory explained. "That kept the competition to a minimum."

The talk and laughter continued as the moon rose and passed across the night sky. They both dished out verbal harassment with great delight, each taking a turn at making the wisecracks. At times the conversation headed toward more serious, sensitive subjects, but some mutual warning system had sprung up between them and truly private ground was never invaded.

Time went quickly, but soon muscles began to ache in protest. Finally, after laboring up a particularly long hill, Tracy stumbled on a low spot in the road. Rory caught her easily, and they stopped together, breathless with exertion. Rory checked his watch, tilting his wrist to the moonlight.

"Two in the morning!"

"Really?" Tracy panted, leaning against him instinctively. "We've been walking all this time, and still nothing?"

Rory was looking around them as he supported her loosely in his arms. "This is getting ridiculous!"

The trees had thinned out a bit, and the landscape was still devoid of human touches, but the road had become smoother. Tall grass grew profusely along the sides, and only the chirping of crickets broke the solitude.

Tracy disengaged herself from him. In so short a time Rory had gotten awfully familiar with her, taking every excuse to hold or touch her. It was pleasant, she admitted, but disconcerting. She tugged her jacket down. "How far do you think we've walked?"

"Far enough," Rory declared.

"What? Where—?"

He took her hand and pulled Tracy to the side of the road, heading for an open space in the grass. "I've had it. I'm hungry and I'm tired of walking, and you need a rest."

"I do not!" Tracy resisted, digging in her heels.

"Well, I do, so we're stopping for a while. Come here."

"I don't want to go in there. If you want to rest, we do it right here!"

"In the middle of this road? Are you kidding? There hasn't been a vehicle through here in months, but as soon as I fall asleep, a bunch of drunk teenagers in a Volkswagen will come along and run me over. I didn't live through a plane crash just to be killed by a VW!"

"I don't want to go in there," Tracy repeated adamantly.

"Come on!" Rory dragged her into the grass. "We can sit down for a few minutes and have a sandwich."

"I don't like this."

"Weren't you ever a Girl Scout? Here! A rock that's perfect. Sit down."

"I don't want to sit." Tracy's teeth were clenched, and she looked quickly around, continuing to sidle nervously around Rory. "I want to go back to the road."

"For crying out loud, you don't have to prove how strong you are, you know. I'll admit you're the toughest little—"

"I'm going," Tracy said firmly, starting back to the road. "There are snakes in here. I know it!"

"Snakes! At this time of year? What self-respecting snake is going to freeze his tail off—don't go that way!"

Tracy decided to make a beeline for the road, not following the short, though winding path they had taken to get to the rock. She hurried through some tall cattails, thrusting her hands through the wisping stuff. It clung to her clothes, and Tracy's heart began to pound with anxiety. She was gasping for breath, nervous and suddenly frightened of the dark.

"Tracy!"

She slipped and fell headlong, splashing. Muck oozed up through her fingers, smelling of dank decay. Having had the wind knocked out of her,

Tracy lay for one horrible moment, too stunned to cry out.

"Tracy!"

Galvanized by revulsion, she scrambled instantly to her feet, shuddering with fright and a sudden nausea. Then she staggered backward.

Rory's arms came around her from behind, preventing her from bolting across the puddle to the road. "Well," he said lightly, "the pioneers must have had a slightly different system for finding water. You okay?"

Tracy nodded, jerking, still too shaken to speak.

"You've soaked your sleeves. Come back here and sit down. There aren't any snakes, I promise. Is that what's got you so nervy all of a sudden? No snakes, honestly. Come back here."

He was gentle but insistent, and Tracy obeyed this time. He tugged his handkerchief from a pocket and pushed it into her freezing hands. Then Rory sat her down on the long rock that jutted up from the grass, and Tracy promptly curled up, hugging her knees tightly and scraping the sticky slime from her unsteady fingers.

"Take off your jacket," he told her, both hands steadying Tracy by her shoulders. "Let's have a look at the damage. It's a lot cooler when we're not moving, isn't it? If you're wet, it'll be worse. I've got the sack thing. Here."

He had stripped off her knapsack, and stuffed it

under his arm to help her with her jacket. Tracy got it unzipped, though her hands were trembling, and Rory peeled it from her body.

"Hmm," he said a moment later, holding it up to the meager light to have a look. He groped along the sleeves for wetness. "Yep. You did it right. Soaked. Less muddy than I first thought, fortunately. Did M.A. pack a blanket or something?"

"Give me that thing," Tracy said irritably, snatching the knapsack from him with her driest hand. "I'll find it."

He laid her jacket on the rock. "Fix us some dinner, all right, Mrs. Boone? I'll be back in a second."

"Where are you going?" Tracy demanded as he started away from her. "Don't go wandering off!"

"Take it easy," he said over his shoulder.

Short of embarrassing herself by begging him to stay with her, Tracy had no choice but watch Rory's tall frame blend and finally disappear into the darkness. She listened intently to his receding footsteps, holding very still to be certain he didn't go too far. In time, there was only silence.

The night breeze rustled eerily in the grass. It was too much. Hesitantly, Tracy called, "Buchanan?"

No answer.

But then he was on his way back, swishing

through the grass purposefully and dragging something heavy behind. Determined not to look foolish, Tracy hastily finished drying off her hands and then dug into the knapsack, coming up with a plastic-wrapped sandwich.

"What are you doing?" she asked, regaining her voice and thanking heaven he hadn't heard her call out for him a moment ago. "What is that?"

"An old branch. I saw it by the road a ways back." He stepped on one end and bent the curling stick upward. It snapped with a dry crack, and Rory held up the shortened limb triumphantly. "Firewood."

"Do you honestly think that's going to burn all by itself?"

He pretended to be offended. "I was an Eagle Scout, I'll have you know. We're invincible. Or inseparable. Or—"

"Insensible was the rumor I heard. Okay, play with your matches. Meanwhile, I'm eating."

"Save some for me," he retorted, setting about breaking up the rest of the dried branch.

"The law of the forest says that the strong survive. You're going to have to fight me for the root beer."

Rory grinned at her, still busy with the wood. "You know, you're no dummy, are you?"

In the act of unwrapping the sandwich, Tracy paused to stare at him. "What brought that on?"

He shrugged, snapping the smallest end of the

branch in one hand. "You play at being something you aren't, then all of a sudden you surprise me."

Tracy gave a gruff "Humph."

"You see? You're either pretending to be John Wayne in a flight jacket, or you're wisecracking like Mae West. But you've got the vocabulary of a Vassar grad. What gives with you?"

"Is this your way of giving me a compliment? Or are you leading up to something?"

He laughed, shaking his head. "I have the feeling you'd head me off at the pass. Any kind of pass," he added heavily. "Tell me, did you go to college or was daddy a secret reader of Voltaire?"

Tracy eyed him as he worked, and she took the first bite of ham sandwich. Mouth full, she said, "I went to college for a while."

"Graduate?"

She shook her head and swallowed. "Two years. Then I got interested in other things, I guess."

He glanced at her measuringly.

"Okay," she admitted, caught in the lie. "We ran out of money."

"Where'd you go? What did you study?"

Tracy sighed irritably. "What's the big deal? I just went to SUNY and took a bunch of courses."

"Good grades?"

Her head came up proudly. "Straight A's since kindergarten."

"No kidding?" Rory looked surprised. "Good grief! What are you doing buried here?"

Tracy looked around them at the forest. "Here? It looks like I'm talking to some nosy character from Chicago. Hurry up with the fire, will you? I'm starting to freeze."

He threw down the pieces of wood and kicked them into a small pile, at the same time stripping off his own jacket. In a moment he came to her and slung it around her shoulders.

Tracy didn't thank him, but she stuck half the sandwich in his mouth. "What's the third degree all about, Rod-er-ick? You looking for a way to get my airplanes away from me?"

He shook his head, taking a bite of the sandwich and thoughtfully studying her as he chewed. "Just thinking about what you're going to do once Shamrock Air doesn't exist."

"Don't worry about it. I'm not losing any sleep."

Rory took a peek into his sandwich. "No mustard, huh? Do you want to come work for me?"

Tracy choked, flabbergasted. "Are you kidding?"

"What's wrong with that? You're smart, and with a little training, you could probably learn how to run an airline properly."

"Forget it," she snapped, growing hostile at that remark.

Watching her askance, Rory cautioned, "Don't

toss this opportunity away without thinking it over. I'm serious. You want a job?"

"Not with you," Tracy said, meeting his eyes.

"Sure about that?"

Tracy nodded, very solemn suddenly. She didn't know why, but she was absolutely sure she did not want to end up working with this man every day. "Yes," she said quietly. "I'm real sure about that."

For a long moment, they were very still, watching each other so steadily that the trees around them seemed to recede into the darkness and disappear. Rory's eyes were bright, flickering with speculation. Another thought seemed to lurk behind his gaze, and Tracy wondered at it. For an instant, it seemed as if he made some important decision about her—a decision that did not please him very much.

By way of apology, Tracy reached and touched his arm. "I don't know why, but I don't want to work for you."

"I know why," Rory said, voice flat.

Tracy put her sandwich down abruptly, afraid to look at him any longer.

Rory lost his reserve, took a step and grasped her wrist. "We'd be fighting this all the time."

He pulled her up. As naturally as if they had rehearsed, Tracy slipped her arms around his neck and recklessly met the kiss. His mouth was quick and familiar, immediately delving deeply into hers. Tracy caught his hair in her fingers and surrendered, parting her soft lips in anticipation of his firm mouth, sensing his loss of control. Rory drew her hard against him, aligning her slight figure to his tougher body and holding her tightly, urgently.

Tracy's head spun. A keen longing welled up in her, a swift, almost painful tremor of desire that rose to her breast. He was strong and hungry, savoring her mouth and sliding one hand provocatively up inside the jacket. His touch was skilled, delighting in the curve of her back while adept in finding the bottom of her sweater. In a moment, Rory's palm was warm against her bare back.

Tracy arched up into his chest, longing to be closer still. Uncertainly, she slipped her hand down the line of his chest. His breath locked under her touch, and he finally broke the kiss, too impatient to be content with that any longer. Aroused, he pressed a string of openmouthed kisses down her throat. "Tracy," he murmured against her skin. "Tracy, I never meant this to happen."

"Please," she heard herself whisper nonsensically.

He continued to kiss her throat, exploring back up to breathe lightly at her ear. "You're a little witch, I swear. I never meant to get tangled up this time. Now I can't keep my hands off you!"

Knees weak, she held his shoulders tightly, too

languid with the pleasure of being held in his arms to get angry. "You're the worst sort of manipulator, aren't you?"

With a breathless laugh, Rory said, "It's got to look that way. I can't help it! You're such a sassy kitten, and you're practically crying out to be taken care of!" He paused, and then murmured huskily, "Kiss me."

She lifted her mouth, and Rory took it swiftly, too excited to make it gentle this time. Roughly, he kissed her lips and sought to caress her under the sweater. His hand curved up, meeting the bare thrust of her shoulder blade and discovering she wasn't wearing a bra. The knowledge sparked something in him, and Rory quickly slipped around to find her breast. She was small and warm and soft, but for her quickening nipple that seemed to burn his thumb when he found it.

Trembling, Tracy let out a short, breathy sigh. His touch was hot on her breast, so welcome that a sharp, stabbing kind of ache shot down through her body. Rory was deft, rousing her nipple and eliciting in Tracy a kind of pain-pleasure that she had never known before. Just as expertly then, he slid down her belly to where the tumult raged inside. His hand was warm and caressing, flat against her one moment and smoothing a gentle circle the next. He was too good, too quick to sense her thoughts and desires. He knew what sensations his touch aroused, for when Tracy sighed again, involuntarily this time, he kissed her temple and murmured, "Yes, I want you, too."

She could allow him to unfasten her belt, for he was already there, dipping his fingers once and twice down into her jeans. He had backed her into the rock, and was gently parting her thighs with his knee. She could let him strip off her sweaters. He had already laid aside the jacket. She could let him make love to her, teaching her all the nuances he had come to know. His shallow breath was warming her neck. His hands were thrilling her; his muscled body felt so wonderful. She wanted him so much that it hurt.

But one thin ray of common sense shone through the dusky haze of passion. Tracy let her head loll back under the rain of nibbling kisses. Softly she whispered, "Don't, please. Don't do this to me. I don't want to be another for you."

"Another?" Rory abandoned his caresses and quickly wound his hand into her long, tumbled hair. Forcefully he tipped her face up to his, scanning her pale features by the cool light of the moon. With his thumb, he traced the tempting curve of her cheekbone. "Tracy, I know how this looks. I'm sorry for that. I've got a reputation, but—"

His eyes were stormy on hers, full of caring, Tracy was sure. But she didn't quite trust them. Voice shaking, she said, "I don't want to be a business conquest. I'm a woman, now, not a company."

"If you only knew how much of a woman!" Rory said sharply, angry with himself. He laid his cheek against hers and pulled Tracy against him once more. "Tracy, you're unique, the most lovely woman I've ever met. I don't want to conquer you. I don't think you'd let me. Just—just—"

Tracy slipped her hands up to hold his shoulders. She laid her head against him and closed her eyes to drink in the sensations. Too quietly for Rory to hear, she breathed, "Just hold me."

"I want you, Tracy," Rory went on roughly, hugging her to him, though he couldn't have heard her plea. "I want your spirit—your spunk. You're not beaten, are you? You haven't realized yet that failure exists. Tracy—" He stopped himself, burying his nose in her wildly curling hair. A shudder rippled through him then, as Rory managed to control himself. On a choked sigh, he added inadequately, "You've got something I need, Tracy."

Perhaps he didn't realize what he was saying. Perhaps he hadn't meant to give away his corporate-takeover strategy in such an unbridled moment. At least he had been honest. He wanted Shamrock Air, and Tracy was apparently part of the bargain. Aching with reluctance, Tracy spread her hands on his chest and pushed. The pressure was weak, but insistent. When Rory loosened his grip on her, Tracy kept her head down, her eyes hidden from him. Her laugh was tremulous. "I'll bet you say that to all the airlines, Rod-er-ick."

He was still, unsure of her meaning. With one finger, he lifted her chin and in the darkness looked deeply into her eyes. "No," he said quietly. "I say what I mean. You're becoming more than just a financial statement, my girl."

She lifted her chin away. "Don't tease me anymore."

"I'm not—" Rory blew an exasperated breath. "Tracy, it was an instant thing with us. It had nothing to do with the business. Ever since you goaded me into kissing you last night, I've been sorry about the airline stuff. I want us just to be a man and a woman. Can't—"

"I don't think you're going to have it both ways," Tracy said, smiling a little to take the sting from her words. She patted him whimsically. "In a cooler moment, I'd ask you to pick one."

Rory did not release her. Giving her arm a shake, he demanded, "You don't really think I could fake what just happened? Do you believe I'm using sex to get your company?"

Tracy's smile broadened boldly. "It's not a bad way to do business, Rod-er-ick. At least, I'm not complaining yet."

He let her go and took an angry pace away. "Damn it!"

"Now, now. Don't give up yet. Your technique is much nicer than what Hallis Air tried."

Rory scowled and braced his fists on his trim

hips angrily. "What's it going to take to convince you that I—that I'm attracted to your mind and yes, to your body, without your stupid airline? Am I going to have to leave you alone?"

Pretending dismay, Tracy widened her eyes prettily. "Oh, what's the fun in that?" She perched on the rock, face upturned to his and smiling. "At least we've got things out in the open. I know what you want. And you...."

He noticed her hesitation and pounced. "And I?"

"And you've found the quickest way to get me hot and bothered." Tracy touched her own lips ruefully. "You're quite the master, aren't you, Rod-er-ick?"

"No," he said slowly. "You just reacted in a very instinctive kind of way."

She plucked up her sandwich again, preparing to munch. She was strangely elated by what had occurred. So he found her attractive! And he couldn't keep his hands off her? Tracy propped her legs up on the rock, unconscious of the pixie-like picture she made there. She cocked her head, tossing her bright hair. "Tell me all the good stuff now. Am I the sexiest girl you've ever known? The prettiest?"

With renewed determination, Rory hunkered down to the fire he had started to build. "If we're not going to bring this conversation to its natural culmination, let's just change the subject, all right? It's become mighty uncomfortable for me the way it's going."

Tracy laughed, her heart swiftly taking wing within her. Watching him work, she said, "I suppose it's one of the hazards of doing business in the particular way you've chosen. Since I'm feeling sorry for you, I won't fight over the root beer. Do you want a swallow?"

Rory looked up at her as Tracy, with a Cheshire-cat grin and a new fire of green in her eyes, sat. Even the layers of clothing that covered her lithe figure did not blot out the lasting sensation of her bare skin against his hands. Her body was young and full of life, just like her spirit.

Rory ground his teeth at the fresh surge of desire for so spicy-sweet a woman. On a growl, he said, "I'm going to want plenty more than a swallow from you, Miss Tracy. Plenty more."

CHAPTER FIVE

THE BIRDS WOKE TRACY before sunrise. Her heart contracted with the momentary fear that came with not knowing where she was, and she was instantly alert. Then, just as quickly, she relaxed, afraid to wake him.

For they had finally fallen asleep, curled together spoon-fashion on the blanket, with Rory's fleecy jacket wrapped loosely over the both of them. His arm was snug around Tracy's waist, elbow riding on the curve of her hip and fingertips lying innocently against her breast. He must have fallen asleep with his nose in her hair, for she could feel the warm caress of his breath near her ear.

Around them, the morning air was cold, so cold that when Tracy expelled a slow unsteady sigh, a misty cloud rose from her mouth. But next to Rory, snuggled deeply against his body, she felt toasty warm. She could feel the gentle rise and fall of his chest as he slept, and her own breathing matched his rhythm. A contented smile curved on Tracy's lips. She closed her eyes again dreamily to relish the intimacy and wait for the sunrise.

Around them the birds were soon clamoring for sunshine, and the sky swiftly turned lighter and lighter. When the first flicker of sun pierced the trees, Rory stirred. He stopped breathing, tightened his arm, and must have remembered where he was. He drew Tracy harder against him and nuzzled her hair. His voice was a gravelly murmur. "You awake?"

She pretended to wake up, shifting against him, then stretching contentedly. She put her knuckles to her eyes and yawned.

Rory gave Tracy a rough kiss on the side of her throat and set her away from him.

She sat up, blushing, and automatically raised her hands to straighten her tangled hair. Tracy kept her head turned to scold him. "We were just going to rest for a minute, remember?"

"You fell asleep like a baby in a cradle," Rory retorted from behind her. Then he groaned and painfully eased himself upright. "Oh, brother."

Tracy looked around at him. "What's wrong?"

Flexing his back gingerly, he winced and grumbled, "I'm older than I thought."

"Stiff?"

"Very," he responded heavily. "That landing last night was just a little rough. Aren't you sore?"

"No," Tracy lied. "Whose bright idea was it to take a snooze on the cold ground after all that exercise?" She crawled around to him and pushed his jacket off completely. Businesslike, Tracy laid her hands on his shoulders and started rubbing with strong, deep strokes. "You'll probably land in the hospital for exposure."

Rory groaned again, with relief this time, and arched his back under her massage. "That's terrific. Lower down."

Tracy obeyed, rubbing the triangle of his back. Even through Rory's sweater, she could feel the hard contour of him. He was gingerly stretching, like a tiger waking from a nap, and Tracy resisted the sudden urge to slide her hands up under his sweater to knead the muscle there. She shook her hair away from her face, clearing her own head, and asked lightly, "Getting better? Are you awake enough to think?"

"About getting out of here? Yes. Are you willing to walk again?"

"I don't think we've got a choice. We've killed several hours here. We had better get going."

Rory checked his watch. "Six-thirty. There ought to be search planes out anytime now. Flares?"

"In the knapsack."

"Okay, Miss Tracy, let's get going."

She let go of Rory's muscled shoulders and sat back on her heels, thinking. It had been awfully easy to touch him and certainly pleasant. She had surprised herself, for she recognized that she wanted to touch him some more, to feel his skin and learn every bone and sinew of his strong frame. In fact, she could feel that awful urgency inside herself again, the desire to hold him as he had held her in the night. The thought was startling in her mind. It made her feel abruptly guilty.

Unconsciously smoothing her palms together, Tracy looked skyward. It was certainly light enough to fly, and the weather was thankfully clear. Had anyone started looking yet? The guys back at Shamrock Air must have been having heart attacks by now and screaming for search parties. How much time would it take to locate the wreckage and get Spin away to a hospital? Tracy bit her lip, wondering.

"Hey." Rory nudged her with his elbow as he tightened the laces on his boots. He noted her silence and turned to look at her with new concern. "Are you really okay?"

Tracy flung her hair over her shoulders quickly. It was the sort of question that Spin would ask her. Spin was always worrying about her state of mind. Flashing Rory a rueful smile, she said, "Sure. I was just thinking, that's all."

He tousled her hair playfully, but with a sort of friendliness that brought a lump to Tracy's throat. "Don't worry," he said gently, obviously guessing the direction of her thoughts. He glanced once up at the sky and gave her a reassuring grin, resting his hand on the nape of her neck. "Spinelli's going to be perfectly healthy when we see him again."

Tracy shook her head quickly, trying to swallow the tightness in her throat. "I—I wonder if we should have left them. Maybe we should have stayed and—"

"Don't," he said quietly, petting her hair. "Don't worry, all right? They could very well have been picked up by now and be having breakfast in bed somewhere."

"In bed?" Tracy repeated dryly, meeting his eyes with disdain. "You're disgusting, you know?"

Rory laughed agreeably, glad to see that her mood had returned to its normal status. He let her go. "As a matter of fact, I'm beginning to wonder if it was safe to leave those two alone together. If you've been teasing Spinelli half as much as you've tormented me, he's bound to have stored up some serious libido in the last few years."

Tracy cracked him on the arm and collected her poise, afraid that Rory might see her anxiety and think she was weak. "Maybe he doesn't take his sex life quite as seriously as you do, Rod-er-ick. Are you capable of walking, or am I going to have to drag you out of here?"

"Come along, Miss Tracy," he commanded, unruffled by her quick tongue. He got to his feet and put a hand down to her. "Let's hit the happy trail."

They doused the ashes of their fire with a little puddle of water they'd collected in the empty root-beer bottle, and found Tracy's jacket to be almost dry enough to wear. She slung it around her shoulders, and in a matter of minutes, they were back on the road. Rory was still stiff, but a few chocolate cookies seemed to divert his attention, and by the time he had eaten, the stiffness was almost gone.

Regaining her humor, Tracy needled him about the eight years difference in their ages, dancing around him like a frisky colt in spite of her own protesting muscles. The morning was very cold, and the fresh color on her cheeks was pretty in the sunshine.

Rory marveled inwardly at her cheerfulness, commanding her once, "Stop that silliness before you trip and kill yourself!"

But Tracy only pretended to be cowed, falling into step with him for several strides before her giggling gave her away.

Exasperated, Rory snatched her arm in hand and held her close to his side. "You're practically a delinquent, aren't you? Behave now, or I'll leave you here in the wilderness."

"Who'll leave who?" Tracy demanded, laughing. "You're the cripple, not me!"

Their progress was steady, and in an hour, they came upon an intersecting road and the sign Noblesboro, with an arrow. Rory tore open the knapsack to get the map, and together they scanned the paper, looking for such a place. Rory found it first and pointed. "Here."

"Can't be!" Tracy objected. "We ought to be farther north somewhere, don't you think?"

"Depends on how you two brought the plane down," Rory said, wrapping up the map again. "I seem to remember losing my stomach somewhere around fifteen thousand feet. You must have brought the plane back around this way. Look." He nodded at the road. "Tire tracks. We must be getting a little closer to civilization."

In another hour they came upon someone's house. It turned out to be a hunting camp, Rory decided, because there was no phone line and no one answered the door. They walked a little farther and came upon a farmhouse. A hostile collie flew out from under a gnarled apple tree, barking his head off, and Tracy dived behind Rory with a strangled squeal. The dog crashed his chest against the gate, taking up his position and barking, barking, barking.

The woman who came out on the porch in pink curlers and a bathrobe was grouchy—they had awakened her, it seemed—and she was suspicious of Tracy's filthy jacket and Rory's scruffy lack of a shave. She yelled at the dog, but that made no difference, so she had to come out into the yard and drag him by his collar before any of the humans could make themselves heard.

Very soon, she understood that there was trouble. With an embarrassed apology for her initial reaction, she ordered the dog to shut up, kicked his tail to emphasize her command, and then asked everyone into the farmhouse. She directed Rory to the telephone and spoke with Tracy about hospitals and airports while making a pot of coffee.

In the kitchen, she turned on the radio and directed Tracy to have a seat at the table—never mind the bucket of apples there; she was going to can some apple sauce this morning. And did Miss O'Hara want any sponge cake? There was some left over from supper.

With Rory's voice rising and falling authoritatively in the next room, the aroma of fresh coffee in the air, and the collie happily curled up in front of the stove, Tracy realized that her whole body was as tightly wound as a new watch. She had kept her composure and acted like an adult until now, but suddenly, with the relief of knowing there was help on the way, she wanted to cry.

The woman of the house chattered on pleasantly, now and then shouting into the bedroom for her husband to hurry up. This picture of domestic tranquility was too much. Tracy sat down on a kitchen stool and pressed cold hands to her face. *Please, no. Don't let me cry now.* Her eyes stung fiercely and Tracy swallowed hard, fighting it.

Rory's conversation was drawing to a close. She heard him say, "In half an hour. Right."

He came into the kitchen then, and Tracy hastily spun the stool around so that she was staring out the window over the sink. Rory thanked the woman for the use of her phone, but she scoffed, "Mercy me, the least I can do!" and pushed a cup of coffee into his hands. Then she bustled out of room, leaving Tracy and Rory alone.

Taking a quick gulp of coffee, Rory walked toward her.

"They're way ahead of us," he reported, coming to a stop behind her. "A plane went up at dawn, and there's a helicopter on its way from Albany."

"Albany?" Tracy asked, trying to sound startled. The tremble in her voice gave her away, though, so for safety she did not turn around to look at him.

Rory hesitated, then passed the coffee cup around to Tracy and laid his hand on her shoulder. Head bowed, Tracy shivered under his steadying touch, but Rory pretended not to notice. Casually he explained, "That's where they come from around here. I talked to the character who seems to be running the show, and I told him about the road we came out on. He knew exactly what I was talking about, so they're sending the helicopter out there as soon as it shows up. Rather than taking a car out there, they seem to think it'll be faster to send the chopper. Here, help me drink this."

Tracy took the proffered cup, and tried a quick, calming sip. Her hands were shaking so badly that she abruptly set the cup down on the edge of the sink. Her voice sounded false. "Let's hope the pilot can find a—a place to land a whirlybird."

Rory recognized the feminine signs of near-tears, but it took him a moment to file through all the possible methods of coping. Deciding to risk getting clobbered, he wrapped one arm around Tracy from behind and pulled her up. Molding her body to fit his, he rocked her gently. "So what do you say?" he murmured in her ear, too low for anyone else to hear over the yammer of the radio. He tickled her with his nose. "You want to go back out in the woods for a while and fool around?"

Tracy poked him with her elbow and laughed unsteadily. "You're just disgusting, aren't you?"

"No, just discriminating," he countered cheerfully, turning Tracy and holding her before him, her back braced against the sink. His eyes were bright, and his slow grin was intriguingly crooked, sliding roguishly to one side. Even with the dark growth of a day's beard on his face, he was very handsome. Lower, he added, "I'd get lost with you anytime, Miss Tracy."

"We're not out of this yet, Rod-er-ick," she said firmly, taking the lapels of his jacket in her hands. Trying to keep a straight face, she tugged at him and said, "You and I may be stuck together for a few more hours, at least."

"Sounds great," he responded, coming inches

closer. His arms tightened around her, forcing Tracy to slide her hands up to encircle his neck. With his satisfied smile coming closer and closer to her lips, Rory said, "Let's make the most of it."

Tracy shouldn't have let him do it, and Rory half expected to get a crack across his face before he started. But she did. And he didn't. Their embrace was spontaneous; a natural, easy folding of one body to another. Tracy tipped her head to watch his eyes, smoke blue and far from solemn. She smiled too, and melted the last centimeter. Their mouths coupled slowly, tentatively, sweetly.

All sorts of delicious sensations swirled in Tracy, like autumn leaves on a breezy morning. The soft, searching kiss was gentle and mellow, strangely satiating. It had been a long night, a pleasant morning, and now she wanted to be held exactly so in Rory's arms. Gratefully, she gave in and lifted herself on her toes to fit intimately to his frame.

Slowly, involuntarily, Rory wound one hand in her hair as he deepened the kiss. He tightened his arm around Tracy's slender figure and pressed her so firmly to him that the contours of separate bodies were melded in one gentle but inescapable embrace. She yielded pliantly.

Caught in the moment, he eased her mouth wider, savoring the first sparks of tenderness in Tracy. She was soft and alluring in his arms, no longer angry or even taunting him with playful words. She was touchingly feminine, her hands slipping naturally around his neck. She made no sound, but her breathing was light, unafraid. Her thick, tumbled hair smelled of woodsmoke and felt soft and silky in his hands. When Rory touched her cheek, the delicate softness of her skin reminded him of the outside petals of a budding rose.

The passion came then, in a slow, building crescendo of coursing blood and quick, eager breathing. Tracy held his face in her hands, keeping Rory's mouth to her own lips, as if the increasing pressure was the only way to contain the fire within. Her body was fairly pulsing with the heat and the anxious need to hold him to her and draw him nearer still. The memory of kneading the muscle of his back was so vivid in her mind that Tracy suppressed a cry of deprivation. She wanted him, she needed to touch all of him and give of herself. The longing was so real, so suddenly exciting, that Tracy was beyond reality. Her senses took command, and she gave a shaken sigh against his mouth.

The woman must have come back into the kitchen by then, for she coughed awkwardly. The world seemed to materialize around Tracy and Rory once again.

Tracy slipped slowly down his chest, relaxing her grasp, and Rory let her go, their gazes remaining locked in stunned, but half-smiling silence.

Tracy was confused, and she blushed a pretty pink. Then the expression in Rory's face made her insides contract with indecision. His answering smile faded and was replaced by absolute blankness.

Tracy tore herself from his arms and tottered one step to lean unsteadily on the table. The woman of the house was staring at the two of them, and her husband, who had finally appeared in his coveralls, looked appropriately bewildered to find a pair of strangers making love when he walked into his own kitchen. Stupidly, Tracy started to laugh.

Rory grasped her shoulders from behind. "Don't mind her," he said calmly, though there was a laugh quivering in his voice too. "She gets a little giddy sometimes. Would you mind giving us a lift to the airfield now? I understand it's about ten miles from here."

CHAPTER SIX

SPIN WAS ALL RIGHT. The helicopter spotted Mary Alice waving a flare at about eleven o'clock, and within a very few minutes they were rescued and on their way to an Albany hospital. For fear that Spin had sustained a concussion, the two of them had kept each other awake all night, so they were very tired. The hospital admitted both Spin and M.A. for observation.

Rory and Tracy hopped aboard a private plane with a young man who had been helping with the search, and they arrived at the hospital about midafternoon. Tracy was relieved to see Spin and talk to the doctor who was treating him. It was a matter of time, she was told. There were X rays to be read, food to be eaten, and sleep to be had. Spin was tired and not nearly one hundred percent, so Tracy left him alone to sleep and went in search of M.A.

Rory was on a pay phone outside her hospital room. He lifted a scrap of paper in greeting when he saw Tracy approach, but he continued to talk on the telephone. Behind his ear sat a stubby pencil that he must have cajoled from one of the nurses. Tracy guessed from the drift of the conversation that he was reassuring Mary Alice's parents. Tracy took a peek into the private room, but the lights were turned out, and M.A. appeared to be sleeping.

Tired herself, Tracy put her back against the tile wall and slid slowly down it to sit on the floor, knees tucked to her chest, arms wrapped around her legs.

"Yes," Rory was saying. "In a day or two. I'll call you again in the morning, if you like. I'm sure she'll want to talk to you before that. Right." He grinned at something that was said on the other end of the line. "Sure. Give my love to Caroline. Tell her I'm sorry I missed her. Right."

Rory hung up the receiver and quickly read down the list of things he had noted on the paper. Without looking around, he said, "How are you doing, Miss Tracy? Still with me?"

A nurse bustled past. The distraction gave Tracy a moment to think, and she tried to organize her thoughts. Still sitting on the floor, she said frankly, "I don't know. I guess I haven't thought about what comes next."

Rory stuffed the paper into the hip pocket of his trousers and walked across to her. "These two have it easy. They're getting the royal treatment. Did you get anything to eat?"

Tracy shook her head.

"Hmm." Rory considered the situation, looking down at her with a thoughtful frown and clearly running several possible scenarios through his mind. Then he went for his back pocket again and came up with a neat leather billfold. Flipping it open, he said, "Unless we turn ourselves over to the nearest Salvation Army, I guess we're on our own. How much money have you got, Miss Tracy?"

Tracy obediently scrounged through her pockets until she had laid thirteen dollars and a quarter on the linoleum in front of herself. Rory gave her a long expressionless look at that, until she protested, "I don't have expensive tastes! I was just running up to Montreal for one night!"

"So was I," Rory retorted, tucking what appeared to be about two hundred dollars back into his wallet. "So we're practically broke, and my credit cards are back at that plane of yours with our luggage. Let's hope some clever chipmunk doesn't decide to go looking for a condo. Come on." He reached down to pull her to her feet. "You're not planning on staying at Spinelli's bedside all night, I hope?"

Tracy shook her head, dusting the seat of her jeans. "The doctor says he won't wake up till tomorrow."

"And you're practically exhausted yourself," Rory added, wrapping his arm naturally around her.

Together, they strolled down the hospital hallway. Tracy leaned against Rory's tall frame, her head resting comfortably on his shoulder. She *was* exhausted, she realized. She had been functioning on nervous energy now for many hours, and everything was finally catching up to her—including the shock of a plane crash. She didn't find being held by Rory Buchanan so strange anymore. It was instinctive between them now.

"Let's go find some dinner, a bed for you and a telephone for me, and we'll get recharged."

"A telephone?" Tracy asked, looking up at him with puzzlement.

"I've got an airline to run, my girl. Despite what you've been taught to think, it doesn't run itself. Have you called anybody yet? Your fan club back home? Your mother? She may have heard about this, and wonder what happened to her little girl."

Tracy was too tired to get angry with his sarcasm, so she answered, "I talked to my cousin Sean and the guys back at Shamrock. Sean said he'd call my mom."

Rory gave her a hard, authoritative hug. "You'll call her yourself tonight."

"Yes, sir," Tracy said, giving up. She yawned.

Shaking his head, Rory took her hand and said, "Come on, before you fall asleep."

Tracy didn't have the energy to ask him where they were going. Rory knew exactly what he was doing, so she let him take charge. It was easy that way. He hustled her into a cab and talked with the driver, making more notes with his little pencil as they drove. The cabbie switched on his headlights, and Tracy saw that evening had begun to fall. It had been a very long couple of days. She stared silently out the window at the state capital, but her mind was on freeze. Soon enough, the car stopped in front of a hotel with a doorman on the street and a brass plate beside the beveled-glass door.

Tracy quailed on the sidewalk, for she was still dressed in her snug faded jeans, boots and utilitarian crew-neck sweater. Her jacket, sleeves streaked with mud, Tracy hastily wrapped up and held before her nervously.

The glass doors parted, and a woman in a fur jacket and suede trousers came out. She called prettily to the cabbie. Rory finished paying the fare, and politely held the cab door for the woman. She tipped her head and gave Rory an enslaving smile, which he returned pleasantly and with plenty of eye contact.

Without a shave, Rory looked devilishly handsome—a gallant scoundrel. He closed the cab door after the woman and turned to collect Tracy, trying to smother his smile.

"Maybe she's got some money," Tracy suggested tartly, looking after the departing cab. "You should have taken her up on that smile, Rod-er-ick."

"Keep it up," he warned wryly, putting his hand to the small of her back and guiding Tracy into the hotel. "I don't know enough about New York law, so we might be about to break one. Act like my wife, little Tracy. Let's hope this place remembers what a good customer my father has been over the years."

Tracy skidded to a stop. "What? Your wife? What are you...?"

But Rory grabbed her elbow and propelled Tracy past the doorman and into the hotel. In an undertone, he said, "For lack of funds, we're going to share a room, so—"

"Are you kidding? You've got a couple hundred—"

"I've got enough to pay for one room and some food and some phone calls and whatever it takes to get you settled until I can have some cash wired here. I'll behave myself, if you behave yourself. Now close your mouth and try not to look fifteen. I don't want to get arrested for corrupting a minor."

By that time he had walked her to the center of the lobby, where Tracy chickened out and twisted from his grasp. When Rory turned on her, she hooked her thumb at a display window and said desperately, "I'll just look around while you take care of the details, all right? I promise I won't run away."

He hesitated, not sure he should trust her.

For the benefit of the two men who stood behind the vast registration desk and the elevator attendant who was almost within earshot, Tracy laid her hand on Rory's chest. Immediately she thought to herself that very soon she was probably going to see that chest bare. The thought gave her pause, and Tracy gulped, trying to muster some courage. She met his eyes and repeated quietly, "I promise I won't run away."

He took the wrist of her other hand. Rory considered her words, and from the brief but wicked flicker of light that passed over his eyes, Tracy knew he was on the verge of making some snappy retort. But he thought better of it, for they had the attention of every hotel employee in sight. With a wry, crooked smile, he let her go.

They walked in opposite directions, then. Listening to Rory's voice at the desk, Tracy wandered to the shop window in one corner of the lobby. It was a gift shop, of sorts. A woman was sitting behind a candy counter reading a magazine, so Tracy did not go inside. She looked at the merchandise in the window: books, toiletries, a display of "I Love New York" T-shirts and a lovely pink negligee, the kind that Tracy was sure only voluptuous soap-opera characters wore. Tracy lingered at the window, not paying much attention to the items there, but straining her ears to listen to Rory.

The men behind the desk seemed to know him

there. Or at least to recognize the Buchanan name. They laughed a lot at the things he was saying, anyway. Tracy sneaked a peek around at him. One of the men was quickly taking notes as Rory dictated the services they required, and the other had collected a key and was crooking his finger at the bellhop. The young man was sent across the lobby to the restaurant entrance.

Curious, Tracy looked after the bellhop and casually started to follow him. There was a menu posted in a glass case just outside the door, and she thought she'd have a look. It was in French, and there weren't any prices listed. A bad sign, her father had always said.

Rory was waiting in the middle of the lobby. Tracy joined him, trying not to look as if she was dazzled by the big-city opulence. He was annoyingly at ease. "Ready?"

Unable to come up with something witty or even sarcastic to say, Tracy mutely allowed him to lead her to the elevator. She felt as if the men at the desk were leering after them, elbowing each other at Tracy's expense. She pressed herself into the corner of the elevator and tried to disappear.

The attendant took Rory's key. "We haven't seen Mr. Buchanan around much lately," the man said, touching the fifth-floor button.

"No," Rory answered pleasantly, easing his hands into his trouser pockets. "My father's retired now, so he doesn't do much traveling up this way any more."

"That so?" the attendant asked. "Buy a place in Florida, did he?"

Rory laughed. "No, no. Too set in his ways, he says. Personally, I think he and my mother don't want to leave their grandchildren."

The attendant nodded. "I know how that is. I've got five of my own now."

They arrived at the fifth floor and the attendant led the way. The corridor was wide, though not long. The key fit the second door, and the attendant stood back to let Tracy enter first.

She walked into the suite uncertainly and looked around. It was not just a motel room like the few she had stayed in, but a real suite, like those pictured in brochures from travel agents. The sitting room was L-shaped and decorated in cherry colonial furniture, some of it covered with pastel fabrics. A pot of flowers sat on the coffee table and a picture of fox hunters hung on the wall above the sofa. Fox hunters! The place looked like a furniture-store display. The flowered chintz curtains stood open, and the view of the city lights was grand.

With determination, Tracy avoided looking into the darkened sleeping alcove, and crossed directly to the window. She leaned her hands on the sill and looked out.

Rory finished with the attendant and came in behind her, closing the door. He tossed the key on the table and dropped his jacket over the back of the sofa.

When Tracy cautiously looked around, he had gone to the desk and was rifling the drawers for some paper. He pulled up the caned armchair and sat, spreading the paper on the desk before him. Over his shoulder, he said, "They're going to bring up some food in about half an hour. I wasn't interested in a restaurant, were you?"

"No."

"So if you want to have a shower or something, go ahead." Rory finally looked around at her. "Maybe you'd better call your mother first."

"And tell her what?" Tracy asked, summoning a hard look at him. "That I'm here in a hotel with you?"

"Never lie to your mother," Rory advised, giving her a quick smile. "It always complicates things. Tell her anything you like."

"That you're a smooth character who's maneuvered me into sleeping in the same bed as him tonight?"

"I didn't crash that airplane," Rory shot back testily, "so I had nothing to do with the circumstances of getting us here. And there are two beds, I'm sure, so your virtue is probably safe." He craned around to look into the alcove where at least one bed was in view.

"Probably?" Tracy demanded, not looking with him at the beds. She stood ramrod straight before him, a picture of outrage.

Rory grinned, then, but it was a tired expression. He sat back in the chair and rubbed his hand over his forehead. "Good. You're back to being the feisty bobcat. Then I'm sure to leave you alone. Any more of that elusive sweet side of yours, and I'd have you in the bedroom by now. Go on, take a shower."

"I don't like showers. I like baths."

Rory sighed, eyeing her with forced calm. "Enough, Tracy. I know my limit, and this is it. I've had a long day, too, and I just haven't got the patience to handle you right now."

Tracy blinked.

Rory got up and peeled his sweater over his head with a swift, angry jerk. Yanking open the top two buttons on his shirt, he walked around Tracy, taking care to keep his distance. He did not notice that she flinched away with the instinctive speed of a jumpy colt. Rory ordered, "Call your mother. Call the Pope, for all I care. I'll be back in a minute."

He went into the shadowed alcove and past the bed, throwing his sweater on the bedspread and disappearing, presumably to the bathroom. A moment later a door closed with a sharp rap. There was silence.

Surprised, Tracy stood still for a long moment. He had nearly lost his temper with her! He hadn't hauled off and smacked her, but he had definitely lost his cool. Until now, he'd taken plenty of razzing, and he'd certainly dished out his share, too.

Yes, until now, it had been a contest of wills between them, but at this point it looked as if Tracy had won! Perhaps youth had its advantages after all. Smiling at her small victory, Tracy headed for the telephone.

Suddenly the bathroom door opened with a jerk. "Call the desk," Rory commanded from the other room. Without coming out to speak to her, he yelled, "Have them send up some aspirin with everything else!"

Tracy didn't flinch when he closed the door this time, and her smile grew. So Rory Buchanan wasn't perfect.

She made her calls. Her mother had not heard about the crash, so Tracy played it down and asked after some relatives to keep her mother calm. Then Tracy checked in at Shamrock once more, giving the other employees an update on Spin's condition. Nothing unusual was going on at the airport. Tracy was on the phone to the hospital again when Rory came back out into the sitting room, drying his face with a white towel.

"Thanks very much," Tracy said to the evening nurse. "If Miss Cooper wakes up, tell her I called to see how she is, will you? Tracy O'Hara."

Tracy hung up the phone and avoided Rory's eyes. She slid out of the chair, saying, "It's all yours, Buchanan."

"Tracy—"

But she was breezing past him, heading for the

sleeping area. She had found a Do Not Disturb sign in the desk, and she waved it under his nose as she passed. "Oh, I almost forgot. The Pope said to say hello. And for you to behave yourself tonight."

At least he didn't shout after her. He was ominously silent, however, thoughtfully tossing the towel from one hand to the other as he watched her smug exit. A moment later, he released a long pent-up breath and sat back down in the chair, reaching for the phone.

Feeling safe, Tracy flipped on the bedroom lamp and looked around. The room was just as pretty as the adjoining one, with the same style of cherry furniture and another well-chosen pastel fabric. No fox hunters this time, but a print of Manet's *Nude in the Park*. Sometimes Tracy surprised herself with the odd information still stored away in the gray cells.

There were, she saw then, two beds after all.

Tracy looked at them with mixed feelings.

"Ann?" Rory asked from the other room. "It's Rory. How are you?"

Tracy ripped off her sweater and headed for the bathroom, not wanting to hear a syllable more. He probably had women in every city! Sophisticated ones, too, like the cab lady in the suede slacks! Ann? And Mary Alice, and somebody named Caroline he was talking about on the phone this afternoon! Cripes! What a Casanova!

The bathroom was immaculate and full of monogrammed towels. Tracy ran a steaming hot bath and stripped down to her bare skin. She tossed her clothes out onto one of the beds, and prepared to have a long relaxing soak. This hotel even provided a little sample size of bubble bath! With a contented sigh, Tracy slid into the water and lay back. Very nice. She closed her eyes and her mind began to wander dreamily.

It was hard not to think about him. Rory was everything Tracy knew she ought to stay away from. He was probably the worst sort of seducing world-beater deep down, and she shouldn't be associating with his type at all. Definitely a heartbreaker.

On the other hand, he was so masculine, so attractive, so darn nice sometimes, that Tracy had a very difficult time not fantasizing all sorts of carnal thoughts.

If there had been only one bed? Tracy smiled lazily at the thought.

But the water grew tepid, and Tracy roused herself from her reverie. With renewed spirits and improved humor, she ran more hot water into the tub and reached for the little packet of shampoo. Might as well get cleaned up right. She washed her hair and took a quick, cleansing rinse under the shower. There were plenty of towels, so Tracy wrapped one around her hair and another around her body. She was starving.

Her clothes, however, had disappeared.

In their place was a wrapped package. Sure that Rory was still busy on the phone, Tracy pulled the towel tighter and tiptoed out to the bed. She unwrapped the paper and discovered all sorts of goodies from the gift shop. Razor, toothpaste, a hairbrush, and at the bottom of it all, the pink negligee.

Tracy picked it up in the manner one might lift the corpse of a muskrat. The nightgown was lovely, that was certain, with cunning bits of lace and delicate straps, and the matching robe was all but transparent. It was definitely the garment of an experienced woman, and Tracy looked at it with great consternation.

Rory laughed abruptly on the telephone. "I know, Leo. Anything for attention. Tell me what I'm missing."

Tracy slipped to the edge of the doorway and peeped around, safely hiding herself from view. She cleared her throat.

Rory glanced over at her.

She held up the nightgown for him to see. "Am I supposed to wear this?"

"You can wear anything you like," he said, not bothering to cover the receiver.

"My clothes?"

"Clean by morning. The manager promised."

"And in the meantime?" she asked, brows raised threateningly.

Rory smiled. "You don't have to wear anything you don't want to."

Tracy glared at him for one second before snatching the nightgown back and disappearing into the alcove again.

Rory was laughing into the phone. "I know, I know, Leo.... No, a redhead. Not exactly red, I guess, but not blond either.... Oh, yes," he said heavily, sighing like a comedian. "Oh, Lord, yes."

Leo, apparently, was laughing at their predicament.

Tracy stared at the filmy nightgown in her hands. This thing was just not her style. The tag was still on it, reading sixty-nine dollars! Tracy hadn't spent that kind of money on clothes since she bought a leather flight jacket from an English mail-order catalog two years ago! A nightgown for that kind of money? She would have been much more comfortable in an "I Love New York" T-shirt. Tracy O'Hara simply was not the sort of woman to wear a slinky negligee.

"Well," Rory continued blandly, unaware that Tracy was still within earshot, "let's just say that I've had more fun at the dentist."

Outraged at that, Tracy ripped off the towel and jerked the nightgown over her head. More fun at the dentist, huh? She stormed into the bathroom and yanked the towel from her head.

She stood glaring at her reflection for a long minute. Then, with a grim sigh, she buffed the worst of the water from her hair with a furious rubbing. A little calmer, Tracy smoothed some cream into her complexion and her hands. It smelled pretty. She slipped into the matching pink robe and looked at herself with a critical eye.

Not bad. She felt stupid, mind you, but she didn't look too bad. In fact, the outfit looked surprisingly stunning. Her thick hair curled damply around her shoulders, the tips wisping gently around the curving sides of her breasts. The lacy bodice covered her to her throat, but the lace plunged to a startling depth, showing pearly skin beneath. Tracy permitted a slight smile. The negligee was actually quite modest, just suggestive, that's all, caressing the slim curve of her hips with fragile fabric. And the effect was anything but innocent.

She felt a bit like a harem girl, all prepared and perfumed for the sultan. Tracy picked up the hairbrush and decided to dry her hair in the sitting room. No use being a timid harem girl.

The bellhop had arrived with dinner, and Rory was on his feet, digging into his pockets for money, and all the while pinning the phone between his ear and shoulder. "Yes," he said into the phone. "What else, Leo?"

Still Leo. Tracy slipped forward silently and lifted the money from Rory's hands. She glanced at the bill and counted out the proper amount, plus a generous tip. She handed over the bills, but the astounded bellhop didn't react for a moment. He stared at Tracy with a slack jaw.

Rory was speechless also.

Feeling a blush start, Tracy shoved the money into the bellhop's hand and ushered him to the door. When he had gone, she fastened the safety chain on the door and then laid the remaining money on the desk. Rory was still on his feet, watching.

Blithely, Tracy approached the tray and lifted a silver lid from a steaming plate. An enormous steak. There were potatoes, too, and salads and dishes of something chocolate—probably mousse—and a glass of some amber liquor, a bottle of wine and a tall glass of iced tea. A book of matches lay in the middle of the tray, and a candle stood beside it. Tracy was not brave enough to light it.

She set a place for Rory at the desk, pushed his drink into his hand and finally stopped and looked up at him. Standing barefoot, she felt dwarfed by him, and suddenly overwhelmingly feminine. He was staring at her blankly, clearly not listening to a word Leo had to say.

When Tracy met his eyes, Rory seemed to get a grip on himself. He tore his gaze from her and concentrated on his telephone conversation. "Uh, Leo, say that again, please?"

Concealing a self-satisfied smirk, Tracy collected her own supper and carried it across the room to the table by the window. She curled up on a chair there and proceeded to eat. She was famished. The salad was crisp and good, with a hint of lemon and not too much dressing. She devoured a hard roll and attacked her steak with zeal. The meat was tender, having been broiled to just the right degree of medium rare. But after several bites, Tracy decided her stomach wasn't quite strong enough to handle the steak, so she finished off her potato and the broccoli with cheese. It was a man's meal, and Tracy couldn't eat all of it. She didn't attempt the mousse, sure that she would later regret eating such rich food. Covering up her dishes, she took her dessert over to Rory for him to eat.

He was still on the phone, eating his meal in fits and starts. Whatever Leo was telling him didn't please Rory at all. He ate distractedly, and finished his drink off in one long swallow. "Okay, Leo, what did Boeing say? Are they going to come down in price to?... Hell, we haven't got that kind of cash! Bernie knows that!"

Tracy handed him the bottle of wine. Without missing a word of his conversation, Rory peeled the foil away from the neck of the bottle and proceeded to thread the corkscrew. While Tracy waited, he drew out the cork and handed her back the bottle, not looking up. Tracy poured him a glass and half of one for herself. The label was French, and the wine was a dry red with a subtle fruitiness. Tracy carried hers to the sofa and proceeded to brush her hair.

In another ten minutes, Rory hung up. He took three quick bites of his steak and jotted more notes on his paper.

Tracy said, "You're going to make yourself sick, you know. Have you got an ulcer started yet?"

Rory grinned at her. "Not yet. Did you eat?"

Tracy nodded, running the brush through her nearly dry hair. "Yes. While Leo bent your ear about your new plane from Boeing."

"It's not mine yet," he retorted, dipping his spoon into the mousse even before he ate his vegetables. "I've got to see my friendly banker first."

"So I hear," Tracy noted, staying where she was. She laid her hand on the top of her thigh and forced herself to remain still. She didn't want to appear nervous before him, for that would certainly give away her lack of sophistication. Lightly, Tracy went on, "Forgive me for noticing, but it doesn't sound as if you're in any better financial shape than I am."

Rory turned the spoon over in his mouth like a kid, savoring his mousse and changing the subject cheerfully. "Your financial shape can't be half as nice as the rest of your shape. Let me see that thing." He leaned back in his chair and propped one foot up on the opposite chair, getting comfortable and taking a long look at her seductively clad figure. His tone changed. "You know, you look very charming, Miss Tracy."

"Don't turn all lecherous again, please."

"I paid for that intriguing bit of lingerie. Surely that gives me some right to inspection?"

"Forget it. I'm wearing this thing under protest. I feel damn silly."

"Silly?" he repeated with some amazement. Rory set down his spoon and with a grin demanded, "In heaven's name, girl, why?"

Tracy struggled with a response. She felt vulnerable and not the least bit in command of herself. His expression was admiring, for once completely lacking the sardonic lift of one brow, or the taunting half smile he so often used on her. Turning pink, Tracy was only able to blurt out an embarrassed, "Just because, that's all!"

Rory sighed. He toyed with the stem of his wineglass and steadily regarded her from across the room. Woefully, he shook his head and observed softly, "You have so much to learn, Tracy."

The look in his eyes could only be described as a smoulder. He was openly admiring the supple way she had curled her long legs under her. Then his gaze traveled slowly up to the soft curve of her small, pert breasts under their inadequate layers of candylike lace. Her pale, pale skin looked scrubbed clean and almost translucent in the lamplight. Tracy put an automatic hand to the throat of the negligee, and the thin fabric of her sleeve fell gracefully away from her slender wrist. The gesture was timelessly feminine.

Rory set down his wineglass purposefully.

Before he could get up, Tracy said swiftly, "Don't plan on teaching me any of your tricks, Rod-er-ick."

Her voice had dropped to an infuriatingly soft whisper, sounding intimate in the quiet of the room. For some reason, Tracy's mind was filled with the scene so many hours ago in a farmhouse kitchen. She had been in his arms then, and thrilling to the mysteries of his body next to hers. He had kissed her sensuously, carefully, deliberately. The memory of those moments came so vividly to her mind that Tracy found herself trembling as she sat in the plush cushions of the sofa. She recalled the way his hands had felt on her body the night before in the woods. He had been expert, arousing Tracy to a point where her body was on fire and her mind had gone blank. As those thoughts crowded in her mind, Tracy's breath came in soft unsteady gasps between slightly parted lips. Her breasts vibrated delicately, causing the fragile garment to shiver against her body. Had he come to her then, Tracy would have been too weak to resist.

Rory considered all his options, and chose to stay where he was. No. He had made a choice, a bargain with himself. He had vowed to draw a line between business and pleasure this time. That was the first decision. The second decision had been that he was going to have Tracy, to possess her in his bed and have her body and her spirit all for himself. He recognized that he desired this young woman in every possible way. But this was one female who wasn't going to fall magically at his feet. Rory Buchanan was going to have to work for this one. To prove himself to Tracy, he was going to have to leave her alone. There was no other way of convincing her that he was being honest with her. She still thought he wanted to seduce her to get her airline. His track record looked mighty incriminating.

Rory shook his head, as if clearing from his mind some perplexing thought. He reached for the phone again and with a certain unwillingness, pulled it toward himself. With a steadiness in his voice that was far from revealing his inner frustration, Rory said, "Okay, Miss Tracy, I've got work to do. Go to bed, why don't you?"

The disappointment that swept Tracy was so acute it was almost a pain. Her fingers tightened at her throat, and she felt a lump rise to the spot. She couldn't speak.

Rory dialed the numbers, saying briefly to her, "Sleep well. I'm sure it will be much warmer than last night."

She couldn't watch him. He was so cold, so calculating, sometimes, turning on and off that charm with such ease that it frightened her. The desire that welled inside Tracy's own body was overwhelming and out of control. She was bewildered by her response to Rory, baffled by her need to touch him, hold him. But for him, sexual attraction was an easy thing.

Into the phone, Rory said blandly, "Buchanan here. Give me Draychak in Maintenance."

Tracy collected herself. She was tired and wanted to go to bed. She uncurled her long legs and got to her feet. A headache had begun to pound behind her temples. She crossed the room and put her empty wineglass on the tray.

Rory watched her approaching, and when she was about to pass him, he stretched and caught her arm firmly. Tracy hesitated, prevented from leaving his side. Slowly Rory drew her arm closer until her palm rested against his cheek. He held it there for a moment, waiting for his call to go through and breathing slowly of the fragrance that rose from Tracy's skin. He closed his eyes, hiding his thoughts from her, his dark lashes falling over the vivid clarity of his gaze. His touch was gentle, tender, as he carefully slid his rough cheek up the silken flesh of her inner arm, savoring the warmth and delicacy.

The gesture brought Tracy's heart to her throat. It was too much. She couldn't breathe, and her legs were becoming so weak that she could hardly keep from crumpling to the floor or throwing her arms around his neck.

A click sounded on the telephone, and a distant voice said, "Draychak here."

Rory collected himself, releasing Tracy with reluctance. "Carl? Rory here." He reached toward the desk where a new cigar lay. "Everything all right?"

Tracy slipped away. She stepped out of the robe and laid it over the bedspread with care. Rory was speaking to Carl, whoever that was, but he wasn't joking around this time. It was all business, and his voice sounded tired. Tracy climbed into the first bed and pulled the sheet and blankets up to her chin. She stared upward for a moment, where the ceiling fixture from the sitting room created a white slash of illumination. She heard Rory strike a match and light his cigar. The aromatic cloud swirled up toward the ceiling.

With a sigh, Tracy got comfortable, curling up on her side and burrowing down into the bedclothes.

Rory stretched. He flipped off the overhead light. The pale glow of the desk lamp illumed him as he said, "Right, Carl. I hate to say it. Your job and my job are riding on this. Get both those planes in the air by morning, or Northstream is in serious trouble."

Tracy lay very still in the bed, feeling the first black haze of unconsciousness envelop her. Had she heard correctly? If so...what did this interesting turn of events mean for her? And for Shamrock Air?

CHAPTER SEVEN

WHEN TRACY WOKE, it was pitch-black. The room was cool, but stuffy, and her throat was scratchy, so Tracy stole out of her bed for a glass of water, and then groped carefully in the darkness until she knew she was in the sitting room. Streetlights shone from outside the window, so she found her way there, and with some difficulty managed to open the window just a crack. The night breeze wafted over the sill, stirring the thin fabric of her nightgown. With an involuntary shiver, Tracy began to retrace her steps.

She hesitated at the foot of her bed and looked across at the other.

Rory was sound asleep, lying on his stomach, with just the sheet twisted around his hips. The tiny bit of light from behind her glowed on the bare skin of his back. His breathing was deep and rhythmic.

Tracy sat down slowly on the edge of her bed and cupped her chin in her hands. How had she gotten herself to this point? A week before, the name Rory Buchanan had been hardly as familiar as that of any of her competitors, and now here he was almost snoring in the next bed! The worst part of it was that Tracy was trembling with the desire to climb in with him.

He was nice enough, after all. What other man would insist she call her mother? What other man would have looked after her once Spin and M.A. were settled at the hospital? What other man would take a room with two beds and then actually insist they sleep separately? Tracy could do worse, she thought. Her love life had been limited, and here was a golden opportunity perhaps to experience some very skillful lovemaking.

She was kidding herself, of course. Tracy was falling in love with Rory Buchanan, and she couldn't stop herself. This was even worse than the crush she had had on Mick Jagger when she was thirteen. This was scarier and more exciting and definitely more upsetting. Every look he gave her, every inadvertent touch of his hand was electrifying. When he kissed her, hadn't she nearly fallen apart?

It would be wonderful, of course, if he felt the same way about her, but Tracy had decided that was impossible. After all, he had his choice of every classy lady in Chicago, probably. He certainly had good taste in everything else. Why not women, too? M.A. was testimony to that. If he had been on the verge of asking her to marry him, well, didn't that prove something?

Tracy didn't know what. Her thoughts had come full circle. She could dive into bed with him and just see what happened. It couldn't hurt. Or could it?

Before she knew exactly what she was doing, Tracy had lifted the corner of the sheet and was sliding in beside him. Rory's body was very warm, his skin radiating a sensual heat that drew Tracy like a magnet. She slipped close, snuggling against his frame and resting her head on the rounded curve of his shoulder. He was wearing his underwear.

Rory stirred sleepily. Without waking, he rolled just enough and wrapped one arm around her body. He released a long breath and subsided into sleep again.

Content to be held against him, Tracy relaxed, resting her hand in the crisp mat of hair on his chest. Her legs entwined with his, and felt small and fragile. He had been in the shower before he went to bed, for he smelled faintly of soap in addition to cigar smoke. Tracy took a long breath, and the subtle scent that clung to him filled her head. Her heart was racing erratically.

Rory woke.

Tracy put her nose to his face—he hadn't shaved yet—and whispered, "It's only me. Go back to sleep."

Rory groaned miserably. "Tracy. What are you doing?"

"Nothing. Just go to sleep."

Rory let her go and rolled onto his back, hands over his face. Muffled, he asked, "What time is it?"

"It doesn't matter. Go to sleep."

"With you here? Tracy, if—damn! Don't touch me!"

Tracy snatched her hand away and sat up, startled by the vehemence in his voice. She strained to see Rory's face through the darkness, but it was no use. Biting her lip, she said tremulously, "I didn't mean to scare you."

"You didn't scare me," he said, sounding a little more awake this time. "Just—go back to your own bed, all right?"

Tracy took a breath. "No."

"What?"

"I said no."

"I heard what you said, damn it, now for crying out—" He stopped. "What are you doing?"

Tracy didn't answer. She was carefully peeling the straps of the soft nightgown over her shoulders, sliding the fabric down to her waist. The quiet rustle sounded like thunder between them, and Rory sat up hastily.

"Tracy!" he warned desperately. "Don't do this to me."

"Please," she murmured, and reached for his hand.

"No," Rory said firmly. "You don't know me.

You don't understand a lot of things about me. And all I know about you is that this isn't the way...oh, God, Tracy!"

She took Rory's hand and brought his palm to her breast, closing her eyes to the sensation that swept through her body when the contact was made. A shudder worked a path down through Tracy, down to the very center of her body where it seemed as if a flame had begun to flicker. She expelled a sigh half in relief, half in want. The warmth of his hand was like magic, and suddenly she felt calm. Calm and sure and determined.

"Please, Tracy," Rory said, his words tortured with pleading. "Don't do this to me. I can't stand it."

"Come on," she urged, unable to say, "Make love to me." She guided Rory's hand until he was cupping her breast, and then edged closer to him. She touched both her hands to his chest. Rory did not pull away, and her nipple bloomed against his fingers. Tracy let her hands slide down his chest, going lower with agonizing slowness. A sheen of perspiration had begun to spring out on his skin. Like a child, she whispered, "I'll be good, I promise."

Rory groaned again.

She leaned toward him and pressed a soft kiss to his cheek, to his mouth, to his strong, pulsing neck. Tracy dropped her hands to his thighs, and there she kneaded the muscle, moving inexorably higher. Rory was frozen still, accepting her touch only because he was too stunned to move away. Shaking his head like a punch-drunk fighter, Rory begged over and over, "Don't, don't."

Boldly Tracy aligned her body with his, kneeling in the bed before him and pressing her soft breasts into his chest. She let her hands slide around his back, arching her slender body to him. "Hold me, please. Touch me."

Suddenly Rory grabbed her shoulders, holding Tracy away from him in a grip that was frightening in its intensity. "Tracy, listen to me. Stop."

"No."

He shook her hard. "Damnation, Tracy, you've never done this before, have you? You're a virgin."

Tracy swallowed. "It doesn't matter—"

"The hell it doesn't!" Rory snapped, his hands moving to her waist. With exasperation, he growled, "I've got too much respect for the way you look at life to make love to you under these circumstances."

"What circumstances would you prefer?" she asked, gathering her courage again and tracing a circular pattern on his chest. Teasing, she rubbed her thumbs over his flat, male nipples and laughed when he tried to escape. "Would you like to be in charge? Shall I lie down and let you ravage me? I'm willing, honestly. I want this. I truly do. Please, Rory."

She had never called him by his name before. Only Rod-er-ick, tauntingly spoken, or chum or pal, or any number of ways to avoid the ultimate intimacy of his first name. The word was softly, breathlessly spoken, a name whispered in the darkness in a way that shook him more intensely than Rory thought possible.

He remained motionless in the bed, holding Tracy hard by her slender waist and wishing to hell he could see her eyes just then. He had come to know her moods, her way of thinking, and her quick good humor in the past few days. This side, this passionate, soft and trembling side, was one that baffled him. Baffled and excited him. Her body was tantalizingly warm, and he felt his willpower crumbling.

Tracy lifted her mouth to his. "Tell me what to do, Rory. Show me."

He let her kiss him, though his lips were unresponsive at first. Tracy's mouth, those generous lips set so prettily in her face, was both hot and sweet, melting the last of Rory's self-control. He wound his hands in her hair and tilted her head up to his, parting her lips and tasting deeply of the young woman who had teased him so thoroughly and so disturbingly in the past few days.

While the kiss mellowed and gained fervor, Tracy thought dimly that she had never known anything so pleasant, so wonderfully gentle and yet so fearfully exciting. She lifted her arms higher around his neck and pressed to him, surprised to find she was trembling as she did so. Against her breast, she felt Rory's heart, and the rhythmic pulse seemed to counterpoint her own quick breathing. Rory slipped his arm lower to circle her waist and crush Tracy firmly to his body.

And then he was kissing her throat, breathing raggedly in her ear and touching, touching, touching. Rory smoothed his hands down her back, cupped her buttocks and then savored the long curve of her thighs. "Tracy, lovely Tracy."

Rory's tight, hoarse whisper carried Tracy over the edge. She heard her own voice answering in a kind of sob as he caressed her legs, wisping his fingertips up and down her supple thighs.

For a fleeting instant she didn't know what to do or how to respond. Then with beautiful simplicity, intuition took over and Tracy explored his body, first with shaking hands, and then covering each place with a soft, breathless kiss. She discovered the ticklish spot just above his hip, the small imperfection in one of his lower ribs that told the story of some childhood accident, and then the hard leanness of his belly.

Patiently Rory endured her exploration. He held rock still for a time, his only reaction to her timid touch being a quick intake of breath or a tightening of his hands on her. Tracy was curious and then wondrous, enjoying each discovery of his body. She nibbled lightly along the ridge of his collarbone and licked whimsically at his earlobes, laughing when he grabbed her bottom in punishment. The sound was low and rippling, so exciting that Rory felt a shudder of anticipation in his own body.

She was inquisitive, but natural, taking pleasure in each small act: kissing his mouth, scratching his raspy cheek with her own softer one, or even tickling his chest with her nose. She was gathering her courage, familiarizing herself with him, learning the basics. She couldn't know what havoc she was creating inside him.

When at last she was brave enough, Tracy slipped her fingers under the waistband of his underwear, the last bit of clothing between them.

The signal was clear. Rory laid her back in the bed. Gently he eased her head into the pillow, but remained above her, one hand slowly trailing up her slender body, up her belly, slowly between her breasts, up the narrow column of her throat to the quivering upthrust of her chin. With his thumb, Rory traced the kittenish curve of her lips.

Tracy grasped his wrist. "Now, Rory. Please. Don't make me wait."

He laughed a little, lowering himself enough to brush her lips with his. "My darling, the waiting is the best. And the worst. Let me do it right. Here." He touched his lips to her throat and moved lower. "Here. And here."

Tracy gasped, for Rory covered her breast with

his mouth in a warm, melting kind of kiss that turned to sweet torture a moment later when his tongue began a slow, erotic arousal that filled Tracy with excruciating longing. A force inside her began to grow, like an ember that strikes a fuel and begins to flame. Thriving on the caresses, as Rory awakened her body, Tracy did not resist, for he was gentle and slow, and she welcomed each new height of pleasure as they gained it.

Rory told her what he wanted of her, and that made it easier. He told her exactly, using words so direct and uncomplicated that each time he murmured to her, Tracy's heart filled to bursting with gratitude for his unaffected ways. He was wise and kind and sure with her, touching Tracy with such respect and tenderness that she was soon pleading for him.

Never had she been so unrestrained, so totally free of inhibition. When the time came, she touched him, marveling that his strength seemed to extend to every part of his body. She took him in her mouth and enjoyed his immediate, involuntary response. She could control him, too, could cause in him the same burning reaction that consumed her. Rory held her small head, saying on an unsteady laugh, "Not yet, little love. Play by my rules this time!"

Tracy laughed too, and wound her arms around his torso, pressing her head against his heart. "I like it better without rules. Show me everything. Rory, don't stop."

Purposeful then, he pressed her hard into the bed and braced her thighs apart. A tremor of excitement shivered through Tracy at that, and Rory took her hands, linking their fingers together in an inescapable grasp. "Don't be frightened," he soothed softly. "Just tell me what you like. Talk to me now."

Before he began, Tracy was nearly incoherent. He nipped the silken flesh of her inner thighs, and Tracy struggled for release of her hands. She wanted to hold his head, to guide him, but Rory would have none of it. Slowly, meticulously almost, he proceeded to tease and torment until the final, exquisite instant when his molten mouth discovered the most sensitive valley of her body. Tracy cried out, arching to meet him, and Rory flicked her with waves so blissfully sweet that Tracy slipped into a state of near unconsciousness. She pleaded with him to stop, but at the same time dreaded that he might.

At last some instinct began to shriek, crying out for the quick heat of him. Tracy heard herself in the darkness, calling to him, commanding this time.

Rory came to her then, tentatively resting at the point she wanted him most. "You're beautiful, Tracy. You're strong and lovely and so full of life. Help me, Tracy," he said, his voice rough suddenly and shaking with an inner turmoil of his own. "Give me some of that fire inside. I need you so badly."

She tensed, preparing for pain, but Rory waited and petted her, coaxing and teasing until she laughed with frustration. Only then did he sink slowly into her body, ignoring her first shudder of misgiving and pressing deeper until Tracy gasped at the sharp, searing heat. Abruptly the gasp turned to a moan of happiness, for Rory took her in his arms and held her, kissing Tracy's mouth with a reverence.

This was making love, the sharing of body and spirit so completely that the world around them seemed hushed with wonder. Tracy's mind swirled with awe for this new miracle. It was the ultimate communication. No words were needed now. She loved him more than any sonnet could express. And he no longer needed to tell her what to do, for Tracy knew. She moved gently with him, her hips rising to the slow thrusts that brought Rory closer to the center of her being. Oblivious to all but the microcosm of sensual warmth, Tracy wrapped her thighs around him and arched until Rory filled her completely. For a time they were still, savoring the peace and pleasure of such gentle union.

The inexorable tempo began. Carefully, Rory moved within her, murmuring her name and plundering her mouth with his. Tracy threw her arms around him. Again and again came the ecstasy of meeting him and the anguish of withdrawal. Rory moved fluidly with her, his voice a barely discernible whisper at her ear. "Tracy, Tracy. You're so good, so sweet. Help me now."

Unconsciously Tracy held his back, gripping Rory with a strength she didn't realize she had left. And suddenly, ridiculously, there it was—the irresistible urge boiling inside, bursting to get out. She was laughing, *laughing* for the sheer joy and pleasure and exhilaration. Tracy was exuberant, jubilant, driven over the edge of excitement and into delight. The act was so wonderful, so beautiful, so good.

Her bubbling laugh was rich and full of unmistakable rejoicing. At the sound, Rory lost his head and was unable to check his own inevitable climax. He gave a low, husky growl of feverish release, then a deep thrust, and one deeper still, seeking some secret place within her. Then a swift, almost agonizing shudder, and he was quiet, breathing raggedly against her throat and struggling with the next words.

Smiling still, Tracy cradled his head. Both were too spent to continue and too thrilled to sleep. His hair was soft and curling slightly in her fingers. Unconsciously Tracy pressed her mouth to his cheek. "Don't let me go."

"Let you go?" he echoed, cupping her shoulders. He seemed captivated by the softness of her skin there. Abruptly overwhelmed by some feeling for her, Rory sought Tracy's mouth with fresh hunger. He kissed her quickly. "After that?" he asked. "After laughing at the most intimate, passionate—"

"I wasn't laughing *at* anything," she protested, hiding her face against his shoulder to escape his criticism.

Rory shook his head in wonder, and his hands smoothed her skin with a new fondness. "I know what you were laughing about. I'm amazed, that's all. Will you ever stop surprising me?"

"I don't know," Tracy whispered thoughtfully, feeling suddenly drowsy under his feather-light caresses. "There's so much that's new, isn't there?"

Rory kissed her once again, gently, but with barely suppressed excitement. "I should have expected you to laugh. Or cry, perhaps. You never do anything by halves, do you?"

"When I do," she said softly, solemnly, "it will be time to give up, won't it?" The vibrancy of her voice was fading with fast-rising languor, and Tracy felt her body begin to drift in dreamy serenity. "Rory, don't let me fall asleep. Not yet. Please...."

He tucked her hair behind her ears and pressed one kiss to her forehead. "Sleep now. We have time later for anything you want."

"It was—you were so gentle."

"Sleep now," he murmured, his lips against her temple and his voice sounding miles away. "We can talk later."

"Don't let me go."

"No."

Drugged with this new happiness, Tracy exhaled one long, contented sigh, and then she was asleep, slipping off into the night sky. In the faraway distance she heard Rory whisper to her, but the words eddied together like lofty breezes above the clouds. She slept, tumbled gently in downy softness, yet anchored by a strong embrace.

WHEN SHE WOKE it was morning and Tracy was cradled on his chest, held loosely in his arms, with his heart beating just beneath her ear. Tracy smiled, blinked drowsily and stretched.

Rory was awake, or else he hadn't slept. His eyes were smoky blue and smouldering with both tenderness and trepidation. His arms tightened around her snugly.

"Hi," Tracy breathed, voice throaty. She could see him now, and it was nicer than the darkness of a few hours before. She arched in his arms like a lazy cat. The movement concealed the fact that she was blushing.

"Tracy," he said abruptly, "I've got to tell you everything. All right?"

Laying her hands upon his chest, she smiled sleepily and said, "All right."

He caught one of her hands roughly, preventing Tracy from caressing him as he spoke. Quickly, he said, "Tracy, I've been married and I'm divorced.

I've got a daughter who is four and lives with me, and while you sleep, you look just as lovely and unspoiled and perfect as she does, and I—"

"Wait," Tracy interrupted, shifting to lie on his chest again and meet his eyes. "Have you been lying here thinking about this stuff all night?"

Rory was disconcerted, his planned speech interrupted. "I don't—yes, probably."

"A daughter?"

"Melora. She'll be four in February."

"Is that important?"

"To me, she is. She's my life, Tracy—"

She laid her finger against his lips, smiling at the agitation showing in Rory's face. "I know *she's* important," she responded softly, waking fast. "I can see that. I mean, is it important to tell me all this right now?"

"You ought to know."

"Yes," Tracy agreed, sliding her fingers up into his dark hair. "But not now. Will you kiss me first?"

Rory hesitated. He complied finally, giving her a slight, nice little kiss on the mouth, the kind that one might give a daughter.

The softness of her lips should not have been unexpected, but perhaps in the space of a few hours Rory had forced from his memory the pleasures he had enjoyed with her. He reconsidered then, as Tracy's mouth curved into a delicious smile. More slowly the second time, Rory bent and tasted her lips with deliberate care. Tracy wound her arms around his neck and pulled him down with her.

Her body was softer than ever and warm with sleep. Her breasts seemed to burn through his chest, and Rory groaned. He tore his mouth from hers. "Tracy, I told myself I was going to be straight with you before I started any—"

"Hush," she whispered, nibbling at his ear. "You're feeling guilty, aren't you?"

"Yes."

"Don't, please. You didn't force me. I started it, remember?"

"I remember," he said heavily, his nose pressed to her throat. "But I can't help it. I've been watching you, and trying not to—to—"

"Yes?"

"To wake you up," he finished in a rush, "and make love to you until we're both exhausted. Tracy, do you have any idea what you do to me?"

Laughing, Tracy passed her palm down his long body. "The evidence is all too obvious!"

Rory moaned and gave her a shake by her shoulders. "You really need a smack now and then, don't you? Get out of here before I—"

"Yes?" she prompted eagerly, holding Rory by his hips. "Will you? Now? And later, too? All day? Everything?"

"Everything?" Rory asked, startled. "What does that mean?"

Tracy smiled guilelessly. "You're the expert!"

"Expert enough," Rory said seriously, "to know that you're going to be hurting later if we're not careful."

"Be careful, then," she urged quietly, seeking to touch him. "I want to stay here forever."

Rory gave up. His carefully manufactured reasoning dissolved so quickly that the tension left his face immediately. The sight of her pert, earnest features transformed with desire was too much for him. He swooped and took her mouth with a new ferocity, pinning Tracy to the bed, though she writhed, giggling, beneath him. He grabbed her wrists and held her still, searing her throat with passionate kisses until she was breathless. Then they were rolling and nipping and tussling with delight, learning the same subtleties of the night before, but this time by the light of day.

It was the beginning of the longest, most exciting two days of her life. They made love, quickly this time, painstakingly the next, with just as much care and tenderness as the first time. It was a magical time, and the world did not intrude upon them. There was no need to leave the sensual solitude of that room. Food came, laundry was delivered. There was music, for Rory loved music, and the bath for Tracy who finally coaxed him to join her there. There was the telephone for talking with the hospital, and there was wine to toast the coming of the second night. And there was the bed. Two beds, in fact.

CHAPTER EIGHT

"WE CAN'T GO ON like this forever," Rory told her when morning arrived again. He had found his shirt and was buttoning it down the front as he spoke. "M.A. probably thinks we've fallen off the edge of the earth."

"She has probably guessed that we're being taken care of by some exquisite hotel," Tracy countered from her curled up comfort in the bed. She smothered a shy, but happy giggle and added with a charming blush, "Making love three times a day and feeding each other chocolate in bed."

"No more chocolates before breakfast!" Rory commanded, and he frowned sternly at her impish image in the mirror.

"But making love?"

Rory met her sparkling green eyes in the mirror, and his expression softened into a smile at her high color and pretended bravura. The pink nightgown somehow accented her healthy sensuality, and Rory felt a tug of remorse. Had he changed this hearty, unspoiled woman? Her spunk appeared undimmed, but was she putting on her tough act again? His own voice caught as he said, "None of that either, for a while."

"All right," Tracy said complacently, but with a gusty sigh. She slipped her legs over the edge of the bed and sat up, stretching her arms overhead and yawning hugely. She was unaffected, as usual. "We'll go see them at the hospital, if you like."

"Aren't you wondering how the Red Baron is doing?" Rory asked, covertly watching Tracy's reflection with an unconscious half smile on his mouth. When she shook out her hair, and the vibrant color flashed in the sunlight, Rory's smile broadened, and he corrected himself, "No, I suppose you're the Red Baron—or the Red Baroness, at least. How is Spinelli?"

"I've talked with him on the phone practically every two hours." Tracy had come up behind Rory and had wrapped her arms around him in a hug. Laying her head against his back, she said, "He's fine—or nearly. He's starting to go buggy in that room by himself, though. He's even starting to complain about the nurses, and I thought they'd keep his mind off his headache for ages."

Rory did not turn around. Tracy's arms felt fragile and small around him. Quietly he said, "Maybe he'll be discharged today."

It had to happen eventually. They both knew it. These two blissful days had to come to an end. The real world was beckoning more strongly with each passing hour. Rory's phone calls were coming more and more frequently, and he had started to look at his watch now and then. Tracy hadn't missed the signs. He was anxious to get back to his work, she knew. And that undoubtedly included leaving Tracy behind.

"Yes," she said softly, unwillingly, her cheek against his back. "Maybe he will."

"Then what?" Rory asked, not moving.

It was a loaded question. Whether he meant Spin's immediate future or the remote possibility of a future between the two of them, Tracy wasn't sure. During their time together there had been no promises made, and Tracy was acutely aware of that fact. She had been careful not to blurt out any imprudent declarations of love herself. But two earth-shattering days had passed, and her life was topsy-turvy.

She slipped away from Rory and tried to sound careless. "I'll take him home, I guess. Let's hope I don't have to play Florence Nightingale during the rest of his recovery!"

Rory turned around, and with a serious expression he watched Tracy gather up her clothes in one quick swipe. As she headed for the bathroom, he echoed with detached thoughtfulness, "Let's hope."

They walked to the hospital this time. The morning was warm and sunny, a perfect day for a happy stroll. Tracy gathered her composure enough to laugh and tease him. She could pretend nothing was different, she supposed. Rory still made her blush one minute and yelp in disagreement the next. Sometimes, though, she held his hand and swung it childishly between them, and sometimes he wrapped his arm around Tracy and hugged her close as they walked. They were always touching, always seeking some small physical contact to prolong the intimacy of the past few days. It was as if neither was willing to let go, and yet they could not speak of it.

"Yes," the head nurse on the floor said, when Rory stopped at her desk to ask about Mary Alice's condition. The nurse took a quick, impersonal look at a clipboard. "She's in her room and dressed. You may take her home now."

"Now?" Rory repeated blankly.

"Now?" Tracy asked, and her fingers convulsively tightened in his.

Mystified, the nurse glanced from his stunned expression to Tracy's and back again. "Yes, of course. Miss Cooper's doctor authorized her discharge this morning. She's very anxious to go, I believe. Will you sign these forms, sir? I'll go get a wheelchair. Standard procedure. And you'll have to go down to the first floor and attend to the paperwork there."

"Yes," Rory said, sounding confused.

"Oh, here comes the doctor now. Perhaps you'd like to speak with him about her condition? If she's going to travel any distance to get home, I think it's only wise—"

Tracy took a pace back and let her hand slip

from Rory's grasp. The doctor was in a hurry, but he paused to speak concisely to Rory about M.A. Tracy backed away from the conversation. By necessity, Rory's attention was focused on M.A. now, and Tracy knew that she shouldn't interfere. He had responsibilities.

Without a word, Tracy slid away and headed for Spin's room alone.

"Boy, am I glad to see you!" Spin exclaimed when she edged inside the door. He swung out of the bed and stood up in hospital-issue pajamas. With a cautious hand on the railing to steady himself, he said enthusiastically, "The doc says I can get out of this place today! I already called home, Trace. Harvey's bringing a plane to get us—"

"What's the hurry?" Tracy asked automatically.

"What's the hurry?" Spin demanded, and he looked around at her tone of voice. "I want to get outta this room! I'm going bats just looking at these walls, and with Mary Alice leaving today, I won't have anybody to—"

"Mary Alice!" Tracy repeated the unfamiliar name. Something weird was brewing here, and Tracy frowned at Spin. "It's Mary Alice now, is it?"

Spin came determinedly around the bed. "Yeah, but don't make a big deal out of it, okay? She's been visiting once in a while, that's all. Get my stuff out of the closet, will you? Harvey'll be at the airport pretty soon."

"Who said you could call Harvey?" Tracy demanded, trying to muster some anger. Things were happening way too fast, and suddenly she was powerless to stop them. There was dismay in her voice as well as outrage. "What plane is he bringing? Who's flying the regular runs?"

"Jeez, Trace! What's the matter with you? We've got things to do! We gotta get back home again!"

Home? The word suddenly sounded strange to Tracy. Where was home now? Anywhere without Rory? Surely not!

Spin was right, of course. They had to get back home and get started on a hundred things. Life couldn't stop completely just because Tracy O'Hara was in love.

Yes, she knew she was head over heels for Rory Buchanan, and the last thing Tracy wanted just then was to go tearing back to Shamrock with Spin and Harvey. There was too much to say, too much to decide! Inside, Tracy suddenly felt as if she was being drawn and quartered. Was this it? Was Rory going to run off to Chicago and marry that drippy Mary Alice Cooper after all? After everything that had happened in the last forty-eight hours?

"Come on, wake up!" Spin exhorted, unmindful of her sudden stillness. "Hand me my pants, will ya? Before the day nurse comes and tries to dress me!"

"Cripes, Spinelli," Tracy snapped, and she threw his jeans right at his sore head. "Haven't you got any class? I'm a lady, you know! What makes you think I have the slightest interest in helping you put your pants on?" She stormed out.

The real world was an unwelcome intrusion for Tracy. She wanted to dig in her heels and call for Rory, but a whirlwind of important tasks suddenly launched her into activity. There was no sign of Rory and Mary Alice anywhere, and Tracy, at the nursing station, was busy with the complicated discharge procedures. She figured that elsewhere in the vast hospital, Rory was similarly embroiled with a tight-lipped pencil pusher in a starched white uniform.

The morning zoomed by, and in no time Tracy found herself in a taxi and heading for the local airport. And Rory had disappeared. Maybe from her life. Without saying goodbye.

Harvey had borrowed somebody's refurbished Piper Cherokee, and for once Tracy had no interest in doing the flying. She sat in the back of the noisy plane with Spin and wondered to herself. Spin was less than talkative also, but halfway to Niagara Falls, he finally noticed that Tracy had fallen into a funk.

"So," he said, trying to sound conversational in spite of the dull roar of the airplane engine. "What happened with you and Buchanan?"

With her face to the window, Tracy muttered automatically, "Nothing. So shut up."

Spin assessed the situation and apparently decided that her mood wasn't foul enough to stop talking. Ignoring the noise from the engine, he asked lightly, "Mr. Northstream didn't change his offer then?"

"What offer?"

"What's with you, Trace? The offer he made to buy Shamrock, of course!"

"Nothing's with me," Tracy snapped, and she glared at Spin until he turned his head. Then, sounding sulky, Tracy said, "No, he didn't change his offer. We didn't talk business."

"Did you see much of him while I was laid up?"

"You're still laid up," Tracy said tartly, and she turned back to the window to hide her expression just in case. "I saw a little of him, I suppose. He's not so bad."

Spin snorted. "That's not what I hear."

"What?" Tracy demanded, angry then. She glanced up to see if Harvey was listening, and then swung on Spin. "What did you hear? From who?"

"From M.A.," Spin retorted promptly.

"You two got real chummy out in the woods, didn't you?"

"Didn't you and Buchanan?"

"Shut up and tell me. What was she saying about him?"

Spin shrugged then, but he had seen the fire in Tracy's eyes. "Mostly stuff we already knew. And that he wants to buy Shamrock real bad."

"How bad?"

Spin had a book of matches in his hand, and he toyed with it, flipping it over and over between his fingers. "Bad enough to try just about any trick to get it."

Annoyed, Tracy said, "Oh, here you go playing father protector again! I can take care of myself!"

"Trace," Spin interrupted, his voice suspiciously gentle, "the guy's practically bankrupt."

"What?"

"Bankrupt. You heard me." Spin kept his eyes on the matchbook and did not watch for Tracy's reaction. He went on carefully, "Buchanan's just about broke. He's overextended his runs, and his planes aren't up to the strain. M.A. says he's—"

"Oh, what does she know? You saw the way she acted after the Grumman went down! Her experience with airplanes is about as—"

"Take it easy." Spin cut her off, still soft. "You don't have to believe it, you know. I just figured you'd want to hear all sides of the issue."

Hardly mollified, Tracy thrust her arms together over her chest in a gesture of irritation. "Gossip hardly qualifies as useful information, Spinelli. If Buchanan really wants to buy Shamrock, and the price is right—"

"Doesn't it sound weird to you? How come he's

trying to buy you out if he's bankrupt? It just doesn't make sense!"

"Mary Alice Cooper," Tracy pronounced the name with sarcasm, "probably heard wrong. If Buchanan really wants to buy Shamrock, and he's got the money to make good on his offer, what's wrong with selling to him?"

"How do you know the price is right?" Spin asked, and he laid the matchbook on his knee. "You've only had two offers, and they're the same. You're going to wait till you hear from a coupla other airlines, aren't you?"

"Of course I am! I'm not as dumb as I look!"

"You don't look dumb," Spin said. "You look pretty, though. Very pretty today, Trace. I just—I'm sure Buchanan has noticed how—what a—well, you're beautiful sometimes, and a—a really sexy girl when you don't even know it, and—"

"Go soak your head!" Tracy burst out, flushing. "What's this leading up to?"

"Nothing!" Spin's voice had risen to match hers over the drone of the airplane, then dropped just as quickly. He went on anxiously, "I just want you to be careful, that's all. You didn't—? You won't go to bed with the guy, will you? If you get mixed up with Buchanan, he'll find a way to get Shamrock away from you for a song."

"Baloney!"

"I mean it, Trace," Spin insisted. "He's been around! He must need Shamrock for some reason.

And if he's going bankrupt, he hasn't got the cash to buy it the right way! Who knows what he'll do to get it."

"What do you think I'm going to do?" Tracy challenged brusquely. "Give him all my airplanes for the privilege of sleeping with him? Cripes, Spinelli!"

"All he has to do is get you pregnant, y'know! It isn't that hard to do! And then—"

"Go to hell, Spinelli!" Tracy shouted, not caring if Harvey or anyone else heard her now. Whether Spin had guessed the truth or not, she wasn't sure. But her pride was burning. Until that moment she hadn't thought about getting pregnant, and that was plain stupidity on her part. Furious, she lashed out at Spin, "Don't play big brother with me!"

"All right, all right! Jeez." Spin rubbed his head with one hand, massaging his headache into submission. "Trace, he's older and a lot more experienced than you. I know you won't— Listen, you can get hurt worse than just having your money and airplanes taken away, you know."

"Now what are you raving about?" she asked caustically.

"I mean," Spin said, choosing his words with deliberate caution now, "that you could get really hurt, Trace. I don't want to see that guy tear you up inside. Just be careful, okay? For once don't do something impulsive."

"Since when have I started being impulsive?" she demanded with impatience. Her heart was jerking painfully, and her breath was short. The news of Rory's financial shape was true. Tracy knew it was true. She had heard enough of his business conversations on the phone in the last two days to confirm everything that Spin was telling her now. With the unpleasant facts and a few unanswerable questions boiling in her mind, Tracy put her head back on the seat and stared out at the brilliant blue sky. There was a dead weight in her stomach that was beginning to hurt.

"You've been impulsive since you were born," Spin shot back finally, and he reached to poke Tracy on her thigh. "And you're not going to change, I know. Just keep the fireworks to a minimum, huh? I don't want you to fall for somebody else while I'm still waitin' for you."

"Spinelli, you must have really taken a crack on the skull," Tracy grumbled. "I think you're delirious."

"Maybe," Spin agreed, and he sat back in the seat with a funny kind of grin. "Maybe so."

"What does that mean?" Tracy asked, seeing the new glimmer of light in his eyes, despite the fact that he dodged his gaze from hers and pretended to look out the window. "What's got you so concerned for my love life all of a sudden? Especially since you've popped a gasket or two over Mary Alice Cooper?"

Something altered in Spin's face just then, some memory perhaps that brightened the gleam in his eyes. But it also brought a queer immobility to his face. Spin was keeping secrets, Tracy saw. He said merely, "Shut up about her."

Tracy shrugged. "Have it your way. You're probably out of luck with her, anyway. Buchanan was going to ask her to marry him up in Montreal but when—"

"What?" Spin grabbed her arm. "He was going to?"

"Hey! Ouch! I take it back! He was going to, but he decided not to after all, so—"

"What's the matter? She's not good enough for him now?" Spin had flown into a rage in a split second, eyes blazing and mouth tight with jealousy. "He'd better not try to take—"

"Hold it down," Tracy begged, frightened suddenly and catching Spin's hand in her own. "I shouldn't have said anything. He isn't going to marry her! He thinks she's great, but he isn't going to marry her. They're just friends. Take it easy, Spin. You'll get sick or something."

Spin jerked his arm from her soothing touch. "He'd better not try anything with her! He can work on you, if he wants, but if—"

Tracy began to laugh. "One minute you're ready to hire a hit man because he was admiring my bottom from a distance, and now you're about to strangle him with your bare hands over Mary

Alice! Wow! You're the one with the fireworks today!"

"It's Buchanan," Spin pointed out gruffly. He pitched the matchbook at the window and watched it hit the Plexiglas and bounce down to the floor. He added, "The man bothers me."

"That's obvious."

"He's after you, Trace," Spin said, kicking his boot absently at the fallen matchbook. "He's already got enough women to keep any man busy for years, but he wants you and Mary Alice, too. I don't like that. He's slick and smart and rich—"

"And bankrupt!"

"Maybe so, but he's got money, you can tell. He was born with money, and—"

"That's what's got your dander up," Tracy noted. "He's different from us. Silver spoons and polo ponies, and you resent it."

"Polo ponies!"

"I made that up. Cool off." Feeling generous suddenly, Tracy added, "You're as good as he is, you know."

"Maybe," Spin repeated, doubtfully this time. He looked down at his own upturned palms for a moment. For once there was no sign of grease or scent of airplane fuel on his hands. As if noting that fact to himself, Spin groused, "Nobody says I have to like him."

"He was a big help after the plane crash," Tracy argued lightly. "And he was honestly concerned about you. I don't think you ought to hate him."

Spin slid a look sideways at her, measuring. "You like him, don't you?"

Tracy managed a shrug. "I don't know. He seems okay on the surface."

"Yeah," Spin agreed dolefully. "But we're sure finding out some interesting stuff about him now, aren't we?"

"Shut up, Spinelli. Why don't you take a nap or something? Your head was weak enough before you broke it!"

When Harvey landed the Cherokee back at the Shamrock airstrip and taxied over to the hangar, Tracy climbed out of the small plane and waited for that happy feeling, that little lift of her spirits that buoyed her each time she arrived at home. But she took two steps out onto the tarmac and saw Rory's twin-engine Cessna parked on the edge of the grass. She faltered to a stop, and her heart did a flip-flop.

No, of course he wasn't here. He had left the Cessna at Shamrock when he hadn't been able to find the key for it. But a tug of loneliness caught at Tracy, and she couldn't shake it off. Rory was gone—back to his own world with his own friends and family around him, and Tracy was home at Shamrock with her airplanes and Spin and the rest of the boys. Everything should be back to normal. Except that Tracy was changed now. She was different, and Rory had made it happen. With a rueful smile, Tracy shook her head and started walking toward the house. She wanted to be alone for a while.

In the few days that passed from that time, Tracy made several important decisions.

The Grumman, they discovered without much surprise, had been badly damaged in the crash in Adirondack Park. The fuselage had been gouged a little, the wings were a dead loss, but more importantly, the engine had been slammed around too much to survive and still function with any degree of efficiency. From an insurance point of view, it was easier to junk the plane.

The FAA investigation team declared they had examined the wreckage to their satisfaction and released the plane from impoundment. With a lump in her throat, Tracy authorized a scrap dealer to haul away the remains after the FAA had completed their required inspection. She asked that the engine be returned to Shamrock, and the man promised delivery within a week or so.

Tracy hung up the phone from that conversation and sat for a long time at her dining table, staring out over the airstrip. This was it. The last straw. With the loss of the Grumman, the poor camel's back was finally breaking. Shamrock Air was not going to survive another three months.

Tracy knew she was going to be forced to sell out. The realization was a heartbreaker for Tracy, but she didn't burst into tears or let depression cloud her thinking. Perhaps it was time to bail out—to get out of a bad situation and start making plans for the future.

Midweek a phone call from Marjorie Hallis surprised Tracy and further convinced her that decisions had to be made.

"Tracy, it's Marjorie Hallis," the airline owner had said swiftly, breathlessly, as soon as the line connected. "I just heard about your narrow escape! My dear, how are you?"

"Okay," Tracy responded. "I'm okay, thanks."

"Goodness, you're braver than I would have been," Marjorie said with a laugh. "It must be your youth. I'd use a crash like that as an excuse to take a long vacation somewhere."

Tracy smiled at the crispness of the other woman's voice. Marjorie was made of tougher stuff than she'd lay claim to, Tracy was sure. "I may take that vacation," Tracy said shyly. "But not for a little while yet."

"I'm sure you're busy," Marjorie conceded. "My dear, what can I do to help? Have you seen the papers I sent you? About our merger, of course."

"Y—yes," Tracy said slowly. "I've seen them."

"I'm sure they're confusing," Marjorie said bluntly. "I'd be glad to explain anything you like, you know. Or I'll keep my mouth closed and leave you alone to think, if that's what you'd prefer.''

Tracy smiled again, though Marjorie couldn't see her. "I appreciate your honesty, Ms Hallis. I just—"

"I'm trying to be as forthright as I can, my dear. We've got to trust each other if this thing is going to go through. Let me assure you that my offer is good for at least another month. I know you've got other parties interested, and I'm sure you're going to take your time making your decision."

"Yes," Tracy said softly as soon as a break came in Marjorie's businesslike conversation.

"Let me give you some advice between girls, Tracy," Marjorie went on, her voice dropping conspiratorially. "Look at all the information carefully. Then put it aside for a week and look again. Take your time and don't let anyone rush you, all right? Not even me." Marjorie laughed once more. "Especially not me! You don't have to hurry the decision, you know."

No, Tracy thought when the conversation had ended. That wasn't quite true. The decision was going to have to come soon. There wasn't time to dawdle over things, that was sure. Tracy was smart enough not to tell Marjorie Hallis that, but Shamrock Air no longer had the luxury of time. A decision had to be made fairly quickly.

As the week progressed, Tracy found determination growing within herself. She called her lawyer cousin, Sean, and asked for his help in reading the agreement papers sent by the Hallis organization. She talked to Miss Harcastle, the bank representative, to get some additional advice. She listened and made notes to herself and began to do some hard thinking. And with her eye on the future in more ways than one, she made an appointment with a local doctor and went for a checkup. And some advice on contraception.

But Rory did not appear. His Cessna sat for days, smack in the middle of everything and acting as a constant reminder for Tracy. Each time she saw the pretty plane, she felt her heart give a quick tick of excitement. She began to carry the Cessna key in her pocket as a kind of charm. Was he going to come get it? Or was the stupid plane going to rust into a heap before he showed his face again?

On Friday night Tracy dragged herself home from the hangar and collapsed onto the couch with an exhausted "Oof!"

It had been a long few days. With Spin out of commission, her work had doubled. On top of the extra work load, the FAA was constantly on the phone with more questions about the Grumman crash—time-consuming questions that were beginning to bug Tracy. She had sent Harvey on the last flight to Pittsburgh, and now she needed some supper. A bowl of soup would be terrific. If she only had the energy to make it.

The phone rang. It was Spin, not the FAA for once. "How're you doing, Trace?"

"Okay, no thanks to you," Tracy responded, trying to sound cheerful. "Are you in bed?"

"Not at the moment. I'm so sick of staring at the ceiling that I feel like hopping a plane and getting out of this place for the weekend—to heck with my headache. You want to come over to my place for some supper? I'll fix hamburgers."

"You just want to hear what's been happening since you landed in sick bay."

Spin laughed. "I guess so. That and—well, I've been kinda worried about you."

Tracy blew an annoyed sigh. "Don't waste your energy on anything that doesn't get you on your feet. I'm tired of running this operation alone."

"Uhm," Spin agreed, sounding dubious. "Okay. You're too tired to come over tonight?"

"Rain check?" Tracy begged, twirling the Cessna key absently in her fingers. "I'm not fit for human companionship, and even you qualify for that these days."

"Shut up," Spin said fondly. "And good night."

Tracy cradled the receiver, and her smile lingered for a time after that. She lay back in the cushions and relaxed there. It was good to have Spin around sometimes. They were looking after each other now, as if they had no one else in the world. Perhaps that was true. Perhaps Tracy

O'Hara wasn't going to do any better in life than Spin. He cared for her, that was clear. Perhaps she had overlooked something in Spin before. Drowsy, Tracy smiled again at the thought of a frustrated Spin laid up for another week. She'd bet he wouldn't make it until Tuesday.

The phone sounded off again, and Tracy struggled to sit. She picked up the phone more quickly this time. "Okay," she said, without waiting for him to invite her. "Hamburgers sound pretty good after all."

"Hmm," came Rory's noncommittal voice in her ear. "Better than chocolates in bed?"

CHAPTER NINE

"OH, RORY," was all Tracy could say. Her breath left her body in one wonderful sigh of release.

"At least you remember my name," he said lightly, and she could hear the smile in his voice. "I thought I'd go down in your memory as one of the many men you've accompanied to a plane crash. How are you?"

"I'm fine, you skunk."

"Skunk?" he echoed, laughing.

"Maybe a—a bat is a better name for you. They disappear into thin air, don't they?" It was wonderful to hear his voice. A week's worth of anticipation flared and burst inside Tracy like a Roman candle. Tension and exhaustion evaporated completely, and though Rory wasn't there to see it, Tracy's smile was wide with delight.

"You did the disappearing act!" he shot back, sounding just as pleased to hear her voice. "I'll buy a top hat and a rabbit, and we'll go on the road together."

"Roderick the Outrageous?"

"And his Irresistible Redhead. What's up?"

Tracy swallowed hard and tried not to sound as elated as she felt. Rory already thought she was a kid without any polish whatsoever. Attempting to match his easy banter, she said, "We've been very busy. The FAA has just about finished their investigation into the crash. Did they interview you?"

"Briefly. They didn't break out the rubber hose to get their information."

"Not yet, anyway." She smiled happily. "And I've been trying to run my airline with an iron hand like you do."

"How's it going?"

"Downhill. We lost the Grumman completely."

"Hmm. As expected. Spinelli?"

"Spin's okay, or at least he will be in another few days. How is M.A.?"

"Good. She's had dinner dates all this week. Everyone wants to hear about her narrow escape."

"Dinner dates?" Tracy repeated cautiously. "With other men, I suppose. Are you jealous?"

"Not of them."

A short silence followed then, in which Tracy did some quick, but careful thinking. Holding the receiver gently in both hands, she lay back on the couch and sought safer ground. She asked, "How did your daughter like the story of the crash?"

"Melora? She wanted to hear it a dozen times, and now she's graduated to drawing crayon pictures of the whole tale. She has portrayed you as a princess with a mop of flaming hair that makes you look like a punk-rock Rapunzel." Rory paused, perhaps getting comfortable in his own chair, and then he added obliquely, "She's gone to my sister's for the weekend."

Tracy digested that information and noted softly, "Then she can't be too worried about her father, I suppose."

"No," he said, amused again. "She's a tough one."

"But with a mushy center, like her dad."

"Don't let that information get around, will you? I have a reputation to maintain in professional circles."

"Hmm," Tracy murmured, imitating his calm. "I guess you've been hobnobbing in those circles all week?"

"A little hobnobbing, yes. And I've been trying to catch up on all the business I should have been doing while I was busily playing—while we were in Albany." Rory was quiet for a moment, and then Tracy heard him strike a match. How could he be so blasted relaxed? He blew cigar smoke an instant later and added, "I have been working. I'm trying to pull off a coup in Montreal, to be honest. But I should have taken a few minutes off before now."

"What for?"

"To call you." Perhaps he sat up straighter, or put his match in an ashtray. There came a short, considering silence, and then in a different tone he began, "Tracy...."

Tracy smiled and crossed her fingers, waiting.

More silence, and then Rory asked abruptly, "Are you letting me squirm?"

Tracy laughed in relief. "Yes."

"I deserve that," he acknowledged, and then he sighed and came clean. "I've missed you—don't ask me why! I should have called before. I'm sorry I didn't. After a day or two I decided that I had made a big mistake with you."

"And after another day or two?"

"I figured you had decided you'd made a big mistake with me." He put his cigar in his mouth again and asked, "Did you?"

"No," Tracy said cautiously, wrapping the phone cord around her hand out of nervousness. "I didn't have second thoughts. Not really. I'm glad we—" Tracy stopped and tried again, "It was...I wish..."

"We ended things badly," Rory suggested, putting a halt to her uncertain stammer. "Everything happened too fast. I suppose that's the way it is between us."

"Is there—" Tracy caught herself, swallowed, and then couldn't stop the words. "Is there still an 'it' between us now?"

Rory laughed, sounding very pleased. "I don't know about you, young lady, but I've been suffering from the most amazing fantasies since I last saw that glint in your eyes. My God, how far away are you?"

"Hundreds of miles. Are you in Chicago?"

"Not far from there. My place is out on Lake Michigan. There's an airstrip fifteen miles away. Called Tall Pines. It's in the Jeppesen manual."

Tracy wondered for a moment. Was he asking her to come? Draining her voice of any hopeful intonations, she asked only, "Is it?"

"Yes," Rory said, and this time he waited. The silence blossomed.

"You're sounding lonesome," Tracy observed softly, and she closed her eyes with a growing smile. Six hundred miles. Perhaps, with a tail wind and light traffic near O'Hare, she could be there before midnight. *Ask me,* she thought. *Just ask, and I'll come.*

"I'm stuck here, unfortunately," Rory said blithely. "I've got phone calls due tonight and in the morning, and there's another obligation I've got on Sunday, too."

"And no one to keep you company."

"Not even Melora. Did I mention that she's gone for the weekend?"

"Yes. You must be very lonesome."

He was smiling again, she knew. He sighed with pretended dejection and said, "Oh, I suppose I'll live. I'll sit around here, maybe play the piano a little—something sad, of course—have a little dinner by myself—"

"You're in a different time zone, aren't you?"

"That's right," he said pleasantly. "It's an hour earlier here. Think of that."

"Think of that," Tracy repeated, teasing him. She got up and dragged the phone with her across to the table. The Jeppesen was there, and she flipped open the manual's loose-leaf pages, searching through the landing charts. What had he said? Tall Pines? *Just ask me, you big idiot, and I'll come!*

"But," Rory continued lightly, "I could use a restful weekend for once. The last few days have been murder."

"You have no stamina," Tracy chided. "Your age is beginning to show. What you probably need is a long weekend in bed."

"Maybe," Rory agreed, "that's exactly what you need, too."

Tracy closed the manual and glanced at her watch. "You could be right."

He laughed a little and said, "Don't let me keep you from your plans. I just called to check on you. You will be careful, won't you?"

"Yes, Rory. Good night."

"Did you say good night or good flight?"

"Good night! You're not going anywhere."

He laughed again and hung up without another word. Tracy reached for her jacket, then went in search of her knapsack. Time was wasting.

The Pitts Special was gassed up and ready, and Tracy climbed into the cockpit not half an hour later. She took off in minutes, and when she'd gained some altitude and opened the throttle, Tracy laughed to herself and executed a victory roll out of sheer delight.

Few things gave Tracy as much pleasure as flying an airplane, and that night the special feeling of independence and exhilaration was intensified. Once in the air, there was nothing but the night sky and an occasional steadying voice on the radio for companionship. Each town became nothing more than a small island of lights in the velvety sea of black. Fields and lakes stretched together in a smooth and faraway landscape, and Tracy was alone with her thoughts.

Up in the sky there existed a unique sort of freedom for Tracy. There was limitless opportunity here, the possibility of traveling to any spot in the world, no matter how distant or unfamiliar. Every airport was the same no matter where the pilot chose to land, with a predictable way of life and a camaraderie that Tracy understood and had come to love. She could set her plane down wherever she wanted, and there she'd be welcomed by the kind of people she knew best.

She could go anywhere, she reflected once she had refueled in Windsor on the Canadian side and took off again. As she pointed the nose to the west and relaxed her hand on the column once more, Tracy admitted inwardly that she *did* have the youth and freedom to do anything she chose.

Except for Shamrock Air.

As she flew, Tracy realized for the first time that she was indeed chained to her airline, to the people who depended on her there, to the memory of her father and the security of the past. Shamrock had once been the anchor of her life, but now suddenly it was a millstone. The business was failing, and Tracy recognized that she wasn't enough of an executive to know how to fix it.

It was Shamrock that kept Tracy O'Hara's life on the ground these days. Since meeting a man as dynamic and determined as Rory Buchanan, Tracy had come to feel a need to spread her own wings, to expand her own horizons. She was frustrated with the same old schedule, the same chores at dawn and the increasingly exasperating tasks that came with every sunset. It was the airline and her ties at the old airport that were keeping her grounded. Perhaps it was indeed time to sell out and get on with a new life. Perhaps it was time to find new people, new family, new sunrises.

"Yes," Tracy said aloud, and the sound of her own voice surprised her. Yes, it was time to give up the old ways. It was time to sell Shamrock Air.

No sadness came with that decision. Perhaps her spirit stayed high because O'Hare Approach was on the radio and the sky was busy around her. Tracy descended when she was told, then skirted the traffic and headed for the small airstrip called Tall Pines. A laconic stranger's voice acknowledged her from the tower, and she found the landing pattern. In a moment the rabbit appeared, the darting arrow of strobe lights that pulsed and pointed the way down the runway. Tracy followed the light and set the Pitts down, bouncing once in her impatience to be on the ground again.

She parked the plane on the end of a line of small private aircraft, and with knapsack in hand she climbed out into the cool night air. The airport was quiet at that time of night, but bright, of course, with floodlights shining on the tarmac. Tracy jumped lightly from the wing.

And Rory sauntered out of the hangar and came toward her.

He had his hands thrust into the pockets of his jacket, and the night breeze stirred his dark hair. He cocked his head, grinned crookedly, and called to her, "Tracy O'Hara! What are you doing here?"

"I could ask you the same question," Tracy retorted, smiling as she strode swiftly across the pavement toward him. Her heart was in her throat. Would he really be happy to see her? Mustering her tough-girl voice, she demanded, "Or do you usually hang around airports in the middle of the night?"

No preliminaries. He took one last pace and caught her up in a hug, one that was surprisingly swift and strong, and Tracy flew into his embrace. She flung her arms around his shoulders and pressed her slim body to his. Inside, she was joyously ready to burst. She couldn't breathe, couldn't speak. She could only feel wondrous delight in seeing him and being held like this.

"I knew you'd come," Rory murmured, half-laughing against her hair. "How could anyone miss the hints I was dropping?"

"Why didn't you just ask?" Tracy blurted out before she could stop herself. She couldn't let go, didn't dare. He'd see that she was in love, that she had fallen like a ton of bricks. His frame felt warm and secure, and she could feel his heart beating against her breast. Her voice sounded choked. "You could have just asked me!"

"Direct questions require a direct answer," Rory replied, and he kissed her head swiftly. "And I didn't want to give you the option of saying no. You're always saying things I don't expect!"

He loosened his grip on her then, and set Tracy away enough so that he could see her eyes. She smiled at him, though she felt her mouth waver. Quickly, she blinked and said, "I'm hungry."

"Oh, for Pete's sake!" Rory exclaimed, hugging her hard once again and letting her go. "See what I mean?"

"I can't help it. I had a cup of coffee on the Canadian side about ten o'clock—oh, and some peanuts before I left." Tracy touched the collar of his shirt as it showed through his jacket, and then her fingertips met the warm skin of his throat. She looked up again, embarrassed this time, and added, "I hurried."

The light in Rory's eyes changed then, and his voice caught oddly. "Oh, Tracy. I feel like a kid, I'm so glad to see you."

Afraid to say the same, Tracy swallowed her agreement. Shrewdly, she asked, "You didn't expect to like me, did you?"

He laughed and cuffed her bottom before pulling her around to walk with him. "No, I didn't expect to like you. I didn't expect a lot of things. Neither did you. Admit it."

"I didn't expect to find you waiting for me."

"What were you going to do?" he asked. "Fly in and go sit in the bar until Indiana Jones came along looking for artifacts?"

Tracy summoned a frown and slanted her face upward. "Are you calling me names, buster?"

"I'd have trouble finding the right one. My car's this way."

Rory drew her with him past the open hangar doors, and Tracy caught a glimpse of more small aircraft inside the vast space. There was only one jet in sight, however—an old one with a flat tire to boot. It was painted with the royal-blue logo of Northstream Airlines, but looked like a derelict. Other than that, the small airstrip was luxurious by Tracy's standards. No Quonset-style hangars with rickety doors and hissing bug-lights for Rory

Buchanan. The place fairly oozed money. The paint on the hangar floor was new, the maintenance stands were strictly spit and polish, and even the gasoline pumps looked clean—maybe waxed, for all Tracy knew. Rory even had those expensive electric rolling doors on his hangar. How could he be bankrupt?

There was a station wagon parked outside the wire-mesh fence in the shadow of the hangar. The car was a jarring note in an otherwise spiffy layout. It was an old Volvo, Tracy saw, with a roof rack and a badly dented fender that was beginning to rust.

When Rory reached for the door handle on the passenger side, Tracy hung back in his embrace to have a better look at the vehicle. "This is yours?"

"You're a snob after all." Rory noted her surprise with a grin. He drew her close again. "I need a car like this for all the stuff my daughter likes to do. Watch out for the—whoops, those are boxes of cookies. Put them in the back seat."

"Girl Scout cookies?"

"No, she's not old enough for Girl Scouts. It's the gymnastics club she's in. Do you want some? I'm told the fudge ones aren't bad."

"I have a feeling this weekend is going to be full of surprises." Tracy accepted his hand to settle down into the front seat of the dilapidated car. She picked up the gaily packaged box of cookies and peeped a look up at him.

"No more than last weekend," he said lightly, with a grin.

Tracy blushed and snatched her hand from his. "I'll go home again if you're going to torment me!"

"You've been tormenting me for the last week in absentia. No, you won't go home tonight. You're tired enough to have an accident again, and if I lost you at this stage, I don't think I'd get over it."

Tracy looked up, her eyes round and turbulent. She couldn't speak for the surge of curious excitement that swept her. Could it be that Rory was as infatuated with her as she was with him? Could he possibly be?

"In?" he asked, checking. Without realizing what he had just said, Rory whanged the door shut and went around the car, pulling the car keys from his trouser pocket. A moment later he got in beside her.

Tracy sat very still in the seat, feeling nervous and awkward and suddenly fifteen years old. She looked straight out the windshield and clamped her fingers around the cookie box to keep her trembling a secret. "Rory...."

He closed his door and turned to her. "Yes?"

"Rory...."

He took a short breath and hesitated, watching her determinedly averted face and the single, anxious quiver that touched her curving lips. Then, very gently he answered her unspoken question. "Yes, Tracy."

And he pulled her across the seat to him.

He kissed her softly, drawing Tracy over until she was almost sitting in his lap, like a little girl in need of comfort. He took the cookies from her and tossed the box over his shoulder into the back seat.

Then he slid his hands up her back and held Tracy by the shoulders until she tentatively slipped her arms around his neck and shifted still closer. Her lips parted out of instinct, and Rory kissed her coaxingly, knowing the response that lay within her. He molded her body to his, deepening the kiss with slow, but ever growing ardor. Rory was gentle and cautious, but unyielding, and he let one hand drop familiarly to the supple length of Tracy's thigh. Without thinking, he followed its long and graceful curve.

The inward fire sparked and grew. In seconds, they were both breathless with relief and urgency.

Time blurred and melted in the darkness while both of them remembered and confirmed each detail, each feeling. Rory caressed her sides, her back, her shoulders, recalling their taut curves and youthful softness. He seared her mouth, desperately tasting all the sensations he remembered and had craved. With Tracy fragile and willing in his arms, he found himself suddenly seething to have her, to tell her a hundred things and hold her bare flesh to his. His heart raced with anticipation.

One palm touched the weight of her breast only briefly—enough to draw a quick tremor and a sigh from Tracy. Her gentle shudder seemed to jolt him, and he remembered where he was. Forcing himself to draw away, he cupped her face, tracing the smooth and delicate contours of her creamy cheek with his thumb. He kissed her twice more, a featherlike contact on her face, then on her temple. When he released a breath, it was unsteady.

Tracy smiled into his cloudy eyes, and a happy rush of wonder tingled in her chest. She touched his face, too, and then she found his mouth again with hers.

He held her breathlessly tight then, and kissed her with a ferocity that transmitted his innermost feelings to her. Quick and anguished, he held her head with barely controlled strength and followed the outline of Tracy's lips, tasting their sweetness with his tongue, savoring. A low murmur of pleasure, of urgency escaped his lips. Suddenly his hands were everywhere—touching, caressing, seeking her bare skin under her sweater.

Tracy felt her body relax into a pool of radiant sexuality. She kissed his mouth, scraped her smooth cheek against his rough one and slipped her hands down his chest. She felt his heart beating swiftly against her palms, and his mouth was warm and tantalizing on her throat.

Then, amazingly, he popped the snap on her jeans, and that brought Tracy to her senses. She writhed away finally, laughing and gasping at once. "Rory!"

"Sorry," he gasped promptly, his voice ragged with laughter and frustration. "I'm sorry, honestly. Tracy, darling, stop me before I do something immature!"

Tracy laughed with him, her eyes alight and her mouth tingling and rosy. "Stop you? I don't think I can. If I had to walk right now, I don't think I could do it. My legs are like jelly."

His smile was warm, though a little weak at the edges, and there was a distinct smoulder in his eyes. Rory gave her thighs a pat that turned into a caress and murmured, "I'm glad. I want you to feel that way. I can't... it's just hard to believe you're here," he finished inadequately.

Tracy's bubbling laugh sounded as breathless as his words. "A lot of this is hard to believe."

"But not impossible. Come home with me?"

She smiled and tipped her head saucily. "That depends. In this car?"

"I promise not to ravage you before we get to the driveway. Unless of course, you'd really like—"

"No, no. At least as far as the driveway, please!" Tracy wriggled off his lap and back into her own seat, swatting his hands away when he tried to balance her with a hand on her bottom. "You're not going to crash this car just to pay me back for dropping you and your fiancée in the Adirondack mountains, are you?"

"She is not my fiancée," Rory shot back, reaching past her for the seat belt. "As you well know. No, I wouldn't crash this fine car for anything. It doesn't exactly belong to me, to tell you the truth. It's on loan from my mother. Buckle up, please."

"I can do it myself," Tracy said, taking the seat belt from his hands. "I'm not your daughter."

"No," agreed Rory, and he kissed her once more on the mouth before he reached again for the ignition. "Now tell me everything, please."

Clicking the mechanism of the seat belt, Tracy glanced around. "About what?"

He shrugged and started the engine. "Anything. Tell me about the crash."

"You mean about the FAA?" Tracy guessed. "And what they've found out?"

"You're a clever girl." He glanced into the rearview mirror out of habit and then threw Tracy an appreciative look. "Maybe brilliant."

"Just intuitive where you're concerned. Wait until I tell you about your fantasies."

"Later, please. When I can act them out. What about the FAA?"

Tracy settled back in her seat, getting comfortable and beginning her explanation.

Long before the Grumman crash, Tracy had known that the Federal Aviation Administration automatically investigated every plane crash in the

United States, looking for evidence of poor maintenance or negligence on the part of airline companies. The agency's purpose was to ensure the safety of all air-traveling passengers. She reported to Rory that they had impounded the remains of her downed Grumman immediately and had meticulously gone over every inch of the plane to look for the cause of the crash.

"I wish they'd let me look at the plane," Tracy told Rory as the station wagon gained the highway and started north. "I'm sure I could find out what caused all that smoke."

"You mean they haven't found out yet?" Rory asked, surprised. "It's been a week!"

"I know," Tracy agreed. "Either they're busy with other business, which would surprise me, or they've found something really fishy and aren't telling me about it yet."

Rory glanced at her, serious suddenly. "No kidding?"

Tracy lifted her palms. "I can't figure it out. All I know is that the plane filled up with smoke but didn't burn. Spin and I crash-landed without any loss of life. Maybe that's why the FAA isn't moving very fast on this. If somebody had died, they'd be screaming."

"It's odd, though," Rory said thoughtfully, as he drove.

"Um. They released the plane, so we ought to hear soon. Did you get your luggage?"

"Yes," said Rory. "It arrived yesterday. M.A. was worried about her makeup case. She'd left a ring or something in it, but there it was. No harm done, I guess. What about the plane?"

"Junked. Some character up there paid me two hundred dollars for the fuselage."

"Ouch."

"You want to put in a bid for it?"

Rory laughed. "No, thanks. I can't afford to be charitable right now. How is Spinelli?"

Tracy told him and asked after M.A., and the conversation evolved easily from there. However, he ignored her attempts at starting a conversation about his daughter. The time would come, but this wasn't it. Rory drove with care, and Tracy felt utterly safe and happy to be with him again. The drive was short, or so it seemed to her, and in a very few minutes, he had drawn up a narrow tree-lined lane.

"That's the lake down that way," he said, pointing past Tracy to show her. "Can you see in the dark? There. And that's my sister's house."

"Where Melora is tonight," Tracy noted, peering through the trees at the darkened shadows of the house. It was too far to see, but Tracy got an impression of a very large building.

"Yes. It's my nephew's birthday tomorrow, and there's some enormous celebration planned for all the cousins. Melora didn't want to miss a minute of it. She stays there a lot when I'm traveling. Ann has been a great surrogate mother."

"Ann?"

"My sister. She's got four of her own kids and doesn't seem to mind one more now and then. I'd be in trouble if it wasn't for her. Here. This is it."

When he touched the electric garage-door opener and the light came on, Tracy could finally see more than just the outline of the house. She released a long quivering sigh and felt the nervousness rise within her once again. The place was huge.

And elegant. It was built of cedar, but not in an outlandishly modern style. There were flowering bushes and a tangle of wild flowers at the corner of the garage, and birch trees stood tall, yet casually around the house, their white trunks shining in the darkness. The uncomplicated architecture of Rory's house blended with the natural setting.

Tracy got out of the car, and when she had closed the door and slung her knapsack over her shoulder again, she walked slowly to the concrete apron outside the garage. A breeze rustled in the trees overhead, but the night was otherwise quiet. There wasn't another house in sight, and the lake shone silver through the trees about a hundred yards down the sloping yard. From somewhere distant, a large dog barked deeply half a dozen times, a sign that the lakeshore was not completely deserted. Perhaps there were other houses within hailing distance, but Tracy couldn't see them.

Rory materialized behind her and wound his

arm around Tracy's shoulders. His nose brushed against her hair. "All right?"

"Yes," Tracy breathed, closing her eyes and leaning against his body. "It's nice here."

"Warmer inside," he suggested lightly. "This way. It's not the grand entrance, but in the dark, I don't want you hiking around the front. You don't mind the kitchen door, do you?"

In fact, the kitchen entrance helped Tracy through that initial rush of nervousness, for they had to climb over a deflated rubber raft, a platoon of tricycles and some water skis in a tangle of nylon line. Rory had left the kitchen lights on, and Tracy blinked uncertainly when they got safely inside.

Rory laid his car keys on top of the refrigerator and crossed to the long butcher-block counter.

Tracy hesitated, looking swiftly around the neat, contemporary-style kitchen. The floor was parquet, the cupboards a sleek, modern white. The ceiling soared high, crossed by exposed beams, and shot with dramatic skylighting, now dark. Plants hung decorator-style from the wood.

Through a tall arched doorway she glimpsed a dining room, complete with a huge table that was nothing more than a slab of glass three inches thick laid across ebony braces. The chairs were teak, Tracy was sure, and over a Chinese buffet hung a picture—a single splash of subdued color on a plain white canvas. Elegant and simple. The whole place was just as spectacular.

Rory had gone to check the telephone answering machine, and he clicked it once. "Sorry for this. Do you mind? I was supposed to hear from someone."

"Go ahead," Tracy said, her voice too soft and throaty.

Rory glanced at her, saw Tracy's stunned reaction to his home and smiled gently. He had been prepared for her culture shock and handled the awkward moment smoothly. "Why don't you have a look around by yourself? I'll be finished in a minute. Want a soda?"

"I'll get it," Tracy said, and she indicated the telephone with a halfhearted wave of her hand. "You go ahead with your business."

He let her go, and with knapsack still over one shoulder, Tracy walked uncertainly through the dining room to the rest of the house. Rooms seemed to sprawl in all directions—a den here, a television room there—but most awesome was the octagonally shaped living room, complete with sunken conversation area and a stone fireplace that commanded one entire wall. There was a glass sculpture on the mantel, but that was the only decoration in the room. Perhaps the minimal clutter was a form of child-proofing the home, but Tracy got the impression that the elegant simplicity of the place was more an artistic concept than common sense. The carpet was thick, the furniture spare and expensive.

Someone with an eye for beauty had decorated the house, and Tracy was suddenly sure it wasn't Rory. Abruptly she felt like the proverbial stranger in a very strange land. Mindful that her boots might still bear the evidence of airport tarmac, Tracy gingerly skirted a beautiful Oriental rug that had been laid down over an already luxuriously thick carpet and approached the great glass doors.

From the kitchen Rory's voice sounded distantly as he spoke on the telephone. Reluctant to go back to him, Tracy slipped the latch on the doors and pushed the heavy glass aside. She stepped out into the night air, leaving the door open behind her.

A patio overlooked the lake and long yard. On it sat a wrought-iron table and a pair of lounge chairs, and through the darkness, Tracy could make out the outline of a child's swing set. With a weak smile, she laid her knapsack on the table and stopped. Taking a deep breath, Tracy tried to organize her scattered thoughts.

They were very different, Tracy reflected with a growing lump in her throat. No wonder Rory had looked around her own home with a derisive eye and a cruel remark about her father's things still hanging on the faded walls.

Tracy O'Hara was so far out of her league here that it wasn't funny anymore. Rory was a man of expensive tastes—expensive in airplanes, in artworks, in everything. In women, perhaps.

Why had he wanted her to come, for heaven's sake? Was he tired of the other women in his life? Did he need someone young and new to keep his interest piqued for a while? Surely there was a reason that a man like Rory Buchanan wanted Tracy around. He could snap his fingers and have anyone, no doubt. Why had he chosen her?

The remote possibility came to Tracy's mind like an ugly creature from a gloomy swamp. She tried in vain to push it aside, but the thought asserted itself in spite of her efforts. Was Rory planning to use her for something? Was Shamrock Air his motivation for bringing an inexperienced and woefully innocent Tracy O'Hara here?

CHAPTER TEN

RORY CAME OUT several minutes later, and Tracy was so lost in speculation that she did not hear him arrive behind her. She sensed his presence, though, and didn't jump or cry out when he touched her.

He put his arms around her and drew her back against his body. Pressing a kiss to the tender spot just below her ear, he murmured, "What are you thinking?"

Tracy thrust up her chin and leaned back against him. Summoning her most cryptic tone, she said, "I was wondering where the hot tub was. I figured you'd have one."

"I'll build one if you want." He kissed her again, just as softly. "What's up?"

"What d'you mean?"

"Come on. Don't start with that routine again." Rory turned her gently until Tracy was facing him. He held her loosely with one arm around her slender figure, and with his other hand tipped her chin up so that he could see her expression in the moonlight. "Tell me what's wrong."

"Nothing's wrong," Tracy said bravely, her green eyes flashing at him in challenge.

"Come on," he coaxed again, smoothing her tumbled hair back from her face with his fingertips. He stroked her throat and said, "I know you now. When you get that look in your eyes I don't see anger anymore. I see fear. You're not frightened of me, are you?"

"You?" Tracy demanded. But her voice cracked and sounded false. Biting her lip, she met Rory's eyes and shook her head as if to throw off some fleeting yet unpleasant thought. Then she was silent, hurting inside.

"Talk to me," he urged softly. "Are you worried?"

"Oh, Rory," she whispered, giving in unwillingly. She brought her hands nervously to his chest and played with the buttons there. She wasn't ready to question him about his motives yet, so she took a breath and asked miserably, "Do we... are you and I going to have anything to talk about? Is there anything we can... something besides... besides...."

"Sex?" he asked, sounding just as tranquil as before. He touched her back, running his hands down the curve of her spine. "You've decided we have nothing in common."

"If we do," Tracy asserted with determination, "it's nothing my father would want his little girl doing without benefit of clergy!"

Rory smiled and touched his forehead to hers. "Darling Tracy. Yes, I find you very attractive. Even passed out in a bowl of peanuts. The first time I ever saw you, my first thought was seeing you in my bed. Yes, we've got a terrific physical magnetism, haven't we?"

Afraid her voice was going to embarrass her, Tracy could only nod. She avoided his gaze.

"But there is more," Rory said softly, his caress continuing down her back. "There's more than sex between us. We've always hit it off, don't you think? You keep me humble and alert and... well, this sounds inadequate, I guess, but you make me happy. You're so full of life. I admire you, respect you. Don't let this damned house and all the things that surround me make a difference, please? This stuff doesn't mean much to me."

"How can you say that?" Tracy asked resentfully. "Everyone is a product of his environment! You can't—"

"So what? Different environments can produce the same kinds of people, can't they? You're frightened by silly things—rugs and chairs and rooms—"

"And you," she declared abruptly. "You're not like anyone I've known before. I feel safe with you one minute, and the next I can't think straight because you touch me or look at me in a way that—oh, hell! I can't explain it!"

"That's a very nice thing to say, believe it or

not." Rory smiled and swung her around as if they were dancing in the darkness. He put his lips against her forehead and added, "Maybe someday we'll find a different way of saying it to each other."

Tracy hugged him, afraid to speak again, afraid to ask about her deeper concern. Was he saying all those things to gain her confidence? To get Shamrock Air?

"Just don't be frightened," Rory said, holding her against him.

"I'm not. Not really. I don't scare easily."

"I know. I have a feeling you'd walk away from me—from whatever we've started together—if you were afraid. Don't leave yet, Tracy. Give it a little time."

"I will go," Tracy promised bluntly. "If I don't like what's happening."

"I know that. Just don't mistake all this for something bad, okay? We'll take it slow and easy and see what develops, hmm?"

Tracy fought the urge that rose inside her. A bubble of tension filled her throat, and for one awful moment she was afraid she was going to cry. The final humiliation. Tracy O'Hara was not the type to be intimidated by mushy talk, so she gritted her teeth and directed a hard look up at Rory again, hoping her eyes did not betray her inner turmoil. "You drive me crazy sometimes, you know."

"Can you settle for that?" he asked lightly. He must have guessed her dismay, for he squeezed her and smiled. "We drive each other crazy, hmm?"

He started Tracy walking back toward the house, his arm firmly across her shoulders. Tracy put her head down, but she slid her arm around Rory, too, her head on his shoulder. "Yes, I can settle for that. Unless it gets worse."

"It's only going to get better," Rory said, handing her through the doorway to the living room. "I predict it. What could be worse than a plane crash?"

Tracy laughed, feeling stronger.

Rory gave her a hug. "How hungry are you?"

"I'm not at all, if you're going to pull caviar and champagne out of your Frigidaire."

Rory pinched her bottom and sent Tracy skipping before him into the room. "You're a pesky little thing sometimes. No, there will be no caviar tonight. I might have a bottle of champagne, though. How about ham and cheese? Or peanut butter and jelly? That's my specialty with Melora. For you, I'll throw in a bottle of Dom Perignon."

"Don who?" Tracy demanded, teasing him.

"You'll learn," Rory promised as he herded her ahead of him through the house. He grinned. "Haven't I taught you all kinds of good things?"

"I can teach you a thing or two, y'know. Don't patronize me."

"You'd probably slug me for it. Forgive me.

Will you allow me to hang up your coat? You will stay, won't you?"

"For a while," Tracy said haughtily, preceding him into the brilliant light of the kitchen. "But I've got an airline to run, don't forget."

"You can count on my memory there." Rory stripped her flight jacket from Tracy's shoulders and headed for the closet beside the refrigerator. Over his shoulder, he added, "I haven't forgotten the business deal we've got hanging in midair, you know."

She felt a thud in the stomach. "Business deal?" Tracy repeated, laughing shakily. "Do you still think you're going to get my assets away from me?"

"I'm doing all right so far, aren't I?"

"I haven't budged, y'know." Tracy climbed up on a kitchen stool and braced her elbows on the countertop. She laid her chin in her hands and tried to master her expression. Flat out she blurted, "I hear you're not in a good position for buying right now."

From the closet he asked, "Have you got a mole in my organization?"

Tracy laughed, stronger this time as she thought of Mary Alice Cooper. "You could say that!"

Rory shrugged and smiled guilelessly. He closed the door and came across the kitchen, pushing the sleeves of his sweater up over his forearms. "I think I'd make a few sacrifices to get you, Miss

Tracy. Shamrock Air might be money well spent."

This was territory that Tracy was unprepared to discuss yet. There was too much she had to learn first. With a casual air she glanced around the spacious kitchen with its expensive appliances and immaculate surfaces. Mastering her initial shock at seeing such splendid surroundings, she changed the subject. "I think you're accustomed to spending well, Rod-er-ick. This is some joint you've got here."

"Don't blame me," Rory said blandly. He had arrived in the work area of the kitchen, and while Tracy watched he set about finding the makings for sandwiches. He tossed her a loaf of wholewheat bread and said, "My ex-wife did all of this."

Tracy smiled at him. "She must have had a talent for making good choices."

He grinned. "Thank you. Are you qualifying me as one of her choices?"

"Well, maybe you weren't one of her better decisions," Tracy corrected herself hastily, teasing him with sparkling eyes. Unfastening the twist tie on the bread, she tipped her head and asked, "How come she left you, Rod-er-ick?"

With an arm load of packages from the refrigerator, Rory came to the opposite side of the bar. He dropped the food before Tracy and countered, "What makes you think she did the leaving? Maybe I walked out on her."

Tracy set about unwrapping a package of ham, shaking her head. "No. You're here with all the goodies. She took off, didn't she?"

"Yes," Rory said quietly, watching Tracy's small hands and avoiding her eyes. "I probably did some pushing, to tell the truth. Our divorce was not totally her fault."

Still busy with the food, Tracy glanced up and asked abruptly, "How come you married her?"

Rory smiled directly into Tracy's eyes. "That bold-as-brass part of you is one of the things I like best. Even when you're making me squirm."

"You dodging the question?" Tracy asked with a grin.

He shook his head. "No. I married her right out of college. We had dated for several years, and it seemed like the logical next step. I was married when I was your age."

Tracy pulled a wry face. "Are you going to start that age junk again?"

Rory laughed and went back to the refrigerator for drinks. "I married because I thought I was in love with a woman who suited me and what my life was going to be. Her father used to be in the airline business. In fact, I got my start with his company before I created Northstream. Margie was—at the time—a nice part of the postgraduate deal. But we changed, as people will. We just grew up a little late and in different directions. We weren't compatible after a while."

"How come?"

Juggling two cans of soda, Rory came back and handed Tracy a bag of peeled carrot sticks cut in child-size lengths. "I don't know," he said on an even sigh. "If I really understood, maybe it wouldn't have happened. I didn't enjoy getting divorced."

"I know." Tracy smiled at him, encouragingly this time. "But...?"

Rory pulled up another stool and sat opposite Tracy. "But...I didn't enjoy living with her after a while. And she was climbing the walls living with me. I—" He faltered, thinking, and then tried again, "When we first got married, Margie was quiet and gentle and the perfect housewife—the perfect wife for an ambitious man. She had few ambitions herself and wanted to make a nice home and family. But she was too smart for that. She needed an outlet, and I thought I tried to help her find one. I thought I'd share my work with her and see what happened. She got interested in the business." Rory hesitated. "Tracy...."

"Business? You mean Northstream?"

Rory nodded. He was motionless suddenly, watching her. "Margie started working with me a little and finally began to research and buy some airline stock of her own. Once she started spreading her wings, there was no stopping her. She's very bright and determined. After Melora was born, Margie just wanted to be out—to be working and wheeling and dealing. I couldn't blame her. Sitting around this house, so far out in the country with nothing but the lake and my relatives for company... it was bound to happen, I guess."

Tracy took a noisy bite of carrot. Still chewing, she cracked open a head of lettuce and began to layer a sandwich on whole wheat. "You're damned understanding now, Rod-er-ick. Were you so nice about it while it was happening?"

Rory grinned out of reflex and shook his head. "Of course not. I have a temper, I'll admit. And Margie got to be just as strong. We had some real shouting matches, let me tell you. Tracy, there's a lot you ought to know about me."

"I've seen a hint of the temper," said Tracy, eyeing him askance, a smile playing on her mouth. She aimed a carrot at him. "Believe me, I've experienced worse. You're an amateur compared to my father."

Rory did not react, did not smile at her words. The truth was very near the surface, but he made a conscious effort to hold it back. Just a little longer. He said seriously, "I want to tell you a great many things about my ex-wife, Tracy. And about our relationship now. But I don't think tonight's the time. It's going to be confusing for you. And I've got Melora to think of first. She's still in the middle of things."

"You've got custody of her though," Tracy said, completely missing the signs of Rory's sudden disquiet as she put the top piece of bread on and gave it a pat. "Take it from an expert on child custody. Dad doesn't get the kids without a struggle."

She had passed him the first sandwich, and Rory took it from her hands without thinking. "I forgot. You must have been in Melora's position once."

"Not quite. I was old enough to decide for myself. Still... there was a fight."

"Margie didn't fight me at the time she left us. She still sees Melora on a relatively regular basis. But my daughter is very grown up. You'll see. She's too mature for her age, I think, and she's got a very busy social calendar. She's quite the butterfly."

Tracy smiled, starting on another sandwich. "Like this weekend and the birthday party."

"Exactly." Rory smiled also, mostly with relief at being over the subject of his ex-wife. His enthusiasm for his daughter shone through as he spoke to her. "Melora misses her mother, but it takes some serious discussion with the kid to make her admit it. There's Ann, who's taken over for Margie with a vengeance. And I'm here most of the time—perhaps not enough, but we're okay so far." Rory snapped the top off one of the sodas and prepared to take a long swallow.

Tracy sat still. With her usual bull's-eye accuracy, she said flatly, "But you were going to ask M.A. to marry you."

Rory choked comically and stared across the counter at her. "You don't even try the subtle games, do you?"

Lifting her nose a notch, Tracy said, "Now and then. Tell me straight now. Why were you going to ask M.A. to get married?"

"Isn't it obvious?" Rory asked, passing her the soda to wash down her first bite of sandwich.

"What's obvious is that you came awful close to asking her, and something's made you back off real fast. It certainly wasn't my arrival on the scene."

"I wish I could say that you changed my mind, but no, you didn't. I'm still confused, to be honest. I told you once before about my feelings on this subject. I just don't believe a marriage to me would be best for M.A."

"She can't fill your ex-wife's shoes, huh?"

"That's not it," Rory said firmly. "M.A. is enjoying her life now. She doesn't need to be tied down like this. Look around. I can't run my airline and be both a mother and a father. Not much longer, anyway. For a while I thought M.A. was the best candidate to help me."

"She's got a lot of talents, hmm?"

"Yes, a lot. She's definitely a class act. M.A. is the nicest woman I've ever known."

"And the chemistry?"

Rory's eyes slid suspiciously sideways at Tracy as she ate. "What are you asking?"

"Have you slept with her?"

Rory grinned. "Should I take the fifth amendment?"

"It would be pretty weird if you were going to marry her for her mothering abilities alone!"

"You're right," Rory admitted. "She's got a lot more going for her than her potential for raising children. But I don't think it's any of your business whether she and I—"

"You're being noble," Tracy decided, interrupting him firmly. She reached for a napkin and continued, "You'd tell me if you slept with someone I didn't know, but because I've met the gracious Miss Cooper, you aren't breaking the gentleman's code of honor. Okay, I've established that you've known M.A. in the biblical sense. Has that been taking place for a long time? Recently?"

"Tracy, this is getting us nowhere—"

"Recently?" Tracy demanded again, harshly this time, but with a smile tugging at her mouth.

"No," Rory said with exasperation. "Not even when we were staying up at your place. M.A. and I haven't really even dated each other since before I was married. We haven't slept together for ten years at least. I just—she's always been around, that's all. I thought a weekend in Montreal might start something nice."

"You mean that Spin and I were delivering you to Montreal so you could have a tryst with Mary Alice Cooper?"

"Partly," Rory admitted, enjoying the fiery look in Tracy's eyes and the outraged purse of her mouth. He said, "I had an important meeting also, though. Another merger, to tell you the truth. You're not the only airline I'm considering buying for myself. M.A. thought she was along for the ride."

Tracy laughed buoyantly. She hooked her heels on the lower rung of the stool and spun, smiling. "You mean she didn't have the faintest idea what you were about to spring on her?"

With a rueful grin, Rory shook his head. "I doubt it."

"Boy, she was really in for a shock!"

Rory sat back, enjoying the delight in Tracy's expression. "Maybe not. M.A. and I get along better than most married couples. We've been friends for years. My parents and her parents vacationed together—all that stuff. She and I probably shared a bath when we were kids. And later we did some natural adolescent experimenting with one another." He rolled his eyes at the memory and added, "She doesn't hold that against me, thank heaven. She's a great lady, you know. Don't underestimate Miss Cooper."

"I won't," Tracy promised, and took a short sip of cola. "Spin might, but I won't."

"Oh," Rory said, lifting his brows. "So Spinelli's got a crush on M.A."

Tracy nodded. "He's also got a very poor self-image at the moment. You intimidated the hell out of him, you know."

"I did?" Rory asked, surprised.

"Sure. You're pretty impressive when you choose to be. You and Mary Alice might make a world-beating couple after all."

"Not if Spinelli can help it, though, right?" Rory drank again and put his elbows on the bar. "He must be a little younger than she is, though. How old is he?"

"Old enough," Tracy retorted with deeper meaning. She took the last bite of her sandwich in one huge chomp and tried to stare him down. For Tracy, it was time to kill the age issue.

"Maybe so," Rory agreed peaceably. He spun the aluminum can on the counter, ignoring the food and musing to himself for a moment before observing, "Spinelli's got a hard battle ahead of him, you know. M.A. is listed in the little black book of most every eligible bachelor in Chicago. Let's hope he's got a secret weapon that's going to charm M.A."

"He's honest," Tracy said naively. Her mood had turned solemn by that time, too, and she defended Spin with all her heart, saying, "He's nice and very sweet. He doesn't play games either. And—and I think he's on the verge of adoring the ground she walks on."

Rory smiled sadly and reached across to caress Tracy's bright hair, comforting her. "Sometimes that's just not enough."

Tracy caught her lip between her teeth. Her eyes were filled with compassion as she lifted them to Rory's. "She's... you don't think she'll...."

"She won't hurt him," Rory said gently, taking Tracy's hand in his own. He shook his head. "She's just as nice as he is, and she'll set him down carefully when the time comes."

"Will that time come? Definitely? There's no hope that she'll fly off into the sunset with him?"

Rory lifted his shoulders and turned her hand over in his. He kissed her palm and with a smile, said, "Who knows? I certainly won't bet money on it either way. But I can't... it's hard to imagine Spinelli having the courage to call her, isn't it? And she's not likely to get in touch with him. It's a long way between here and Shamrock, you know."

The yawn escaped before Tracy could stop it, and she clapped her hand over her mouth belatedly. Laughing ruefully, she nodded. "Yes, I know!"

Rory let her go and got to his feet then. "It's been a long night for you. I've kept you talking when I should probably have tucked you into bed with a glass of warm milk."

"Oh, please!" Tracy shuddered in revulsion.

"You're not getting champagne," he retorted, starting to clean up the leftovers. "One drink and you'd be giddy for hours. No, I think you'd better go straight to bed. In the morning—"

Tracy caught up with him at the refrigerator, and slipped her arms around him from behind. "Are you having second thoughts?"

He dumped everything haphazardly into the refrigerator and closed the door, glancing down at her over his shoulder. "What do you mean?"

Tracy laid her head on his back, needing to hide from his searching gaze when she asked the important question. "About asking me to come. Now that I'm here, you're pretending I'm practically your daughter."

Rory turned around and gathered Tracy up in his arms. The contact was easy and familiar once again. He tried to frown and said, "That's silly."

"It isn't. Half an hour ago you were fondling me like I was your mistress or something, and after we've talked about all the other women in your life, I'm suddenly being sent to bed with a glass of milk. Don't I measure up after all? Do I really get shuttled off to bed by myself for a good night's sleep while the adults stay up?"

Rory smiled, holding Tracy in an embrace that was far from fatherly. Voice low, he asked, "What alternative have you got in mind?"

"You haven't got a hot tub, huh?" Tracy inquired slyly, slowly sliding her hands up his chest.

He shook his head and linked his hands behind her back, amused. "Sorry, no. Just the lake. And at this time of year, the temperature of the water is not balmy. There is the bathroom, however. Are you in the mood for one of your Tracy O'Hara patented two-hour soaks?"

She dropped her eyes bashfully. "No. Not alone, anyway. I might fall asleep. But...."

He jiggled her lightly. "But...? Have we got to work on your inhibitions, Miss Tracy? The young lady who nearly exhausted me last weekend is still too shy to tell me what she'd like to—"

Tracy got her fingertips to his mouth in time to stop him. "Don't tease me now. I'm not one of your sophisticated women, you know."

"Yes," Rory said kindly, and he kissed her forehead fondly. "I know. In fact, we've got a little matter to discuss on that score, but not here."

Tracy lifted her mouth provocatively to his. "Where, then?"

Rory touched her cheek, caressing her and looking into the emerald depths of her laughing eyes. His own eyes grew warm. He smiled and took her lips with gentleness, but his embrace changed, getting stronger. He pulled her body to his and kissed her long and deeply, filling his hands with her tousled hair and holding her head firmly, as his emotion grew.

Tracy weakened and relaxed in his arms. Her head swarmed with lovely, delicious sensations, and she felt her thighs meld warmly into his as an involuntary tremor of passion grew within her. Her lips parted to let him explore her mouth. His tongue was sure and savoring, and he was deft and arousing, already filled with desire himself, Tracy knew.

Releasing her gently and with a sigh, he met her eyes again and smiled ruefully. "You're so lovely, Tracy. So full of fire. I can feel it. Are you sure about this? Sure you want to be here with me?"

"Do you think I flew all the way out here to have a sandwich? Yes, I'm sure."

He stroked her hair and dipped his nose to nuzzle her ear. "You've thought this through carefully? Do you really want to start something with me?"

"We got started last weekend," she reminded him with a small unsteady laugh. Tracy tipped her head back and let him kiss her jaw, her throat. It was too wonderful, too intoxicating. She closed her eyes and let the pleasure sweep her like a sun-warmed wave. Did he know how glorious he could make her feel? Her voice caught. "There's no changing that now."

"This is different," Rory murmured, finding her patterning pulse with his mouth. He kissed her there warmly. "We could call it an accident, an impulsive, reckless mistake. This is calculated, Tracy. It's not a one-night stand anymore."

"Was it ever?"

"No," Rory said quietly, and he touched his mouth to Tracy's cheek. "Not for me."

"Not for me either," Tracy whispered, and she found his lips again with hers, feverishly this time.

She kissed him with vibrant emotion trembling in her throat, and when she could, implored, "Rory, please...."

"Think now, Tracy," he urged, matching the intimate, raw quiet of her voice. "There are responsibilities that come with this territory."

"It sounds like you aren't sure yourself."

"I'm not," he said truthfully. "I'm still working this thing out. If you have as much sense as I think you have, you're still thinking, too."

"Yes, Rory," she said, and Tracy took him by the hand. "But I've come to a few preliminary conclusions."

Rory smiled hesitantly. "So have I, Tracy, but they're not all good. I keep thinking I need more time to decide how I—to figure out what's happening between us."

"You're worried about consequences."

"You should be, too."

"What could go wrong?" Tracy laughed softly. "Rod-er-ick?"

He allowed her to pull him toward the doorway, holding her all the while. "Tracy, I'm serious. You've got—before I never thought about it, but there's something very important—something I don't take lightly. I was a fool not to do something about it last weekend, but—"

"Hush, now," Tracy whispered. "Don't fuss. Is this your little matter to discuss?"

"Yes. I—we—"

"Don't fuss," Tracy said again, though a blush appeared prettily, high on her cheekbones. "I need my knapsack."

"What?"

She found the light switch with her palm and doused the lights behind them. "My knapsack. I've taken care of your very important something. I won't get pregnant, I promise. I went to a doctor this week."

In the half light he started to smile, then laughed against her mouth. "Did you? Tracy!"

"What kind of child do you think I am? It's in my knapsack. I just—I was supposed to practice this week, though, and I didn't have time. I might not—it's hard to—"

"It's all right," Rory intervened then, and he gave up trying to be logical. He picked her up lightly in his arms and carried her straight through the dining room. Kissing her throat, he added, "I'll help you."

CHAPTER ELEVEN

His bedroom was all white with spectacular shadows thrown by mysteriously concealed lights. An enormous bed was set high on some kind of a recessed dais and Tracy burst out laughing when she saw it.

"What in the world—?" Rory asked, when he had set her on her feet.

"What a place!" Tracy exclaimed, exploding with laughter again. Within the confines of his embrace, Tracy looked around the room. "This is better than the Poconos! Where's the mirror on the ceiling? Do martinis pop out of a hidden compartment somewhere? Is that a water bed?"

Rory expelled a long-suffering sigh. "You have absolutely no manners, have you? No, that is not a water bed. Go bounce on it, if you'd like. Melora loves to."

In vain Tracy tried to master her amusement, but it was no use. Soft music had magically begun to emanate from somewhere as soon as the shadowy lights were turned on, though the sound was beautifully muted by the luxuriously thick carpet and elegantly furled draperies. The coverlet on the bed was white satin, and there were ruffles on each of the dozen pillows tossed casually at the headboard. Tracy tipped a pixie smile up at Rory. "You can't take this room seriously, can you? It's like something out of a movie!"

"A bad movie, no doubt. I've gotten used to it, I guess." Rory stood back and glanced around his exotic bedroom with a fresh perspective. "It is a little, a little...."

"Hilarious. I'm going to feel like a sacrificial lamb up there. Is that a spotlight? I bet it is!"

Rory grabbed her hand to keep Tracy from going in search of more things to laugh about and spun her neatly back into his arms. He was smiling, though, at Tracy's undaunted attitude. "You're the farthest creature from a lamb that I can think of. And the only thing that's been sacrificed here is my dignity. You are absolutely a vixen, Tracy O'Hara!"

"Thank you," she countered winsomely. "I think you need fewer lambs in your life right now."

"Maybe so," Rory admitted, kissing her forehead once. "But I wonder if you need someone like me in your life at the moment?"

"Let me worry about that," Tracy responded, letting her voice drop softly. Her hands found the small of his back.

Rory filtered the curling mass of her hair

through his fingers, and said, "More amazing partnerships than ours were brought together by sheer animal attraction, I suppose."

"Sure. Anthony and Cleopatra, Laurel and Hardy."

Rory smiled, but the amusement didn't last. "It seems to me that Anthony and Cleo ended in disaster. Tracy—"

"Let's stick with Laurel and Hardy, then. At least their kind of mayhem was enjoyable."

Rory kissed her mouth, half to quiet her foolishness, half because he couldn't stop himself any longer. His lips were warm with pulsing blood, and Tracy could feel his heart swiftly beating against hers. A long pleasure-filled moment later he released her from the kiss and gazed candidly into Tracy's limitless eyes. "Tracy, I don't want to subject you to disaster. I can't promise otherwise, and that's tearing me apart. I want you, but I don't want to hurt you."

Touching his face, slipping her fingertips through his short dark hair, Tracy murmured with a smile, "I'm very strong, Rory. Don't forget. I'm not a good victim."

"It's your brand of strength that's so unique. It—it seems so fragile, Tracy."

"Bend me, then," she urged, holding her body pliantly to his. "You can't break me, Rory."

"I wonder," he said.

"I think you like me because I'm tough, don't you?"

Rory smiled. "Yes. Tracy, maybe this doesn't make sense, but before I met you, I felt—I thought I had become jaded, perhaps. I had my head buried in my airline, and business still wasn't as good as it should have been."

"You're obsessed with me, so you're neglecting your business?" Tracy suggested with a grin.

He pinched her and laughed. "No, you idiot. You've made me realize that the airline isn't so important—that I shouldn't become obsessed with it, I suppose."

Tracy frowned, not quite understanding. "I work hard, too, y'know."

"I know," Rory said, and gave her a soft kiss on her mouth, unable to stop himself any longer. Stroking her hair, he continued, "You work hard, and you play hard, and you laugh and torment me constantly. Being with you, I feel as if I've been dead inside for too long."

Tracy melted against him and laid her head on his chest, afraid to speak for fear she'd say something stupid.

"You're different," he went on softly. "And sometimes I feel I can't get enough of you."

"Even if I'm a century younger than you are?"

"You are young," he agreed, arguing gently. "More than just in years, you're so much younger than I am. I'm not unscathed by life the way you are. I've made mistakes, and I can't promise you that I'm not making one right now. I just—I want you more than anything, Tracy."

"Then that makes two of us," Tracy whispered, running her hands up the strong muscles of his back. "What could be wrong about that?"

"Nothing, I hope!" Rory groaned, and he hugged her, squeezing Tracy's slender figure with barely suppressed ferocity.

Tracy lifted her face and sought his mouth with her own suddenly. She kissed him, pressing her mouth to his quickly, almost fiercely. "Stop worrying, please, Rory. Make love to me now. I need you as much as you need me, maybe more. We can give each other so much. Please."

Whether he heard her plea or finally gave in to his own raging ardor, Tracy wasn't sure. But in the next instant Rory had gathered her up, burying his nose against the delicate, pulsing flesh of Tracy's neck. He hugged her hard and smoothed one hand up her narrow back, seeking to mold her body even more intimately to his own.

"Yes," Tracy breathed, and she smiled, lifting her head high in surrender to him. "Make the sun shine inside me again."

Laughing lightly, Rory found her mouth and murmured, "Someday it will be better than sunshine, Tracy, darling. A solar flare, if you like. Supernova."

"Someday?"

He sighed regretfully. "You want me to—you ask me to make love to you, but there's this look in the back of your eyes. It—you've still got doubts about me. You don't trust me, do you? And yet you want this." He laid his hands around her hips and pulled her pelvis up against his.

"I like making love with you," she whispered.

"But you're holding something back. I know," he said quietly. "It's good that you're doing that, I think. But when this mess is all over, when we can put aside the airline business, you and I could have something very special, Tracy."

"Until then?"

He smiled once more. "I suppose we'll have to make do with what we've got, hmm?"

"Y—yes," Tracy said quietly.

"Let's go to bed," Rory murmured, his mouth seeking hers again. "I want to feel your skin against mine."

Tracy sank into the soft ticking with a sigh of complete pleasure. She looped her arms around his neck and smiled up into his eyes, her mouth soft and tremulous. Rory kissed her gently, firmly, and slid his hands under her sweater, peeling it up and off her body in one slow tantalizing motion.

After kissing the hollow of her throat, he lifted Tracy up, bringing her lips to his in a lingering exploration of her mouth. Skillfully he unclasped her bra and drew it off one shoulder. He kissed her there, and Tracy shivered, then laughed. In a moment he had her breasts free, and whimsically he ran his nose around one and then the other.

Tracy made a grab for the hem of his sweater, and while writhing under his searching mouth and teasing hands, she pulled the garment over his head and let it fall over the edge of the bed. Giggling, she started to unbutton his shirt.

"You amaze me," Rory said softly when he reclined beside her on the bed, patiently waiting while she worked at the buttons. "You have no preconceptions about this, have you?"

"About what?"

He touched her breast with his forefinger and smiled when it tautened with excitement. "Sex. We both know how far your experience with the opposite sex extends, but you seem to have overcome that handicap very quickly."

"Ooh, you make me angry sometimes!" Tracy wriggled away, though he captured her easily. She braced her hands on his shoulders, holding Rory off long enough to glare into his eyes. "I haven't been completely inexperienced with the opposite sex, you know."

He laughed and continued to undress her as though there was no interruption. "Are you going to tell me about boys in the back seats of their fathers' Buicks?"

"I have had a boyfriend or two."

"In junior high?"

"No," Tracy snapped tauntingly. "I had two serious relationships with—with—"

"Boys," Rory supplied with a grin as he drew off her jeans.

"Maybe so," Tracy said firmly. "But I haven't been totally without—hey!" She struggled to sit up, failed, and lay back down under him. "I think I know why you talk this way about my past love life. You're jealous, aren't you?"

"Jealous?" he demanded, hooting. "Of who?"

Tracy managed a prim expression. "Never mind. We don't need to get into names, I'm sure. You like to think of me as your own personal conquest, I think."

Rory considered the question for a moment, his head cocked to one side. "You may be right. Well? Who was he?"

"Who?" Tracy asked, playing dumb with a sparkle in her green eyes.

"The guy you were serious with. In college?"

"Yes," Tracy said slowly as she pulled off Rory's shirt.

"Why didn't you sleep with him?"

Tracy looked shocked. "I have a few morals, you know! I was raised very strictly. Falling into bed with you was a shattering event in my life, I'll have you know, Rod-er-ick."

"Was it?" he asked, smiling into her eyes.

"Yes," she said lightly, avoiding his piercing gaze. She touched his bare shoulders, caressing him there.

"Why did you?" he asked curiously. "Why did you pick me out of all the men that must be panting after you?"

"Because," Tracy said shyly, "nobody ever made me feel the way you do."

"Purely animal attraction after all?"

"N—no," Tracy murmured.

"What then?" he asked, teasing her. "If you tell me that I remind you of daddy, it will really make my day. Am I so much like your father that your deep dark Oedipal—"

"Stop," Tracy begged quickly, urgently. "Don't talk like that."

Rory's grin faded at her sudden seriousness. He cupped her shoulders tenderly. "Okay," he said softly. "Easy, now."

"You do not remind me of my father," Tracy said after a long pause. She could not look him in the eyes, so she traced tiny, aimless whorls on his chest. "He wasn't anything like you, Rory. Believe me."

"When I first met you," Rory said carefully, "I thought all you wanted was to have your father back in your life. Was I right?"

"I miss him," Tracy said quickly. Anxiety was apparent in her tense expression when she began to explain, "Yes, I'd like to have him back. But...."

Rory touched her face, tipping her chin so that she had to meet his gaze. "Tell me."

Tracy smiled ruefully. "It's nothing, really. You don't remind me of my dad. I think that's why—why I was attracted to you, Rory. You're not rough with me, or mean."

Rory couldn't keep the surprise from his face. "Was your father rough with you?"

"Sometimes," Tracy admitted uncertainly. "He was very strict, you see."

"He didn't hit you," Rory said suddenly, and there was a menace to his tone.

"No," Tracy said, too fast. Then, "Well, once in a while if I had done something stupid or—"

"Good grief," Rory muttered, and he closed his eyes at the thought.

"I know, I know," Tracy snapped in sudden anger. "We're not the blue-blooded Buchanans who'd never dream of smacking each other unless the chips were really down, but—"

Rory interrupted, "I would never hit anyone no matter how far the chips went down, Tracy. That's a promise."

She touched his face quickly, her fingertips quieting his lips with a fresh gentleness. "I know," she murmured, trying to smile. "You were something really new for me in a lot of ways, you see."

"I'm beginning to see," Rory said roughly.

She sighed softly, unwillingly, and went on, "You're so gentle, Rory. You're the gentlest man I've ever known, and it's been a wonderful discovery. But the way you treat me physically is not all that's been unique, you know. First, you make me feel like an intelligent person—the way you talk to me and listen to what I say. And then you make me feel. . . ."

He kissed her once, gently, on the mouth. "Yes?"

Tracy expelled a long sigh and breathed, "Like a woman, Rory."

The tension suddenly seemed to melt from his body, and Rory relaxed against her once more. He gathered Tracy up in his arms and kissed her long and softly, with meaning. Parting her lips, he tasted the essence of her mouth, tested the texture of her full lower lip and found it warmer than ever before. When he released her, Rory smiled into her eyes. "You *are* a woman, Tracy, love. I think of you as unspoiled and fresh—like—" He searched his imagination for the right comparison as he caressed her face. Inadequately, he said, "You're like an apple tree that's just come out in all those pretty pink blossoms in the springtime. With all that potential just getting started."

Tracy smiled, blushing. "Here goes the master again."

He laughed. "What?"

"Don't deny it. You're a master at making love," Tracy said. "At making a woman feel this way."

"What way?" Rory asked, coming slowly closer until his breath was warm and caressing on Tracy's ear. "Tell me how you feel, Tracy, darling."

"I feel like scratching your eyes out," she said with a small, shaken laugh. He had laid his palm over her breast, a perfectly innocent touch except that his pulse beat subtly against her heart. Tracy felt herself arching instinctively against his hand, and she added, "And I want to give you great pleasure."

"A great combination of feelings," he said, and nestled close to give her earlobe a surreptitious lick. "But at the moment, I think you ought to tuck in your claws, little kitten. I vote for great pleasure right now. Kiss me."

Tracy obeyed, of course, and the searing heat of Rory's mouth on hers was as delicious as every time before, perhaps more so. They rolled together, wrestling Rory out of his trousers and making a mess of the bed.

Tracy laughed when he pinned her on the pillow and ravaged her breasts with tiny, erotic kisses. She bit her lips to keep from speaking again, thankful that he had stopped his sweet talk before it was too late. He was going to get the words out of her yet—this wonderful, understanding, gentle man. She was going to tell him soon, she was sure. She was in love. She was falling deeper and deeper, and she was afraid to tell him. Surely that admission would be the final proof of her lack of sophistication!

With an unconscious smile, Tracy succumbed to the dictates of her senses. Being with Rory was always exciting. Like this, in bed, it was ecstasy. She looped her arms around his neck and drew him down to her body. His heart raced against her breast so strongly that Tracy found herself repeating the incessant words in her head along with that powerful rhythm. *I love you. I love you.*

Rory kissed her mouth, teased her breast, and then caressed the long curve of her thighs. He cupped her bottom, lifting Tracy off the bed to meet him, and then he was deep within her, unable to wait. His breathing was deep as he savored the warmth of her body, the silken texture of her skin, the thick floss of her hair as it slipped between his fingers.

Softly he murmured his appreciation, but Tracy was too full of pleasures to hear his words. She touched him everywhere, delighting in his quick intake of air when she explored with tentative hands and then kissed him lightly. This was love between man and woman, she was sure. As the room darkened and narrowed to include only the two of them clasped in a wondrous embrace, Tracy bit her lips to hold back the final, sweetest words of all. *I love you,* she nearly cried. *I love you.*

CHAPTER TWELVE

PERHAPS IT WAS THE DIFFERENCE in time zones that brought Tracy awake first the following morning, but she did surface from the cozy muffle of sleep with Rory's bare back pressed smoothly into her own and the fragrant scent of fruit wafting with a subtle sweetness from the silver bowl on the night table. There was sunshine just beyond the white curtains, and around the bed the white fabric and striking contemporary furniture shone in the morning light.

Tracy smiled drowsily at the sunlight, for she thought it would always remind her of that first morning with Rory—when the forest appeared around them as the sun rose over the horizon. It had been a magical morning then, and now it seemed there might be other mornings with Rory just as delightful.

He was sound asleep, too deeply unconscious to even stir when Tracy turned over. She touched a soft kiss to his shoulder and slipped from the bed without disturbing him. Her stomach was very empty, and breakfast was definitely in order. Let Rory sleep.

His shirt from the night before lay crumpled on the floor, and Tracy plucked it up and put it on. Buttoning it, she walked barefoot through the silent elegant house to the kitchen. The morning sun was streaming down through the skylight, illuminating the only evidence of their supper of the night before: the pair of empty soda cans. Tracy tossed them into the trash and began to forage through the refrigerator.

She gathered her supplies together and laid them out on the counter. A black-box radio stood on top of the refrigerator, and Tracy flipped it on to listen to the familiar weather reports from NOAA—National Oceanic and Atmospheric Administration—as she worked. Though he made light of his abilities, it appeared that Rory was as much of a pilot as Tracy was. It was instinct that made flyers monitor the weather at all hours of the day and night.

With the muttering voice of the weatherman to keep her company, Tracy made a pot of coffee and began to measure out her ingredients just the way her mother had taught her. She cut prosciutto ham into tiny chunks and did the same with two kinds of cheese, a little onion, those nice mushrooms. This was going to be one fantastic omelet. Someone even kept Rory supplied with homegrown herbs. Wonder who? With a shake of her head and a wry smile for the women who looked after this very charming man, Tracy put a widebottomed pan on his stove and turned on the gas.

The kitchen, Tracy noticed while the pan gained the proper temperature, doubled as a kind of family room and office for Rory and his daughter. A collection of childish drawings was thumb-tacked to the back of the pantry door, and under the counter by the telephone lay a stash of papers and folders that must have represented work that Rory had brought home for the weekend. She spied a chart half-folded under the knife rack, and unfurled it while waiting another minute for the pan to heat.

It was a map of the Midwest and east coast, Canada included, and someone had inked in a series of check marks at various locations. Chicago, Detroit, Cleveland, Louisville, down to Washington and up as far as New Hampshire and through New York. LaGuardia as well as Kennedy airport had been marked. With a flash of realization, Tracy knew that she was looking at a map of Northstream Airlines' landing ports. This was Rory's empire. She studied it for a long time, and gradually her expression grew solemn with understanding.

The pan was more than ready, and Tracy tore her attention from the large piece of paper. She set a pepper mill on one end of the map to keep it flat, then crossed to the stove and set to work on the omelet.

But at a crucial moment, Rory arrived in the kitchen, wearing his jeans and pulling a shirt over his head. He emerged looking sleepy, but pleased to see her. "You're beautiful in the morning," he said, giving her a quick kiss on the back of her neck. "Even in that creation you're wearing."

Tracy laughed and leaned back against his body briefly. "Oh, it's just something I threw on. Don't pester me now. I'm too busy."

"Too busy?" Rory echoed, outraged. He grabbed her around the middle and pulled, hauling Tracy's slight body around and bending her over his arm in a classic dip. Her hair tumbled out behind, and Tracy laughed up at him, clutching uselessly at his shoulders to keep from falling. He growled, "I'll show you busy, my lovely lady!"

"Stop it!" Tracy cried, flashing the spatula to fend him off. "Your breakfast will burn!"

But he was undeterred and kissed Tracy long and deliciously, suspending her body dangerously over the floor, but holding her with an unbreakable embrace. It was too wonderful to resist, of course, so Tracy lifted her arms around his neck and melted. The rush of nearly liquid sensations, a kind of bubbling revival of the previous night's passions, warmed her veins, pulsing sweetly. Tracy sighed and gave up the struggle, returning his kiss with languid pleasure. A moment later, Rory reluctantly set her on her feet again. His smile was warm and intimate, and Tracy knew her own expression must have mirrored his.

"Well," Rory murmured quietly as he nibbled at her cheek, "how was that for breakfast?"

"Oh!" Tracy exclaimed, breaking the blissful moment. She jumped comically, as if touched by a live wire, and struggled free of him. "The breakfast!"

No damage had been done, and Tracy flipped the omelet with a deft flick of the spatula. "There are certain things that shouldn't be interrupted, you know."

"Yes, I know," Rory said meaningfully. With his arms still around her from behind and his nose buried against her throat, Rory suddenly became aware of something other than Tracy's slim and unusually attired body. He abruptly asked, "What are you making? Tracy, that smells wonderful."

"Of course it does. Did you think my talents were limited to pampering greasy airplane engines?"

"You've learned to pamper me," Rory rejoined, nuzzling another kiss into the wild tangle of her hair. He was distracted, though, and asked again, "Honestly, Tracy, that looks fantastic. What are you doing?"

"Get a plate or stay out of my way," Tracy commanded lightly. She lifted the pan from the flame an instant later. "You can have a bite if you behave."

"You won't eat all of that yourself," he said

with confidence, as he loosened his grasp on her. Uncertain suddenly, he asked, "Will you?"

"Get a plate!" Tracy laughed, giving him a thrust with her hip.

"And real coffee, too," Rory said prayerfully when he had gone to the cupboard. "My love, your talents are beginning to overwhelm me. Where did you learn to do all this? Taking care of dad?"

"Be careful," Tracy warned, checking the edges of the omelet with the spatula. "You'll have cold cereal and frozen juice if you don't watch it."

"Tell me the truth," Rory said. He laid two plates on the counter and went back for cups and silverware. "When did you have time to learn to cook?"

"My mother is French," Tracy answered, as if that explained everything. With a practiced flare, she slid the steaming concoction onto the waiting plates. "I learned to cook about the same time I learned to fly. Dad kept me in the hangar with him, and my mother demanded equal time in the house with her. They didn't spend too much time together, you see, so I met with them one at a time—even before they were divorced. Funny, huh?"

"Maybe," Rory said doubtfully. He picked up his plate and inhaled the aroma of perfectly selected and cooked ingredients. "Wonderful," he said again, eyes closed. "This is definitely a surprise benefit, Tracy love. I never imagined you had talents like this. Let's eat."

"Just wait, please." Tracy was quick with a small knife, peeling off two slices of an orange and twisting them each into pretty garnishes—one for each plate. "There. Eat."

Smiling, Rory gave her one more kiss, a sloppy one on her mouth. "You're terrific. I'm in awe."

"Are you?" Tracy asked, smiling saucily.

"Yes," he said simply, pulling out a stool for her. In a moment Rory had her settled at the counter, and poured her a cup of coffee. Without asking if she took it, he fetched milk from the refrigerator and then showed signs of taking even greater pains for her comfort.

Before he could go looking for juice, Tracy caught his sleeve and pulled him to the other stool. "Sit down and have your breakfast," she commanded gently, feeling uncomfortable that he was suddenly being gentlemanly and therefore strange. "Before it gets cold. I'll eat it myself, if you don't."

Rory saw the familiar flicker of uncertainty in her eyes despite the tartness of Tracy's tone. He had come to recognize her flashes of temper as Tracy's way of covering her weak moments. To put her at ease again, Rory obeyed with a relenting grin. "I wouldn't doubt it. You've done very little but eat since you got here. Do you intend to keep up the pace today?"

"I can't help it if I'm hungry. I'm still a growing girl, you know," she said, digging him about his age once more.

He laughed. "All right, all right. Eat as much as you like, but surely there are other things we can do while you're here."

Mouth full, Tracy blinked at him and let her eyes drift appraisingly down his body.

Rory laughed again. "Besides that, too, you little fiend! What do you say? A walk around the lake? A drive into the city?"

"I've seen cities before," Tracy said primly. "They all look the same to me. No, show me the rest of this place, will you? I'd like to see the lake. It's darker than Ontario, did you notice?"

"Is it?" Rory asked, working on his omelet with great gusto. "I hadn't seen that. Lake Michigan is bigger, that's for sure. And not quite so dirty."

"Lake Ontario is not dirty!" Tracy claimed in outrage. "It's lovely, in fact. Don't go criticizing, please."

"Heaven forbid that either of us criticizes anything about the other," he said heavily. He lifted a mushroom out of the omelet with his fingers and took it in his mouth. He swallowed and grinned. "Okay, a walk along the shore is on our agenda. What else?"

"Aren't there any airplanes to look at?" Tracy asked, concentrating on her food. "We could go flying."

"Sure. You could take me up in your Pitts."

With a wicked smile, Tracy said, "You'd better skip the rest of your breakfast, then, Rod-er-ick. I like to cut the capers, you know."

"You'd enjoy making me sick, wouldn't you?" Rory's grin was wide. "You'd roll a dozen times and finish with a loop just to see me turn green."

"Are you challenging me to do it?"

"No," Rory said quickly, taking another bite of his omelet. "This food is too good to pass up. It really is terrific, you know. My compliments to your mother."

Insulted, Tracy narrowed her eyes. "My mother! I think I will take you up and make you sick! I did this myself, you know!"

"It's in the blood," Rory teased her fondly, before all the compliments went to her head. "What else did she teach you? How to darn socks and clean house?"

"Don't get your hopes up," she shot back. "I'm not going to take Mary Alice Cooper's place in your plans, Rod-er-ick! Getting married is definitely not on our agenda for today!"

Rory burst into laughter at that, and he set his coffee cup down on the counter before he spilled it. "Getting married! Good grief! I let this young lady wear my favorite white shirt once and already she's talking about—"

"Put a cork in it, my friend," Tracy commanded gruffly, reaching for the map that she had been studying before Rory arrived in the kitchen. She pulled the paper across the counter, set her own cup on one corner, and shifted his plate on the other. She tapped the map with her finger. "I found this and had a look. Very interesting."

Rory's smile did not fade, but his eyes were sharp on hers. "What does that map have to do with getting married, may I ask?"

"I should ask you that question," Tracy retorted, deciding that now was as good a time as any to establish his motives. She gathered her strength and said with a surprising amount of lightness, "I'm inexperienced, but I'm not stupid. Remember, I was raised by a man who ran an airline. After a look at this map of yours, I know what you're doing, Mr. Northstream Airlines."

Rory went back to his food, elbows on the counter, but he was amused by her discovery. "Okay, tell me what you think you've learned."

"Okay," Tracy said gamely. "I already know that you're in financial trouble. But by studying this map, it's easy to see that you're on the verge of making it big. Aren't you?"

Rory lifted his brows. "How?"

Tracy drew a line on the map with her finger. "Chicago to New York. A very nice, expensive run. All commuter airlines like to build networks. It's the only way to compete with the big airlines. You have landing rights at all the big airports in the Midwest. You're moving east, and you've nearly got it sewn up, haven't you?"

Rory drank his coffee, listening.

"Except you need Pittsburgh," Tracy said firmly. "And you need to break into Canada, and Philadelphia or Newark wouldn't hurt. Once you get those locations, you're in the big time, aren't you?"

"Not quite," Rory said judiciously.

"Almost," Tracy corrected herself. "You're working a nice little spider's web, in fact. I congratulate you. It's a tough thing to do. Not many commuters could have expanded the way you have."

"But they're still solvent," Rory noted with a suddenly wry smile. "And Northstream...." He shrugged and let the implication remain.

Tracy nodded. "I know. You can't afford to buy the planes you want. So what? Take care of the old ones for a little longer."

Rory was quiet again, going for his coffee.

Tracy took a deep breath and decided to go all the way. She had a great deal to lose, and she knew it. But confronting Rory with what she knew and getting some answers was better than living with the doubt any longer. It had become too much of a strain. Tracy watched his face and kept her voice just as light as before. "You're almost as big as Hallis Air and some of the other regional commuters now. There's only two things that are stopping you from breaking into their marketplace."

"And those are?"

"This Canadian merger you're working on, for one. I'm guessing it's with Air Norland."

"Good guess," Rory said noncommittally. "And the other roadblock on my highway to success is?"

"Me," Tracy said evenly. "If I don't sell Shamrock to you, you're not going to make it, are you?"

Rory set his cup down very, very carefully. He did not meet her eyes. "Tracy...."

"It's obvious," Tracy went on quickly. "You need my landing slots at Pittsburgh and at Montreal. Those two acquisitions will complete your circle, won't they? The real question is what you'll do to get them."

Rory's eyes turned cold. With warning in his tone, he said quietly, "Tracy, if you say what I think you're about to say, I'm going to be tempted to strangle you."

"Strangle me?" Tracy asked. But her attempt at a chuckle failed miserably. She shrugged pushing her plate away. "I guess it's something I've got to risk, isn't it?"

The silence was long and pregnant, and during that awful stretch of time Tracy decided that she had lost him. Even before Rory was truly hers, she had lost the man who had become so perfect in her eyes. But then Rory managed to muster his composure, and in a flat, accusatory tone he said, "I'm not starting a relationship with you so that I can have your silly little airline. Don't think it, Tracy."

"It has crossed my mind before," Tracy said pointedly, as she met his steady gaze again, her eyes clear and fiery. "Don't underestimate me, Rod-er-ick."

"No," he said with sudden ferocity. "Never that."

"You've had relationships with women before. Not just M.A. and your wife, like we talked about last night. You—you've been with other women in the industry, Rory. Libby Stone, for one."

"Libby Stone was a while ago, and it had nothing to do with business." Rory got off the stool and paced away, as if not daring to stay close to Tracy any longer.

"It doesn't matter," Tracy intervened before he could continue. "Whatever you had going with any woman before doesn't mean much to me. But I have to wonder in the back of my mind, don't I? I'd be very stupid if I didn't think you were being—being nice to me so I will sell my company to you."

"Being nice to you?" Rory echoed in disbelief. He turned around to Tracy with a perfectly blank expression.

"I don't want to believe you'd do it, Rory—that you'd use me." Tracy was trying very hard not to sound pathetic. She clenched her teeth and fought to stay calm. Very mature. "I'd like to think we've got something started that's purely animal attraction with a little good conversation thrown in. But that isn't the only thing that's got us together, is it? With you, I think business always comes very high on your ladder of priorities. It's the same with me, you know. It...it would be a lot easier to...to have this kind of personal relationship if I was a cook in a restaurant somewhere and you played the piano in the bar."

"Yes," he said. "But it isn't easy—this thing between us. It's always going to be complicated, Tracy. You're clever and beautiful, and I love those things about you. But...."

"But you still want Shamrock," Tracy guessed. "You want me here like this, and you want Shamrock."

He wagged his head unhappily. "I wish the two of you were unrelated, but you're not. Yes, I want you here with me, and I want Shamrock, too. I think I'll get it from you, Tracy, but I want to do it right. I'm not pulling tricks, and I don't want you to give me something because of the way we made each other feel last night."

Tracy looked down, linking her hands in her lap. "That's honest. I hope."

"Yes. I have been honest." Rory paused, thinking hard and finally adding with great unwillingness, "And at the moment, dear Tracy, if I had to choose between you and Shamrock, I'm not sure which I'd take. It's a decision that would affect the lives of many people, including my daughter, who is the most important other soul in my life. I couldn't take you and let Shamrock go. Don't... you're not going to make me choose, are you?"

Tracy's smile was bitter, and she knew it, so she kept her head bowed.

So he didn't love her. He didn't feel the way Tracy did about him. The realization came like a hard blow to her heart, and she had to steady herself before she could respond to his question.

She said, "No, I'm not going to make you choose. I don't want to hear the vote, to tell you the truth. Not now, anyway. I like you best when you're honest with me, Rory, but a part of me wishes to hell you hadn't been quite so honest this time."

Approaching, he touched her hair, sliding it over her shoulder with one finger. "You'd like to hear me say that I love you and want you with me forever?"

"No, no," Tracy said, laughing weakly, trying to sound convincing. "I'm not ready to hear that at all. I'd bolt for home if I thought that's where you were headed."

"Good," he said softly. "Neither of us is ready for that. I'm glad you're not a foolish kid, Tracy. But you are a woman, and a woman deserves to hear the right things from a lover. I'm not—I haven't been good to you on that score."

"Good enough," Tracy said, but she remained

involuntarily rigid under his hand. "I haven't had enough experience to judge you. But then, I'm not exactly the best lover myself, am I?"

"Better than you know." Rory kissed the top of her head and murmured regretfully, "Darling Tracy, I'm very sorry."

"Don't," Tracy ordered, holding very still. "Don't feel sorry for me, please. It only makes me furious."

"Of course," Rory said solicitously. "Look, Tracy, I'm not feeling sorry for you, I'm just regretting that you're who you are and I'm still Northstream Airlines."

"Maybe you won't be for long," Tracy countered irascibly, shooting him a quick, pretended glare. She shrugged out from under his hand and reached to pick up her fork again, trying to deaden the ache inside herself with a steadying breath. She said caustically, "Maybe you'll go bust, and I'll hire you to sweep out my hangars."

Rory moaned with exasperation and gave her hair a tug before he let go. "You are the most wicked young lady I've ever known!"

"Eat your breakfast," Tracy told him as she made a show of digging into her own food again. "If you're going to seduce me for my company, you might at least do a proper job. You're going to need your strength, you know."

"See what I mean?" Rory demanded, sitting down beside her again.

Though her words were light and taunting as usual, Tracy found that she was still wary inside, still uncertain. And perhaps at the bottom of that well of emotion lived a certain spark of anger still. She resented the fact that he couldn't separate his business from his love life. Why couldn't he just forget Shamrock? To Tracy, one financial setback was an easy price to pay, if the reward was having Rory in her life. Couldn't he see things the same way? But no, to Rory, Tracy was not nearly as important as Northstream. He hadn't fallen for her the way she had gone head over heels for him.

So Tracy made a silent vow to herself. She could enjoy the time spent with him, taking pleasure in verbal sparring with him, and delight in the hours of lovemaking. But she had to withhold a little something. She couldn't give in and tell him of her feelings yet. She needed some insurance against getting burned in this relationship, and that was going to be it. She wasn't going to fall desperately, irrevocably in love with Rory Buchanan. She couldn't let herself do it. Not while Northstream and Shamrock hung in the balance.

Rory had some telephoning to do after they had eaten, and Tracy took a long bath while he was busy. She took pains to apply a bit of makeup and brushed her hair until its vibrant color rivaled those in the spectacular works of art in Rory's lovely home.

When she had dressed in her jeans again, he

took her for a walk along the lake, and later for a short, very cold boat ride. At the airport he showed her an old Shorts plane that had come in for repairs, and Tracy enjoyed looking over that out-of-the-ordinary craft.

All the while, however, Tracy was ever so slightly subdued. Her smile wasn't as quick, and her eyes seemed to hold a shadow of misgiving each time Rory sought her gaze with his. Rory sensed the change, but he did not mention her quieting spirit. He understood, perhaps. He held her hand and touched her often, hoping to assuage her doubts through wordless communication.

Yet still there remained the quick repartee, the raucous humor and endless ribbing. Even over dinner at an intimate and horrendously expensive restaurant that overlooked the lake, they exchanged barbs and taunts and laughter, and finally the single look that conveyed a message full of passion and desire. Without finishing the bottle of wine, they left the restaurant and drove in silence back to Rory's home. In bed, Tracy thought her heart would burst for the wild, yet distressing flood of emotions that surged along with the final, pulsing moments of ecstasy. Still, she kept silent and held him tightly, wondering if a time might come when Rory cared as deeply for her as she did just then for him.

Sunday dawned even warmer than the previous day, and they ate breakfast together on the patio in the sunshine. Tracy did not speak of her departure for home. That would come soon enough. She had to get back to Shamrock, but putting an end to this blissful weekend was an unhappy thought. When Rory suggested she go get another sweater for herself from his drawer, she perked up.

"What for?"

"I told you, didn't I?" he asked, stacking their dishes together. "I've got an unbreakable engagement today, and you had better come along."

"What is it?" Tracy sat up with interest. "Time to meet Melora?"

Rory smiled, pleased, and he nodded. "Yes, Melora and a few others. My family is having their annual football game today. Lunch and a chance for my father to demonstrate that he can still put away a sixty-yard touchdown pass."

"Oh," Tracy said, suddenly full of doubts. "Your family?"

"Don't start looking like that," Rory admonished firmly, cocking an amused eyebrow at her. "They're not a bunch of trolls and ogres, you know."

"I know that!" Tracy began hotly. She squirmed, and lifted doubtful eyes to Rory. "I just wonder if... well, what are they going to think of you and me?"

"They're going to think I'm still a rotten, seducing son-of-a-gun, and that you're adorable—if you watch your language, at least. Keep a rein on the expletives, please. My mother may still know how to wash out a foul mouth." Rory carried the plates inside the house.

"I...but, Rory!" Tracy called, scampering after him. "What will they think of you and me together? They're going to know that we—that I—"

"Don't worry," Rory told her bluntly, though a grin had started to assert itself around his mouth. "They're used to me by now. You're not the first, Tracy love, I'm sorry to say."

"Nor the last?" she demanded resentfully.

He kissed her forehead. "Go get another sweater, please. Anything but cashmere. We're liable to get dirty today."

Tracy found a soft green sweater of Rory's that looked very pretty against her red hair, and while in the bedroom, she packed her things into her knapsack. Sweater and all, she went back out to the kitchen and Rory.

He looked wordlessly at the knapsack, but did not mention the fact that Tracy had to leave today. Perhaps he was just as unwilling as she was to end the weekend. He put his arm comfortingly around her shoulders and led Tracy out of the house to the garage.

In his car a while later, Tracy asked, "Is this an annual affair, did you say?"

"A picnic," Rory confirmed with a nod as he

drove. "Yesterday was my nephew's birthday, and tomorrow is my father's. It's their wedding anniversary around this time, too, though I can never remember which day it is. It's just a convenient time to get the clan together."

"Your sister Ann..." Tracy began a list of the people she should know.

"Yes, and her husband is Brad," Rory explained helpfully. "My brother Rick and his wife Dorothy will be there, also. They've got three kids, and then there's Ann's brood. The Coopers usually show up—you may see M.A. again—and a couple by the name of Randolph, also friends of the family. Maybe some cousins, too. It'll be a mob, now that I think of it. Are you terrified?"

"Me?" Tracy asked, trying to be insulted. "Terrified?"

"Nervous, then," Rory said with a grin, glancing across at her. "A little anxious?"

"No," Tracy said softly, with a sheepish look at him. "You were right the first time. Terrified."

Rory laughed and pulled her over for a quick, hard kiss. In another three minutes the car had nosed down a long lane with tall trees on either side and the lake dazzlingly bright in the distance. The lawn was huge and perfectly groomed, and Tracy wondered what the name of this lovely park might be. Before she could ask, Rory pointed. "There. See the volleyball net?"

Most of the family had already arrived, it seemed,

and when Rory pulled the car to a stop in a line of perhaps a dozen expensive automobiles, many heads came up and greetings were called.

"Oh, dear," Tracy murmured to herself. Thirty people or more were milling cheerfully amid the picnic tables.

"Have strength," Rory said lightly, giving her a pat on the thigh. "And stay away from my brother, all right? He's a fast worker, I'm told."

"Faster than you?" Tracy demanded, but Rory was laughing and climbing out of the car.

He pulled her out with him and closed the door, and holding Tracy by her hand, he pulled her down to the lawn to meet his family.

CHAPTER THIRTEEN

THEY WERE ALL GRACIOUS and perfectly mannered and very attractive, but just slightly cool during the introductions. It took Tracy several minutes to decide that they didn't dislike her, but that Rory's family was just a standoffish bunch of upper-crust types who didn't warm up real fast. Rory was absolutely at ease, of course, and everyone seemed genuinely fond of him, so they couldn't be all bad, Tracy reflected.

His mother was a small, deceptively fragile-looking woman with a stylish haircut and a pair of mannish trousers that flattered her whiplike figure. She took Rory's head in her hands and pulled him down for a proper kiss and hug. Then she shook Tracy's hand and looked her right in the eye with a piercing gaze that told Tracy a lot. This woman didn't want any sweet young thing messing up her son's life.

His sister Ann, it turned out, was angular like her mother, but tall and in possession of the same vivid blue eyes as Rory. She had a slow, reserved smile for Tracy, but she gave Rory a sisterly pinch on the behind that made him jump in surprise.

Mr. Buchanan was just as big as Rory, but his jolly manner temporarily disguised the fact that he also had a disconcerting directness in his eyes, which probed deeply into Tracy to determine her motives for being among the Buchanan clan. He smiled at her, however, and held her hand while he led her down to meet some other guests. Tracy cast one desperate look over her shoulder to see Rory being dragged in another direction by his sister to help carry the beer keg. He was not going to help her through the ordeal of meeting all these Old Money relatives, but Tracy wanted to go running after him like a frightened child.

Mary Alice Cooper came out of the sea of aristocratic faces, a sight for sore eyes. Tracy smiled with genuine relief.

"We meet again, Miss O'Hara," M.A. called cheerfully. "Under better circumstances, this time!"

"Hi!" Tracy greeted her with more enthusiasm than she should have. Perhaps her fear of blundering among these sophisticated people was starting to show, so Tracy made an effort to match M.A.'s easy manner. She collected herself and agreed, "Yes, better circumstances this time. How are you feeling?"

"What do you mean?" asked Rory's father, obviously confused that the two young women should know each other.

"Oh, it's nothing, Richard," M.A. teased, laughing attractively. "You go warm up the football, all right? I think the younger generation is finally going to beat you old coots this year!"

"Blasphemy!" Richard Buchanan crowed. He relinquished Tracy into M.A.'s care and went off into the party.

Tracy stayed cautiously at M.A.'s side for a time then, trying to get her bearings and sort through the names and attach them to the right faces. The picnic had been laid out in a pretty assortment of baskets on two long tables with real linen cloths and china service. The plastic cups for beer clashed with the highly polished silver coffee urn, but no one except Tracy seemed aware of the fact. There was food of every description, and Tracy wouldn't have been surprised to find caviar beside the fried chicken. Big slabs of shad were smoking over an aromatic fire, and there was even a pot of chowder bubbling over a camp stove. Rory's brother-in-law Brad was tending an array of hot dogs on the grill for those with more mundane tastes.

And underfoot were the children. They ranged in age anywhere from twelve years down to just a few weeks, for Ann had a very tiny baby lodged in a kind of knapsack arrangement that she wore on her chest like a reversed papoose. Tracy watched the children tear around the tables, snatching food here and there and clumsily spilling cups of cider on the grass. A lanky black Labrador puppy had appeared from somewhere, and it galumphed after the shrieking children in search of discarded pretzels. Tracy hung in the background and watched, taking in everything.

Mary Alice Cooper had a huge camera around her neck, and from time to time she crouched to snap a picture of a child or of two adults engrossed in conversation. Tracy decided that she must be the unofficial family photographer, for everyone behaved naturally before her camera, hardly batting an eye when she sought to capture some candid shot. M.A. moved with confidence among the many guests, introducing Tracy now and then, and including the younger girl in all the conversations. Tracy was very glad to have someone's apron strings to cling to that afternoon.

Rory returned for a time and joined the casual saunter among his relatives. Tracy was sure that he sensed her unease, because he didn't make a public show of affection toward her, and for that Tracy was very grateful. She remained timidly, watchfully, by his side.

Finally Rory came upon his brother in the crowd, and introductions were made over the keg of beer. Rick was older and bigger than Rory, heavier through the waist and with a thick cord of muscle across his sloping shoulders. He was attending to the tap, wearing a loud pair of expensive trousers, a spiffy sweater and a ridiculous baseball hat advertising an imported beer—a hat

Tracy was sure Rick would never wear except among his family. He filled Rory's cup with the foaming lager.

"What's this pretty thing's name again?" Rick demanded with a grin, removing his cigar from the corner of his mouth long enough to speak. "Stacey?"

"Tracy," Rory corrected, accepting his drink. "Be nice to her, please."

Rick had smiled knowingly down at Tracy, his blue, half-lidded eyes so like Rory's in a seductive mood. "I'll be very nice, little brother. She's cute. How old are you, Tracy?"

"Old enough," Rory countered, stealing Tracy's line. He bumped her shoulder with his own in a silent attempt to give her support.

Rick let his gaze slide appraisingly down Tracy's figure before he winked at his brother. "Well done, Rory, my boy. Get 'em young and train 'em right, I always say."

Tracy gritted her teeth and counted to ten, hardly able to hold back a hundred retorts that came boiling to her mind. What a boor this one was!

Rory was smooth, however, in the face of his brother's sly humor. "Actually, I defy anyone to train this young lady, Rick. She is definitely her own boss. Watch what you say. You're liable to have your ears pinned back."

"What?" Rick asked, laughing delightedly down at her. "This pretty little thing? Why, she could hardly hurt a fly, I'll bet. What do you say, Tracy? Would you like to try pinning back my ears?"

"No," Tracy said, trying hard to be harmless.

"You're too easy for her, Rick," Rory intervened before Tracy could add a more heated comment. He could see her clenched teeth and head held firmly bent to hold back the torrent of abuse undoubtedly filling her head. Rory controlled a smile, amused at Tracy's attempt to be good.

"I'm very easy," Rick said, and he slid his arm around Tracy's shoulders, steering her away from his brother with a laugh. "Come along, my girl. Let me show you around a little."

Rory was not coming to her rescue, much to Tracy's dismay. His mother had arrived and touched his elbow authoritatively for a talk with him about some matter. With a last, beseeching look over her shoulder at him, Tracy was led away by brother Rick, who asked, "Have you seen the house yet?"

"House?" Tracy asked, trying to pull out from under his arm. "What house?"

"You are a newcomer, aren't you?" Rick asked delightedly. "My parents' house, of course. Up there through the trees. Would you like me to give you the grand tour?"

Tracy hadn't seen the house until then, it was so well camouflaged by the thick trees. When she did see it, she was astounded. Until that moment,

Tracy thought the picnic was being held in a lakeside park, for the grounds were so extensive and beautifully kept. Clearly this was the Buchanan ancestral palace, if such places existed in America. The building was spectacular, like those old fortresslike country manors in English picture books. The trees and flowering bushes had been professionally planted to look like the landscaping around Windsor castle. The effect was beautiful and bespoke money—plenty of it.

In her stunned silence, Rick was able to get a firmer grasp on Tracy's narrow shoulder. He hugged her close, purely brotherly, of course, and murmured, "I'd be glad to show you the family jewels, little girl, if Rory hasn't already."

Tracy yanked free of Rick, and threw up her chin, scorching him with the green fire in her eyes. Suddenly, too much was happening all at once. Rick's implication had been blatant and crude, and Tracy responded in kind, her words snapping with sarcasm, "You'd better keep your jewels under lock and key, big brother. They might get hurt otherwise!"

Rick's eyes popped, and he stepped a hasty pace away from the firebrand before him. "Easy now, little lady. I was just fooling with you."

"Rick!" Ann called then, spotting the two of them and the signs that fireworks were about to begin. Her baby still slung around her body, Ann approached with a smile on her beautiful mouth.

She teased, "You're not trying to kidnap Rory's young friend, are you?"

The word kidnap contained an equally objectionable connotation, and Tracy swung on Ann, ready to do battle with her as well. Fortunately, however, she remembered her manners and her vow to behave herself for Rory's sake, so she bottled her anger with an effort.

"No," Rick answered his sister. He gave Tracy a quick, wary look, on his guard finally. He said, "I think I'm safer out here in broad daylight with her. Have you met Tracy yet, Ann?"

"Yes, we've met," Ann said with a gracious smile at the younger woman. "You seem to have a calming effect on our brother, Tracy. Rory looks very well today."

"Yes," Rick said, glancing in Rory's direction. Rory was still talking with his mother, several yards away and out of earshot. Rick continued, "He's looking much healthier these days. Is that your doing, Tracy?"

"We haven't known each other very long," Tracy answered stiffly.

"Well, it's been a hard year for him," Ann explained. "He's been working very hard, you see. We've been a little worried about him. He doesn't do anything unless he can do it well, you know. Perhaps you've noticed."

"Yes," Tracy said, reserved and quiet again. Maybe they were rubbing it in that she was a newcomer.

"I'm glad to see he's looking so happy," Ann added, and she also watched Rory for a moment. Tracy thought she detected a genuine concern in Ann's face just then, and a shadow of worry in her eyes.

Rick was eyeing his cigar. Bluntly, he said, "He's rid of that damned woman for good. That helps."

"For good?" Ann asked sharply, turning to Rick.

He shrugged. "It's all but sewn up. I'm representing him as usual of course. The custody hearing is Wednesday. It shouldn't be a problem."

For Tracy's benefit, Ann said quickly, "Rick is Rory's attorney, both personal and in business. They're trying to get permanent legal custody of Melora, you see." She turned back to her brother. "Rick, be straight, now. Do you mean Rory will definitely be awarded custody by the judge? Even if Margie contests the decision?"

Rick stuck his cigar back in his mouth, speaking around it. "It was part of the split when the divorce was final. Rory got the kid, and she got a big chunk of Northstream Airlines to keep her happy."

Tracy lifted her head and stared at the two of them. What were they talking about?

"But that was just a verbal agreement. Now Margie wants both, right?" Ann asked.

"She thinks he's weak right now," Rick admitted. "Rory's in trouble with the banks—we all know that. Margie's trying to pull a fast one to get Melora and the rest of Northstream away from Rory while his defenses are down."

"Rory won't give Melora up for anything, though. And Margie would have to buy him out to get the company, right?"

Rick nodded. "He's not desperate enough to sell Northstream just yet. I think he's got a slick maneuver up his sleeve at the moment, so don't write him off."

"None of us will write him off, of course," Ann said firmly. Her amused curiosity was evident, however. With a grin, she inquired, "What slick maneuver is he ready to pull?"

"He's got a sucker on the hook, I hear." Rick's smirk was unpleasant. "Some big deal that's going to put Northstream back in the horse race if he can pull it off without spending too much of that precious capital of his." Rick laughed. "I'm sure he'll find a way to charm a merger into taking place. That ought to settle his business and improve his love life at the same time!"

Tracy found herself staring at Rick Buchanan in a kind of fascination. She couldn't be hearing this, she thought to herself. Rick couldn't be talking about Shamrock, could he? Had Rory been bragging about snaring Tracy and her airline for a song and dance? Or just a dance? The sexual kind? A huge painful lump rose in Tracy's throat. A sting began to hurt behind her eyes, but she stared at the older Buchanan brother without blinking. So it was true. Rory was using Tracy to gain Shamrock Air.

Rick was completely unaware of Tracy by that time. The conversation had become a candid exchange of family information between brother and sister. He had forgotten that Tracy was listening, and continued, "Rory's getting his wits collected again. The divorce and all the hullabaloo that went with it had him shaken up for a while. Maybe emotionally, but definitely financially. Now he's getting back on the right track."

"And now Northstream's gaining strength again?" Ann asked, clarifying the situation in her own mind.

"Not yet, but it will, if this merger thing goes through." Swelling his chest out pridefully, Rick added with great satisfaction, "I think my little brother is going to give that Hallis babe a much deserved kick in the pants."

"Hallis?" Tracy repeated, before she could stop herself. No, no! This was too much. Tracy's small, suddenly frightened voice shook and from inside came a shudder of dread. He wasn't going to say it. It couldn't be true. The facts were too perfect, too neat, too horrible.

"Sure," Rick said agreeably. "Margie Hallis owns another airline. Maybe you've heard of it. It's a big successful commuter—half of which she inherited from her father, and the other half she got from Rory in one of the worst divorce settlements I've ever heard of. She calls it Hallis Air. She's his ex-wife, you see. Rory's ex-wife."

Tracy stared.

"Rory taught her all about the airline business," Ann added, coming to her brother's defense. "Now she's trying to put him out of business because she's angry over the child-custody thing. It's a really messy situation."

Marjorie Hallis was Rory's ex-wife. They were both vying for Shamrock, both offering the same amount of money. And Rory had kept his ex-wife's identity a secret. What else had he lied about? Even Rick knew that Rory was using his charm to gain a merger with another airline.

Tracy stumbled backward, her hand automatically at her mouth. No, no.

Rick was staring at Tracy as if she was about to be sick, and Ann made an instinctive move to touch Tracy's arm. But Tracy shook them off. She was too upset to make an excuse or apology, and she turned and half ran away from the group. It was too awful. How could he have done it?

The lake was a hundred yards down the lawn, and Tracy found herself stumbling toward the water, toward the silence. The party noises faded behind her as she hurried away, not daring to look back. The last thing she needed was for Rory to come tearing after her. She didn't trust herself not to make a scene.

At last she came to an unsteady halt, her legs trembling beneath her. How could Rory have kept such a secret? Why? He'd had a hundred opportunities, and not a word. If Marjorie Hallis was his ex-wife and his largest competitor, surely he must have realized the information might at least interest Tracy a tiny bit!

With her head full of jumbling, angry possibilities, Tracy set off, walking swiftly up the shoreline, her hands thrust into the front pockets of her jeans, her shoulders hunched. What could it all mean? Besides that Rory was just using their almost-love affair to further his precious business? Tracy had seen that coming since she had first laid eyes on the man. Why hadn't she kept that foremost in her mind? Of all the stupid, naive, childish mistakes to make! She'd known all about Rory from the start, and yet she'd allowed her growing emotional attachment for him to change her mind. Just as he'd intended all along! What a fool—a young stupid fool!

Tracy stumbled and nearly collided with M.A. and a little girl. They had been talking together, M.A. crouched on the beach to speak with the child on her own level. Tracy halted in her tracks and backed away uncertainly, blinking to come out of her daze. "Oh," she gasped. "I'm sorry."

"Oh, hello, Tracy," M.A. said smoothly, though she remained down beside the little girl. She turned her eyes to look deeply into the child's face. "Melora, this is Tracy, the lady your daddy and I told you about."

The child had been crying. Her face was pinched, her eyes red and streaming, and her nose had just been wiped with M.A.'s dainty handkerchief. She was small and thin-boned, her Oshkosh overalls hanging a little too loosely on her long narrow body. Her face appeared rounded, an impression accentuated perhaps by the dark wedge of her short hair, and she had Rory's fine eyes and a perfect little mouth that was scrunched tightly to hold back more tears. When she looked up at Tracy, though, her face relaxed a little and her eyes cleared.

Tracy stared back into Melora's eyes, trying to wipe the pain out of her own expression for the child's benefit. She said the first thing that came into her mind, though her voice sounded weak and shaken. "Hi. Looks like you've been playing."

Melora's face fell again. She had been playing with a lipstick, for her mouth and half of each cheek was liberally streaked with a coral red. The gold top of the tube lay in the sand at M.A.'s knee, and Melora looked forlornly down at it.

"Yes," M.A. responded with matter-of-fact tone. "Melora found her Aunt Dorothy's handbag and helped herself. We've been talking about it."

"I—I—" Melora gulped hard. "I shouldn't have."

"It's okay," M.A. said soothingly, smoothing

Melora's short brown hair under her palm. "Everybody does a silly thing once in a while. You're allowed to make a mistake."

"I—I'm sorry," Melora said miserably.

"I know you are. Sometimes we do dumb things when we know better, but it's okay now and then. Right, Tracy? We've all done stupid things in our lives, and I suppose we'll keep on doing them."

Tracy didn't answer, couldn't answer. Her own chest had become so tight and aching that she thought she was going to burst at any moment. She stood stiffly above the sniffling child, heard M.A.'s calm and sympathetic voice, and the tears just started to come. Everyone does stupid things. The heat filled her eyes and spilled in scalding streams down her cheeks, and there wasn't any way to stop them.

"Goodness!" M.A. exclaimed.

Melora's eyes widened even more and she clapped her hands over her mouth.

Tracy spun around as if to bolt, but M.A. had the foresight to grab Tracy's belt loops, and she hauled hard, digging in her heels. Tracy staggered around again, her face in her hands. She gulped, "I'm sorry."

"Don't be sorry," M.A. said brusquely. "What in the world...?"

Melora was fascinated by the sight of an adult dissolved so thoroughly into tears. Her high little voice with its Midwestern flat vowels piped up inquisitively, "My daddy says you're the bravest girl in the world!"

Tracy laughed brokenly and tried to halt the sobs. "I'm not very brave right now, am I?"

"Everybody's allowed to cry," M.A. interjected, still trying to teach a lesson to Rory's little girl.

Melora's pert face remained upturned to Tracy. "How come you're crying?"

Tracy couldn't quite get a grip on herself, so she shook her head slowly. "I don't know exactly. I feel stupid, I guess. Gosh, M.A., don't let me make a fool of myself in front of these people!"

Mary Alice Cooper took command of this situation just as swiftly as she had managed a weeping child. She put her arm around Tracy and turned her back on the now-distant party. "Take it easy, Tracy. What's up?"

"I've been so dumb! Such a complete patsy!"

"Melora, be a sweetie and run get a glass of water for Tracy, will you? And not a word to anyone, okay, honey?" M.A. put her head close to Tracy's once more. "Unless you'd like Rory to—"

"No!" Tracy objected in horror. "Lord, no!"

M.A.'s face changed when she said to the child, "Run for the drink, Melora. Don't tell about Tracy being upset, okay? Can you keep a secret?"

The secret idea appealed to the little girl, and she pelted off up the beach, leaving M.A. in charge. They could hear her sneakers beating back along the sand, and then the sound evaporated.

"Well," said M.A. with authority. "What's got you so rattled? An earthquake or something? I never thought I'd see you crack!"

But M.A.'s kind humor only made things worse, only made Tracy feel more like a little kid at the wrong birthday party. Tracy shook her head again, unable to put the right words together. "I've been—I just heard who Rory was married to before, that's all!"

"What?" M.A. asked, mystified. "What's so—? Oh! You mean you didn't know he and Margie—?"

"No, I didn't know!" Tracy cried, keeping her head bent, her face hidden. "He didn't tell me, so how was I supposed to figure out that the two companies that are trying to buy me out are practically the same family?"

"I see," M.A. said thoughtfully, her arm tightening around Tracy's waist. "He should have told you, hmm? Rory never mentioned his wife?"

"He mentioned her, of course. We just... apparently it didn't suit his purpose to tell me who she was! And he's had a lot of chances, M.A."

"I see," M.A. said again. "He deliberately kept you in the dark. What for? Business? Or maybe something personal?"

"How should I know?" Tracy demanded bitterly. "I can't imagine what he's been planning all along. It's obvious he's got me right where he wants me, though, isn't it?"

"I don't know," M.A. said with a flash of a grin. "Where does he want you?"

"In bed," Tracy snapped. "With my airline safely signed over to him, of course!"

"Oh, God," M.A. murmured, and it sounded as though she meant it as a prayer. "I hope this isn't happening. Tracy, my dear!"

"Don't feel sorry for me!" Tracy exploded. "I'm feeling sorry enough for myself!"

"It's okay," M.A. soothed once more, holding her tight. "Be as angry as you like. Or as sad. If it were me, I'd be screaming right now! He isn't really trying to get your airline by starting a relationship, surely? Maybe there's a reason for him not telling you about Margie. I can't imagine what, though. Such a rotten trick, Rory!"

"The worst part is that he's probably got a lot more surprises up his sleeve!" Tracy burst out, angrily dashing the tears from her face. "He's been sneaky and slick, and I've been an incredibly stupid mark. Lord only knows where I'd be next week if I hadn't just heard the big news. He'd probably have me tied up like a damned calf in a roping contest!"

"Easy now," M.A. advised. "Rory's basically a nice guy, Tracy. I'm sure his intentions toward you personally have been completely honorable. But the business stuff isn't my area of expertise. Are you sure he's been sneaky? Maybe it doesn't matter that Margie and he—"

"I can't figure it all out now!" Tracy cried, clutching her head in her hands to shut out the world. "I can't think straight. I only know that I want to kick him or something!"

"You are furious," M.A. noted. "Come on. My car's right up here. I'll take you somewhere, if you like. You don't really want to confront him here, do you? With his whole tribe watching?"

"I don't ever want to confront him," Tracy moaned, allowing herself to be dragged up the lawn. "I want him to fall off the edge of the earth!"

"That won't last," M.A. predicted. "You'll want to have your say in this, I'm sure. Just give yourself enough time to gather your arguments, all right?"

"Then hit him with both barrels!" Tracy declared, striking both fists against her own head. "Oh, I could—could—"

"Scream?" M.A. suggested. "Or cry?"

Tracy hiccuped. "Cry. Cry and cry some more. Oh, M.A.! I really—I thought we—Rory and I—"

"You thought you were falling in love," M.A. said evenly, drawing Tracy laboriously up the slope to the driveway. "It happens, you know. And with Rory, it's not hard, is it? He's such a dear."

Tracy staggered against the hood of a car and laid her hands on the hot metal to catch her balance. She lifted her tear-streaked face and stared at M.A. "He thinks you're wonderful, too. Why don't you take him? Marry him and get him off the market, will you? So he won't be bothering every woman in the airline business anymore!"

"Me?" M.A. laughed. "Why me, for heaven's sake?"

"Because he likes you."

"He likes you, too," M.A. said with a friendly grin. "And you're better suited to coping with him than I am. Tracy, this thing may work out, you know."

Tracy shook her head. "No. I don't think so. The only way it'll work is if I sell my company to somebody else."

"What?"

"Yes," Tracy said steadily, grinding her teeth as she looked down the lawn at the party below. Rory was down there somewhere, laughing no doubt, and enjoying himself. Rory always enjoyed himself, and he seemed to get what he wanted all the time. Tracy shook her head and added, "We'll see what he thinks of me when I'm broke. He may be back on your doorstep, M.A., if he thinks I've got nothing to offer."

CHAPTER FOURTEEN

M.A.'s CAR was a small Japanese model with a sunroof. She helped Tracy climb into the passenger seat, and ran over to get Tracy's knapsack out of Rory's station wagon. By that time Melora arrived with a half-empty paper cup of apple cider.

"I spilled a little of it," the child told Tracy diffidently as she passed the cup through the open door of the car. "But not too much."

"Thank you for bringing it," Tracy said, accepting the cup with both shaking hands. She smiled tremulously at the little girl. "Sorry I'm not as brave as you thought."

"It's okay," Melora said cheekily. "If you took me for a ride in your airplane sometime, though, I'd be really brave, y'know."

Tracy laughed and glanced up at M.A. before giving Melora another, stronger smile this time. "I bet you'd be very brave indeed. Next time I come back here, I'll see if you still want that ride."

"I will," Melora said firmly. "You won't crash again. But if you did, I'd know just what to do in the forest. I got a sleeping bag for my birthday!"

M.A. laid her hands on the child's shoulders. "Miss O'Hara is going to go for a ride in my car now, Melora. Will you tell your daddy for us?"

"Sure," Melora answered with a big smile up at M.A. "But he's gonna play football with grampa first."

"Let's hope he doesn't get hurt," M.A. said, laughing. She pushed the car door closed and sent Melora on her way back to the party.

Tracy waved at Rory's child as the little girl trotted back to the party. Then, when Tracy was sure she couldn't be overheard, she muttered fiercely, "Let's hope he breaks his blasted head wide open!"

M.A. climbed behind the wheel of the car a moment later. "Well? How about it? A drive back to my place so you can think things over?"

"Not much to think about, is there?" Tracy asked bitterly. "I think I've been taken for a long ride already."

M.A. sighed and reached for the ignition. "I hope Rory isn't pulling something fishy with you, Tracy. It just isn't—well, I don't like to think that Rory's become a hard-nosed businessman completely. He's got an awfully nice side to him, you know."

"Believe me," Tracy shot back, "I know. At least, I thought I did."

"He's got to have a reason for not telling you he was married to Margie Hallis."

"Sure," Tracy agreed with an irritated sarcasm in her tone. "If I knew his ex-wife was his biggest competitor, I'd be more likely to sell out to a third party, wouldn't I? I don't want to get involved in his messy divorce and his wife's crummy attempts to get their child away from him. All that situation needs is a few more people mixed up in it!"

M.A. nosed the little car around until they were facing out toward the highway, and then she put it into first gear and started driving. "Relax. He won't get you involved in his divorce. It's long over with now. It's just Melora and the airline business that's left to haggle over."

"And it sounds like Rory's been doing a great deal of haggling over business lately," Tracy said, slouching angrily back into her seat. "Rick knew all about a potential merger with another company—a company run by a woman who would improve Rory's love life as well as his balance sheet! Rick said it himself."

M.A. winced. "Perhaps Rick wasn't talking about you. Maybe it's someone else."

"That's just as bad," Tracy snapped. "If he's romancing me and somebody else at the same time, I—oh, rats!" Tracy buried her face in her hands again, determined not to cry once more. She groaned. "How could I let things get so far out of hand when I knew the score from the beginning?"

"Maybe things aren't too far out of hand yet,"

M.A. said softly. As she drove, it was clear that she was thinking. "Maybe you've still got some options, Tracy."

Tracy frowned at the road, her own mind beginning to turn again once the initial shock was past. "Maybe so," she agreed.

M.A. drove, and Tracy sat quietly in the seat beside her.

There were options, of course. But none of them gave Tracy much pleasure. In the last half hour it had become painfully obvious to her that little Tracy O'Hara was not going to have her cake and be allowed to eat it, too. She wasn't going to get Rory Buchanan, and she wasn't going to be allowed to keep Shamrock Air. The only right she still had left was to choose who got to buy Shamrock from her. And Tracy was willing to bet the ranch that neither slick Rory Buchanan nor his fair and overly friendly ex-wife was going to take over Shamrock Air.

The real world was suddenly not very rosy for Tracy. She was a natural optimist, but this blow had really knocked her for a loop. How could Rory have been so deceitful? To what purpose had he kept his marriage to Marjorie Hallis a secret? And was Rick right? Was Rory really using Tracy to strengthen his own company? After all those wonderful things he had said to her. And the way he had made gentle, but earth-shattering love to her.

In silence, Tracy let the facts wander back and forth across her mind. M.A. was quiet—perhaps occupied with her own concerns. Tracy appreciated the time to gather her thoughts. And her respect for Mary Alice Cooper continued to grow. M.A. was an understanding, willing friend, and Tracy found a deep affection developing for the lovely blond woman.

They drove to what must have been the edges of Chicago before M.A. pulled off the major highway and found her way through the streets to a large community of condominiums. The small, clustered buildings all looked the same to Tracy, but M.A. drove quickly through the crisscross of parking lots until she came to the last building by a clump of evergreen trees—the only trees in sight.

M.A. whipped into the last parking space and pulled up the emergency brake with a yank. She sat still and stared out the windshield for a split second. "For Pete's sake!"

Tracy followed her gaze, then sat up straight in surprise. "Hey! It's Spin."

Spin—of all people to find here in Chicago—was sitting calmly on the concrete stoop of the condominium, looking all gussied up in his best pair of jeans and a new sports jacket. He had polished his cowboy boots and carefully combed his hair. When he saw M.A. behind the wheel, he climbed to his feet and lifted his hand in wary greeting.

As Tracy got out of the passenger side of the car, though, Spin's expression turned to one of surprise, and then relief. Swiftly he strode down the sidewalk to her. "Trace! Are you okay?"

"Of course I'm okay," Tracy said roughly as he arrived before her. "What are you doing here?"

"I came—I had to find you," Spin answered distractedly. M.A. came around the hood of the car then, and he turned bashfully to her. "Hello, Mary Alice."

"Vincent!" M.A. said. Her tone was friendly, polite even, but not quite enthusiastic. She held out both her hands and clasped his with just a shade of uncertainty. Tipping her mouth up, she kissed him lightly on the cheek. "Good heavens, what a surprise."

Spin accepted her kiss. "Hi. I—I'm glad to see you, Mary Alice."

She smiled tentatively. "Are you?"

With a grin, Tracy realized that Spin was actually blushing. She covered her mouth and decided to keep quiet for the time being.

"Yes," he said firmly, staring her down in spite of the color that slid up his cheeks.

M.A. smiled in earnest then, watching poor Spin fight his emotions and his I'm-the-toughest-guy-on-the-block attitude. She lowered her eyelashes and said softly, "Then I'm happy that you came, Vincent. I didn't think you would."

"I wasn't afraid," Spin said stubbornly.

"I never said you were," M.A. replied composedly. She dropped one hand, but continued to clasp his other gently. "You said you wouldn't be comfortable with me."

"I didn't say that," Spin said quickly. "I meant that I—well, that I—"

"I know," said M.A., squeezing his hand. "We can talk about it later, if you like. Or not at all."

Spin had been holding his breath, but he let it out finally in an uncomfortable "whoosh." He glanced at Tracy and scowled at her inquisitive expression.

"Don't take anything out on Tracy," M.A. intervened before the two of them could start snapping at each other again. She said, "You and I can work out our own problem, Vincent. I'm glad you came to talk about it sensibly."

Spin sighed again, and in his thickest Oklahoma drawl, repeated, "Well...it's good to see you, Mary Alice."

M.A. laughed and swung his hand. "You said that already. Will you come in now?"

Spin flushed again and dropped her hands. Hastily he explained, "Well, I...it wasn't...I had to come for Tracy, y'see, and when I couldn't find out where she was, I figured I'd come get some help from you."

"So you didn't come to see me after all," M.A. said, teasing him with a sparkling light in her eyes. "I see. Well, what luck that Tracy's right here with me. All your troubles are in one basket for convenience. Perhaps we can start détente for nuclear arms as well as everything else!"

Deciding it was safe to interrupt this not-very-loverlike scene, Tracy demanded, "What's this all about, Spin?"

He turned to her, trying to unscramble his brain. Blankly he asked, "What?"

Tracy punched him insistently on the arm. "Why'd you come looking for me? Something wrong at Shamrock?"

And suddenly Spin was with her, forgetting his own situation with Mary Alice and composing his face into a serious, but comforting expression. He took her arm just above her elbow. "Sort of. Trace, can we...? I think we'd better sit down and talk."

There was something hiding in Spin's eyes—something bad and frightening. Tracy felt her stomach lurch again with fear. "Something is wrong," she blurted out, grabbing his sleeve. "Oh, Spin, tell me now. Is somebody hurt?"

"No, no," he assured her quickly. Dropping his arm around Tracy's shoulders, Spin turned to M.A. "Do you suppose we could have a cup of coffee or something, Mary Alice?"

"Of course," M.A. said briskly, leading the way up to the sidewalk without any questions. "This way. I've got a terrific herb tea I think you're going to like, Vincent."

"Herb tea?" Spin echoed doubtfully.

"What's going on?" Tracy demanded, tugging at Spin's jacket. "Cut the conversation, Spinelli. I'm going crazy! What's wrong at home?"

"Take it easy," Spin urged gently, pulling Tracy with him into the foyer of M.A.'s condominium. "Nobody's hurt. Nothing blew up. We're okay. It's something weird, that's all. The FAA wants to see you."

"The FAA?" Tracy repeated, astonished. "Now what for? Still the Grumman crash?"

Spin nodded. "They finally finished their investigation into the wreckage."

"They did? What took so long? What did they find?"

"Easy, easy!" M.A. laughed. "He'll answer those one at a time. Shall I take your coat, Vincent?"

Tracy practically wrestled Spin out of his jacket in an effort to get him to hurry up. "Tell me!" she cried. "I'm going nuts! What took the FAA so long to get their report done?"

"There was something suspicious, of course," Spin said as he passed his jacket to M.A. for her to hang up. "There wasn't anything wrong with the engine. There wasn't even anything wrong with the plane."

"Then why was there smoke?" M.A. asked in confusion, turning around again. "If the cockpit was full of smoke, there had to be a reason."

Spin nodded. "There was. A smoke bomb."

Tracy stared.

"Smoke bomb!" M.A. exclaimed. She dropped the jacket on the floor.

"Holy hell," Tracy breathed, leaning back against the doorjamb.

Only Spin wasn't shocked by the news, but then, he had known for several hours. He bent to get his jacket. "Yep. Somebody must have planted it up in the nose before we took off. A timer set off the thing finally, but not until we were up in the air. It was calculated."

"What?" M.A. cried. "You mean someone intentionally—?"

Spin nodded. "It sure wasn't a practical joke, that's clear. Somebody wanted that plane to crash that night."

Tracy's thoughts burned through her mind like wildfire. The possibilities were endless, but unbelievable. Who would want to crash the Grumman? Why? To ruin the plane? To kill someone? For kicks? And who would do such a thing? An employee at Shamrock? No one else had access to the planes but Tracy's own maintenance crew! She shook her head in stunned silence.

"I can't believe it," M.A. was saying swiftly. "It's like something that might happen in a movie! Why would anyone want to crash your airplane?"

"I don't know," Spin said softly, directing a

slow, measuring look at Tracy. "There are a lot of questions to answer. And the FAA wants some of those answers before they turn the whole thing over to the FBI."

"FBI!" Tracy said, astonished. "Why?"

Spin shrugged. "It's foul play, and that's not the FAA's jurisdiction. The FBI treats it just like they handle skyjacking cases and things like that. It's their ball game now, and the FBI won't mess around. Trace, we're going to be awful busy, you and me."

"They don't think we did it!" Tracy exploded. "Why would you and I actually plan to crash-land a half-million-dollar airplane? That's crazy!"

"They don't suspect us," Spin said quickly. "But we were the victims—and the ones most likely to provide information. We've got to get back home, Trace. They want to see you as soon as possible—tonight even."

"Let's have some of that tea before either of you goes tearing home," M.A. suggested firmly. She took Spin's hand and then Tracy's, too, and began to pull them into the spacious apartment. "I think we've had a shock."

M.A. led the way back through the apartment, and the other two followed docilely—Tracy dumbfounded and Spin in a new kind of daze. At the time Tracy might not have noticed much about the rooms if it hadn't been for Spin's startled, then intrigued reaction. His usually confident swagger faltered as he looked around.

The apartment was neat and filled with sunshine from the tall windows, and lush greenery that thrived on the abundance of light. Lacy curtains, a set of pretty china cups on an Oriental table, a lovely spray of fresh flowers—all very feminine decorations—marked this place as the home of a very ladylike lady. The walls were white and absolutely covered with framed photographs. It didn't take a genius to figure out that M.A. had taken the shots herself. Spin wasn't brave enough to start looking closely at any of them, however. He simply twisted out of M.A.'s grasp and walked determinedly toward the kitchen by himself. Apparently, he wasn't going to let the apartment intimidate him.

M.A. arrived in the tiny kitchen first, and plucked a painted kettle from a suspended wrought-iron rack of shining cooking utensils. Unaware of Spin's growing consternation with her home, she put the kettle under the tap and turned on the water full blast. Shaking her fair hair, she remarked, "I can't believe the FBI and everything, Vincent. It's incredible, isn't it?"

"I certainly think so," Tracy muttered.

Spin must have caught the bitterness in her voice, for he seemed to remember himself and Tracy. He pushed her gently by her shoulders into one of the kitchen chairs, and then pulled one up for himself so that he was sitting close with his knees against hers. He laid his hands just above Tracy's kneecaps and watched her eyes for her reaction. "The FBI thinks it's a mighty strange situation. Trace, honey, we've got to think. Did anything out of the ordinary happen that night?"

Tracy rubbed her palms against her forehead. "I don't remember anything funny. It was a last-minute trip. Rory was going to fly his own plane up to Montreal, but I had... he couldn't find the key for his Cessna. I volunteered to go with you at the last minute. Who looked over the plane before we left?"

Spin shook his head. "The whole crew was there. They all remember having a look, so the Grumman was practically on public display."

"But somebody had time to slip a smoke bomb into the engine before we took off that night."

"Right. I took it to Niagara Falls the morning before, so it had to have been within a thirty-five-hour time period that somebody got to it. But the plane is parked right under our noses all the time."

M.A. appeared beside them, setting cups on the counter. "So it was an inside job?"

"One of our employees?" Tracy asked in amazement. "I can't believe it! Why?"

"It's not our place to figure out who," Spin said heavily. "The Feds have already started combing through every bit of dust in that hangar."

"What!" Tracy objected, bolting upright. "They're snooping around my property and I'm not there?"

"Easy, easy," Spin soothed, holding her on the stool. "Why do you think I'm here? I couldn't get you on the phone, so I came to find you and take you back."

"Oh," said Mary Alice with an odd, involuntary sigh. She turned abruptly away and went to the stove, leaving Spin with Tracy.

Tracy glanced at M.A.'s back before she sought Spin's worried face with her eyes again. She had been holding her breath out of anxiety, and she let it out with a long gust of air. Sincerely she murmured, "Thanks, Spin. You've gone to a lot of trouble."

He shrugged, not looking at Tracy. He was watching M.A., who was puttering uselessly at the stove, waiting for the water to boil. Without really thinking about what he was saying to Tracy, Spin explained haltingly, "It's okay. I caught a commercial flight up this morning. I didn't know how to find Buchanan's operation, so I came here instead. I...I thought Mary Alice could...could help." Spin seemed to catch himself then, and looked back at Tracy, taking a split second to focus his eyes on her. He said, "We'll take the Pitts back home as soon as you're ready to fly."

"I'm ready now," Tracy said promptly. But a quick thought struck her, and she shot a second look at M.A.'s back. Tracy's instincts were not failing her now. There was definitely something in the wind between these two, no matter what Rory had said. M.A. had been genuinely disappointed when Spin declared that the purpose of this visit was purely on Tracy's behalf. And the two of them certainly had something to clear up between them. Hoping that she could sound convincing, Tracy faltered and said, "B-but I guess I could use a little rest and maybe a cup of tea or something before we go. And maybe you two want to talk."

"Us?" Spin asked, acting surprised. "Mary Alice and me? We've got nothin' to—"

"Hush, now, Vincent," M.A. intervened.

"Yeah," Tracy added. "Shut up and listen to the lady, Spinelli. If the two of you have something on your minds, just get it out in the open and see what happens."

Spin shot a look at M.A. "I'm not so sure I'm going to like what she's got to say."

"Oh, for heaven's sake!" M.A. burst out. "If you would just stop worrying about your precious ego for one minute—"

"My ego!"

"You heard me," M.A. said steadily. "If you weren't so darned worried about the differences between us, I think you'd soon realize that the differences don't matter."

"To you, maybe," Spin shot back. "You're the one who's got everything your heart desires, so I—"

"Oh, damn and blast and go to hell!" M.A. shouted suddenly, shocking Tracy into staring dumbly at her. M.A.'s blond hair flew about her usually composed face in a furious quiver. "I pegged you wrong from the beginning, I can see!"

"What d'you mean by that?" Spin demanded, getting slowly to his feet.

"I thought you had a deeper sense of life—what's important in life!" M.A. snapped. "If all those wonderful things we talked about in the forest that night were just empty words to you, then—"

Spin flushed angrily. "I never say anything I don't mean, Mary Alice."

"Then you honestly feel the sentiments in those poems you memorize so carefully?"

"Poems?" Tracy asked, bewildered.

"Shut up," Spin said to her.

"Don't tell her to shut up!" M.A. commanded, her eyes flaring with angry lights once again. "If you think you can get away with ordering women around like obedient dogs, then you can just—"

"I do not treat anyone like a dog," Spin said quickly. "Tracy never listens to me, anyway. I have never ordered you around, Mary Alice, and I don't intend to start trying. If you can't get used to the way I am, then maybe this idea is for the birds after all."

"Are you looking for an excuse for us to step out of each other's lives now, Vincent?"

"I don't need an excuse. Mary Alice, I just think that you and I have too many—"

"Stop it, stop it, stop it," M.A. said. "That decision is not one you can make all by yourself, sir! I think I have half an interest in this—this—this relationship, you know."

"Relationship?" Spin echoed carefully. "Is that what you fancy people call a friendship? Or a love affair?"

This was Tracy's cue to leave. She slid off the stool and tried to close her ears to the argument. This was none of her business anymore, that was sure. She said blithely, "I think I'll go take a walk, if you don't mind. Just around the building, maybe. Can I go out this way?"

Neither M.A. nor Spin answered her, for they were too busy glaring at each other and breathing as if they'd just finished a hundred-yard dash. Surreptitiously, so as not to disturb them, Tracy edged uneasily around the counter. A large sliding glass door stood beside the stove, and she gently slipped the latch and let herself out of the room. Whew!

The shouting resumed as soon as she was out, so Tracy quickly scooted away from the door.

A small patio lay beyond, and then a wide expanse of common grass. Tracy walked slowly to the rim of the patio. She put her hands into the pockets of her jeans and stood for a long time, staring at the grass.

Someone had forced the Grumman to crash. Rory was wooing his way into her life so he could have Shamrock and save himself from bankruptcy. His ex-wife was rich and powerful and using Rory's present, precarious position to steal away their daughter and take a good piece of Northstream at the same time. And Marjorie was also trying to head off Rory's merger with Shamrock by buying Tracy's airline herself. What a mess! What a complicated, stinking mess!

Tracy shook her head and stepped off the patio onto the grass. Her boots sank into the soft turf a little, so she paced slowly out into the middle of the lawn, thinking. It was too much of a mess to try sorting out all at once. Tracy realized that she'd be better off taking one strand of the knot at a time. The unraveling might go a bit easier that way. The place to start was with the plane crash. Rory was going to have to wait. Anyway, Tracy didn't want to think about Rory just yet. She was afraid she was going to cry again.

The big question at the moment was why anyone would put a smoke bomb into the engine of an airplane. There were plenty of ways to cause a crash, ways that didn't leave many traces. It certainly sounded like an amateurish job to Tracy. An aircraft mechanic would know any number of methods for crashing a plane. Why try something that was sure to leave evidence behind?

Shaking her head, Tracy started back to M.A.'s

condominium. It was time to get back to Shamrock and try figuring out this mystery for herself. She wasn't going to trust this to the FBI. Those turkeys were liable to really confuse things!

But when Tracy arrived in the kitchen, the room was empty. Spin and M.A. were not in sight. The teakettle was whistling to beat the band, but no one was there to take the boiling water off the stove.

Tracy was at first frightened. Where had they gone? But then, with a rueful smile at herself for being so jumpy all of a sudden, Tracy took up a pot holder and removed the kettle from the stove herself. The apartment was very quiet. Very, very quiet.

Half a minute later Spin arrived in the kitchen looking frazzled and breathless and sheepish at the same time. He was raking his hair back with one hand, trying to make his hair neat again. It looked as if someone else had ruffled her fingers through it in a passionate moment.

Spin did not look Tracy in the eyes, but indicated the teakettle. He was breathless. "Gosh! We heard that thing go off, but we were looking at some pictures in the living room! Did you know M.A. was a photographer, Trace? She's really good, too. Really good. Boy, you should have a look at some of her stuff. Nice stuff, Trace. She's really good."

"I'm sure she's excellent," Tracy said dryly,

putting an end to his nervous talk. "Are you finished yet, Spinelli? Or do you want to go kiss her some more before we get out of here?"

"You're a real nuisance sometimes," Spin snapped in exasperation. "I thought you might have learned something this weekend, Trace!"

"Oh, I've learned plenty," Tracy said softly. She let her gaze travel to the window, to the blue patch of sky that showed through the curtains there. Full of regret, she repeated, "I've learned plenty, Spin."

CHAPTER FIFTEEN

TRACY AND SPIN ARRIVED back at the Shamrock hangar on Sunday evening. Almost from the moment the Pitts set down on the tarmac, Tracy's attention was devoted to the federal investigation into the crash of her Grumman G1. Both the FAA and the FBI wanted to find who had sabotaged the charter flight, and Tracy stayed up late that night talking with the investigators.

Rory did not call on Sunday night, nor did he phone on Monday.

On Tuesday afternoon, however, he arrived.

Without knocking, he walked straight into Tracy's house where she sat having a late lunch at the table by the fireplace. She nearly swallowed her tongue with the last bite of sandwich when she saw him. She was alone—hiding from the FBI fellows, actually, because she hadn't had a moment's peace since they'd arrived. When Rory strode through the door looking like a thundercloud, Tracy held her ground and tried not to cringe.

He dropped his jacket over the opposite chair and pulled Tracy to her feet with a powerful yank.

"Wh—what are you doing here?" she demanded, gulping, automatically fighting to get free of him.

"What the hell do you think I'm doing here?" Rory's voice was hard and angry, his eyes a stormy blue. He didn't pull Tracy against his body, but held her inescapably before him. "You don't suppose this is a social call, do you?"

"I can think of half a dozen reasons why you might show up," Tracy countered, keeping her chin up and her own expression hostile in spite of the sudden tumult inside her. Just the sight of Rory's tall and handsome figure standing in the middle of her life was enough to transform Tracy into a stuttering teenager. But she forced herself not to fly into his arms and weep with joy. She glared upward at him. "I bet you've got some new scheme to try out on me, haven't you?"

"A scheme?" Rory snapped, grabbing her arm in a grip that really hurt. "Do you honestly believe that crap, Miss Almighty O'Hara?"

"I don't know what to believe," Tracy retorted, stepping back a pace. "But I'm sure not listening to a word you've got to say, buster!"

"All right then, you won't object if I do the listening for once, and you do the talking, right?" Rory let her go, almost pushing Tracy back into the chair. He towered over her, furious, his dark hair spilling over his forehead, looking like a war god about to spur his charger into battle. His clothes were rugged—khaki trousers, a sweater with a shirt and tie underneath. It was clear he wasn't on business. His voice thundered suddenly in the empty house, "Explain to me, please, why you went roaring off without a single word of explanation Sunday. Did you chicken out? Decide my family wasn't bizarre enough to suit you? Did my brother Rick make a pass at you and shock innocent little Tracy?"

"Nobody made any passes—except you, of course! And I had gotten pretty used to it by that time." Tracy clenched her hands around the arms of the chair and sat tight, glaring up. "I knew from the first night I met you what you were out to get, but I let my better judgement get a little clouded. If you want Shamrock Air, Buchanan, you had better get in line with all the other bidders!"

Rory swore and kicked a chair out from the table. He sat and looked stoically angry, cold-eyed and taut around his mouth. "What's got you back singing that song for heaven's sake?"

"Rick didn't tell you?" Tracy inquired sarcastically. "M.A. didn't spill the beans either?"

"About what?"

Tracy folded her arms across her chest and summoned an imperious look. "Your brother was generous enough to recount some family history for me, that's all. About your wife, for starters."

"My—?" Rory's rage faltered then, but didn't

dissipate. He never took his eyes from Tracy's. "I see. And you've drawn some conclusions, have you?"

"About you and Ms Hallis Air? Yes, certainly."

"Tracy—"

"Don't bother explaining." She cut him off sharply. "The mere fact that you chose to keep your relationship with Marjorie Hallis a secret from me is information enough. Whatever your motive, it doesn't matter now."

"It doesn't?" Rory asked sharply, and he reached for her wrist with a swiftness once more. With Tracy's arm firmly in his grasp, Rory pulled her closer across the table. The planes of his face were hard, marshaled strictly from within, but his tone was wary. "What have you done, Tracy?"

"I haven't sold Shamrock yet, if that's what's got you worried," Tracy retorted curtly. She did not struggle in his grip. It would have been useless to do so. She held herself rigidly however, and didn't avoid his glare. "I haven't decided what to do with my airline. But I have decided that I could care less about you and your ex-wife. If the two of you want to bicker over Shamrock, I'll just keep away from the fight until the winner steps out of the ring and offers me a whole lot of money. I can't lose, can I, Rory?"

"Yes," he said, the words coming from between gritted teeth. "We can both lose something,

Tracy, something we'll never have a chance at again if we're not careful."

Tracy felt the fear bubbling in her stomach then, and knew her eyes were flickering. She tried to keep the anger in her voice. "Are you talking business now?"

"No," he said, "and you know it. I'm talking about us. You and me."

"There isn't any us."

"You're wrong." Rory's fingers bit deeply into Tracy's slender arm. "You can't even say that without getting that little kid's pout on your mouth! We've started something, Tracy, and neither of us really wants to end it."

"Forget it!" Tracy shot back, practically spitting the words at him. "I'm not falling for any of your smooth lines anymore."

"This isn't a line. I know better than to try something phony with you, Tracy. You'd see through me, just like I can see the truth in you right now. You're in love with me."

"What?" Tracy objected, blustering it out. She wrenched free of him and stared, rubbing her wrist.

He let her go and sat back, watching. "Deny it, then. Look me in the eye and deny it."

"I don't have to obey your commands," Tracy snapped. Instinctively she rose to her feet and cut around the chair, putting it between herself and Rory. This, she hadn't expected. How to react?

What to say? Were her foolish feelings so obvious to him?

He didn't chase her. He didn't come after her. He sat perfectly still and said, "Grow up, Tracy."

That was too much. Tracy blew her cool. "Grow up?" she exploded, wheeling around to face him. "Dammit, I wish you'd stop that stupid age routine! What does it take to prove what kind of adult I am?"

"Adults have honest feelings, Tracy."

"Don't you think I do?" she demanded in a shout. "Do you want me to say that I love you? All right, I love you! But that doesn't mean I trust you any farther than I can throw you. You're a blasted liar and a sneaking son of a—"

"That's enough," Rory said sharply, as if reprimanding a child. He got up from the chair but stayed several yards from her. "If you'd just control your temper for half a minute and think straight, you'd probably realize—"

"Don't patronize me!" Tracy shouted. "I hate it and it's uncalled for! I can think as clearly as you can—maybe clearer in this case! I'm not going to listen to another word from you, Rory, until I've settled my business and fixed things with Shamrock. In the meantime, you can go to blazes."

"That attitude is understandable," Rory responded, sounding calmer this time. He came slowly around the table. "You haven't any reason to trust me, I suppose, though I wish you'd believe that I have nothing but the best intentions where you're concerned."

"Forgive me if I withhold my opinion."

His smile was bitter. "Forgiven. Do you want explanations now? Or do you expect me to walk out of your life today?"

"Walk wherever you like," Tracy snapped. Angrily, she wrestled the blasted Cessna key out of her pocket. "Here! Take your stupid plane and go!"

He caught the key effortlessly, but didn't look at it. He didn't even appear surprised at its sudden reappearance. Instead, he watched her eyes and the emotions that battled there. Quietly he said, "What I'd like is to take you back to Chicago with me, but I realize that's crazy. You see, Tracy, I've fallen pretty hard for you. I'd like to have you with me. I'm probably in love with you, in fact, but I'm not sure either of us is ready for the kind of relationship we seem to have tumbled into."

"Listen," Tracy began hotly, chokingly, "I'm plenty old enough for—"

"I know you're old enough. I'm talking about me this time." Rory took a breath and held it, preparing himself. Then the explanation came. He said evenly, "I was married to Marjorie, and I'm still settling that situation—not very successfully, as you've probably heard. Until I met you, I figured I was never going to get myself so deeply involved with a woman again. I've seen what can go wrong, Tracy. I don't want to go through that again, I don't want to put my daughter through that kind of trauma again, and I don't want you to be a victim either. Being in love with someone isn't easy."

Tracy flung herself away, retreating behind the wing chair for security.

"At first I thought I was keeping my feelings to myself because I didn't want to hurt you," Rory went on. "But you're not as vulnerable as you look, Tracy. You're strong, very strong, and more resilient than any woman I've ever known. That's why I couldn't imagine what made you run off the way you did on Sunday. You're tough, but you're still immature at times—don't look at me like that! So I figured something silly sent you into a tailspin at the picnic. You're not the type to run away because your feelings got hurt."

"Well, for once my feelings were a little wounded," Tracy replied caustically. "You weren't honest with me, Rory, and after what we—we've done together, that really hurt."

"Because I didn't tell you I was married to Marjorie Hallis?" He put his shoulder to the mantel and nodded. "All right, I deserve whatever punishment you think for that. I didn't tell you at first because you and I had a business deal in the balance—a business triangle with Hallis Air, a company that just happens to be run by my ex-wife. Then things heated up between us, and I didn't think the identity of who I used to be married to should make any difference. I intended to tell you a lot about myself on Saturday night, but we got busy with other things, didn't we?"

Tracy blushed. She remembered all too well what "other things" Rory meant. She spun away from him and said over her shoulder, "So you let your big brother drop the bomb."

"It never occurred to me that any of my family would bring up Margie in conversation. I wasn't thinking straight. I made a mistake."

"You seem to make a lot of those."

"Don't start with the glib remarks."

"All right," she said, swinging on him. "I may or may not accept that explanation from you. Give me a few days to think it over. In the meantime, tell me what you're doing here. Come to change your offer for Shamrock? Or are you hoping I'll take you to my bed for a—?"

"I came for my airplane," he interrupted swiftly, the cold light of anger appearing in his eyes once again. "I flew up from Pittsburgh on your commercial run to take my Cessna home again. And I wanted to see you face to face if you intend to break things off. It's only fair that you say goodbye in person."

Tracy ducked her head and looked away, holding her breath. She could barely make her voice heard for the tightness in her throat. "Is that what you want? To say goodbye?"

Rory shrugged then. "That's your decision, not mine. I've already told you what I'd like... to take you back with me. I do love you, Tracy."

Before she could stop herself, Tracy put her face into her hands. She was trembling and cold and feeling half-sick inside. If this was the path of true love, it was awful. When she took a breath, it sounded suspiciously like a sob.

Rory came to her then and put his hand at the small of her back. Tracy tried to step away, but she collided with the chair and was trapped there. Rory said quietly, "Tracy. Tracy, love."

"Don't touch me," she said, unable to lift her face from her hands to look up at him. "I can't think when you touch me."

He sighed, but there was some amusement finally in the way he expelled that long breath. "That makes two of us. All right, my girl, let me make a logical choice, hmm? Trust me this far? Let's give it some time. Two weeks? Will you decide what to do about Shamrock in that time?"

"I don't know," Tracy said, slanting a cautious look upward. "It depends on the investigation. The FAA has frozen me until they decide about the plane crash."

"That can't take too much longer," Rory said, touching his forefinger under her chin. Almost caressingly, he lifted Tracy's face higher so that he could appreciate the clarity of her green eyes and the soft curves of her cheeks. With a smile, Rory said, "And once you're out from under Shamrock, we'll see, all right? We'll get the business out of the way, and then I'll come back."

"Are—" Tracy swallowed hard, forcing her voice to come out normal "—are you still going to try to buy Shamrock?"

"Yes," he said firmly. "I can't afford not to. It's up to you to make the best decision for yourself, and I intend to do the same for me. Can you keep the two Rory Buchanans straight in your own head?"

"I—I'm not sure," Tracy said with all honesty.

"It won't be easy," Rory agreed, a grin starting on his mouth finally. He bent and pressed an impulsive kiss on her forehead. "But I have a feeling you can do it better than anyone."

She pushed him back then, for her heart was hammering so violently she was sure Rory could feel it. The tension was almost too much to bear. Tracy ducked out from his almost-embrace and fled the rest of the way around the wing chair. Throwing him a fierce look, she said, "Just don't expect any preferential treatment!"

"No," Rory said with another regretful sigh as he picked up his jacket. "I won't expect that, certainly. In fact, I'd better leave now before I try a little preferential treatment on you, Miss O'Hara. You look wonderful today. I've never known a female who could look so charming in the same grungy sweater and jeans."

"I do not wear the same sweater all the time!" Tracy objected, glad suddenly that they had something less emotional to talk about. The rush of relief washed over her like a cleansing wave. Then, remembering, she smacked her hand to her hip and said, "Wait. I've still got the sweater I borrowed from you on Sunday. Don't leave yet. I'll go get it."

She escaped into her bedroom, glad to have a brief time to get a grip on herself. Rory's sweater was neatly folded on top of the dresser, and Tracy took it in her arms, hugging it to her chest for a moment. She saw her own reflection in the mirror above the dresser. A young, green-eyed woman with a nervous flush of pink across her high cheekbones.

So he loved her. He had said it. He loved her and he was starting to respect her, too. If only.... Tracy sat down on the edge of her bed, her legs suddenly too shaky to support her any longer. She sat back on the coverlet, buried her nose in his sweater and wondered. Was it possible? Could the mess with Shamrock work itself out and let them live happily ever after? Could she imagine that Rory might show up on her doorstep in two weeks with a ring in his pocket and that smile of pleasure in his eyes? Or was that too much to hope for?

Of course, the way he had said those magic words hadn't been too romantic. As usual, a shouting match had gotten the truth out of both of them. It was a disappointing realization for Tracy. Perhaps she was tough and strong and resilient, but she enjoyed a little romance now and then. Had he meant it? Did he love her? Or was it just the right thing to say at the right time in the argument?

"Tracy?" Rory called, just outside the room. He poked his head through the door, in the act of shrugging into his jacket. "Tracy?"

She stayed on the bed.

He came in and stopped, looking down at her. "Are you okay?"

Tracy nodded, the full impact of what had passed between them hitting her like a bulldozer. She was in love with him. Here was the man she wanted to spend the rest of her life with. Here was his sweater, feeling soft and itchy at the same time under her hands, and smelling faintly of autumn afternoons. Tracy's eyes were wide and startled, turbulent as a stormy sky. She couldn't think of a thing to say. She loved him. And he loved her back.

"Oh, Tracy," Rory said softly, dropping down on one knee before her. He pulled her against his chest, wrapping both arms so tightly around her that she could feel the pressure of held breath being squeezed away.

She laid her head on his shoulder and whispered, "I love you."

He laughed and filled his hands with the soft

tumble of her hair. "I'm glad," he murmured, touching his cheek to hers. "I don't know which one of you I love more—the foul-mouthed little kitten with a brain that works faster than quicksilver, or the soft, apprehensive woman who melts me inside."

"You make me feel like I'm two different people sometimes. Or three, or four."

"You're still growing, darling, no matter how old you'd like to be. I just don't want you to change. I don't want to make you different from what you really are. I love you this way."

"Shrieking at you one second and—and dying to make love the next?"

"You don't shriek. And as for making love—well, if this wasn't the worst possible time between us, I'd forget about being the cool voice of reason and—" Rory interrupted himself this time, and scanned her face as if to memorize the jumble of emotions reflected there. With a gentle smile, he said softly, "Tracy, darling, kiss me just once before I go."

He didn't have to ask. Tracy found his lips with her own, silencing Rory with a soft, trembling kind of kiss that soon grew into a long, insistent melding of souls. Tracy let fall the sweater, and wound her arms high around Rory's neck. She parted her mouth and savored. He was here with her now, holding her, kissing her just the same as before. No matter what had happened in the interim.

Rory smoothed his hands down her back as if recalling the lithe curve of her body. He hesitated, then deepened the kiss. Conveying a new message, he slid his hands around her bottom, as if asking a gentle, but urgent sexual question. He ran one palm slowly down her thigh, appreciating the supple length of muscle there. Breaking the kiss by millimeters, he murmured, "Tracy, I missed you. Two days felt like years."

"Like centuries," Tracy agreed, smiling hesitantly as she touched her mouth to his once more, her eyes lazily lidded to conceal the glow of emotion a while longer. Biting her lip, Tracy asked, "Rory, are you going to turn out to be a fink?"

He laughed softly, regretfully. "Are you calling me names so I'll leave?"

"N—no," she answered, after catching a sigh. He had brought his hand to the curve of her breast and it hovered there, tantalizing. It was foolish to imagine he might come clean at a moment like this. Tracy felt her willpower crumbling. With discretion thrown to the winds, she touched his face and urged softly, "Stay a while longer."

Message understood, Rory hesitated. It wasn't the right time. But he couldn't stop himself. He eased her back onto the bed in a slow and gentle motion until Tracy was reclining there.

His body was hard and powerful against hers. Kissing her mouth hungrily, he muffled the small moan of pleasure that escaped her throat. His own sigh mingled with hers when Tracy smoothed her hands down his back.

Carefully, though his fingers were oddly clumsy with haste, Rory unbuttoned the top of Tracy's sweater and pulled it over her head. He left her trapped in the garment for an instant and swooped to touch his lips to the bare skin of her chest. "This isn't the right time for this," he admitted.

"Is once more going to make a difference?" Tracy asked, with a small nervous laugh, struggling to get free of her sweater.

"There are good times and bad times to go to bed," Rory said, unable to stop himself from kissing her collarbone, her throat. "And this time it's just plain lust, I'm afraid."

"No," Tracy said, smiling. "It's the first time we've admitted that we love each other."

He met her eyes then, marveling at the sparkle that never seemed to leave the emerald depths of her gaze. "I've been in love with you from the start, I think. What a combination of qualities! You're a crazy mixture, Tracy O'Hara, and I can't keep my hands off you!"

Giggling, Tracy wrenched out of her sweater and clasped Rory to her. There was laughter on her face, but inside a familiar and exciting tension had already begun its inexorable spiral. She tugged at Rory's sweater, and together they began to undress each other. Quickly, a pile of discarded clothing grew on the floor beside the small bed, and in no time, Rory was tucking Tracy under him, covering her slender body with his longer frame.

"I'll be miserable," Tracy said quietly, nipping his earlobe as she spoke, "if you turn out to be a real rat over this airline business. Please, Rory—"

"Don't talk," Rory murmured, lifting her to meet him. "We'll only start another argument. Just enjoy. We'll have this to remember until we can really be together. Making love with you... Tracy, can you feel what you do to me?"

Tracy brought her hands to his chest, there sensing the tripping beat of his heart. His breathing was deep, yet piqued, and she could see the warmth of passion in his eyes. "Yes," she responded. "It makes me happy. You've taught me so much, Rory, and I want you to feel good, too. Here. Let me."

Rory lay back and helped Tracy roll on top of him. She covered his body, teasing his chest with the long curling tendrils of her hair. He wrapped both arms around her, kissed her throat, and sighed with pleasure. Closing his eyes, he savored the weight of her slender body, the silken texture of her thighs as they clasped him, the liquid heat of her lips as they trailed an exciting path down his chest.

"Oh, Tracy," he whispered.

She couldn't wait. With disarming uncertainty, Tracy eased him inside her until she was filled with a sort of white-heat that pulsed with every contraction of Rory's heart. Her own sigh of welcome was unrestrained. Here he was within her once more, a union of love so complete that Tracy felt a soft, stealing haze of contentment surround them.

She played her small hands along the line of his shoulders, running her fingertips back and forth across the contours of muscle and bone. She touched the spot on his throat where an artery beat the echo of his heart, and then moved to brush his skin with her lips. Tracy smiled and felt the fluttering insistence of her own body begin. Moving gently above him, she enjoyed the repetitions of separation and reunion with her eyes closed, head cast back, her hair tumbling down her naked back in a blaze of color. Her breathing was soft, but quick.

When Rory touched his warm palms to her breasts, Tracy heard her own moan of response. With a smile, he said, "I love you, Tracy. I need you with me. It can be like this for a long time to come."

The crescendo of pleasure came upon her in a slow, delicious wave then, and Tracy surrendered with a cry that sounded of wonder and pain at the same time. She shuddered, and Rory took her swiftly, comfortingly, in his arms. Gathering her to his chest, he rolled, pinning Tracy into the warmth of the bed. Gently he smoothed her hair back from her face and pressed soft kisses to her temples. He soothed her with quiet talk, yet stayed firmly inside her body.

Weak with pleasure, Tracy looped her arms around his shoulders and drew him more securely within her. Rory thrust gently then, gradually seeking her darkest core. Deeper and deeper he thrust, until the energy created by their own exertions caused its own inevitable burst of flame. Rory groaned and found the warmest, securest depth of Tracy's body. He clutched her, as if to prevent losing himself within her. Then he was still, spent and sated.

Panting lightly, they slowly returned to earth. The wonderful haze cleared in time, and they relaxed, melting into each other once more.

There was much to say, yet Tracy was quiet. The wrong word might lead to the wrong discussion, and she'd never see him again. Rory, too, was reluctant to speak. They lay in peaceable silence, each occupied with troubling thoughts until sleep edged closer and closer.

CHAPTER SIXTEEN

RORY SAT UP, and Tracy woke instantly, surprised that she had fallen so soundly asleep. It was dark beyond the window of her room, but Rory was reaching for his clothes. Evening had fallen.

Tracy touched his bare back. "What's wrong?"

Surprised, he turned and then bent to give her another gentle kiss on the mouth. "I thought you were dead to the world. Nothing's wrong. I've got to go, that's all."

"Go?" Tracy repeated, trying to keep her voice from sounding petulant in the half light. She sat up, drawing the sheet to her breasts. "Why? You mean back to Chicago? Tonight?"

But Rory had found his trousers in the heap of clothes on the floor and began searching for his socks. "I have to. There's a meeting in the morning that I can't miss."

With Marjorie Hallis. Tracy remembered the conversation between Ann and Rick Buchanan. They had spoken of a meeting between Rory and his ex-wife over custody of Melora. Tracy sighed shortly and said, "Oh. I see."

"How about an 'I'll miss you terribly and can't wait to see you again'?"

Tracy smiled unwillingly. "All right. I'll miss you terribly."

Rory glanced around at her. "There's a distinct lack of validity in the way you said that."

Tracy hugged her knees and watched him dress. "I'm just wondering what's going to happen when I see you next, that's all. Will there be a big showdown, I wonder?"

"Let's not speculate," Rory suggested lightly, "until it happens, all right? I'm a firm believer in the ostrich theory."

"Bury your head in the sand, and all the bad things will go away?"

"Exactly." Rory pulled his sweater over his head and threaded his arms through the sleeves. "Discussing airlines with you is guaranteed to start fireworks. Get rid of Shamrock, Miss O'Hara, and I'll be happy to talk with you about anything."

"Eventually you and I are going to have to talk about our airlines, you know," Tracy pointed out.

"Eventually," Rory agreed with a gentle laugh.

"Are you going to change your two-million-dollar offer?"

"Now, now. Never talk business in bed." Rory tousled her hair, but the rough gesture turned into a caress. With a suddenly serious darkness in his eyes, he added, "You've received my formal offer on paper, haven't you? I'm not changing anything."

Tracy nodded. "All right. But do you understand that you're not the only bidder? And that you're not exactly top of the heap?"

He grinned. "Money-wise, perhaps. Make your best decision, Miss Shamrock Air. We'll all sleep easier if you keep your feelings out of it."

"How can I—?" Tracy caught herself, stifling the angry retort that boiled in her mind. She shook her head swiftly. "Blast it!" she muttered. Then, with a quick, frowning look up at him, she said, "I've got one question, though. Will you answer it?"

"We'll see," Rory said warily.

"Have you discussed Shamrock Air with Marjorie Hallis?"

Rory eyed her solemnly. "Tracy—"

"Just a simple yes or no will be enough," she said firmly, not flinching from his gaze. "Answer me, Rory."

"Okay," he said with amiable compliance. "No, I haven't talked about Shamrock with Margie."

"Will you? At your meeting tomorrow?"

Rory kept the surprise from showing in his face, but his hands were suddenly stilled in the act of picking up his shoes. He said, "How did you know I was seeing her tomorrow?"

"Are you going to ask her about buying Shamrock?" Tracy pressed, sounding curt.

"I don't know," Rory said finally. "It's possible."

"I have a feeling," Tracy began slowly, tracing her fingertips through the sheets and avoiding his look, "that I'm on the verge of becoming a pawn, Rory."

"A pawn?"

"That both you and—and your ex-wife—are using me somehow."

Rory sighed again, but he did not reach to touch her. "Tracy, I could explain and deny until I was blue in the face, but I don't think that's enough for you, is it? You're going to have to wait and see, I think."

"You make yourself sound awfully suspicious," Tracy responded bitterly.

He pulled her toward him then, and kissed the top of Tracy's head. "Good. Keep your guard up a little longer, my love. It can't hurt."

Tracy closed her eyes and relaxed against his chest just a little longer. The fact that he was leaving was suddenly an awful ache inside her, one that grew and grew with each passing heartbeat. The next words escaped involuntarily. "I wish you wouldn't go."

"We're in agreement there," Rory said, sighing with regret once more. "But tomorrow is one meeting I can't ignore, though Margie would be delighted if I did. The tigress would pounce if I let my guard down for an instant. She'd like me to miss a lot of meetings these days."

Tracy touched his chest with her fingertips, turning over his remarks in her head. Without looking up at him, Tracy asked softly, "Rory, will you tell me all this stuff sometime? Am I allowed to know about your life with her? And with Melora?"

"Of course," he said roughly. "I wish I could take the time to tell you now, if it would make you feel better. Try to trust me, my love, if you can. I've got to straighten out my life before I can share it with you."

Tracy gave him a shove then and sat back, trying to sound gruffly humorous. "Just hurry up, all right? I'm—"

"I know, I know." Rory cut her off, laughing. "You're the impatient type!" He cuffed her shoulder lightly and got off the bed. "You've got your own affairs to settle, Miss Tracy, so get started, will you? Get rid of the FAA and figure out how best to dispose of Shamrock. Forget about me and my conniving ex-wife for a while and concentrate on selling your airline, hmm?"

Tracy saluted. "Yes, sir!"

He leveled his forefinger at her in chastisement. "And none of that nose-in-the-air stubbornness of yours, my girl. Ask for some help if you need it. Talk things over with Spinelli if it will do some good. Or the boy-wonder cousin who's the lawyer."

"Yes, Rory," Tracy said, gentler this time. Not moving from her tumbled bed, she smiled hesitantly at him as Rory finished buckling his belt and bent to tie his shoes. Demurely, she finally asked, "Are you going to kiss me goodbye?"

He climbed across the bed then and caught her head between his hands to give Tracy one of the most smashing kisses she'd ever remember receiving from him, one that left her limp and panting for air. He tasted her lips one last time and set her back down among the bedclothes.

She met his blue eyes and smiled. "I love you."

His face changed, the emotion suddenly raw and obvious in his expression. Rory caressed her cheek, kissed her lightly again and murmured, "I love you, too, Tracy O'Hara. Just keep your wits about you, hmm?"

And then he let her go, giving her hair a final, funny tug before he caught up his jacket and sweater and headed out of the bedroom. He didn't look back. The front door swung, squeaking, then closed with a bang, and Tracy could hear his footsteps sound as he headed for the hangar.

Tracy lay back in the bed. There was no smile on her face, though, just a drawn mouth and tightly squeezed eyes. A confusing parting. There was too much to think about.

Tracy relaxed her body finally, one limb at a time, once she was sure she wasn't going to cry. In the quiet darkness of her own bedroom the bewildering bits of the puzzle seemed to swoop and whirl around her. A month ago things were smooth and uncomplicated, and then Rory Buchanan had come tearing into her life, and her world was in an unbelievable uproar. What to do?

The biggest question was also the most heartbreaking: Would Rory dump her if she sold Shamrock to him? Would he take the airline and leave her with cash and a lot of memories?

And what was Marjorie Hallis's role in all this? Was she a villain or not? Tracy was betting that Rory's ex-wife was willing to pay more than the two million she had offered for Shamrock. Financially, it might be better to sell out to the highest bidder. Rory had told her not to make an emotional decision. Selling out to him would definitely be emotionally motivated, and probably not the best business policy.

But was Marjorie out to ruin Rory? Could Tracy make a difference in that conflict? Why was Rory so reluctant to talk business with Tracy now? Rory was careful to keep their discussions of a Shamrock-Northstream merger to the barest bones. He didn't want Tracy to make an emotional decision. He had said so repeatedly.

A thought bolted through the jumble of facts to light up Tracy's mind like the proverbial hundred-watt bulb. What if Rory wasn't begging for Shamrock because he didn't want to get Tracy mixed up in the larger mess with his ex-wife? What if he was playing a gallant part here? Could he be protecting Tracy?

From what? From Marjorie Hallis? To warn Tracy off a deal with Hallis Air would be unethical, not to mention illegal as far as the FAA was concerned. Suddenly Tracy's brain was seething. What if? What if Rory was protecting Northstream and Melora and himself and now Tracy from Marjorie Hallis? Was it possible?

What had he said just minutes before he left? "The tigress would pounce if I let my guard down for an instant. She'd like me to miss a lot of meetings these days."

"Oh, my God!" Tracy scrambled out of the bed, shouting, "Rory!"

Though he couldn't possibly hear her, she shouted again, "Rory! Stop! Oh, God!"

Her jeans were on the floor, boots beside them. Tracy had them on in seconds, and she was shoving her sweater over her head even as she ran out through the house. How much time was there? Had he gotten to his plane yet?

She pelted across the yard, hit the tarmac and kept running. The lights of the hangar showed brilliantly against the black sky, and the rotating beacon on the steel tower shot a blazing glare over Tracy's head before swirling off into the night. She heard the first plane engine fire up. Tearing around the corner of the hangar, Tracy screamed, "Rory, no!"

Two mechanics in the hangar turned around, startled. Tracy bolted right past the open door and out onto the runway. The Cessna had hesitated, brakes set, while Rory made the last preflight check. He revved one engine with an ear-splitting roar, and the small plane stood on its toes, ready for flight.

Tracy ran directly into the path of the plane, waving frantically. Her hair blew around her head like a tornado, the propellers were driving the air with such thunderous power. Then the revving engine faltered, for he must have seen her.

"Get out!" Tracy cried, foolishly trying to make herself heard over the incredible roar of the engines. She ducked around the wing, running past the prop as if it was standing still. "Get out before it blows up!"

Rory popped the door, leaned across the right-hand seat and poked his head out. He was laughing at her, clearly unable to hear a word she was saying. He was amused that she'd come chasing after him. "What are you doing, you crazy little—?"

Tracy flung herself at the wing, ignoring the steps and scrambling up the handholds. Her face was white, her eyes bright with terror. Clumsily, she pushed the door wide, hands shaking. She grabbed his arm. "Get out. It's going to blow up. Rory, please! Get out!"

"What?" he demanded, perhaps seeing her expression for the first time. With the instincts of a pilot, he reached back and hit the red knobs to shut down the engines. Above their dying whine, he asked, "What's wrong, for Pete's sake?"

Tracy hauled him hard. "Just get down! Get down and away! Hurry, Rory!"

Obeying without thinking at first, Rory climbed free of the cockpit. He swung Tracy down ahead of him, then clambered off the wing and followed. Half a dozen running steps later, he caught her arm and pulled her around to face him. "What's the matter? Tell me now. Tracy—"

"It's in the engine, I just know it!" Tracy gasped, staggering in his arms and struggling to pull him farther from the slowly dying whine of the aircraft engines. "Get away before it goes up."

"Before what goes up? What are you talking about?"

But Tracy didn't take the time. She ran, pulling him as hard as she could by his sleeve. At the hangar door, she shouted, "Harvey! Call the fire company! Get the fire extinguishers out of the Jeep! Don't get too close to—"

Suddenly Rory swore in astonishment behind her. Tracy spun around to see the first of the smoke start pouring from the nose of the twin-engine plane. She seized Rory's arm, for he had started automatically toward the Cessna. "No, wait!"

He wheeled back and grabbed Tracy by her forearms. He shook her hard. He was angry and scared, his face taut, his eyes furious. "How did you know? What's going on?"

"It's happened before," Tracy said breathlessly. "Somebody put a bomb in the Grumman before we crashed that night. I just—"

"A bomb?" Rory shouted, astounded. He loosened her fractionally.

"A smoke bomb," Tracy corrected. "It was a smoke bomb. It had been hooked up to a timer. When I realized—"

"Who would do such a thing?" Rory demanded. "How did—?"

Then the explosion: a tremendous growling roar that suddenly grew to a rocketlike concussion. Rory hugged Tracy to him, but they both found themselves staggering backward into the hangar because of the force of the blast. Fire spewed out along the tarmac in the blazing red of exploding fuel. Black oily smoke billowed out, blanketing the whole plane for an instant before surging toward the sky. The runway lit up like daylight as the Cessna was engulfed in flame.

As Tracy clutched Rory, her hands on his back were warmed by the heat of the fire behind him.

The two mechanics had taken off, running in opposite directions. Moments later, the fire alarm went off in a horrendous, blasting shriek.

Rory swore again, prayerfully this time, as he hugged Tracy hard once more. "You could have been killed!"

She laughed drunkenly, hysterically, and countered, "You could have been killed too, you idiot!"

He hugged her again, this time so hard he might have cracked the ribs of a lesser woman. Tracy buried her face against his jacket and breathed her heartfelt thanks. Too close a call to be the least bit funny. She had nearly lost him. He could have died, and Tracy knew just then that nothing in the world would have made her feel like living without Rory.

Harvey was shouting at them and waving like a maniac. Tracy loosened her grip on Rory, her purpose suddenly changing. "C'mon," she shouted. "We've got to move those planes!"

There was work to be done before the emergency got worse. Men were pouring out of the bar by that time, and everyone lent a hand in shifting the line of aircraft that stood perilously close to the burning Cessna. Tracy started down the line of tie-down rings, frantically fighting the knots of nylon rope loose so the men could heave the wings and shove the planes away from the danger zone.

The next half hour blurred together in a frightening kaleidoscope for Tracy. She worked alongside the men in moving the airplanes and ground vehicles, then directing the puny extinguishers to be used as soon as anyone could get close enough to the Cessna. She was sure the FBI would want to see what was left of the plane, and she was determined not to let it burn itself out before the local fire company arrived.

The FBI was certainly concerned. The two investigators had been in the bar with the other men when the explosion occurred, and even before the fire was completely out, they started asking questions. Long before the chief FBI investigator found her standing inside the hangar nearly an hour later, Tracy had realized just how complicated things had become.

"Do you want to tell me what you know, Miss O'Hara?" the investigator named Bailey had asked. "Or are we going to keep playing games with other people's lives before the truth comes out?"

Tracy was tempted to tell the investigator everything that she knew. But one question hung queerly in the back of her mind—a question she wanted to know the answer to before she started talking with the federal agents.

Just why would anyone want to kill Rory Buchanan?

It was obvious that someone had tried. Twice.

CHAPTER SEVENTEEN

RORY LEFT THAT SAME NIGHT on one of Tracy's Metros, though he was obliged to take an FBI agent in tow. Tracy hadn't been allowed a moment alone with him before he left, and that frustrated her no end. There were so many questions to ask, and Tracy had an odd feeling that she was the only one who knew all the angles. So she kept her mouth shut a little longer.

The FBI and the FAA were understandably interested in the explosion of Rory's plane, though the Cessna was not a commercial craft. Since Tracy's Grumman and Rory's small Cessna were similarly sabotaged, the two federal agencies stepped in before the wreckage was cool.

At midnight Tracy stumbled into the bar for a cup of coffee before she went to bed. The place was thankfully empty of federal employees, so she pulled up a chair at the table by the window. Spin was there.

"Hi," he said to her, obviously as completely bushwhacked as she was. His eyelids were heavy, and the cigarette in his mouth had an ash about an inch long dangling from it.

"Hi, yourself," Tracy said, reaching for his coffee cup without asking permission.

"You okay?" he asked briefly. "Not hurt?"

Tracy took a swallow of lukewarm coffee and set the cup abruptly down on the table with distaste. She shook her head, making a grimace at the coffee. "Not hurt. You?"

It was a conversation of monosyllables, the sort of talk that existed between two old and close friends. Spin wasn't worried because Tracy didn't run at the mouth. He looked her over carefully, though, reassuring himself that she really was okay. Nodding, he told her, "I'm good. Pooped, but good."

"You did some nice work out there," Tracy said as she relaxed back into her chair, stretching her legs out before her. "I didn't remember about the fuel we had stored in those two barrels. They could have blown sky-high if you hadn't said something."

Spin's smile was weak with exhaustion. "I figured you had enough to think about."

Tracy grinned, too. She nodded. "Yeah."

Spin had a large manilla envelope on the table, and a set of five-by-seven black-and-white photographs were fanned out alongside it. He had been looking them over, perhaps even when the explosion occurred. He dropped one hand over them, as if casually hiding them from Tracy.

She had noticed the photos immediately, of

course, but had taken her time bringing the fact to his attention. She sat forward and pulled one picture from the batch. "What's this?"

Spin didn't answer for a moment. In fact Tracy got a quick impression that he had been about to snatch the picture from her fingers. But he said with a more exaggerated drawl than usual, "What's it look like?"

"Like a picture of you," Tracy said, studying the photo through narrowed eyes.

It was a good picture, really. Someone had caught Spin in a natural pose outside the hangar, with his aviator glasses pulled ruggedly down around the strong base of his neck and his hair tousled by the breeze. It was an unexpectedly virile picture—a romantic picture. With that in mind, Tracy said, "Mary Alice Cooper took this, didn't she?"

"How did you know?" Spin demanded defensively, making a grab for the photo.

"Take it easy," Tracy commanded, withholding the picture for a moment. "Lucky guess. What do you have it for?"

Frowning, Spin gathered up all the pictures with a swift gesture. "She sent a bunch of them, that's all. I told her I liked her work, so she sent me some of the pictures she took when she was here with Buchanan a few weeks ago."

"Not bad," Tracy said generously, as she studied the photograph a second time. "Considering the subject matter, anyway."

Spin ignored the taunt. He was obviously angry about something, and Tracy guessed it was unrequited love. With a kind of sullen growl in his voice, Spin said merely, "She's good with a camera, y'know."

"Yeah," Tracy said, looking at the picture again. It really was a nice photo of Spin. It had caught a certain strength—a certain power or personality, showing that M.A. either had an artistic gift or a budding love affair with her model. Tracy supposed from Spin's mood that the love affair was not getting off the ground.

Not being a person who drags confessions out of others, Tracy kept her silence. Spin would work things out for himself, she reasoned. She reached for the other photos, and he handed them over without protest, without much interest any more. Spin was tired and getting depressed, it was clear—not from the explosion and seemingly endless questions from the FBI. He was feeling low about Mary Alice Cooper. With a long sigh, he got up from the table and went to the bar for a drink.

Tracy leafed through the pictures with only half her mind functioning. She was too tired to think, too tired to notice what she was looking at. But suddenly her brain focussed. Tracy stared at the picture in her hands. Her eyes popped, and she bent closer, closer until her nose was practically pressed to the paper.

"Cripes," she muttered to herself.

"Now what?" Spin asked, as he sat down again beside her. He had a tall glass of Irish whiskey in his hand, no ice. "What are you lookin' at?"

"You won't believe it," Tracy said, voice low and excited. She threw the picture down on the table. "What do you see?"

"Your airplane," Spin said, glancing at the photo. "The Pitts."

"No, no," Tracy said tensely, pointing. "In the background. Look, Spin! See it?"

Spin bent closer, puzzled, then his body stiffened. He picked up the picture and squinted. "Well, I'll be damned," he whispered.

It was evidence. Or almost, anyway. The picture was a portrait of the Pitts Special. But in the background of M.A.'s photograph stood the Grumman G1 before it had taken off on its ill-fated flight for Montreal. Tracy guessed that M.A. had unintentionally snapped the picture sometime late in the afternoon, judging by the way the sunlight slanted across the tarmac. And under the nose of the Grumman stood a man, half crouching as he tinkered up inside the plane.

"Who is it?" Spin whispered, staring at the picture. "Can you tell?"

Tracy glanced furtively around the bar. Out of the corner of her mouth, she said, "I think it's Harvey, don't you? Our own man!"

"Harvey?" Spin repeated in disbelief, peering

closer yet at the photo. "What in Hades would Harvey be doing...? Trace, you don't think...?"

"That Harvey planted a smoke bomb in the Grumman so we'd crash it? I wouldn't have guessed it ten minutes ago. But Spin, what else would he be doing? This is proof!"

Spin wagged his head. "I don't believe it. Why would Harvey want to do something like this? He's been a pilot for Shamrock almost as long as you and I have! I'd trust him to fly my mother!"

"But he's always broke," Tracy said swiftly, thinking as fast as a locomotive. "Spin, he's got a bunch of debts and is always looking for ways to make an extra buck."

"So what?"

"So what?" Tracy repeated, grabbing Spin's arm. "Don't you see? Somebody paid him to sabotage that airplane!"

"Who?" Spin demanded, not ready to believe her theory yet. "Who'd want to crash the Grumman?"

"Not just the Grumman," Tracy said shortly. "But Rory's Cessna, too. And I think I know. Spin, how about waking up your girlfriend? I think we need to talk to M.A. tonight!"

TRACY AND SPIN took a commercial flight to Chicago the next morning, and Mary Alice Cooper met them at the airport. She gave Tracy a fond embrace in greeting, and for Spin she had a full-fledged hug.

"I'm glad to see you," she said to Spin, still holding his hand and smiling up into his eyes. Then, turning back to Tracy with concern on her face, M.A. asked frankly, "Should I be glad? Or afraid for you?"

"Don't be afraid," Spin said, gathering them both up, one woman in each hand. "Tracy's not afraid, and she's got the most to lose, I think."

"What's going on?" M.A. asked as they headed up the crowded airport concourse toward the main terminal. O'Hare, as usual, was a madhouse, and M.A. expertly sidestepped a squadron of travelers making a mad dash for their next connection.

"That seems to be everyone's line these days," Tracy observed, striding quickly along with Spin as they made their way through the throng. "None of us is absolutely sure what's happening."

"Except that someone is trying to crash airplanes," Spin added. To M.A. he said confidentially, "Do you have any idea what it took to convince the FBI that we should be allowed to come out here today?"

"I don't get it," M.A. interrupted. "I always thought it was the FAA that took care of plane crashes and airline mergers."

"They do," Spin explained, "but in cases like this—where foul play is clearly indicated, the FAA turns things over to the FBI. Did you bring your photographs?"

"Every last one of them," M.A. said. "Three dozen on top of the ones you already have. Are you planning on going through the whole batch?"

Tracy nodded. "We've got to. It's very important, M.A."

"Are you sure this isn't a job for the FBI?" M.A. asked anxiously, glancing up at Spin. "Do you think it's wise to jump into something as dangerous as this by yourselves?"

"By ourselves," Spin corrected, taking her arm more securely. "Wise or not, we're in the soup now. And Tracy's the only one who's giving the impression she knows what's happening."

"That's a relief, believe it or not," M.A. said with a friendly, yet teasing grin. "For some reason, I'm very secure with Tracy in command. It must have been the night she ditched that airplane in the Adirondack Park—"

"Wait a minute!" Spin objected, wrapping his arm around M.A. as if to punish her with a squeeze. "I was the pilot that night!"

"Were you?" M.A. asked innocently. Then, with a burst of laughter at his wounded expression, she said, "Oh, Vincent, you're such a... a...oh, a man sometimes! Come on. My car's this way. Will you at least tell me where we're going, since I'm the chauffeur today?"

They had made it as far as the doors to the parking lot, and Tracy hesitated there and checked her watch. "Rick Buchanan's office is on Wacker

Drive. We've got some time to kill before we crash the meeting."

"How much time?" Spin asked with authority. "Enough to look over the rest of M.A.'s pictures?"

"And some extra, I'm sure. Two whole hours," Tracy said, sighing and looking up. "Is there some place we can go and look at the photos carefully?"

"I've got an idea," Spin said assertively as he turned to M.A. "Let's have a quick look at the pictures in the car and go someplace else for a while. Mary Alice, can we call upon your expertise this morning? I think Tracy could use your help, but she's never going to ask for it."

"For what?" M.A. asked, puzzled anew.

"Yeah," Tracy cut in, her tone full of suspicion. "For what, Spinelli?"

Spin took Tracy's elbow and spun her away from himself, displaying her body for M.A.'s approval. "What do you say, Mary Alice? This young lady's got a business meeting in two hours with some of the most important people in our industry. Do you think she's dressed for the occasion?"

"Spinelli, pick a Great Lake and go jump in it!"

"She's definitely not dressed for the occasion," M.A. said firmly as she cast a discerning eye down Tracy's jean-and-jacket-clad figure and ignored Tracy's outraged expression. M.A. quickly took stock of the situation, tapping her finger against her upper lip as she contemplated Tracy. Then, she came to a decision and pronounced with confidence, "I know just the place to go. This way, folks. You came to the right woman. I know all the best shops in Chicago. Michigan Avenue, here we come!"

In spite of Tracy's protests, M.A. drove with all speed to a busy shopping district somewhere in the confusing tangle of Chicago streets. In the back seat Tracy tediously studied each of the photos M.A. had brought along, and passed them one by one to Spin in the front seat for further scrutiny. They carefully examined each picture, but nothing earth-shattering showed up. Fighting down the first wave of apprehension, Tracy sat quietly in the back, not paying much attention to where they were going. Without any more evidence, her task this morning was going to be even more difficult.

M.A., however, knew just where she was headed and was impervious to Tracy's declarations that she had no intention of buying any clothes on this trip. She whipped into a parking space in one of those enormous parking decks and reached for her handbag. "This way, everyone. Vincent, we're going to need your opinion, so don't go hiding in a corner."

"Me? Hide? Mary Alice, you don't know how long I've waited to see Trace in something besides jeans. I wouldn't miss this for anything!"

M.A. was suddenly a missionary with a cause. She took charge of the shopping party with the undaunted air of an evangelist. "This way," she said. "I have a special saleswoman in this store whose taste I trust implicitly. Between the four of us, we ought to find something suitable."

Tracy might have bolted, but for Spin's firm hand under her elbow. He even provided the strong arm when it came time to coercing Tracy into a dressing room with a supply of suits and dresses to try.

M.A. was more delighted by each succeeding outfit, until Tracy came slinking out of the dressing room in a shocking red dress with a prim white collar. M.A. had taken over Tracy's transformation with determination. Firmly, she declared, "Oh, no! The color's all wrong. Try this one, Tracy. What do you think?"

Somehow M.A. and her helpful salesclerk had conjured up a wool suit in a muted hunter green with a velvet collar on the cleverly cut jacket. As soon as Tracy slipped into the slim skirt, she understood the value of well-made garments. The skirt was flattering, floating about her knees when she walked, and clinging with a subtleness to her thighs. The jacket was elegant without being prissy, and a plain silk shirt with an understated ruffle at the throat completed the outfit.

Tracy studied her barefoot reflection in the mirror. Definitely feminine, yet businesslike—a new feeling for Tracy O'Hara, yet one she wouldn't mind getting accustomed to. She caught sight of Spin's face in the mirror, and he winked at her and grinned. Perhaps he could see that she had grown up completely. This was no longer a little girl in a stunt plane.

With an odd rush of mental images, Tracy suddenly realized that not only had she grown up since she'd met Rory Buchanan, but that she still had some growing to do. Standing before a mirror in clothes selected by Mary Alice Cooper—a woman Rory respected—Tracy realized that she herself could be a poised, intelligent woman just like M.A. or Marjorie Hallis. Her mind cleared slowly. Tracy looked at Spin. Nodding, he gave her a thumbs-up signal and a grin.

"Shoes next," M.A. said, taking their silent nods for a decision to buy the green suit. She said, "Let me pay for this and we'll run up the escalator."

"You can't pay for the suit," Tracy objected immediately. She grabbed up the tags and peered at the amount printed there. Aghast, she exclaimed, "Cripes! Is this the price or somebody's social-security number?"

Spin arrived between the two women then. "Neither of you is paying for this. I am, and there isn't going to be an argument. Go get some shoes, Trace. Time's running out."

"You're not going to pull the charitable brother routine," Tracy snapped without thinking.

"Brother?" Spin asked, and his eyes sharpened on Tracy's face.

A rush of color flooded up her cheeks, and Tracy said quickly, "Just an expression. I don't need your charity."

Spin came forward and dropped a soft kiss on her forehead. "I wouldn't mind being your brother, Trace. Sometimes I wish I was."

Tracy swallowed hard. It seemed the worst possible of times and places, but suddenly she wanted to know. "Spin...."

He hugged her; it was a real hug, too, the kind that bespoke a great deal of emotion. Over her head, Spin said, "I wish you were my sister, Trace. That would explain the way I feel about you and—and your dad. I admired him so much, and I used to wish that he was my own father, too. But he wasn't, and I just had to pretend."

With her face pressed to Spin's chest, Tracy said softly, "You're a lot like him, you know."

Spin laughed shortly. "I practised, believe me. He was quite a guy, and I used to look in the mirror while I shaved and imitate his voice, the way he said things, the way he... well, I loved him the way you did, Trace. If I could... listen, I'd give a lot to be your brother now."

Tracy stretched and kissed his cheek. "I'd like to be your sister, too, Spin. I wish we could make it true. I love you."

"But not the same way you love Buchanan." Spin grinned, and gave her a gentle shove. "I know. Hurry up, Tracy. We've got to work things out so you get to keep him, I think. Come on. You've got important business today."

WACKER DRIVE was a prestigious address, Tracy saw immediately. Rick Buchanan's law offices were so tasteful that Tracy felt like a pauper in a Dickens novel as she stood on the sidewalk outside clutching Spin's hand for support. Even in her new finery, she felt like an intruder.

"Well?" Spin asked. "Do you want me to come along?"

With a rueful smile, Tracy let go of his hand. "I do, but that wouldn't look right, would it?"

"We'll come up with you," M.A. said positively, leading the way into the building. "We can wait outside for you in case you need reinforcements."

Rick Buchanan's imperious secretary stopped them with a disdainful look. "Have you an appointment, Miss Cooper?"

"No, I haven't," M.A. returned with an equally haughty demeanor. "Miss O'Hara has business with Mr. Buchanan's client, though. I'm sure Rick won't mind this interruption."

The secretary got to her feet, as if anticipating that Spin might make a rush for the conference-room doors. She also reached for the telephone. "If you'll please take seats in the waiting room, I'll just ring through for Mr. Buchanan's permission. Your name again, please?"

Spin gave Tracy a quick, firm look and he nodded once. "Go for it, kid."

So Tracy took a breath and cut around the secretary's desk, while M.A. and Spin blocked. She let herself through the huge mahogany doors.

Rick was startled by the interruption and stood up automatically. His stenographer was shocked enough to drop her eyeglasses onto her note pad, and Marjorie Hallis spun her seat around at Tracy's entrance and blinked. Immediately she identified the newcomer to her attorney.

Rory looked up and didn't move. In fact, he froze.

Tracy had never felt cooler. Once she was in the lion's den, she wasn't afraid. She walked straight to the conference table, laid her envelope there and looked directly at Rick. "Good morning, Mr. Buchanan."

Rick collected himself and came around the table warily. "Uh...it's Tracy, isn't it?"

She extended her hand. "Tracy O'Hara. I'm sorry to interrupt. I think I can make this meeting much simpler, however."

"Simpler?" Rick repeated, a mystified smile starting. He took Tracy's hand and couldn't stop an instinctive glance down her splendidly clad figure. His jovial demeanor returning, he replied, "Well, I'm always looking for ways to simplify my work. You...you certainly look different this morning, Miss O'Hara. You've brightened up my day already."

Marjorie Hallis had stood up and was on her way around the oval table. "Tracy! What a pleasant surprise! I wasn't sure when we'd get to meet again. How are you?"

Tracy shook Marjorie's hand solemnly. "Very well, thank you."

Marjorie was tall and in ten years would be described as statuesque. She had a face that was beautiful in a well-maintained, sculpted sort of way. Her eyes were dark, her hair had been expertly frosted, and she wore a vivid shade of cranberry lipstick on a full and lovely mouth. She had dressed in a honey-colored jacket that matched a kiltlike skirt, and in very high-heeled shoes she was several inches taller than Tracy. She wore two bracelets on one arm and a gold pendant watch on a thin, expensive chain. Her smile displayed teeth, which were perfectly straight and even. "It's so nice to see you, my dear. I thought you never left your home unless it was for an airplane."

The joke fell flat. Tracy let the remark sail by, and glanced instead down at Rory. Her heart jumped, as if every vein in her body had suddenly convulsed with emotion. But now was the time to be firm and adult. "Hello," she said coolly.

"Good morning," he said back. Though perfectly composed, Tracy knew he was dying to shout, "What are you doing here?" But he kept quiet and watched her every move.

"I thought we might as well lay our cards on the table," Tracy said to them all then. She turned to Rick. "Perhaps you won't mind acting as the moderator for this?"

"Certainly," said Rick. "I have a feeling this meeting is about to get interesting."

"Not to mention illegal," Tracy added guilelessly. "Shall we get started?"

"I think I'm in the dark," Marjorie muttered as she subsided into a chair as far from Rory as possible. She stared at Tracy. "What are we starting?"

Tracy sat at the head of the table and laid her hands flat on the surface. "Are you still interested in buying Shamrock Air?"

"Yes," Marjorie said, smiling. "Of course."

Tracy turned to Rory and fixed him with a direct look. "Are you?"

"Yes," he said.

"Your two-million offer stands?"

"Yes."

Tracy looked at Marjorie. "And you? Are you standing by your original offer?"

Marjorie smiled again, cagily this time. "I think we can negotiate."

"Good," said Tracy. And she opened her envelope. "I'll sell you Shamrock for two million if you give me some information first."

"Information?" Marjorie asked politely. Perhaps her smile wavered then. "What information?"

Tracy threw the photograph down in front of Marjorie Hallis. "Will you tell me about this photograph?"

At a loss, Marjorie picked up the picture. She was laughing prettily. "This is certainly a bizarre way of negotiating a merger, but I suppose I'm game. This is an airplane. A stunt plane, isn't it?"

"Look closer," Tracy said curtly. "In the background."

"Another plane," Marjorie said, holding the picture closer. "A larger one."

"A Grumman G1. See anything unusual?"

Rory sat forward slowly, his interest sharpening on Tracy's face. He didn't say a word.

"There's a man under the nose," Marjorie said, sounding very casual. "I can't quite make out what he's doing."

"We can have the photo blown up," Tracy offered calmly. "In fact, blowing up seems to be awfully easy these days."

Marjorie laid down the photograph and regarded Tracy across the table. "I don't quite follow you."

"Neither do I," said Rick. "Miss O'Hara, perhaps you'd explain just what you—"

"Let her go on," Rory said, cutting off his brother's protest. "Let her talk."

"I don't think I need to explain anything to Ms Hallis," Tracy spoke in a perfectly level voice. She was surprising herself with her own calm. She said, "We've learned a lot from one photograph in just a few hours. In fact, once I started talking with some of my employees, things fell into place very nicely. The FBI and the FAA are anxious to—"

"What are you talking about?" Marjorie asked loudly. "Are you accusing someone here?"

"Accusing?" Tracy asked innocently. "I thought we were negotiating."

"What do you want?" Marjorie demanded, going cold. Hastily, her attorney leaned over to whisper in her ear. But she persisted, "Why are you here?"

"To get the facts," Tracy said. "Before I go to the federal officials and ground Hallis Air for a long time."

CHAPTER EIGHTEEN

THE CHAMPAGNE CORK EXPLODED off the bottle with a wonderful pop, and Spin bolted backward to catch it in his hands. The group cheered when he made the catch and Rory—in a most ungentlemanly gesture, probably prompted by the fact that he was so euphoric himself—presented Spin with the first fizzing glass.

The party had come directly to Rory's house after a rousing good dinner at a popular Chicago restaurant, and the host was happily distributing glasses of champagne to celebrate the day's events.

"Who's going to make the toast?" M.A. cried above the hubbub of celebrating Buchanans and their guests. "Rory? What have you got to say after today's excitement?"

"I'm speechless," Rory countered, laughing as he spilled champagne on the floor tiles while trying to fill his sister's glass. "Get Rick to say something philosophical. He's the orator."

"Not today," Rick denied, lifting his glass high in a mocking salute. "Today I had to talk fast to keep a lot of us out of jail. What a day! Is this the kind of excitement you planned when you came barging into my office this morning, Tracy?"

Tracy was sitting on the counter where Rory had lifted her not long after their arrival in his home. She smiled, swinging her long legs, her green eyes sparkling. "I shook everyone up today, didn't I?"

"Yes," Rory said emphatically, wrapping his arm around her waist. He smiled at her, his gaze warm and flickering. "To put it mildly, you shook us up."

M.A. lifted her glass. "I'll propose a toast if none of the rest of you will."

"Don't toast Tracy," Rory said with a laugh as he patted her thigh and let her go. "Her head's already too full of praises."

"Deserved ones," M.A. shot back promptly. She raised her glass and swept on, "All right, then, I think we should toast the FBI. Weren't they wonderful?"

"That depends upon your point of view," Rick said laconically, lighting up a cigar. "I think Marjorie would disagree if she was with us at the moment."

"Bite your tongue," said Ann angrily. She had come to help celebrate her brother's victory, but she was still shaken by the information that had been discovered during the day. Ann said, "With any luck, Margie will be in jail before morning."

Rick drank his champagne off in three long swallows, and relaxed into one of the stools at the kitchen counter—just an arm's length from Tracy. "Don't count on Margie going to jail for attempted murder, sister dear. I think Margie's smart enough to insulate herself with henchmen very well. She undoubtedly took all sorts of precautions when she started this crazy campaign against Rory. My guess is that nobody's going to be able to prove she had anything to do with those plane crashes. At least, we won't find enough proof to stand up in court."

"But she's going to have a heck of a time getting her airline back in the air," Spin said heavily, aiming his cigarette at Rick to make his point. He was already a little drunk, and had lost enough of his inhibitions to slide his arm across M.A.'s shoulders as he spoke to the group. "I think the FAA is going to keep Ms Hallis very busy for the next few weeks. Even if they never prove her involvement in the destruction of both airplanes, she's going to be under a lot of suspicion for a long while."

"Do you really believe it, Rory?" Ann asked, seriously, placing her glass on the counter before her. "Do you really believe that Margie—that she meant to—?"

"To kill him?" Rick supplied bluntly.

Rory shook his head and left Tracy's side for the first time in an hour. He touched his sister's back, comforting her. "No, I don't think so, Annie. I think she planned to stop me from attending the meeting I had scheduled in Montreal. She had a smoke bomb planted in Tracy's Grumman so we wouldn't take off. She was trying to block the merger I was working on with Air Norland, and she succeeded. Last night, though, when my Cessna blew up—"

"I have a theory about that," Spin interrupted. "I think she had the Cessna rigged with the smoke bomb first, and when you couldn't find your key and decided to take the Grumman instead, she had Harvey sabotage our plane, too."

"So the Cessna was rigged to explode the whole time it was sitting at Tracy's airport?" M.A. asked, turning to look at Spin's face without sliding out from under the loop of his arm.

Tracy spoke up when it looked as if Spin was too engrossed in studying M.A.'s face to respond. She said, "The FBI told me that the Cessna probably wasn't supposed to blow up. There was a smoke bomb in it, too, but it had been laid too close to the fuel lines. The explosion was a mistake. The plane was only supposed to smoke and keep Rory on the ground. I'm sure she never meant for anyone to die."

Ann shivered, and Rory gently, affectionately, turned his sister toward him. They hugged, and Rory said lightly, "Don't take it so hard, sis. Next time, you might really get rid of me."

Ann tried to laugh, and boxed his ears in reprimand.

"Two very close calls if you ask me," M.A. said. "It was pure luck that nobody was hurt when we crashed in Adirondack Park. And last night, Rory...." She shivered at the thought.

"Count on Tracy to be thinking," Spin said proudly.

"I may be broke," Tracy added with a deprecating laugh, "but I'm smart."

"Broke?" M.A. asked in surprise. "Really? You mean Shamrock Air is in trouble? I didn't know that."

Tracy hooked her thumb at Rory. "Ask the efficiency expert over there. It's a miracle that Shamrock is still flying, I'm told."

M.A. turned with expectation to Rory, as did his brother and sister. M.A. said brightly, "Well, how nice for you, Rory. Since your merger with the Canadian airline fell apart, here's a perfect opportunity! Why don't you buy Shamrock Air and solve everyone's problems?"

Rory glanced around and saw Tracy's ambivalent expression. He burst out laughing at the look on her face. Tracy had the grace to smile, too.

"What did I say?" M.A. asked, mystified by Rory's uproarious reaction.

Tracy put her nose in the air with pretended haughtiness. "I'm not sure I want to sell out to him, M.A. He's been a skunk about everything from the beginning, you know."

Rory eyed Tracy with a grin lurking on his mouth. "I'm not so sure it would be wise for me to buy a failing airline right now, either. I'm almost broke myself. Maybe I'll just sit tight and wait for a better opportunity to come along."

"Like what?" Tracy challenged immediately, her eyes fiery with outrage.

He lifted his shoulders innocently, teasing her. "Who knows?" he asked the group at large. "Maybe I'll get more for my money if I wait a little longer for the right deal."

"It sounds to me like the two of you are made for each other," M.A. pointed out firmly. "Two almost-bankrupt companies like yours are a perfect match."

"A perfect match," Rory repeated thoughtfully. His gaze rested on Tracy with amusement. The light of deeper emotion seemed to glimmer in his eyes, however.

"We'll see about that," Tracy promised darkly, not about to commit herself in front of all these people.

"Time will tell," Spin added with a broad smile.

"Time!" Ann exclaimed, craning around with agitation to look at the kitchen clock. "What time is it? Oh, heavens, I've got to run! Baths and bedtime stories, and I promised I'd make hot chocolate for all the kids tonight!"

"It's time we were all heading for home," Rick agreed, sliding off the stool. He looked from Rory to Tracy and back again with an amused grin, and laid a congratulatory hand on his brother's shoulder. "I can see there's still some business to attend to here tonight. We'll all get out of your way and let you clear up the details, Rory."

Rory shook Rick's hand. "Thanks, big brother. I appreciated your help today. And all along, too."

"Glad to be of service," Rick said blandly. "Now that you've officially got custody of that kid of yours, maybe we can finally take the vacation I've been promising my wife as soon as I got things caught up at the office. Working for you has kept me busy for the last year!"

"I'll fly you anywhere you want to go," Rory promised magnanimously. "In fact, I may take a long vacation myself."

"Hmm," said Rick, sliding his eyes at Tracy. "I don't blame you, little brother. Take a very, very long one, all right?"

Ann was next to say goodbye. She kissed Rory swiftly, holding his arms. "Good night, sweetie. I'll keep Melora one more night, okay? I'm sure you've got your hands full tonight without her underfoot."

Rory grinned. "Thanks, Annie. We'll come get her early in the morning."

The rest of the goodbyes were quick and pleasant as everyone gathered up jackets or handbags. Both Ann and Rick gave Tracy hugs, genuine kisses and—from Rick—a bemused wink as he helped her down from the counter.

"Don't let my brother wiggle out of any commitments the easy way," Rick advised as he set Tracy on her feet. "You stick to your guns, Miss Tracy O'Hara. Make him give you what you want."

"No coaching, please," Rory said decisively, coming across the kitchen to lay claim to Tracy by taking her hand. He lifted her fingers to his lips and kissed her there, smiling into her eyes as he did so. "She's hard enough to convince as it is."

At the front door M.A. turned and gave Tracy a quick, affectionate hug. "Good night, Tracy. We all—we're very grateful for what you've done. Don't listen to Rory. He's going to make light of this whole thing and tease you forever, you know. It's the way he is."

"I think I can give him the same treatment," said Tracy. Then, with quiet sincerity, she continued, "Thanks, M.A. We owe you a lot, you know."

"Only because I take pictures without looking at them very carefully." M.A. held Tracy's hands a moment longer and sought her eyes with a steady look. "You're good for each other, you and Rory. I wish you all the happiness in the world, Tracy. You both deserve it."

Spin didn't waste any time. When M.A. let her go, he gathered Tracy up in a huge hug and held her hard. "Take care of yourself, Trace."

"Cripes," Tracy muttered, trying to ignore the lump that rose quickly to her throat. Saying goodbye to Spin like this was foolishly difficult. Tracy tried to bluff it out, but she held him around the neck to hide her face an instant longer. She said, "You'd think we were never going to see each other again! I've got to get back to Shamrock tomorrow, and you'd better be there, too, or I'll fire you."

"I have a feeling you're not going back quite so soon," Spin said with an odd smile. He kissed her on the forehead. "Call me if you need me."

Rory stepped behind her then, and Tracy leaned back against him. He shook Spin's hand and said, "I'd promise to take care of Tracy for you, but she'd probably belt me for saying it."

"Her bark is plenty worse than her bite," Spin confided. "You can't take Tracy too seriously, you know."

"I think I'll belt you instead!" Tracy threatened, pretending anger once more.

Rory laughed at her show of temper, then remembered his manners and offered sincerely, "Say, Spin, do you need a place to stay tonight? You're not going back to Shamrock now, are you?"

"No," M.A. intervened smoothly for him, tucking her hand into the crook of Spin's arm. "I've asked him to help me tonight. A publisher wants to see my photographs for a book about flying, so I've got to put together a proposal. Vincent said he'd look through them with me tonight. Just to help me organize them, of course."

"I see," said Rory, smiling benignly at his longtime friend. "You won't turn into a stranger, will you, M.A.? After all you and I have been through?"

"You're never going to be rid of me, Rory Buchanan." M.A. kissed him on the cheek. "I'll be the bestperson at your wedding, if you think it won't upset the social columns! Good night, you two."

Tracy cuddled back deeper into Rory's chest, and together they watched the others walk down to the driveway and get into their cars. Rory waved good-night, and when M.A.'s little car pulled down to the highway, he drew Tracy inside with him and closed the door to the outside world.

She didn't speak, but molded pliantly to Rory's frame, sliding her arms around his neck and smiling up at him.

Rory's answering smile was pleased and relaxed. The taut lines of his face had smoothed themselves in the past few hours, as if the weight of his assorted troubles had been lifted and no longer worried him. He bent without speaking and kissed Tracy lightly on the mouth.

She sighed and tightened her arms around him. Softly she said, "That's not good enough, please. I've had a long day."

"And now you're ready for your reward, is that it?"

"Yes, Rory," she murmured, lifting herself up on tiptoe to kiss him properly, gently, but with fervor.

Rory swept her up against him in a long and savoring kiss this time, holding her inescapably in his arms. His mouth was sure, seeking the warmth within her. His heart accelerated—as it always did when she was so close and soft in his embrace. Rory kissed her gently, but with a power held just barely in control.

A long delicious moment later, he loosened her fractionally, and put his lips against her cheek. "Tracy, love."

She closed her eyes and smiled. Her heart felt ready to burst with delight. "Oh, Rory. Is it over?"

"The bad stuff?" he asked, rocking her in his arms. "Yes, darling, we've got only the good things ahead of us now."

She nestled close and murmured, "Your family has a lot of notions about you and me, I think."

"Shall we surprise them?"

Tracy's forehead wrinkled as she looked up into Rory's eyes in wary puzzlement. "What do you mean?"

He traced the curve of her cheek with his thumb and said, "They're expecting me to buy you out in a few weeks' time and to set up housekeeping with you here."

"So?" she asked cautiously. "How are we going to surprise them?"

"I'll buy Shamrock tonight, if you'll let me."

"Rory—"

"Easy now," he soothed before she could protest or even question him. In a rush, he explained, "You've got better things to do with your life than managing a hopeless operation like Shamrock. You've got talents, Tracy. Big talents that even I didn't recognize until you came sailing into Rick's office today looking like a million dollars and talking like a negotiator for the teamsters' union. You're going to go places, my love. It's time to get on with the rest of your life. Sell Shamrock, and go back to school."

"How did you know about that?" Tracy demanded, her voice trembling.

He smiled, drawing his hand up the length of her spine in a fond caress. "That you wanted to go back and finish college? It was easy to figure out. Did Marjorie offer to help you get in somewhere? And to pay your bills?"

Tracy's look was cautious. "We didn't discuss details. She—she said she could help me, though."

"You don't need help," Rory said firmly. "You can get into any school in the country all by yourself. Engineering? Business? You can name your own ticket, I'm sure."

"I—I'd like to study engineering," Tracy said cautiously. "Aerodynamics and design, maybe."

"Good. We can start checking with colleges right away if you like."

She avoided his eyes for a moment. "Somewhere near here? Near you?"

Rory blew a long sigh as he considered the best way to phrase his next questions. Finally he said, "Tracy, I want you to be absolutely sure about this. Do you need some time to spread your wings a little? To experience the things that other young women—"

"I know my own mind, Rory," she intervened harshly, with a suddenly angry look up at him. "I'm in love with you, and you're not going to talk me out of it. If you're not ready to get tangled up with me after what you've just gone through with your ex-wife, then—"

"Don't put words in my mouth," he said firmly, giving her a shake.

"I know you've had a rough time," Tracy continued stubbornly. "I can understand that you want to be sure this isn't another fling. Just don't expect me to wait around patiently while you—"

"I'm not asking you to wait," Rory said softly, nuzzling his nose into her hair. He laughed softly. "In fact, I planned to spend the whole night convincing you, if need be."

"Convincing me of what?"

He kissed her roughly on the ear. "I can't have you living here with me, Tracy. Not with Melora in the house."

"I'll live with M.A. then—"

"No," Rory said, laughing as he squeezed her against him once more. "Tracy, darling, you're going to have to marry me, that's all. I don't want you to get any farther than the next room for a long time, please. If it takes me hours to convince you of that, then—"

"M—marry you?"

"Yes. It will make life much simpler, my love. I want to be with you forever. Shall we surprise my family and do it right away?"

"Marry you?" Tracy repeated dazedly. "Really, Rory?"

"Good grief," he said with a laugh. "I believe you don't have a snappy comeback for once!"

Tracy laughed with him then, and shook her head. "I thought I was going to have to twist your arm and force you to—to ask me to live with you, but I—"

"Give me some credit, darling. I know a good thing when I see it." Rory gathered her closer, seeking her mouth with his. "And you're the best thing that's happened to me in a long, long time, my love. Will you be my wife?"

"Yes, Rory," she whispered, melting into his kiss once more. Her breathing was shallow, but easy, matching Rory's. Their hearts beat in quick, delighted syncopation. Tracy pressed into his body and felt the passion roll in like a tidal breaker. Her instinctive sigh caught in her throat and turned to a quiet, funny moan.

Rory laughed at the sound and loosened her just enough to gaze deeply into her eyes. "You're so complicated and so simple, Tracy. You're full of vinegar, and yet you're sweeter than any woman in the world. You're good for me, and I need you—probably more than you need me right now."

"No," Tracy disagreed softly.

"I think so," Rory argued, and then he added, "I want to make you happy, though. Tracy, love, I don't give a damn what happens to Shamrock, I'm ashamed to say, but I do want you here with me."

"You'd have a hard time getting rid of me now," Tracy whispered. "I love you."

"We'll get married soon?"

"As soon as we can."

"Then what? Shall I take you away somewhere?"

Tracy laughed, teasing him. "Can you afford to take a vacation, Rory?"

"A short one," he said, smiling good-naturedly. "In fact, there's an air show in Amsterdam I should go to. I'm shopping for a new plane, you know. We could make a honeymoon out of it."

"Can I suggest one condition?" Tracy asked, playing her fingertips along his shirt buttons slowly.

"No, you may not fly the Pitts to Amsterdam," Rory responded with a laugh, guessing her condition.

"Not even close," Tracy countered smugly with

a smile. She lifted her eyes to his and bravely asked, "Could we take Melora along?"

Rory's face changed, going from surprise to pleasure and then apprehension. His embrace was suddenly stronger as he began hesitantly, "Tracy...."

"I'll never be a mother to her," Tracy explained quickly. "I'm just not the mothering type. Not yet, anyway. I'd like to spend some time with her, though, Rory. We...I feel as if we've been ignoring Melora, and she's part of you—a part of you I think I could learn to love if we had a chance. Please, Rory?"

"On our honeymoon?" he asked, his eyes squinched up as if he was in pain. "Are you sure that's a good idea?"

"We'll have time for lots of trips," Tracy said gently. "And I don't want Melora to feel as though she's being pushed out of your life. Trust me on this, Rory. I think it would be nice if we took her."

He sighed. "I don't think I'm ever going to be able to deny you anything. You're spoiled already, and I'm only going to make it worse. Yes, of course. You can both stuff yourselves with chocolates and sleep till noon every day."

"Hmm," said Tracy, purring as she tugged his shirt collar seductively. "Maybe not. I like to see the sunrise with you, Rory. It...waking up with you always makes me think of that first morning after we slept together."

"At the hotel in Albany?"

Tracy blushed. "No. After the plane crash. In the woods, remember? I felt...I think I knew I was in love with you even then."

Rory held her close once again. "Then I will promise you many more sunrises like that one."

"Tomorrow?" Tracy asked, peeking upward.

Rory smiled. "Are you suggesting we go to bed early tonight?"

With a laugh, Tracy nodded and said ingenuously, "It has been a long day, hasn't it?"

"And I haven't made love to you in at least twelve hours," Rory added, swooping her up in his arms. With Tracy snuggled securely against him, Rory started for the bedroom. He touched a kiss to her cheek and said softly, "And I want to make love to you, Tracy, without that shadow of doubt in your eyes for once."

"No doubts anymore," Tracy whispered. "You're stuck with me now, Rory. I love you."

ABOUT THE AUTHOR

Flight into Sunshine is Nancy Martin's eighth romance, although she has only been writing for two years! Originally an English teacher to gifted students, Nancy retired several years ago to raise her family, and turned to romance writing as an outlet for her energies while her two daughters were small.

Nancy's father, who is in the commuter airline business, provided much of the detail and ambience of this story, and the experience of working with him drew father and daughter closer, according to the author. Although *Flight into Sunshine* took only ten weeks to write, Tracy O'Hara, its heroine, inhabited Nancy's imagination for fifteen years. This author feels strongly that romance writing has become the perfect occupation for her: she can stay at home with her family, gain satisfaction and stimulation from a self-disciplined career, and work with wonderful men such as Rory Buchanan every day!

Just what the woman on the go needs!

BOOKMATE

The perfect "mate" for all Harlequin paperbacks!

Holds paperbacks open for hands-free reading!

- **TRAVELING**
- **VACATIONING**
- **AT WORK • IN BED**
- **COOKING • EATING**
- **STUDYING**

Perfect size for all standard paperbacks, this wonderful invention makes reading a pure pleasure! Ingenious design holds paperback books OPEN and FLAT so even wind can't ruffle pages—leaves your hands free to do other things. Reinforced, wipe-clean vinyl-covered holder flexes to let you turn pages without undoing the strap...supports paperbacks so well, they have the strength of hardcovers!

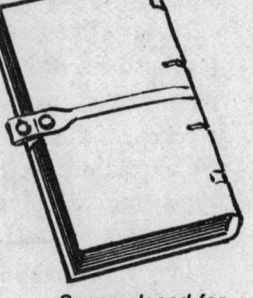

Snaps closed for easy carrying.

Available now. Send your name, address, and zip or postal code, along with a check or money order for just $4.99 + .75¢ for postage & handling (for a total of $5.74) payable to Harlequin Reader Service (to:

Harlequin Reader Service

In the U.S.A.
2504 West Southern Ave.
Tempe, AZ 85282

In Canada
P.O. Box 2800, Postal Station A
5170 Yonge Street,
Willowdale, Ont. M2N 5T5

TAKE THESE 4 Harlequin Romances FREE

as advertised on TV

Delight in **Mary Wibberley**'s warm romance, MAN OF POWER, the story of a girl whose life changes from drudgery to glamour overnight.... Let THE WINDS OF WINTER by **Sandra Field** take you on a journey of love to Canada's beautiful Maritimes.... Thrill to a cruise in the tropics—and a devastating love affair in the aftermath of a shipwreck—in **Rebecca Stratton**'s THE LEO MAN.... Travel to the wilds of Kenya in a quest for love with the determined heroine in **Karen van der Zee**'s LOVE BEYOND REASON.

Harlequin Romances... 6 exciting novels published each month! Each month you will get to know interesting, appealing, true-to-life people.... You'll be swept to distant lands you've dreamed of visiting.... Intrigue, adventure, romance, and the destiny of many lives will thrill you through each Harlequin Romance novel.

Get all the latest books before they're sold out!

As a Harlequin subscriber you actually receive your personal copies of the latest Romances immediately after they come off the press, so you're sure of getting all 6 each month.

Cancel your subscription whenever you wish!

You don't have to buy any minimum number of books. Whenever you decide to stop your subscription just let us know and we'll cancel all further shipments.

Your FREE gift includes
- MAN OF POWER by **Mary Wibberley**
- THE WINDS OF WINTER by **Sandra Field**
- THE LEO MAN by **Rebecca Stratton**
- LOVE BEYOND REASON by **Karen van der Zee**

FREE GIFT CERTIFICATE
and Subscription Reservation

Mail this coupon today!

Harlequin Reader Service

In the U.S.A.	In Canada
2504 West Southern Ave.	P.O. Box 2800, Postal Station A
Tempe, AZ 85282	5170 Yonge Street,
	Willowdale, Ont. M2N 5T5

Please send me my 4 Harlequin Romance novels FREE. Also, reserve a subscription to the 6 NEW Harlequin Romance novels published each month. Each month I will receive 6 NEW Romance novels at the low price of $1.50 each (*Total–$9.00 a month*). There are no shipping and handling or any other hidden charges. I may cancel this arrangement at any time, but even if I do, these first 4 books are still mine to keep.

NAME _____ (PLEASE PRINT)

ADDRESS _____ APT. NO.

CITY _____

STATE/PROV. _____ ZIP/POSTAL CODE

Offer not valid to present subscribers
Offer expires December 31, 1984   R-SUB-2X

116-BPR-EASV

If price changes are necessary you will be notified.

Yours FREE, with a home subscription to HARLEQUIN SUPERROMANCE.™

Now you never have to miss reading the newest **HARLEQUIN SUPERROMANCES**... because they'll be delivered right to your door.

Start with your **FREE** LOVE BEYOND DESIRE. You'll be enthralled by this powerful love story...from the moment Robin meets the dark, handsome Carlos and finds herself involved in the jealousies, bitterness and secret passions of the Lopez family. Where her own forbidden love threatens to shatter her life.

Your **FREE** LOVE BEYOND DESIRE is only the beginning. A subscription to **HARLEQUIN SUPERROMANCE** lets you look forward to a long love affair. Month after month, you'll receive four love stories of heroic dimension. Novels that will involve you in spellbinding intrigue, forbidden love and fiery passions.

You'll begin this series of sensuous, exciting contemporary novels...written by some of the top romance novelists of the day...with four every month.

And this big value...each novel, almost 400 pages of compelling reading...is yours for only $2.50 a book. Hours of entertainment every month for so little. Far less than a first-run movie or pay-TV. Newly published novels, with beautifully illustrated covers, filled with page after page of delicious escape into a world of romantic love...delivered right to your home.

Begin a long love affair with
HARLEQUIN SUPEROMANCE™.
Accept LOVE BEYOND DESIRE **FREE**.
Complete and mail the coupon below today!

FREE! Mail to: Harlequin Reader Service

In the U.S.
2504 West Southern Avenue
Tempe, AZ 85282

In Canada
P.O. Box 2800, Postal Station "A"
5170 Yonge St., Willowdale, Ont. M2N 5T5

YES, please send me FREE and without any obligation my **HARLEQUIN SUPEROMANCE** novel, LOVE BEYOND DESIRE. If you do not hear from me after I have examined my FREE book, please send me the 4 new **HARLEQUIN SUPEROMANCE** books every month as soon as they come off the press. I understand that I will be billed only $2.50 for each book (total $10.00). There are no shipping and handling or any other hidden charges. There is no minimum number of books that I have to purchase. In fact, I may cancel this arrangement at any time. LOVE BEYOND DESIRE is mine to keep as a FREE gift, even if I do not buy any additional books.

NAME _____ (Please Print)

ADDRESS _____ APT. NO. _____

CITY _____

STATE/PROV. _____ ZIP/POSTAL CODE _____

SIGNATURE (If under 18, parent or guardian must sign.)

SUP-SUB-22

This offer is limited to one order per household and not valid to present subscribers. Prices subject to change without notice.
Offer expires December 31, 1984

134-BPS-KAPX